AFTERLIFE

GHOSTLAND 2.0

a novel

Duncan Ralston

SHADOW WORK PUBLISHING

Cover and interior art by
Ascending Storm www.ascendingstorm.com
Sanitarium BB font by Blambot,
used by permission.

ISBN 978-1988819211

Also by Duncan Ralston

Gristle & Bone (Collection)
Salvage (Novel)
Wildfire (Novella)
Woom (Novella)
The Method (Novel)
Video Nasties (Collection)
Ebenezer (Novella)
Ghostland (Novel)
The Midwives (Novel)
In Every Dark Corner (Collection)

For more, visit
www.duncanralston.com.

Greetings from
DUCK
FALLS

PARK LEGEND

"I like to scare people, and people like to be scared. It's a funhouse sort of thing. I'm the florescent ghost—or actually, I'm more like a stage manager or a puppeteer. I'm running the ghost, which is more fun than being the ghost. I know where all the trapdoors are that people are going to fall into."
— Stephen King, interview excerpt,
Twilight Zone, April 1981

"Whoever said death can't be a blast?"
— Rex Garrote, foreword to *Shōki*

PROLOGUE:
THE TERMINAL MAN

Ghostland
April 20th, 2019

G AME OVER, HE thought, blinking through the cracked lenses of his glasses. The entire park was in full meltdown, and the brats had just left him behind, escaping with the psychiatrist. Now he was broken and probably dying, trapped in the control room with that insane, frenzied *thing* they'd called *Alpha* in the lab, but the kids had called *the Swarm*. It had already murdered Ms. Amblin, pinning her against the monitor wall like a heretic nailed to a cross. Any second now it would be coming for him.

"*HARRISON.*"

The voice boomed over the blare of the alarm and the sound of chaos and destruction, driving a spike of terror into Harrison's heart. It was *his* voice. He was here in the control room, among the dead and the dying. He was *here*. Was it even possible, after everything that had just happened? How could *anyone* have survived?

Of course, it's possible, he thought. *All those long*

nights I spent coding made it possible. This... all of this... it's as much my fault as it is His.

"*HARR-I-SONNNNNN*," the voice said again. *His* voice.

Harrison Greely raised his head, the pain in his neck and lower back and broken nose causing stars to shoot across his vision. The emergency lighting flashed in the cracked, dandruff-flecked lenses of his glasses. He took them off and wiped them on his shirt, streaking them with blood that had spilled from his nostrils. He settled the glasses back on the bridge of his nose and blinked into the erratic light.

Hiding somewhere in the front row, Nia Dearwood—with her dull pink hair and fake-vintage Pokémon T-shirt—let out a prolonged, high-pitched scream. Was she still at her terminal? *God, it'd be just like her to die at her computer*, Harrison thought. Not that he was any different, he supposed.

He raised himself onto an elbow, feeling weak, every muscle like wet spaghetti. All he wanted was to lie back down and sleep for a week, even if it cost him his life.

"*GET UP, HARRISON.*" Mr. Garrote's voice boomed over the comm system speakers. "*GET. UP. YOUR WORK HERE ISN'T FINISHED JUST YET.*"

The programmer rolled over onto his butt, managing to prop himself up on shaky arms.

"*There you are,*" the writer said, lowering his voice. "*Welcome back to the land of the not-quite-living.*"

The control room looked like an explosion in an office supply store: a mess of broken computers, loose paper and pens, a shoe with a foot still in it—*God, that's Bishop's Reebok, isn't it?*—torn off above the ankle, keyboards and ergonomic LED mouses, desk toys and orthopedic office chairs.

Sara Jane Amblin herself lay sprawled on the floor in front of the monitors. The entity that had murdered her—*Alpha, the Swarm*—still hovered over her remains, twisting itself back and forth as if examining her, looking for signs of further life to drain.

Above them, Garrote's massive face was displayed in mosaic over the entire wall of monitors, missing only the screens blacked out and cracked by the impact of Ms. Amblin's body. He looked like a religious maniac who'd painted his face with a giant black crucifix from forehead to lips, the paint chipped and cracked. His dark grin filled the second row from the bottom.

"Hello again, Harry. Did you miss me?"

The writer bellowed laughter. Everything was a big fat joke to Mr. Garrote. He was probably having a blast, laughing it up in that fish tank of his in the labyrinth of servers beneath his creepy old house.

"You crazy boomer *asshole*!" Nia cried, peering up at Garrote from the front row of computer terminals, accusation in her eyes.

Alpha Entity darted toward Nia at the sound of her voice, writhing and pulsating, leaving Ms. Amblin's remains behind. Nia leaped to her feet and ran, tripped over a desk chair and sprawled across the aisle. Panting, she rolled over and screamed one final time as the Swarm—as *Alpha*—descended upon her.

Harrison closed his eyes. He didn't like Nia. He didn't like any of his former coworkers, but having seen the Alpha suck the life out of Ms. Amblin made him realize he didn't dislike any of these people enough to delight in watching them die.

Her scream ended abruptly, almost as if Garrote had

pressed Stop on a Hallowe'en horror sounds tape.

"*That's better now, isn't it?*" the man himself said, his dark grin widening into a smile. "*We can hear ourselves think.*"

Harrison opened his eyes again, cautiously. The Swarm hovered between himself and Nia's dead body, convulsing like an unstable element, a dark mass of dead energy hungry for the life pumping through his veins.

For a moment he wondered if the featureless faces swirling within the cloud were scrutinizing him, sizing him up, the way they seemed to have studied Ms. Amblin's corpse only moments ago. He had no doubt Garrote would let it do the same to him, if he didn't follow the man's orders to the letter.

"I did what you asked! You promised you'd let me live!"

"*And so I shall,*" the face spread across the monitor wall said. "*But we have much to do before nightfall, Harry. There's still the little problem of getting me out of here and that, unfortunately, will require some assistance. The children who just left—can you keep track of them?*"

Harrison nodded. "As long as their headsets are on, they should be easy to ping. If not, we'll have to use facial recognition from the security cameras—" He frowned. "You know, this would be a lot simpler if you didn't *kill everyone* who could have actually helped me!"

"I'm *helping you, Harry. The rest of the team were an impedance to our Great Work. We'd have to explain how we got from there to here, and you know I find backstory oh so tedious.*"

Harrison bit his tongue.

"*Find the children, Harry. I want you to keep an eye on them. Don't do them any favors, though. When they*" *survive, I want it to be by the skin of their teeth. It can't be made easy for them. Life isn't easy. Nor should death be."*

"Okay," Harrison said. "But why them? Why not someone stronger? More capable?"

The smile stretched across the screens grew wistful. *"Because the boy was my Number-One Fan, once. I believe he'll do what needs to be done without even being aware I've been pulling his strings. And the girl has moxie in spades. She reminds me of myself, in my youth."*

Whatever "moxie" was Harrison didn't think he'd seen it. She'd seemed like a typical stuck-up teenaged girl to him. A spoiled princess.

"But I could do it so much easier," he said. "I know the tunnel system, the server grid, the hatch code…. I could be with you in less than an hour, depending on—"

"Tut, tut, Harry, my boy. You're far too delicate. My park would eat you alive. You'll be safe in here, as promised. And I need you at your terminal. I'll have my hands full with all of my new toys."

That smile again, as wide and deadly as a California fault line.

"Oh, there's a man here today by the name of Alex Fischer. The twisted little freak is lingering around the Transportation building, by the mobile home exhibit. I suspected he wouldn't be able to stay away and indeed, I was right. I want him, Harry. I'll send his image to your terminal."

"What's so special about this guy?" Harrison asked, burning with jealousy. First the kids and now this Fischer guy. It was almost like Mr. Garrote didn't think of him as a partner at all.

"Nothing much," the writer said offhandedly. *"I simply despise loose ends. Get busy now, my diligent little*

beaver."

Harrison pushed himself shakily to his feet.

As if attracted by his movement, the Alpha darted toward him, as swift and menacing as a school of hammerhead sharks.

Feebly, Harrison threw a hand up in front of his face to protect himself, as ineffectual as tissue paper held in the path of a heat-seeking missile. He let out a frightened little scream and squeezed his eyes shut, waiting for the cloud of death to squeegee the life out of him.

Mr. Garrote giggled.

Harrison lowered his arm and opened his eyes.

The Alpha floated inches from his face, so close he could reach out and touch it if he temporarily lost his grip on sanity. A reckless part of him wondered what it would feel like. If it would be an agony in every pore and nerve ending in his body or an icy numbness lulling him sweetly into oblivion. Of all the ghosts in the park Mr. Garrote could have sent to kill everyone in the control room, the fact that he'd chosen these faceless assassins, the Alpha to His Omega, spoke for itself.

"Oh, be a dear and let my pets out, would you, Harry?" Garrote said. *"They're quite hungry."*

Harrison did. Gladly.

Harrison Greely had never been a popular boy.

He couldn't dance, couldn't bring himself to talk to girls without stumbling over his words, couldn't play sports outside of table tennis, couldn't speak up in class without a stutter, couldn't make friends, couldn't impress his teachers with physical prowess or mental aptitude or even gain their sympathy when the other kids picked on him.

What he *could* do was program. He'd been a whiz with computers ever since he stripped his older brother's PlayStation down to its individual diodes and chips at the age of nine, reprogrammed it via their dad's Pentium III, and put all of the pieces back in the correct order. The only difference, other than a slight crack in the gray casing, was that young Harrison had suddenly been able to beat his brother Tommy in any game by using a simple cheat code and still make the win look natural.

Tommy hadn't played with him much after that.

While Harrison was sad to lose his brother's sporadic companionship, the time alone gave him the opportunity to formulate what he'd already begun to think of as his Great Work. With rapid advancements in technology during the early-2000s, old motherboards, casings, RAM and various spare parts were often tossed into dumpsters or left in boxes on front lawns, providing enough supplies to keep Harrison busy between school and supper, when no one was home besides himself and Tommy—and once Tommy left for Penn State in 2004, Harrison alone.

Young Harrison dreamed of supercomputers with enough raw intelligence to subjugate every one of his bullies. Somewhere between his early and late teens the idea of creating an AI Superintelligence began to feel too risky. Nanotechnology could theoretically repair and maintain the Machines just as easily, perhaps easier, than any human. He'd read Kurzweil, von Neumann and Moravec's thoughts on technological singularity and "transhumanism," the theoretical merging of Man and Machine. He'd read about neural networks and "deep learning," which had still been in its infancy when James Cameron's epic techno-fantasy film *Avatar* had been unleashed upon a world Harrison considered woefully unprepared for its genius, breaking every single box office record and forever changing his life, shaping his destiny.

He'd left the theater that night feeling a deep sense of excitement—*my Great Work, at last!*—but also a terrifying urgency. His invention would change the world, the way Cameron's film had changed the definition of what a Blockbuster Film could be, but only if he lived long enough to complete it. He was especially careful on the way home, looking twice before crossing the street, holding his keys in a fist to prevent potential thieves and murderers from harming him, locking the door and returning to check on the locks multiple times throughout the night as he worked alone in semidarkness.

The world would never know they had lost a Great Mind if Harrison Greely died before his Great Work was done. He vowed that someday, the world would know his name. They would fall at his feet and grovel.

In his second year at MIT, a Mormon transhumanist group discovered his work and offered to fund his studies. He'd worked with them throughout the next few years of his PhD, but their partnership had never reached a place of synergy. They were too nice. They'd all wanted eternal youth and happiness. And while Harrison would have been fine with eternal youth, happiness was the furthest thing from his mind.

It wasn't until the Hedgewood Foundation poached him in his last year at MIT that Harrison discovered his true value. They'd offered him a deal: they would pay for his final year of tuition and provide a per diem of fifty dollars a day—far more than Harrison had ever seen in his ramen-and-Gatorade life—in exchange for his Friday evenings and weekends. He'd gladly accepted, not even caring that Hedgewood had a reputation for overworking and underpaying its employees. After all, he wouldn't technically be an employee. They needed his brain more than he needed them, and Harrison certainly didn't need his Fridays and weekends.

His liaison had picked him up that first Friday after class and every subsequent one in a private helicopter. The following Monday, he'd noticed jealous looks from fellow co-eds. Suddenly, people who'd had no interest in him were full of questions. Who was he working for? What was he working on? Could he get them on the team?

All of the employees at Hedgewood, from the janitors to theoretical physicists, ate in the same stark white cafeteria. Non-disclosure agreements prevented them from revealing details about their work to others who weren't on their team, which left most conversations consisting of things happening in the outside world, much of which— since most of these people appeared to live at the facility— was secondhand information from TV.

Did you see what happened on Lost this week? Did you hear what Obama said in his speech? Isn't it awful what happened in Haiti? Can you believe how much oil spilled in the Gulf of Mexico? What about this Julian Assange guy? Is he a hero, a cyber terrorist or what?

Like the sudden keen interest from fellow students back in Cambridge, people at Hedgewood seemed eager to talk to him because of his weekly returns to the outside world. Harrison had stumbled into popularity, yet he still preferred to keep to himself. He listened. He nodded. He didn't have much to offer by way of conversation and when he did, when he'd start to discuss his interests in the Singularity and classic PlayStation vs. next-gen systems, and his favorite movie in the whole world—which had been *unfairly panned* by the critics and *James Cameron was shooting four sequels simultaneously, did you know that? FOUR!*—he would notice their eyes begin to glaze and their attention start to wander, as if they'd suddenly found something extremely interesting to look at on the blank white walls of the cafeteria.

It wasn't long before he fell once more into the role of Pariah, which suited Harrison just fine.

In his third month at Hedgewood, sitting alone at a corner table eating chicken tenders and bright-orange macaroni while the others discussed things he cared absolutely nothing about, Rex Garrote sat down opposite him. In that moment it seemed as if the entire cafeteria had fallen silent.

"I've heard about your work," the writer said—though at the time, Harrison had no clue the man was a writer, nor who he was at all. He was still just a man, not the demigod he would become to Harrison in later years. Harrison had only seen him in passing once or twice, heard people whisper about him secretly, rumors and speculation he felt no need to pry into. Strange things about faking his own death and living here like a hermit since the early 2000s. Stories that couldn't possibly be true—though, in time he would discover they were true, and much worse.

Harrison chewed his food quickly, swallowed hard and choked on it. He washed the blockage down with a mouthful of Gatorade Glacier Freeze. "O-okay," he said finally, not exactly sure how to respond.

The man sitting across from him smiled, and though the smile didn't crease the skin around his eyes it didn't seem to hold a trace of condescension. "You're a man of few words," he said. "I like that. You're a thinker. A *dreamer*, like myself. I see big things in your future, Harrison Greely." He held out his hand. "I'm Rex Garrote."

Harrison wiped his greasy fingers on a stack of napkins and shook the man's cool, dry hand. "Harrison—oh, right. You already…" His skin whispered against Garrote's palm as he let go of it.

"Don't fret, my boy. It's not my intention to poke fun at you or make you feel inadequate."

They sat in silence a moment, Garrote watching him, Harrison feeling scrutinized. Awkward. "There sure are a lot of people here," he said to fill the silence. "Must be a lot of other projects—"

"Not a single one as important as yours." The writer smiled lightly and patted Harrison's hand, which held a forkful of neon macaroni. "Well, perhaps the one other. I'd like to be your partner, Harry. Take you under my wing, so to speak. I feel your work could be incredibly important—could be *great*, in fact."

It was thrilling to hear those words from someone else's lips. That his work could in fact be *Great*.

"You just need a little nudge in the right direction," the writer said. He grinned then: a dark, sardonic half-smile Harrison came to know intimately in the following years. "That, and the proper motivation."

In the control room, Harrison placed the Pandora neural mesh on his head and connected it to the port he'd installed on his terminal without Ms. Amblin's approval. The emergency lights stopped flashing and the backup lighting flickered on overhead. In the eerie silence that followed he remembered all of the dead who lay here with him. His former colleagues. Some of them he might even have considered friends, in another life. It was a graveyard— both in here and outside.

He'd known all the while that this time would

eventually come. That he would stand alone in a room full of death. That he would remain behind, helping a dead man who'd provided him with a sense of purpose he'd known from the moment he'd torn apart his brother's PlayStation would one day be recognized.

This was his Great Work. Right here, right now. The dead were inconsequential.

He called up the Pandora program. On a separate monitor he scanned all active devices, looking for the serial codes Garrote had provided him. On a third he pulled up 3D schematics of the park, showing each of the cameras, every mechanism, door and trick. A fourth showed the main program code, the cursor blinking.

Results pinged back quickly and two separate camera feeds appeared on the device monitor: POVs from the headsets of the boy and the girl. They were running, the images erratic and somewhat blurry. He caught glimpses of the woman they'd come in with, the psychiatrist—as well as two meathead security guards.

A moment later, two flashing red dots appeared on the schematic, very near Bright Falls Sanitarium.

"*There* you are," he breathed. In that moment his grin reflected in the matte black of the coding monitor looked very much like Rex Garrote's own.

PART 1
GHOSTS ARE PEOPLE TOO

It is uncertain exactly what caused the so-called "Ghostland Disaster." Speculation has run the gamut from mass psychosis, to natural disaster, to chemical attack. At this point, it is doubtful the cause will ever be determined, and if it is, whether or not the public will be informed.

— Ducks Falls *Squawker*
April 24, 2019

War was inevitable, now. Samson felt it in his bones. All he'd ever known was blood. He'd gotten a taste for it soon after he and his brothers set their feet on the shore in Danang, lugging their M-60s, rucks and equipment, greasy sweat sticking their uniforms to their skin. The ghosts of his fallen brothers would fight at his side… and the ghosts of their enemies would stand along with them: Charlie and GIs, shoulder to shoulder, razing the whole godforsaken world to ash.

— Rex Garrote, *Shōki*

THE GIRL WHO PLAYED WITH GHOSTS

Placid Oaks Cemetery
Berkeley, California—October 31st, 2019

ONLY A PSYCHO would spend Hallowe'en at a graveyard," Lilian Roth said, bundled up against the evening chill. Passing under the soft glow of a cobwebbed streetlamp, she cocked an ear to her left, as if to listen to the autumn wind rustle dead leaves through the tombstones. Her laugh was a bright and cheerful counterpoint to the aura of death and decay. "Yeah, you wish, dork."

To most people it might have looked like she was speaking to herself, with no one in the desolate graveyard to hear her.

Lilian wasn't like most people. Her once dull, normal life had been irrevocably changed twice: first, on the day in April when her best friend Ben Laramie and her therapist Dr. Allison Wexler, along with more than two-thousand others, had lost their lives at Ghostland. The second, the night Ben returned to her as a ghost.

He paced alongside her now, mimicking the actions of her arms and legs. The illusion of life wasn't quite perfect:

his feet hovered an inch or so above the ground, for starters. Lilian had already gotten used to him occasionally forgetting to breathe or blink or walk, and the fact that he never felt hungry or thirsty or tired. Ben thought it made her uncomfortable when he behaved like any other ethereal being, so he continued to act like the living around her. He'd suddenly puff out his chest as if he was taking a deep breath, or pretend to stumble upon noticing he'd just walked through something at shin-level that would have tripped a living person, and she'd have to try hard not to laugh.

Just a few months ago she never would've imagined she'd be working with Ghosts Are People Too, stalking through a graveyard on Hallowe'en with the ghost of her best friend, in search of a dead woman to free from the woman's own personal Hell. But here she was ascending the low, tree-covered hill in the center of Placid Oaks, where a columbarium stood with a view of the entire cemetery. The mist had grown thick around her feet, and the stone building housing dozens of urns filled with cremated remains shone stark white under the crescent moon. This was where people claimed to have most often seen the so-called "Woman in White."

"Is she even here?" Lilian asked.

"I'm not sure, there's a lot of interference," Ben said, sensing the presence of multiple ethereals lurking among the headstones. "Hey, did you hear about Miss Delyse?" he asked, remembering what he'd heard earlier in the day.

"What about her?"

"She committed suicide."

"*Are you serious?*"

"Dead serious," he said.

It had become one of his favorite phrases, lately. Lilian

would've kicked herself for setting up the joke but she was too bothered by what he'd said to even roll her eyes. For a short time after Sara Jane Amblin informed the world about the existence of an afterlife there had been a sharp rise in suicides, especially among teens—but that was over a year ago. The spike had tapered off since, with a drastic drop following the Ghostland Disaster. The world seemed to be slowly returning to normal.

The sweet, middle-aged Caribbean psychic from TV she and Ben used to watch ironically seemed like the furthest thing from suicidal. She was a grandmother. Grandmothers didn't commit suicide.

"That's awful," she said finally.

"News said she like decapitated herself in her car or something," Ben said.

"She cut off *her own head*?"

"Well, like, she tied a rope around her neck to a tree and backed out of her driveway. There were people watching from across the street, they said."

"Why didn't they try to stop her?"

"I dunno, I guess they didn't—" He paused, listening as the wind whistled, rattling bare branches like rolled bones. "She's here."

Lilian startled. "*Miss Delyse?*"

"Jessica, dumb-dumb. Why don't you set up the Ouija on that crypt over there?"

Lilian tugged on the strap of her knapsack, drawing it closer to her body. "I still don't get why we have to use this thing."

"It's the only way anyone's been able to contact her. Like Professor Hermann with that old phone, 'member?"

She remembered Claus Hermann, the bespectacled Jewish scientist originally from Berlin, with his odd little obsessive-compulsive tics and the sporadic outbursts of static electricity that formed around him. They'd only been able to contact him using the old rotary-dial phone in his apartment, which was now part of a historical tenement museum in New York's Lower East Side.

Professor Hermann had witnessed the Third Reich's rise to power in the '30s and fled Germany to America before the situation grew dire. Despite this, he was afraid to join their fight against Rex Garrote—a war Ben and Lilian felt was inevitable, and would reach them before any of them were ready.

Sadly, there were more ethereals like Hermann than Ben and his friends at GRP2. Content with the status quo, repeating the same trivial tasks and motions day after day, hiding themselves from the living who shared their space, often unknowingly. Afraid to fight back, before it was too late for any of them.

"Take me back," Professor Hermann had said after a short time among them. "I prefer my home. *Bitte*."

Ben had taken him back to the museum, where guests would marvel at their hair standing on end and the static shocks he'd unintentionally give them. The next day two others from their group had fled.

"I'm gonna wink out for a bit," Ben said, hovering among the graves. "See if I can shake her loose." Without awaiting Lilian's response, he disappeared from her side.

She still found it sort of weird to see him "wink out," as he called it. The way he acted with her she could almost believe he was still alive, aside from his little mistakes. Then he'd disappear and she'd remember her best friend was the Dead Kid. The kid she'd shunned for so many years to avoid the sting of embarrassment for being his friend.

She sat on the crypt, a cold, dulled-granite block in the vague shape of a coffin with the name UNTERGANG engraved in its side. The plastic planchette rattled inside the box as she heaved her knapsack off her shoulder. She laid the Ouija board on the cold granite beside her, placing the planchette at the center of the board. She lit a candle and laid the tips of her fingers gently on the planchette's plastic, heart-shaped surface. Closing her eyes, she moved it in concentric circles, wider and wider, like a splash in a pond.

It was strange how something so simple could contain so much power, like a cross to a vampire—less magic, Lilian assumed, than psychological conditioning. Like Claus Hermann's telephone. Or the ghost they'd tried to liberate from the supermarket, who would only communicate through condensation on the glass in the frozen food aisle. The Woman in White—also known as the "Singing Woman," due to claims of witnesses hearing the phantom singing of an indistinct song—had only ever responded to the Ouija.

"I wish to contact the spirit of Jessica Kissimon."

She widened her circles, the light scratching of the planchette on the board the only sound aside from the wind in the trees and the swish of dead leaves in the autumn evening chill.

"Jessica Kissimon, the spirit called the Woman in White, I wish to communicate with you! If you are here," she said, projecting her voice, "speak to me through the board. Tell me why you remain in this cemetery. Tell me what you require to move on."

The planchette jittered under her fingers, so lightly it could have been from her shivering. It stopped circling and swept across the board, pausing for a moment with the viewing aperture above the M. It moved to the A and stopped there.

MA.

"Your mother? Did your mother do something to you, Jessica?"

The planchette cycled rapidly between M and A, M and A—*MAMAMAMAMA*. Then it stopped. Lilian held her trembling fingers over it with a creeping sense of dread, her breath caught in her throat.

Jessica Kissimon died in a head-on collision in 2011 on her way back from Vegas, where she and her new husband had eloped. Her husband had been drunk and survived the crash. The family of four in the other car died. Jessica's mother had been sitting in their living room on the other side of town, watching *America's Got Talent*. She later told the papers she hadn't approved of their marriage but she would have tolerated him if it meant she'd have her baby back.

The planchette moved again, very slowly, dragging across the board, as if some force was pushing against the spirit she'd summoned. It came to rest on the N.

She waited. The planchette held there.

"Man?" she said aloud.

The candle guttered with a low rumble. The clouds parted in the same moment, revealing the stark-white sliver of moon.

"What man, Jessica?"

She covered her ears from the sound of a high-pitched shriek. Stone cracked nearby and she jumped, turning toward it in mid-air. The grave marker directly ahead of her had cracked down the middle. The shriek stopped abruptly. Reluctantly, Lilian lowered her hands, wondering if that was the sound witnesses had spoken about.

"Jessica, I'm a friend," she called out, a nervous quaver in her voice. "I'm trying to help you."

She tried to conjure the calm demeanor Allison had as she'd spoken to the dead man at the farmhouse in Ghostland, drawing him gently out of his body. But she was frightened. No matter how many ghosts she'd encountered since that day, when an ethereal acted out, even out of fear themselves, she couldn't help but worry.

"Jessica? You said man. What man, Jessica?"

The shriek came again, louder this time. Headstones cracked and tipped around her, like the ground splitting on a fault line. The planchette circled, tracing the path of the stones as they toppled one after another. Bare branches whipped and the moon disappeared under a scud of dark clouds.

Lilian drew her knees up to her chest. The second her fingers left the planchette it shot off the board and clattered at the foot of the columbarium steps. The remains of the family of four in the other car were stored in there. The theory was that Jessica haunted the building due to her guilt over their deaths. That she mourned the loss of their lives as much as her own, if not more.

The voice fell silent.

"I've got her!" Ben cried.

He reappeared suddenly, hovering at the top of the steps, holding the Woman in White in a bear hug from behind. She struggled against his grip, the gauzy material of her white, Victorian-looking wedding dress moving languidly, like dancing underwater. Jessica's mother denied her daughter had ever owned such a gown, and it wasn't something she might have picked up for a quickie Vegas wedding. Even the police report had confirmed she hadn't been wearing it when she died.

It made Lilian wonder if Jessica had imagined it into being. Most ethereals wore what they'd been wearing when they died, or what they were buried in. Lilian looked at her own clothes: a pair of loose-fitting gray TNA joggers, one of Blake's bulky Stanford hoodies, her puffy winter vest and her worn Converse. If she died right now and had to wear this outfit for eternity, the afterlife would be pretty embarrassing.

"Jessica, listen to me," Ben said. "And please, *please* don't scream again." He paused a moment, waiting for a reaction. She remained silent, continuing her slow-motion struggle. "I'm like you, okay? Only I never got trapped like you did. I'm not stuck, get it? Don't you ever wonder why you're always wandering around this graveyard night after night? Wouldn't you rather be somewhere else? *Do* something else?"

Her lips moved soundlessly. Lilian thought it looked like someone calling for help in a nightmare. The spirit's eyes widened in absolute terror. A deep red stain began to bloom in the middle of her dress.

"She's trying to say something," Lilian said.

Holding her as tight as he could, Ben tried to look over her shoulder to see if he could make out her words. Her gown fluttered into his field of vision. "Can you tell what she's saying?"

Lilian watched her lips. "It looks like she's saying *Easter*." She squinted, watching the Woman in White repeat the same words as the red stain spread over her breasts and down the length of the gown. "Please pear?"

"'Please pear'?" Ben scoffed. "Yeah, that's probably what she's saying. Totally makes sense."

"Well, I'm not a lip reader! Why don't you Vulcan

mind meld her?"

"Because that's an invasion of privacy, Lilian."

"Okay, then just hold her in a bear hug all night. Maybe she'll tire herself out, like, never."

"*Fine*."

Ben squeezed his eyes shut. His mouth opened and a young woman's voice came from his lips, warped and thick-sounding, like when Lilian had played one of her dad's old 45 records after she'd left the box too close to the radiator.

"*Heeeeeee's heeeeeere*," Ben said in Jessica's voice.

Lilian felt a chill straight through to her bones. *He's here.* Was "he" the man Jessica warned her about with the Ouija board?

Drained of energy, Ben let his arms drop from around Jessica Kissimon's waist. She immediately vanished in a blinding white light. The columbarium dome cracked. The weathervane tilted, the rooster and arrow issuing a rusty squawk. The final headstone split and the upper half collapsed on the grave mound.

No way could the Woman in White be this powerful.

He's here, Lilian thought. *Garrote? Is that who she means by "he"?*

Ben winked out. For a terrifying moment Lilian worried he'd abandoned her, that he'd run away and left her for dead. He reappeared at her side a moment later. "Come on!"

She leaped off the crypt, knocking the Ouija board aside, and hurried down the hill, the low mist whipping up around her legs. Ben flew ahead of her, quicker than any living person could move.

As they neared the gate, a dark figure stepped out from behind a weathered stone angel. Lilian skidded to a halt, tearing up clods of damp grass. The man was maybe twenty feet from her, two rows away.

The dark figure stepped into the gateway, barring escape. Something in his hand caught a glint of light from the streetlamp beyond the brick wall.

This is it. Nowhere to run. He's come for us. It's all over now.

The man belched.

Lilian allowed herself to relax, but only somewhat. It wasn't Garrote. But Jessica had said, *He's here*. Who was this man? What kind of nutjob hung out at a graveyard on Hallowe'en? Not the kind of man she wanted to meet alone in the dark, she knew that much.

"That's no ethereal," Ben said.

The man raised whatever he held to his face. Liquid sloshed against glass. He was drinking. He lowered the bottle, staggered forward a few steps. Not just drinking, he was *plastered*.

"A drunk idiot in an empty cemetery," she muttered. "That's just great."

"Jessica?" The drunk man sounded uncertain. "S'that you?"

She could see his face now, unshaven and grayish in the moonlight. His shirt collar stuck out of his heavy jacket and the tails were pulled from his jeans. The laces of his boots were untied. Lilian recognized him from photos she'd seen in Jessica's file: it was Eddie Frazier, her husband.

"You ruined my life, you know that? Why'd you have to keep hitting me, huh? You knew I was trying to watch the road. I get six years in prison and I gotta see those people we killed—*we* killed, Jessica—I gotta see their faces every night before I fall asleep, that's *if* I fall asleep.

So why'd you do it, babe? *Huh?*"

He threw the bottle. It smashed on the gravel a few feet from Lilian.

"I'm not Jessica," she said, sounding braver than she felt. "And you drove drunk."

"I know I shouldn'ta done it." She heard him sob. "I knew it was wrong. But we was celebratin. We just got *hitched.* How come Jess gets away with it, like she didn't do nothin wrong? Like she's an innocent victim? It ain't fair. The news made me out to be this bad guy. Nobody believes me when I tell them she turned the goddamn wheel as a joke." He laughed bitterly. "As a fuckin *joke.*"

"She's looping," Ben said. "She knows she's guilty. She's punishing herself, that's why she can't leave here. The white gown covered in blood isn't pain, it's guilt. Tell him that."

Lilian repeated what Ben told her.

"What? You can't know that." The husband's voice rose in anger. "How would you know that?"

"The song," Ben said. "The one she sings. I figured it out. I think it's 'Hold On Lucy.'"

"'Hold On *Loosely*,'" Lilian said. Her dad had the single on vinyl. Whenever he put it on, he'd start that awkward wiggling dance he did and drag either her or her mom into the living room to dance with him until they just about died of laughter and embarrassment.

The husband's anger evaporated. "What did you say?"

"'Hold On Loosely,'" she said again. "That's the song Jessica sings, the one nobody can figure out. Does it mean something to you?"

"Jesus…." He staggered further into the light. "You *do* know. That was on the radio when it happened. She was singing it when she pushed the wheel. Like a joke. Like a sick *joke*."

"Tell him she stands beside their urns reliving that moment every night." Lilian repeated what Ben said. The drunk man's face crumpled and he began to cry, weeping into his hands.

"I wish she never met me," he moaned. "Her ma was right. We were poison for each other."

"You can't help who you love," Lilian said, feeling the sting of those words, thinking of Ben and how she knew he still loved her even though he tried to hide it, even though she was seeing someone now and Ben pretended to be cool with it, pretended to even like Blake. She hoped he never looked into her mind, because if he knew what she thought sometimes it would push him away, drive him away from her for good.

They left the cemetery, leaving Jessica Kissimon's husband to his grief and guilt. His punishment had been imposed on him by the state: six years for vehicular manslaughter. Jessica's penance was self-imposed, and if she wouldn't allow them to help her, it would last much longer. Her guilt tied her to Placid Oaks, to mourn the lives she helped to take.

Ben sat silently beside Lilian on the hour-long drive back to campus. He left the seatbelt off, even though he'd always worn it when he was still alive. It took far too much effort to hold it for such a long drive. Especially with so much on his mind.

As they crossed the Oakland Bay bridge, he turned to Lilian and spoke. "She cracked all those headstones. The mausoleum roof."

Lilian nodded, gripping the wheel tighter. "She's pretty powerful. Would've been good to have her on our side."

He agreed with a nod. "When she said 'He's here,' I

swear she meant—"

"I know," she said, cutting him off. "I did too."

"I was worried for a minute I won't be able to sense him when he does come. That he'll ambush us and we won't even have a chance."

"I thought about that, too."

The silence drew out between them, without even the stereo in Lilian's old family Chevy to dampen its oppressiveness.

Ever since Ben came back, ever since he warned her that Garrote had escaped, she couldn't help but think the end of the world was inevitable. Her destiny and Ben's were inextricably linked with the architect of the coming Armageddon. Thinking of this depressed her. She'd wonder why she couldn't have a normal life like other girls her age, whether friends and grades really mattered when they were all so close to the end. Why had she spent Hallowe'en in a deserted graveyard a hundred miles from school instead of getting wasted with the girls in her dorm before meeting up with Blake and his friends at some trashy college bar for cheap shooters and all-night dancing in slinky costumes? Even hanging out with the kids in the Geek Squad to watch the Ghost Brothers in the first of their two-night live television event *Return to Ghostland* would have seemed normal compared to this. Blake had texted her an hour ago, wondering why she'd ghosted him, and she'd tucked the phone back into her jacket without replying.

He wouldn't understand. I don't even understand.

Normal wasn't possible anymore. Not with Rex Garrote out there, dead yet deadly.

That was why they needed to gather up as many capable ethereals as they could. Not just to free them, as the people at GRP2 expected her to, but to fight beside them when the time came.

"I know we can't save them all," she said finally. "And maybe not all of them deserve to be saved. But it doesn't stop it from hurting when we lose one."

Ben agreed—though he worried that if Lilian knew what he'd done she would change her mind about whether or not even he'd deserved to be saved. If she knew this was all his fault, would she ever forgive him?

Am I poison for her? he wondered.

They drove the rest of the way in silence.

CHASING GHOSTS PT. 1

S.P.D. West Precinct
Seattle, Washington
October 29th

Y O, RINGO! DESK phone's ringin."

Sam paused at the lobby door with one arm in her jacket. That damn desk phone. She was certain she'd forwarded her calls but half the time it didn't seem to work. She'd be at a crime scene, a grisly suicide or a murder, and her mom would call wondering why she wasn't picking up her desk phone even though she'd always told her mother not to call during regular work hours unless it was an emergency. She'd have to step under the police tape and push through a crowd of looky-loos to call her voicemail, only to discover six to a dozen messages waiting.

It was aggravating, but not half as aggravating as just about everyone in the department still calling her "Ringo" after all these years.

Why not McCartney? she thought, putting her jacket back on the rack by the door, beside the umbrella stand with a puddle around it, the WET FLOOR sign propped up beside it. *Why not Lennon or Harrison? Why the drummer with the goofy grin? Why the comic relief? No, it had to be Mr. Shining Time Station. Mr. Octupus's Garden in his Yellow Submarine.*

Detective Sam Beadle heaved a dramatic sigh at the desk officer and returned to the bullpen. And of course, that damn phone stopped ringing as soon as she reached it.

Probably Mom again, anyhow. Seems like she knows exactly the wrong time to call. Must be psychic.

The thought brought her current predicament back into focus. She was headed out to speak to the witness, the Hemming woman.

Let Mom deal with the machine, she thought, with only a trace of guilt.

"Win some, lose some," Detective Borden said, shrugging up his broad shoulders behind the desk across from hers.

Sam agreed with another heavy sigh as she headed back to the lobby. It seemed like far more losing than winning these days.

Ever since Stan passed away at Ghostland she'd felt a strange sense of melancholy. She told herself she wasn't grieving. Stan and her mother had been divorced since she was sixteen, and after high school they'd drifted apart entirely. Estranged.

As the daughter of a cop and a nurse, it seemed inevitable Sam would follow in either of their footsteps. Ending up in the same job as the father who'd all but abandoned her had more to do with aptitude than torch passing. That she'd made detective in the same precinct where her father had held the same rank made her Ringo instead of Detective Beadle. All these years later and the nickname still stuck.

When she'd still been in uniform, she used to run into

Stan every so often. They might pass a few pleasantries over a break-and-enter with an unintended double homicide or a domestic dispute ending in murder-suicide. He would fumble with some fatherly words of advice he had no right to offer and they would go their separate ways. That was that.

Why so glum, then? Maybe it was the rain. *Liquid sunshine*, some people called it. She used to love the rain when she was little. She used to jump and splash in puddles in the yard. Now it was just an inconvenience. Just another damper on a miserable day.

Sam couldn't pinpoint the exact cause of her depression. All she knew was that she wasn't grieving. Certainly not for a father she barely knew.

She hurried to her car, soaked before she opened the door, and slipped behind the driver's seat. The passenger seat was piled with case notes, her computer, crime scene photos, lab reports, and the shoe box full of small white envelopes. It was her office away from the office. Since she'd never been assigned a partner, she'd never needed to make an excuse for the mess and clear it so someone else could sit.

Sam didn't regret being alone. She'd always worked better on her own. Even in school, when everyone else had paired off, she would hang back, make herself part of the wall so no one would pick her and the teachers would have to assign her to a group or let her work on her own. Being a "lone wolf," as she liked to think of herself, allowed her to work through her cases without someone else's opinion coloring her own. It gave her time to deliberate, to rely less on instinct and more on facts.

Her father had been old school, falling back far too often on hunches and gut feelings. His gut ended up getting him killed. Stan Beadle, sixty-eight years old, had driven all the way across the country to that ridiculous amusement park in Maryland, and the two cases that had dogged him through the latter third of his career had literally crushed him to death, trapping him under the collapse of that damned house alongside the lead suspect in the Doll's Head murders, like the witch sisters of East and West Oz.

Everyone in Sam's precinct knew her father believed that obscure horror writer from the '80s was still alive after all these years, that he was out there somewhere, in hiding. And for no real reason other than Stan's gut told him it was so. The body had been burned to a crisp but the dental records had matched. It was suicide. Self-immolation. Open and shut.

Old Stan had refused to let it go. Suddenly he was the number one fan of this Rex Garrote, always reading one of his trashy novels with the luridly painted covers at his desk, on the road, in his recliner at home.

Guys on the force started to wonder about his sanity. Guys who'd once respected him and whose respect was important to maintain if you wanted to rise in the ranks.

After Stan retired, years went by with the two of them passing barely a word. When they tore up that damned house from its foundation—only the word her father had used was *exhumed*—and took it to that park, Stan suddenly started reaching out to her again. Not to catch up or mend fences. His gut told him something weird was going on and could she maybe look into it, put out some feelers to her colleagues.

Eventually Sam had broken down and gone out to the grounds to meet him, despite her better judgment. She'd found Stan peering into the overgrown foundation where Garrote House once stood, his expression distant. He'd looked even older than the last time she'd seen him, at his retirement sendoff, his white hair even more sparse and his skin speckled with liver spots. His eyes looked bleary and tired and his back was hunched beneath his beige trench coat.

Sam cleared her throat to announce her presence he looked up, startled and embarrassed.

"They moved it," he said.

"Apparently," she grunted.

He didn't react to her sarcasm. "Some town called Duck Falls in Maryland. Like, *duck*, *falls*," he said, ducking slightly and acting out something falling into the hole with a withered hand. "Folks are saying it looks like a junkyard for old buildings and cars and carnival rides. I talked to someone on the town council. She said the land's been rezoned for an amusement park." He frowned, his bushy eyebrows creasing together under the crumpled brim of his fedora. "What kind of an amusement park has old houses in it? What is that?"

"I don't know, Stan."

He took off his hat and regarded her with bleary eyes. The flesh on his face and under his jowls was sallow and doughy. "When did you stop calling me 'Dad'? When did that happen?"

Sam shook her head. "You can't just come back into my life and ask me that like you've been there the whole time. And you really need to drop this Rex Garrote business."

Even the guy's name was ridiculous. Stan's partner Detective Edelweiss once called him "Sex Parrot," and he and Stan's buddies had laughed about it for a week straight.

"He's *dead*, Stan. He's *been* dead for over a decade."

Stan scratched his mostly bald head, shifting the sparse

blond hairs. He put the hat back on and pulled it down over his ears. "Maybe you're right. Maybe that's all this is: a dead end. It's different when you retire, Samantha. Some guys can pick it all up and move down to Florida, fish for marlins, live for their kids and their grandkids. Me, I'm stuck on one case. It's my Moby Dick. I am Ahab."

He was peering down into the hole again, like the proverbial abyss.

"You're not Ahab," Sam said. "Ahab had a hobby."

Stan chuckled. "When I had you and Lucille, that was all I needed."

"You didn't need us," Sam shot back. "That was the problem. You needed your work. You needed cases. You needed to be *right*." *Pot meet kettle*, she thought, but continued anyway, because she needed to get it out and he needed to hear her. "But you're wrong about this. You're chasing a ghost."

Her final words to him came back to haunt her as she drove the wet streets toward Marjory Hemming's house. *Chasing a ghost*. Here she was, doing the same damn thing. Letting her gut lead her down a blind alley.

She glanced at the box of envelopes on the passenger seat. It felt too much like grief to keep them in the house. She'd lost her father long before he'd shuffled off his mortal coil. The man who died at Ghostland was already a ghost to her.

Stopped at a red light, she opened the box. Inside was a collection of small white envelopes, Stan's childlike script in all caps scrawled on their faces. She grabbed the envelope off the top of the pile, slipped the card out and read it.

SUSPECTS INNOCENT, WRITER DID IT.

She'd read them all several times over since Stan died,

all seventy-eight of them. At first, she'd assumed the inscriptions on the envelopes and the cards within were regarding his own cases. Eventually she realized what she was reading, and it began to paint a portrait of the father she barely knew. A man who lived for a good mystery. For policework. Deduction.

She returned the card into the envelope and put it back with the others. She nestled the lid on the box and dialed her voicemail, went hands-free as she turned right at the lights.

"Hi, Samantha, it's Mom. I guess you're not at your desk. Call me when you get a chance—"

She skipped it.

"Detective Beadle, it's Marjory Hemming, calling back about Regina Delyse. If you could swing by the house today, I'll be around between eleven and two—"

She skipped the message, already on her way to meet the woman.

"Sam. It's Gun. Your pop's partner. Former partner."

She recognized the old man's gruff voice right away. He didn't need to say it, nor to elaborate.

"Look, I need to speak with you, kid," Gunnar said. *"It's about your dad. Call me, okay? Or better yet, swing by the house. It's been a minute."*

She couldn't remember the last time she'd seen Stan's partner, fellow retired detective Gunnar Edelweiss. Likely would have been one of the backyard barbeques they used to have back when Stan and her mom were still pretending to be happy. When Sam herself was maybe twelve. Guys on the force had called him Gun or The Gun, like he was Mike Hammer or somebody. He'd had a mustache and sideburns and always wore Hawaiian shirts open at the collar like Magnum P.I. when he wasn't on duty, but he'd still end up with a deep-red farmer's tan. He'd spend most of those sunny afternoon parties in the yard spraying kids with the hose in a smokey haze from a menthol Kool hanging out of his mouth. Sam's mom said the cigarettes would kill him someday, but he'd already outlived his partner—her ex-husband and Sam's father. Some of their colleagues never made it as far as retirement, passing away from some illness or dying on the job.

Sam parked her tan '96 Cutlass Ciera in the street near Regina Delyse's two-story house and got out. The rain had stopped on the drive out to Bellevue and sunlight glittered on the wet streets and rooftops.

She figured it would probably be spitting again by noon. Winter in Seattle. God love it.

The police tape had been removed in the week since the woman known professionally as Miss Delyse had passed away. Suicide, the coroner had declared it when Sam went down to see the so-called psychic's remains. Her severed head had rested in the nook between her neck and shoulder.

"Terrible way to go, decapitation," Ron Thibodeau, the medical examiner, told her. "That thing about being able to see for thirty seconds or so after death? I hear that's a myth. It's all just reflexes, like the legs of dead frogs. Still, it can't be pleasant."

There had been a brief period of speculation in the precinct and the news that it was a racially motivated murder. Regina being a Jamaican-born black woman and the actual method of death being a rope tied to a tree, the conclusion was natural. But witnesses had seen her tie the rope to the tree herself and enter her car alone.

It was definitely a puzzler. Sam was still having trouble wrapping her mind around it. Stan would have appreciated the case, in a macabre way. He would have called it a "real head-scratcher," as he literally acted out the phrase.

Sam opened the screen door and knocked on the inner door of the bungalow directly across the street from Regina Delyse's house. Marjory Hemming answered right away. She was between shifts, dressed in nurse's scrubs with her hair tied up, the heavy bags under her eyes shiny with a lavender-scented lotion. Under less inauspicious circumstances Sam might have considered asking her out. Cops and nurses seemed as natural a pairing as life and death.

"Detective." The woman smiled warmly. "Come in, please. I'm just having lunch."

The living room was dim, a bowl of tomato soup steaming on the coffee table and the television on at a low volume. *General Hospital*. Sam couldn't imagine doing her job all day and coming home at lunch to watch *Law & Order*. Then again there weren't any soaps about police stations, as far as she knew.

She sat on a rattan chair facing the tartan sofa where Marjory sat to the sound of squeaky springs. The furniture all looked to be secondhand or hand-me-downs. Marjory owned a home on a single income in a market that had skyrocketed in the last ten years. Sam still rented. She couldn't afford to buy anywhere near town on a cop's salary.

The witness ate her soup, lifting the spoon from the bowl on the coffee table to her lips and slurping while she watched the TV, as if she'd just invited Sam over to watch her soap.

"You wanted to talk to me about Regina?"

"Oh," the woman said. She laid her spoon across the rim of the bowl. "Sorry, I got sucked into my stories." She nodded at the television and Sam nodded back amiably, despite her eagerness to take her statement and leave. "Back when we first talked, you asked if anything seemed odd about Regina that day. I just got off shift, I was running on about two hours of sleep and six coffees, so I forgot the most important part."

"Oh?" Sam said. She wanted to prod her but it was important to let a witness speak at their own pace. As a trauma ward nurse, Marjory had probably believed she'd seen it all. A decapitation was on an entirely different level. Sam had seen her share of them as a first responder at car crashes, but witnessing the head fly off in a jet of arterial blood was unfathomable to her.

Only two others had witnessed the death. They were just curious, wondering what Regina Delyse was doing with the rope. "It was like out of a Road Runner cartoon," the Amazon delivery guy who'd been dropping off a package three doors down told her. "I thought she was trying to pull down the tree or something, ya know? Stick it to city hall."

Then blood had spattered the insides of the windows and the rope went loose, the car rolling up onto the opposite sidewalk and crashing right into the fire hydrant in front of Marjory Hemming's house. Marjory had been watching from her window as she washed dishes between shifts.

"I said then it seemed like she was having muscle spasms, or myoclonic seizures. I never saw her act like that before so I was watching her pretty closely. Figured I'd talk to her about it when I had a chance, see if she might want to come in to the hospital and get checked out. But then…" She trailed off. "Anyways, I was looking at symptoms online, seizures and Parkinson's and ALS and whatnot, diseases that attack the body, the nerves and muscles. And just on a whim I typed in *miss delyse suicide*, you know, to see what people were saying about her online. I know, never read the comments section. But I did, and that's where I found the video."

Sam's ears perked up. "What video, Marjory?"

"You know the Rock and Roll Psychic?"

Sam didn't, but she nodded for Marjory to go on.

"Well, he had this Facebook Live thing he did every week where he'd talk to his fans. Anyway, so halfway through this video he starts acting like his body's fighting itself. Or there's something inside of him, like a parasite controlling his movements, and he had to fight it off." She nodded, satisfied with her description of what she'd seen. "I turned the video off before, you know… But that was exactly how it looked when Regina left her house and tied that rope around the tree. *Exactly*."

Sam was unsure how to reply, nor what Marjory was implying.

"Don't you see?" the witness said finally, picking up her spoon from the bowl. "It was *ghosts*. Not suicide. *Ghosts* killed Regina and the Rock and Roll Psychic."

Back in the car, Sam pushed aside a heap of papers, opened her laptop, and looked up this Rock N' Roll Psychic. Some of the hits were puff pieces about his charitable contributions, his famous psychic cases or his appearances on talk shows and medical shows. Most were about Drew "The Rock N' Roll Psychic" Agnew's suicide.

Sam found the connection to Regina Delyse tenuous at best. The two had committed suicide within a week of one another, over twelve-hundred miles apart: Regina in Seattle, Agnew in San Diego. The only similarity other than a gruesome manner of death was the fact that they were both professional psychics—*Con artists*, Sam thought derisively—and that extremely slim connection was a coincidence at most.

She didn't believe in psychics or telekinesis or spoon bending any of that supernatural crap. Growing up with a nurse and a cop for parents, both of them lapsed Catholics, there was precious little room for superstition in their house.

To think that evil spirits were guiding them to kill themselves was not only farfetched, it was a full-blown psych ward delusion. She could just imagine bringing it to Captain Brewster and getting laughed right out of his office. Likely with a week's leave for her mental health.

Just like her dad, they'd all whisper. *Convinced a suicide is more than it seems.*

It took a bit of finessing in her search terms before she was finally able to find the video Facebook had pulled for violating its terms of service. She pressed play, bracing herself for the worst. The video was twenty minutes long and the first fifteen or more involved Agnew bigging up himself, talking about his show on TLC, his recent "collabs" with famous musicians, and hanging out with Richard Branson and the Obamas on Necker Island.

Sam skipped ahead and caught the knife already dragging, the flesh unzipping, spilling blood. She thought of kids watching this on a dare or out of morbid curiosity. Stuff like this was so easy to stumble across. Somewhere along the line the internet had become a proxy for public executions and lynch mobs. The thought of it turned her stomach.

She skipped back to the first big spike in views indicated on the timeline and played it from there. Drew

"The Rock N' Roll Psychic" Agnew had brown hair in a "more on top" style, a California tan, whitened teeth and a chiseled jawline. He looked like just about every single white guy on a reality-TV dating series.

"I'm grateful for every single day, for every gig I've been fortunate enough to play, for every success I've had," he said. "And that's the key to life, in my opinion. If you want to stay grounded, you gotta be grateful, you gotta—"

His left hand flopped off the acoustic guitar in his lap, flicking across the strings discordantly. He stared down at the hand, fearful, like a spider that had just crawled out from under the sofa.

He stood abruptly, the guitar falling off his lap with another discordant twang as he turned away somewhat robotically and headed off screen. The laptop camera refocused on the wall behind his desk, on rows of books and comics on his shelves, the Funko Pops and horror movie figurines and a psychedelic Hendrix Experience poster beside the bookshelf.

Finally, Agnew returned, visible only at the waist. He moved the laptop, positioning the camera so it faced the oval Persian rug at his feet.

A metallic glint along his leg was the first indication that something wasn't right. Those who were quick with the Pause button might have seen the silver blur of a slightly curved Japanese short sword in his hand.

He sat cross-legged on the rug. Even this movement seemed to be a struggle against an unseen force. His jaw worked but his lips barely opened, as if his mouth was wired shut. It looked like his lips were smeared across his face, as if he was pressing them against exceptionally clear glass.

He gripped the blade's haft in both hands, his fingers

trembling. It darted an inch forward, then back. Forward, then back. Tears welled in his eyes. He cried out as the blade plunged into his abdomen. Whether it was in terror or to give himself the courage to go through with it, Sam couldn't tell. Either way the sound was muffled, as if he was screaming through a gag.

The same push-pull motion accompanied the blade's sideways incision across his gut, almost like he was sawing at the flesh, though the blade didn't appear to be serrated. Intestines spooled out, hot and wet with blood, oozing bile and half-digested food onto his lap.

He fell backward and the blade clanged against the hardwood floor. The laptop camera struggled to keep his jittering body in focus, shifting between him and the edge of the keyboard until he fell still.

Sam closed her computer and sat for a long moment looking out through the drizzle-spattered windshield. It was definitely bizarre, the way he seemed to be fighting his own hands. How his lips appeared to be flattened against his face and his voice muffled when he screamed.

Occam's razor, she thought. *Simplest explanation. What's the simplest here, considering the struggle? A schizophrenic episode? Epilepsy, like Marjory said? And that muffled scream, it could just be bad audio. Overmodulation.*

But how to explain why Regina Delyse suffered a similar fate, according to the Hemming woman?

Easy. Marjory's misremembering now because she's been fed new information. She couldn't understand why Regina would've acted the way she had. When she saw it, her thoughts went directly to medical problems. That's what she knows. Her brain's way of making sense of what she saw. Then she sees this video, there's the immediate connection of the two of them being psychics, and now she has new information to process what she saw. It's like that study they talked about in Police Science, that thing about reconstructive memory. "War of the Ghosts"—that's what they called it, right? Okay, it's another creepy coincidence, but that's all it is: a coincidence. Watching the Rock N' Roll Psychic video shaped Marjory's memory of Regina's suicide—it changed her memory. War of the Ghosts. Open and shut.

A light rapping on the passenger window startled her. Marjory Hemming stood under an umbrella, ducking to peer into the car, looking both frightened and excited. Sam reached over and rolled down the window.

"Forgot something, Marjory?"

"They just showed on the news," the nurse said. "It's another one, Detective. Another psychic just killed herself."

INVISIBLE FRIENDS

Las Vegas, Nevada
October 31st

ANDY PARK HURRIED into the little shop just off the Strip and jerked the door closed. He locked the bolt and watched through the tinted glass and beaded curtain, sweating and panting heavily as the two goons in black suits from the Palais Royale ran past.

Only then did he turn and look at his surroundings. There were dozens of places like it throughout Vegas, most of them close to the Strip. Everyone wanted to know if their lucky streak would stick, if they should bet it all on red or black or cash in those chips while they were hot. Everyone wanted to know which machines would pay out, if their new love warranted a quickie wedding officiated by a guy dressed like Elvis, if the luck they'd come here to find would finally arrive.

Andy had always been luckier than most. Sometimes it seemed like this luck wasn't fully under his control, as if someone else was guiding him. Like the time he felt himself pushed back onto the sidewalk while crossing the street with his attention on the scratch ticket in his hand, just in time to see a Humvee blow past.

"Would ya look at that," an old man nearby had said. "Looks like you got yourself a guardian angel there, fella."

Andy had called these little moments of luck his Nudges for as long as he could remember, and had never ascribed any supernatural attributions to them. When he was a toddler his mother had told him he was blessed with a *gwisin*, a friendly spirit. She'd said one day she'd left him sitting in a supermarket shopping cart to grab something she'd missed. A stock boy had come out from the back pushing a dolly stacked with boxes of frozen dinners and hadn't seen the shopping cart. As he began unloading them into the freezer the pile tipped over. Everything fell, dozens of Swanson frozen dinners and fish sticks and DiGiorno premade pizzas.

The stock boy freaked out when the shopping cart shot out from under the collapse with a toddler in the back, kicking his feet happily, blissfully unaware of how close he'd just come to death. The stock boy hurried around the skid, expecting to find the kid's mother buried under a pile of frozen food, but there was nobody. The cart had moved on its own. At least that was what he told Andy's mother as she returned from the breakfast aisle with the box of Cheerios she'd forgotten from her list.

He said her son must have had a guardian angel. Misook Park believed a *gwisin* had saved her son's life.

As an adult, Andy often felt as if he was being pushed toward the perfect slot machine at the casino, and the reels seemed to roll back or forward of their own accord after they'd already stopped, as if some cosmic hand were twisting them just for him, to give him that next big payday right when he needed it most.

Usually he wouldn't even will it to happen… and it just sort of would.

Like back at the Royale, when his bucket of coins had fallen just in time to drop the pit boss on his ass, giving him one last chance to run. Or right now, when he could have hidden in any of the small businesses off the Strip and the Nudges pushed him right into a psychic's shop.

"Jeez, you came in just like the wind," the woman at the front desk said. "You all right, dude?"

She looked like a surfer chick in need of an ocean. Blonde fringe, deep tan, cut-off acid-wash jean shorts and a loose Pink Floyd tank top. She was sitting in the lotus position and painting the toenails of her left foot gold with the right foot already dried.

"Sorry," Andy said, leaning against the door as he caught his breath. The small waiting room was covered in posters, wall hangings and painted sigils, palmistry charts, astrological signs and Tarot designs. It smelled like sage and fragrant patchouli. "Can I just hang out here for a few minutes?"

She shrugged, applying paint to her big toe. "This is Vegas. You could run naked down the strip singin the Star-Speckled Banner and I bet nobody'd even bat an eye."

"Spangled."

She looked up. "What's that?"

"Nothing. Thanks." He pointed to three empty chairs set up against the wall, below a poster naming the chakras. "Mind if I sit? I ran all the way from the Palais Royale."

"Dang." She pointed the nail brush toward the chairs, indicating for him to feel free. "Ain't that the French place on Flamingo?"

He nodded and sat, stretching out his aching calves and rolling his ankles.

"Whatcha run all the way from there for? Somebody chasin ya?"

He tried on a smile. "Shouldn't you already know that?"

She gave him a challenging look. "And why would I know that?"

"Well, you're a psychic, aren't you?"

The girl laughed. "Do I look like a psychic to you?"

He laughed, embarrassed. "I mean, no. I guess not. Do I look like the type of guy who'd be running from casino goons?"

She shrugged. "I dunno. You kinda look like that cute l'il guy from the *Oceans* movies." She raised an eyebrow suggestively. "You know, the real limber one."

Andy didn't think he looked like Qin Shaobo. For one thing, Shaobo was Chinese. For another, Shaobo had a round face and widely spaced eyes. If anyone, Andy liked to think he looked more like Will Yun Lee from *Witchblade*, but shorter and nowhere near as buff. At least hers was a far more flattering comparison than Dr. Chow. Being an Asian man in the casinos he'd garnered at least a few references and *Hangover* quotes from ignorant tourists.

"The Amazing Yen," he said with a nod, not wanting to disappoint her.

"That's the guy." She smiled. Her teeth were movie-star white against her tan. "My mom's the psychic," she said, nodding toward the beaded curtain leading into a darkened room. "I just handle the business side."

"Well, thanks for letting me hang out. I'm Andy, by the way."

"Lamb." She seemed to read something in his face. "I know, it's a weird name."

"For a white girl, sure."

She smiled, letting out a little laugh through her

nostrils, and went back to painting her nails. "Lamb with a B," she said. "Like 'Mary had a little lamb its fleece was white as snow.'"

"Oh, that is weird. How did you—?"

"Long story. Have to ask my mom."

As if on cue an older woman's hand poked through the beaded curtain, the long-painted nails and wrist with heavy bracelets parting the strands. Lamb's mother stepped out, a woman in her mid- to late-fifties with streaks of gray in her braided dark hair. She wore a loose, flowing satin gown of soft pink, violet and orange. Her eyebrows were thick and her blue eye makeup made her gaunt, lined and tan face look slightly skeletal. Still, Andy could see where Lamb got her looks. A pair of bifocals hung from a lanyard around the woman's neck.

"Who are you?" the psychic asked, though it seemed more of an interrogation than a friendly question. "What are you doing here?"

Andy felt caught. "I can leave if you—"

"*Mom*. He's in trouble. I said he could stick around a while."

"*You* said." The woman sputtered. "Whose name is painted on the window? Does that say *Lamb's* Psychic Readings? Have I been wasting the best years of my life doing your job for you?"

Lamb rolled her eyes and painted her left baby toe gold.

"No? Good. Then I say who can 'stick around' and who can't. And *you*," she said, twirling a jeweled hand in an all-encompassing gesture at Andy. "You and all of your friends are not welcome to stay."

Andy peered out through the glass window and door, worried the goons had come back. They were nowhere in sight. "What—excuse me, what *friends* are you talking about?"

The psychic popped her dark eyes and turned to her daughter. "He doesn't see them?"

Lamb looked up at him then, letting her gaze drift from one side of him to the other, then back down to her toes. "He doesn't see them."

"You don't see them," her mother said.

"Who am I supposed to be seeing?" Andy asked, vaguely annoyed by their comic routine.

The psychic shook her head and clucked her tongue. "Come," she said, waving him toward the back room with a jingle of her bracelets. "We have much to discuss."

"Tell me… how long have you had this 'strange luck'?" Psychic Sonya asked once he'd sat down at the small table beneath a carnival-glass lamp which cast a warm orange glow over the room. The walls were draped with dark-violet velvet and the small table was covered by a long red tablecloth. In one corner was a small shelf with various instruments of the woman's trade: a crystal ball, several Tarot decks, candles in various colors, incense sticks and bundles of sage, even an old Ouija board and planchette tucked in behind it all. The room smelled like a Bath & Body Works, with incense sticks burning in each corner.

"For as long as I can remember," Andy said, feeling awkward in the tiny chair. "My mom used to say I have a *gwisin*—a ghost, but like a friendly one," he added with a self-conscious chuckle.

Sonya hummed noncommittally, sitting in the small chair opposite him, across the red table. "I suppose we'll have to see. Give me your left hand, please."

She laid her right hand flat on the table, palm up. Andy

laid his left hand in her palm. She clucked her tongue, peering at it through her bifocals.

"Your fate line is very faint. You don't believe in destiny, do you?" She looked up without raising her head, her dark eyes in shadow reflected on the lenses of her glasses.

"How could you tell?"

"It's all in the lines. Your life line is broken. You've had many ups and downs, and will continue to experience them throughout your life."

"I mean… doesn't everybody?"

She ignored his jibe, adjusting her glasses on the bridge of her nose. "This square here—" She touched the outside of his palm lightly with one long, curved fingernail painted violet. "—this indicates protection and good luck from outside forces. I suspected I might see this. Do you have any health issues?"

"No."

"Just as I thought," she said with a nod. "This square here—" She touched the pad below his middle finger. "—indicates protection, as well. The star in the center suggests protection from a fatal accident or punishment, since you have no current health problems."

"That's good."

She shrugged. "Perhaps. Although you may come to wish you were dead, in hindsight. You may remove your hand."

He did.

"Now I'm going to speak plainly," she said, peering at him above her glasses. "Your guardian angels—your *gwisin*—they're in the room with us right now."

Andy looked around. He saw nothing but hadn't expected to.

"You can't see them but they see you. Your mother was correct. They are ghosts, Andy. Ethereal beings."

He laughed. She gave him a serious look.

"You're fucking with me, right?"

"I am not *effing* with you, Andy. Some people act like spiritual magnets for the dead. I suppose they're most often attracted by a certain energy. A certain aura. Your aura is indigo. Ethereal beings appear to be drawn to this color. Mine is violet. Another hue favorable to spirits. I can reach out to them, if you like. Ask them why they're attached to you. I am a certified medium. But I don't want to upset them unduly, and I don't want to dissuade them from protecting you, if it so happens they've attached themselves to you for a specific reason."

Andy had sat through her entire spiel, wondering when would be a polite time to leave the room. He stood eagerly. The chair almost toppled but righted itself in time. He knew that it would without even looking at it. It always did.

"Thanks… for this. Really." He began backing out of the room. "I think I should get going though. Lots to do… and stuff."

"Andy, I believe your friends would like for you to stay. They've clearly brought you to me for a reason."

"Nobody brought me here. I just ran in. It was a coincidence, that's all."

Sonya favored him with a smile she might have given a dull child. "There's no such thing as coincidence."

Andy staggered backwards through the heavy velvet curtain and into the bright Vegas sunshine, his heart drumming like a dancehall beat. He turned and almost ran right into Lamb.

She smiled, leaning up against the door, several strands

from the beaded curtain draped over her shoulders like long cornrows.

"It's creepy, isn't it?"

"What—what's creepy?"

"My mom. She really has a gift, you know? And that's scary. Believe me, I know. I grew up with it."

"I don't believe in psychics. Or guardian angels. Or ghosts or any of that… stuff."

She cocked her head and studied him. "You will, though. Maybe not today, maybe not tomorrow. But if Mom thinks your friends brought you here for a reason, they'll let you know what it is real soon."

"You see them, too?"

Lamb shook her head with slight disappointment. "More like sense them. I'm not like my mom. She's been able to see ghosts since she was little, since my grampa's plane crashed. Both my grandparents died in the crash. My mom was the only survivor. Eight years old, walked right out of the burning wreckage and fell straight into a coma."

"Wow. That's—that's lucky."

"Yeah. My mom had a guardian angel, too."

Lamb crossed her arms over her chest, allowing Andy another glimpse at her tank top without her thinking he was looking at her breasts—which truthfully, he would also have liked to.

"Floyd Lamb Park," he said, referring to the spring lake oasis near Gass Peak, just northwest of the city.

"Huh?"

"Pink Floyd," he said, pointing at the flecked and faded band logo. "Lamb—" He pointed at her, then to himself. "—and my last name is Park. Floyd Lamb Park. That's weird."

Her eyes lit up as she smiled, wiggling her freshly

painted toes on the tile floor. "Wow. Yeah, that is kinda freaky, isn't it? Like, of all the tops I coulda wore today, I ended up puttin this one on."

"Of all the shirts," Andy agreed, smiling back. "Your mom said there's no such thing as coincidence. Maybe that's why I came in here. Not for a reading… but to meet you."

Lamb winked. "Still unsure about those guardian angels of yours?"

When he asked, she took his number.

After Andy left, Lamb's mother returned from the back room in a funk. Something had troubled her more than her usual clients. Whatever happened between them, the reading had disturbed her.

"That boy," she said, squinting out through the front window. "You were right to let him stay. I just hope he'll be all right."

"Is it that bad?"

"He's had at least two spirits close to him since early childhood. Possibly more that I can't see. He's a powerful conduit, but he doesn't understand his power. He doesn't *believe* in it. Power like that could be dangerous in the wrong hands. If someone were to manipulate him for their own gain."

"I dunno, Mom. He seems like a smart guy." She shrugged. "And he's cute."

"Cute, maybe. Foolish, definitely. You remember my accident?"

How could she forget the accident? Not the plane crash. She meant the car accident, while Lamb's mother was pregnant with her.

"Those guardian angels of his could turn on a dime if

he's not careful," Sonya said. "I nearly lost you when I didn't heed what mine tried to tell me. Because I took a Lucky cab to the hospital that day instead of calling your father at work. Well, you know what happened next. And out you came on the side of the road—"

"—on Lamb Boulevard," they both finished together.

Lamb had heard the story a hundred times, told to various customers and friends. It was practically a local legend how Psychic Sonya had survived not one but two accidents and gave birth to her daughter on the side of the road.

Lamb told her mother about Andy's Floyd Lamb Park connection and Sonya agreed it was very auspicious. But she still wasn't convinced the ethereal beings attached to the boy hadn't led him in here for more dire reasons.

The young man and woman, Korean like the boy—possibly related to him, though perhaps not—had worn identical expressions of fear or dismay. They both appeared to be victims of a shooting, and held hands as if they were a couple. If he'd stayed a while longer and let her commune with them, Sonya might have learned what they wished him to know. What knowledge they wished to impart. Why they had attached themselves to him in the first place.

In Sonya's experience, spirits were very in tune with the astral world, from whence psychic phenomena and other mental gifts sprung forth. It was possible, like the little dead boy who'd appeared to her when she woke from her coma as a child, that his spirits knew of some portentous future event, and had brought him here to prevent it from occurring.

She supposed now she might never know. Lamb had taken a liking to him, but she was flighty when it came to men. She was just as likely to share a drink with him, maybe even share her bed, only to never speak with him again.

Was that what his spirits were trying to prevent? Was the danger something related to Lamb?

Only one way to find out, Sonya thought.

"I'm gonna go get lunch from the crepe place," Lamb said. "Want somethin?"

"I'm fine, love. Thank you."

She stroked her daughter's hair—soft as a lamb's, as she always told her, despite the occasional bleach job—then kissed her forehead and returned to the back room with the bell tinkling above the exterior door. As she crouched in front of the shelves, both her knees popped like snapped twigs despite her morning yoga. She moved aside the crystal ball and the candles, and plucked the spirit board and planchette from the back.

With the board set up on the small table, she began moving the planchette in methodical concentric circles. The incense smoke in the corners of the room flickered and twitched, as if disturbed by a gust of air, though Sonya felt no such thing.

She called out to the spirits, reaching out to anyone who might be eavesdropping from the astral world. At any given moment it was possible to connect with any number of ethereal beings. Sonya had come to realize some were able to communicate with her from as far as the other side of the material world.

The beaded curtain in the hall rattled. She looked up from the board to see the thick velvet curtains still rippling as though someone had just passed through.

"Lamb?"

Her daughter didn't answer, and she hadn't heard the

bell chime above the door, signifying Lamb's return. There was no one here but herself and the spirits.

She asked the presence to identify itself as the planchette circled wildly beneath her fingertips—*swish, swish* across the board, unbidden by her touch. When the communication began it came in a flurry. The planchette rested briefly on the H, moved quickly to the E, then to the S.

That's easy, she thought. Not many words started with H-E-S, and it wasn't likely a spirit would begin communication with *hesitate*. It had to be *He's*.

The planchette swished to the H, the E, the R—

And then the spirit she'd summoned grabbed her by the wrists, squeezing them so hard she could see the shape of its fingers outlined in cream on her tanned skin. Sonya gripped the planchette in both hands as it lifted off the board.

It felt as if the floor had dropped out from under her feet. Of all the times she'd been in contact with the astral plane, she'd never been physically touched before, save for a wisp of breath through her hair or a bristle of cold on the nape of her neck. This was new and frightening. She felt both electrified and repulsed.

Whoever this spirit was, it was much stronger than any Sonya had encountered before.

Which meant she was in danger.

She should have been more cautious. She'd been so eager to make contact she'd clearly conjured something malevolent. Some dark otherworldly force. An invisible enemy.

She struggled to keep the planchette on the board. The phantom hands wanted her to let go but she wouldn't give in to its demands. She held fast, and when the hands jerked violently on her wrists, the pointed end of the planchette shot directly into her right eye.

She let go, screaming in terror and pain—half of her world red, the other searching madly, scouring the small room for any sign of the spirit that had harmed her, had blinded her right eye.

The hands let go of her wrists and her flesh regained its color. Cold fluid oozed down her cheek as she felt for the planchette, still sticking out of her face, and twisted it free with a bright flare of agony. She tossed the broken plastic to the floor.

"*Show yourself!*" she cried, turning round and round in tight circles, seeing only out of one eye. If only her guardian angel was with her now. But Rupert, the little Victorian-era orphan who'd been at her side for over a decade, had long since moved on.

Sonya doubted even he could have protected her from the force that had latched on to her now.

Was this why the Park boy's ghosts had brought him here? To warn her about this insidious presence? Was it possible they'd known?

The presence shoved her from behind, launching her staggering through the curtains and into the hall. Sunlight temporarily blinded her remaining eye. The other had gone completely dark.

She stumbled forward and sprawled against the wall. Gasping for breath, she groped the wall to steady herself. The malevolent force struck her again, harder than the last. She hit the beaded curtains and staggered through, blood pattering on the grungy tiles at her feet.

The presence thrust her sideways, behind the counter. She tripped over Lamb's chair, scattering pamphlets and business cards and packaged bundles of incense as she gripped the side of the counter to keep from falling.

Her braid pulled roughly upward in an invisible grip.

"No, no, no—"

It slammed her headfirst into the counter. She felt her nose burst open and stars shot across her vision, even in the blackness on her right side. Blood poured out of her, spilling over her lips and splashing the counter.

Lamb came in just then, carrying a white plastic bag from the crepe shop and a cream soda. The bell chimed above her head.

Sonya cried out her name. Her daughter's eyes went wide and she dropped her lunch. The can of pop struck the floor and spun, shooting a pink fountain at her feet as she ran to her mother's side.

The presence smashed Sonya's face into the counter again—*SLAM!* She swam in and out of consciousness.

"Mom, stop!" Lamb cried.

"It's not—"

SLAM!

"—not—"

SLAM!

"Mom!"

Lamb grabbed her arm but the presence tore Sonya's left hand free of the desk and backhanded her daughter across the face. The poor girl staggered back two steps, holding her cheek in shock, her beautiful blonde hair falling in her face. Blood trickled from the cut on her cheekbone.

Sonya was able to say, "I love you, my little La—"

Before she could finish, the insidious presence smashed her face into the sharp corner of the counter, sending shards of cartilage into her brain.

Psychic Sonya's luck had run out.

THE HAUNTING OF BENJAMIN LARAMIE

Ghostland
April—August, 2019

BEN WAS DEAD. He knew it even before the ghosts began to surge over them, wave after wave of dead energy slamming against the hatch and crackling over Lilian's keeper suit. He'd known it the moment he'd set fire to Garrote's corpse and watched the flesh burn off his once-favorite writer's comatose body. His heart was giving out. There would be no more second chances.

Even as he convinced Lilian to lay down her life with him, he knew it was wrong to ask it of her. But there didn't seem to be any chance of survival, not without the hatch code. Convincing her to sacrifice herself for the greater good seemed to be the only way to turn their tragedy into a victory.

He'd taken her hand and asked her to die at his side. As partners. The decision hadn't sat well with him, but he'd convinced himself it was the only way.

While his heartbeat slowed, as his life ebbed away, his final wish was that the keeper suit would protect Lilian long enough to live through the final surge. That the batteries would hold until rescue came. He doubted it would, but hope was all he had.

His legs gave away and he fell to his knees, dragging Lilian down with him. He tried to let go of her hand but she held firm. Her mask had fogged but he could see her well enough that her tears were visible through the clear plastic.

"Don't let go, Ben!" she cried, barely audible over the tumult of voices as the ghosts surged over them and the fizz and crackle as they struck the keeper suit. "Get behind me!"

Ben shifted as she moved out in front of him. He scooched backwards with his hands and feet until his back pressed up against the cold metal of the hatch.

His eyelids were already drifting closed. He opened them wide, sucking in a deep breath, hoping to wake himself, to hold onto consciousness for just a little while longer. But his peripheral vision was already washing away to fuzzy gray.

He peered up through the hole in the ground where Garrote House once stood, where the writer had made himself as big as his ego, his colossal face filling the sky, a Titan towering over his terrible army. Garrote could reach into the hole and grab them if he wanted to, but for some reason he hadn't. He'd only watched them, his dark, malevolent eyes never leaving Ben, a sardonic, sadistic smile creasing his enormous face.

I did this, Ben thought. *I let him free. I should've left his body to rot.*

This wouldn't end here no matter what happened. He knew that now. Taking revenge on Garrote had released his spirit from his body, making him far more dangerous.

Dying here wouldn't prevent Garrote's escape. What

had happened here was the opening salvo in the War to End All Wars. It was the beginning of the end.

Sooner or later, someone would open the hatch from the outside and the police, the FBI, the Army or the National Guard would come storming in without regard to protocol. In their eagerness to rescue any remaining survivors they would release Garrote and his ghosts, and nobody would know what had happened until it was far too late to stop him.

With the last of his remaining strength, Ben pushed himself to his feet. Lilian sat with her head between her knees, her back turned to him, focused on the ghosts pummeling them from all sides. She hadn't seen him stand.

The smile on Garrote's gargantuan face flattened. His brow creased.

Ben had decided. If Lilian lived to pass on what they learned, there would be further opportunities to fight. His own death wouldn't be in vain.

He turned back defiantly to face the hatch panel. Its strange, indecipherable glyphs blurred in front of his eyes. He blinked away tears and looked again. This time, somehow, he was able to see them for what they represented: *an alphanumeric sequence*.

His vision growing narrower, the gray constricting around the edges, he entered the digits slowly, the same code they'd found on the typewriter, corresponding with the signed and numbered hardcover in the library.

S-H-O-K-I-2-3-7.

The panel beeped.

The red light flashed green.

The heavy clunk of the maglock echoed throughout the underground arena, the only real sound aside from Lilian's low sobbing and the crackling of her keeper suit, the occasional rumble of more earth falling into the hole. The screams and howls of the ghosts hurtling themselves at them was only a digital mimicry of electrical impulses from dead energy through his headset.

He collapsed again when the heavy door swung open, went sprawling over the threshold as the last light of day spilled into the alcove, flickering with the red and blue lights of emergency vehicles.

"*SURVIVORS!*" a voice boomed over a megaphone. "*THERE!*"

Ben tried to raise his head, tried to turn to see who the man was talking about, even as he realized he must have meant Lilian and himself.

As Lilian cried out for them to stay away, as she tried to pull the door closed only to realize Ben was in the way, that he could no longer move himself and she had to tug at his shoulders, at his dead weight, the last of his life ebbed away and darkness overtook him.

When consciousness returned, or something very much like it, Ben found himself standing in front of the hatch. Instinct made him gasp for breath but he discovered he couldn't breathe. After a moment he acclimated to the sensation. He wouldn't die from lack of oxygen. The body he saw when he stretched out his arms—dressed in the same clothes he'd been wearing that day, down to his backpack—was nothing more than an echo, an avatar of the Benjamin Laramie he'd left behind.

Is this a dream?

For a moment he grasped on to the idea that he was asleep, that every single moment since his heart attack as Garrote House rolled through Duck Falls had been an elaborate dream. He wasn't dead. He would wake up in a hospital bed any minute now with a pain in his chest where the surgeon had cut him open.

No, he thought. *I really am dead. All those years people called me the Dead Kid, it's finally true.*

The truth of it settled in. He was dead and Ghostland was real. It had to be—he stood in the empty parking lot behind its north wall now. Judging by the sun, it was mid-afternoon. The emergency vehicles were long gone. To his left stood two tall outbuildings, a smaller one labeled SECURITY to his right, each windowless and made of cinderblocks like the control room inside the park. A thick sheet of burnished metal now covered the hatch, riveted in place. Danger signs stood around the perimeter, like at the entrance to a mine shaft that had collapsed and released clouds of poison gas. On the wall to the left of the sealed hatch, someone had spray-painted "ReX GARROTe LIVeS" in three-foot-tall letters the color of horror movie blood.

How long was I gone?

He remembered everything now. Lilian doing her best to undo what he'd done, to pull the door closed, still willing to give up her life for the chance to prevent Garrote from escaping, even with freedom a footstep away. He remembered the emergency vehicles spotting them and the elation that had washed over him, which he felt again now.

Lilian's alive! She made it out!

True, she was alive somewhere, but he knew she wouldn't be able to see him as he was now. Even if she'd kept her AR glasses, they wouldn't work without the Ghostland program feeding them data.

The weight of this realization was heavier than anything he'd had to bear in life. *Is this what the afterlife is? Wandering alone in a half-world between death and whatever comes next? Not able to interact with anyone I've ever cared about? This is nothing like the brochures. Where's the tunnel of light? Where's Grandpa Laramie and my fluffy ol' boy, Rollo? Why didn't my life flash before my eyes?*

He laughed. *That'd be the most boring highlight reel in history. Except for the day I died, I didn't do much of anything.*

The hollow clatter of a plastic cup skittering across the parking lot startled him.

Is someone here?

"*HELLOHHHHH!*" he shouted. Cupping his hands around his mouth didn't seem to project his voice any louder than without them. He repeated his cry, beginning to walk across the lot.

The only response was the caw of a crow a good distance away, pecking at something stuck to the asphalt. When he moved close enough to see that the thing it was pecking at was a desiccated mouse carcass, the crow cawed again and flew away. He couldn't be sure the bird was responding to his presence or if it had left of its own accord.

As with breathing, he realized he no longer needed to move his arms and legs for forward momentum. He hovered the rest of the way to a wet ditch blooming with summer flowers at the edge of the lot. Something there caught a wink of sunshine as he approached, drawing his attention. He floated over to it.

A broken AR headset lay in the loose gravel, the Ghostland logo nearly scratched away. He tried to pick it up but his fingers slipped right through. Following the ditch toward the main road, he found a *Know Your Ghosts* guidebook fluttering in a stream of tea-colored water trickling from an irrigation pipe. He left both relics for someone else to find or to weather away and disintegrate, the way he supposed his body must have, six feet under the cemetery grass on the far side of town.

When he reached the southern edge of the parking lot, he was struck by a sudden horrific certainty that an invisible barrier would prevent him from ever leaving Ghostland. That he'd be cursed to an eternity trapped on Burt Bucklebee's old farmland, like the ghosts in the park looping in the places where they'd died. Their *hauntings*.

Something he'd said the day he died came back to him now. *You can't get rid of me that easy*, he'd told Lilian. *If I die, I'd probably still haunt your ass.*

The memory made him chuckle—but it also made up his mind.

He'd made a promise, and he told himself he would follow through whatever the cost. More than anything, he needed to tell her she hadn't survived for nothing.

They had work to do. A war to prepare for. He didn't know how he knew but he was certain Garrote had escaped, and many ghosts had gone with him. Some still remained beyond its high walls, he knew. He supposed he could sense them. But the thought of passing through that wall to find others like him was unsettling. Just *looking* at it made him want to put as much distance between himself and this place as possible.

Cautiously, he stepped one foot over the edge of the asphalt. From all of the horror fiction he'd consumed over the years he'd expected resistance, but there was none. No invisible force thrust him back onto the Ghostland lot. No debilitating flashbacks to his death froze him in place. No sudden shift took him from where he stood—floated, really—back to the place where he'd awakened.

Marveling over this, he planted both feet on the road and began the long trek back to Duck Falls.

The town had changed so much since he'd last seen it. Even before he reached the outskirts, he'd noticed the changes. A good-sized encampment had assembled at the eastern edge of the old Bucklebee farm. People moved in and out of tents and campers and caravans, cooking food on hibachis, drinking and chatting, tossing frisbees, sitting with their dogs with books or tablets in their laps while small enclaves played various types of music from reggae to classical. A small group sat in a drum circle and elsewhere, a woman with orange hair and camo cargos played guitar while others sang along. Many of them wore T-shirts with #GRP2 stenciled in white letters. Ben considered giving them a thrill but he didn't suspect he'd be able to even cause the slightest flicker in a candle flame so early in his afterlife. He could barely frighten a crow.

Downtown, the streets were filled with traffic, the sidewalks bustling with life. In the courtyard behind the town hall a small market had been set up, where people Ben recognized sold fruits and vegetables, arts and crafts and various other items. Businesses that had floundered before Ghostland were doing brisk business now, despite the tragedy—or more likely because of it. Call it New Salem. Duck Falls was in the tourist trade now, whether her citizens liked it or not.

He paused on the sidewalk at Main Street as people swished by on both sides. The anonymity didn't bother him. He'd gotten used to being ignored when he was alive. At least now he had the comfort of knowing he was literally invisible.

It gave him the opportunity to study people as they passed without having to worry they might think he was a freak for staring. Several people in the crowd wore Ghostland T-shirts or peak caps. A few even held park maps. Unless all of these people had been at Ghostland on opening day, someone must have been making a killing selling unlicensed merch at the market or out of the back of a van. Wherever they'd gotten them, none of these people appeared to be from town.

A news van had parked out front of the library on Kubler Road. Half a block to the north, people milled in and out of the abandoned church. Vehicles crammed the curb up and down the street.

What's going on there? Some new Sunday service?

He drifted further down Main Street toward the Roths' apartment, reminding himself to investigate the church when he was done.

Pigeons cooed in a poop-stained roost above the 86 Diner's neon sign. The restaurant itself was packed with midday customers, far more than Ben had ever seen outside of a Saturday night. He watched for several minutes before confirming Mrs. Roth wasn't on shift. While he wondered how his parents had fared in the wake of his death, his first concern was what had happened to Lilian. He would go to their apartment next.

An elderly woman walked right through him as he turned around, and for a moment it seemed as though his mind had tuned in a distant radio station. He heard a scrap of what he assumed must be the old woman's thoughts— *cat food, Wilbur's medication, a loaf of good bread*—and then the voice was gone as she continued on her way to the grocery store.

He marveled over it a moment. *Did I really just read*

her mind?

Yet another thing to investigate once he was certain Lilian was safe. Business first, then fun.

Upstairs in apartment 3B, Mrs. Roth—Maddy—ate lunch at the kitchen table with her husband, Hiram. She was wearing her work uniform, the one that made her look like a waitress from a '50s diner. He felt a little creepy about barging right in, but he couldn't exactly knock. Even if he was able to, he would have scared the life out of them. He was just glad not to have caught them doing something private he didn't want to see.

"It's just so sad, Hi," Maddy said. "I keep thinking how this was partly our fault. We should've known Michael and Wendy wouldn't let Ben go to that place in his condition. If we hadn't pressured Lilian to go with Dr. Wexler, they might not have gone at all. The two of them would still be alive."

Hiram took his wife's hands and kissed them both. "My dear," he said, "we can't know what would have happened. He might've gone with or without her. And we can't change the past. 'The moving finger hath writ and moved on,' as the philosopher said. What's done is done. I know you loved Ben like he was our own, but dwelling on it won't bring him back."

Ben blinked at this, feeling a chill run up a spine he no longer possessed. The thought that he was here, at this exact moment, for this exact discussion… even if it had happened a dozen times before, it felt like a sign.

He moved down the hall to Lilian's room. As soon as he entered, he could tell she hadn't been living here for quite some time. Her room was clean, for one thing. The Lilian he knew—which he had to admit was not the same Lilian who'd come with him to Ghostland—kept a messy room.

Maybe she'd changed. Still, there was evidence she'd packed up and moved on. The shelf of knickknacks beside her dresser was mostly bare. Her favorite teddy bear with the bell on the ribbon around its neck from when she was little was also missing. If he could have opened her drawers or her closet door, he expected he would have found most of her clothes missing.

Where did she go?

He thought of the old woman in the street, listening in on her thoughts like tuning into a radio station. The Roths wouldn't have Lilian's current address just lying around for him to find. If he wanted to figure out where she was, as wrong as it felt to him… he would need to do some snooping in one of their heads.

Hiram was putting the dishes in the dishwasher and Maddy was washing a pot in the sink when Ben returned to the kitchenette. It felt like a violation to touch Lilian's mom, despite knowing her on a more personal level than her dad. Ben wasn't even sure it would work.

But he had to try.

"All I'm saying is, the boy died a hero," Hiram said. "Hundreds of people are alive today because of the sacrifice he made. Our daughter is alive because of him."

If they only knew, Ben thought, reaching out with both hands to touch the man's balding head.

"That's more than he ever could have hoped for in life," Mr. Roth went on. "Now granted, he was a mensch. He was a very bright boy. But those parents of his never would've let him shine."

Maddy's shoulders slumped and she stopped her relentless scrubbing. She knew it was true. Ben had heard her say so countless times, over fries drowned in ketchup and greasy burgers at the 86.

"He's got his own memorial at the high school, Maddy, my love," Hiram said, rubbing her back between the shoulders. "He's up there with the jocks and the scholarships. Suddenly he's Mr. Popular. How many kids like him leave a legacy like that?"

"You're right. It's not fair though, is it? He was such a good boy."

"That park was full of good boys and girls. And women and men and everything in between. It was a terrible, senseless tragedy, and someday those bastards are going to have to reckon with what they did to this town. That son of a bitch Hedgewood—"

"But Ben was *special*," Maddy said, and Ben felt himself begin to cry, though when he reached up to touch his face, he felt nothing at all.

Hiram squeezed his wife's shoulders. "I know, my sweet." He kissed her on the forehead and she leaned into his chest. "When Lilian gets back from school—"

School, Ben thought. Now was his chance. He touched Mr. Roth's temples. His fingers went directly into the man's head and his mind was filled with a swirl of thoughts: the words *Stanford* and *co-ed dorm* and *this new boy*. He pulled his hands free while Hiram consoled his wife, oblivious to the fact that the sanctity of his mind had just been violated.

"New boy," Ben said, disturbed by the thought of Lilian with some guy—*any* guy, let alone This New Boy. He left the Roths' apartment in a daze and returned to the street, not knowing what to do next. He was drifting across the road, undisturbed by the traffic passing through him in both directions, when he first saw the man looking directly at him from the crowd.

He was a black man in his early to mid-forties. Muscular, with a soul patch beard, wearing stonewashed jeans and a tight black T-shirt with frays above the cuffs.

He can see me….

"Hey!" Ben shouted, hurrying down the middle of the road. "Hey, you!"

He lost the stranger among a group of teenagers emerging from the new ice cream shop between Green's Antiques and his mom's realty office. When he reached the alley between the shop and the antique store, the man was already gone.

That was weird, he thought.

Only then did he notice everyone around him appeared to be moving in the same direction, toward the west end of downtown. *Where's everybody going?*

He followed the crowd, weaving through them with ease, picking up slight signals on what he jokingly began to call WESP, Psychic Radio. The snatches of inner monologue mostly confirmed what he'd already begun to notice, that they were headed toward the evangelical church abandoned by its congregation after the land the Hedgewood Foundation had purchased for Ghostland was rezoned for an amusement park. Why people were headed there, he still couldn't tell.

The church itself had been freshly painted, the lawn and gardens made vibrant in the time since he'd last walked by on his way to the diner from his house on the Duck Bill. Someone must have taken it over. Maybe turned it into apartments, like they sometimes did in big cities. Whatever the reason, the driveway and back lot were full, and people milled about on the sidewalk and in the street, with a couple of local deputies holding back traffic.

At the foot of the steps a large rectangular object stood

covered by a light-beige tarp. Ben assumed it was a sign or plaque of some kind. Speakers had been set up on the grass, a podium with a microphone in front of the chapel door. A crow cawed twice from the top of the steeple, eyeing the crowd below like a demon or vampire in animal form. For some reason, Ben thought it was the same crow he'd seen earlier, though they all looked relatively the same, and he couldn't possibly know for sure.

The TV news crew had planted themselves on the outskirts of the crowd, a blonde woman with eyes as blue as her blazer and pencil skirt in the blazing camera light, repeatedly brushing her hair with her fingers.

"Are we good? Are we ready?" she asked the man behind the camera set on a tripod. He wore his Red Sox cap backwards to see through the viewfinder, and a vest jampacked with various camera equipment. He indicated he was ready with a raised finger.

"I'm here at the Duck Falls, Maryland, headquarters of the activist group Ghosts Are People Too, or GRP2 as they call themselves, who are about to unveil their latest project, a memorial for the lives lost during the tragic events of April 20th, 2019—what's since come to be known as the 'Ghostland Disaster.'"

The correspondent glanced over her shoulder as the heavy front door of the church creaked open and several people stepped out. "Now, we're being told that Ghosts Are People Too are at the forefront of the fight for compensation for the families of those who lost their lives during this terrible tragedy. Their leader, Thea Petralia, heir to the Kismet dating app fortune, claims to have a personal stake in the struggle, alleging to have lost several close friends during the tragedy."

The large speakers whined with feedback as a young

woman at the podium neared the microphone. She had thick, dark hair tied back in a ponytail and smoky, dark eyes. She wore a black tank top and black cargo pants, and aside from the makeup—her glossy, pouty lips and incredibly shiny hair—her whole ensemble made Ben think of a revolutionary soldier in a music video, or a celebutante cosplaying war.

That must be Thea Petralia, he thought.

"Thank you all for coming," she said. "Today, and each day forward, we mourn the loss of more than two thousand of our friends, relatives and loved ones who passed away in a single day less than five miles from where we now stand. We still don't know exactly what happened," Thea Petralia said, looking over the crowd. "But we *do* know who's responsible—"

"The goddamn ghosts!" a man in the crowd shouted. "Goddamn ghosts got em, that's who!"

She regarded the man with a tight smile. "In these dark, unprecedented times, it's only natural to want answers. We think, there *has* to be someone to blame. We point fingers toward the Other—"

"*Spooks!*" the man shouted.

"Jerry Dougan, hush now," a woman said.

Thea Petralia smiled patiently. "It's okay. We're all grieving. We're all scared. But before we continue, I'd like to assure you that there is no reason to be afraid. My people and I were informed, from an inside source, that what happened at Ghostland was caused by a computer malfunction. A virus that spread throughout the system, causing various exhibits to malfunction."

"You weren't there!" a young woman called out. "You didn't hear their screams!"

"I'm sorry," Thea said. "I understand your pain, your

frustration. I lost people there that day, too."

"You lost Twitter followers," the first heckler—Jerry Dougan—scoffed. "We lost *family*!"

Voices joined him in agitated agreement.

"You say ghosts are people," the man said, pushing his way to the front of the crowd. "My son-in-law, Dustin, *he* was a person. He was on crew. He welded those cursed fuckin places back together from spare parts like a fuckin Frankenstein."

The heckler shuffled to the steps with a loping gait and turned toward the crowd. His face and neck were sunburnt, stubbly with salt-and-pepper bristles. He wore a trucker hat with a Shell gas logo and his silver hair poked out over his ears.

"Dusty was there when they shipped them spooks in, every damn one of em in a crate sealed in lead. He seen a man get thrown through a plate glass window when they opened one of em, another guy scratched all to hell by goddamn invisible claws, just 'cause that machine of theirs wasn't *calibrated* right. Dusty never came back from work on opening day. Now you're gonna stand there with a straight face and tell us a fuckin *computer* killed my son-in-law? Our *family*? Our *friends*?"

More angry voices met this. Thea waited for them to quiet before she spoke again.

"I can't bring back your son-in-law," she said. "I can't bring back your family and friends, or mine. But we can try to *move forward* together."

The heckler spat at his feet.

"You all know me," Thea Petralia said. "I've spoken to many of you personally. We've had fresh milk and cookies together. We've done shots of rye whiskey."

There were a few chuckles at this, as some in the crowd

warmed to the mention of their comfort foods.

"You know my intentions are pure. Whether you believe in ghosts or not, whether or not you believe in our cause—that doesn't matter. What matters is that we try to move forward. We *fight* for compensation. And we continue to put pressure on the Hedgewood Foundation, to hold them accountable for this senseless tragedy."

Cheers and whistles erupted from the crowd. The man in the Shell hat descended the steps with a hangdog look. He took off his hat and scratched his balding head and for a brief moment Ben was reminded of Stan Beadle. He felt his heart ache, even though he had no physical heart to hurt.

"Without further ado," Thea said. The two men who'd stepped out of the church with her pulled the sheet off the plaque, revealing a massive list of names chiseled onto a glossy block of granite, along with a dedication:

THIS MEMORIAL IS DEDICATED TO THE 2139 SOULS WHO LOST THEIR LIVES AT GHOSTLAND ON APRIL 20TH, 2019. MAY THEIR MEMORIES LIVE ON FOREVER.

The crowd applauded. Only a few jeered, and were quickly hushed by their companions. They surged forward to scan the names, searching for friends and relatives and neighbors. Some placed flowers at the foot of the memorial, others trinkets, photos, letters and votive candles. In the coming days there would be candlelit vigils here, as there had been at Ghostland, and crowds from all across the world would gather to pay homage to the victims of the Ghostland Disaster, which had made worldwide headlines.

Ben mingled in with the crowd, looking for his name, his head filling with random scraps of thoughts from people he inadvertently touched, men and women and children in mourning, their grief and memories of their loved ones overwhelming him until he was moved again to tears which couldn't manifest in his ghostly eyes.

And then he spotted it, his own name right at the very bottom, not last to be remembered but the only name to be inscribed with a personal note:

> *For Benjamin Laramie—*
> *who gave his life to hold the door.*

He turned to the leader of GRP2, an organization he'd once considered a joke. Thea Petralia surveyed the crowd with tears streaking her makeup, wearing the smile of someone whose life work had finally been given meaning.

He wanted to tell her the inscription was a mistake, well-intended or not. That he was far from a hero. But he knew she wouldn't be able to hear him. So he promised himself he'd return, if he ever discovered a way to communicate with the living. And after he confessed to Lilian, Thea Petralia would be the next to know his secret shame: that he'd unleashed untold evil upon the world, and soon they would all pay for this mistake.

Ben was on his way home when he began to feel like he was being followed. He turned to find the man he'd seen earlier watching him from the front lawn of the Edisons' house, where Lilian had lived until the recession. Except he wasn't *standing*, Ben realized. He was hovering a few inches above the crisp, brown grass in front of the rose trellis Maddy Roth had planted when Lilian was born, which the Edisons had upkept.

"Are you dead, too?" Ben called over. A small group of middle school girls passed on the sidewalk between them, laughing and skipping, oblivious to his shouting.

The man disappeared. Ben looked up and down the street for him, but he was gone.

He reappeared a few feet from Ben, hovering in the middle of the road. "You new, huh?" the man said, with a trace of what Ben thought might be a Louisiana accent.

"New?"

"Newly woke," the man said, nodding. "Fresh dead."

"Yeah, I guess I am."

The man nodded, stroking his soul patch. "Yeah, I figured you was. Always seem to sniff out the new ones." He stuck out a large hand. "Name's Leon Moncrief. My friends call me Le Mon," he added, pronouncing it like a French word rather than *Leemon* or *lemon*.

Ben looked at Le Mon's hand.

"Go on, shake it," the man said, chuckling. "It ain't gon' bite."

Ben stuck out his hand and grasped Le Mon's. He could actually *feel* it: warm and prickly against his skin. It was the first thing he'd felt since he awakened from death, and it comforted him to know he wouldn't be unable to feel anything for the rest of his afterlife. "I'm Ben," he said.

Like the MJ song, Le Mon said with laughter in his voice, holding his gaze as firmly as his hand. It took a moment for Ben to realize the man wasn't moving his lips. *Not too happy about that memorial, I see. Don't fancy yourself the hero type, do you?*

Ben jerked his hand away. "Don't do that."

"Sorry," Le Mon spoke aloud, smiling sheepishly.

"Just a little trick some of us use to get our thoughts across quicker. No harm intended."

"I just don't like the idea of people looking around in my head, that's all."

"Understood. You been to see your mama and them yet?"

Ben looked up the street. "I was just heading there."

Le Mon nodded. "You'll want some privacy then. I'll be around, when you need me. Only… you best be careful. I'm not the only one got a nose for new blood. You see a reflection in anything that looks like it don't belong? You get out of there lickety-split."

"What do you mean, a reflection?" Ben thought of the hall of mirrors in Rocky's Fun House, and the severed body parts he'd seen in the glass.

"You'll know when you see it. We call em imagoes. Some folks call 'em mirror people, or glimmers, or shades. Whatever you wanna call 'em, you best hope you see them before they get a whiff of you, youngblood."

Ben thanked him for the advice—although the idea of "mirror people" seemed somewhat silly to him, like something the man might have made up just to scare the new kid—and he set off down the street again, paying close attention to the windows of houses and parked vehicles just in case. He called back before he'd gone too far: "What are you doing here, anyway?"

"I didn't know at first," the man said, "but I suppose I was waitin on you. Like I said, I always sniff out the new blood."

Ben's dad was sitting in his recliner with his feet propped up, drinking a can of Natty Boh. His dad never drank during the day, especially not on a weekday, which Ben knew it must be due to the talk show on the television: *Susan & Jessie in the Morning*. His dad never watched talk shows. His dad also never cried, but right now his puffy eyes were red and glistening. His face was sallow and almost gray. It looked like he hadn't shaved in days, whereas he's always been clean shaven when Ben had lived under their roof.

The kitchen door opened and his mom entered with an armload of groceries.

"Mom!" Ben hurried to her, glad to see she'd held up better than his dad in his absence. Her hair was done in shiny brown curls the way it looked in her realtor photo, on FOR SALE signs around town, and she wore a freshly pressed off-white pantsuit. Not a single smudge in her makeup.

She nudged the door closed behind her with the heel of a strappy sandal and dropped her keys in the loose change dish by the door, then set the grocery bags on the island.

In the living room, Ben's dad quickly wiped his tears with the heels of his hands, embarrassed and ashamed.

"Come help me with the groceries," Wendy Laramie called from the kitchen, picking up a crushed can of Double Duckpin IPA with a huff and tossing it in the recycle bin under the sink.

Michael Laramie lowered the recliner's footrest, knocking his beer off the side table as he stood. It glugged foamy and wet onto the carpet and he dropped to the floor beside it muttering, "Shit!" His dad rarely swore. He grabbed a *TV Guide* and used it to feebly pat the puddle dry.

"Michael?" Wendy called, irritation in her voice.

"I'm coming, goddammit!"

Ben startled. His dad *absolutely never* swore at his

mother.

Wendy tore open the door and returned to the car while Michael drank the remains of the beer and placed it and the sodden magazine on the coffee table. Ben followed him to the kitchen.

His mom entered with two more armfuls of groceries, which his dad took from her. "Thank you," she said curtly, not meeting his gaze. She went back out to the car.

He brought them to the counter and started rooting through the bags, not putting anything away, clearly just looking for something. "You gotta be kidding me," he muttered, his eyes growing dark and his jaw clenching.

When Wendy returned, he went right at her. "Where are the Snyder's?"

"Store was out of pretzels."

"Goddammit, Wendy, Snyder's were the only thing I wanted on the whole goddamn list. You might as well not have gone at all—"

"Well, maybe you'd like to go store to store to find them? Oh, that's right, you're too drunk to drive. You never do anything but *drink* anymore."

Michael jabbed a finger toward her. He looked about to say something but instead he fumed, exhaling sharply through his nostrils like an enraged bull.

"You're grieving," she said. "So am I. The difference is I'm *taking charge* of my grief. I *refuse* to let it define me."

"You want me to do something? *Fine.*"

Michael tore open the door and stormed out into the yard. As Wendy shook her head, beginning to unpack the groceries, the eggs, the lettuce, Ben followed his dad out back.

His old bikes were leaning outside the garage on their

kickstands, his dad already rummaging around inside as he crossed the once immaculate, now shaggy lawn. Tools and plastic clanged and clattered within.

"Where is it? Where the hell *is* it?"

Michael slapped an open palm at the underside of a shelf full of old paint cans and the shelf came off one of its brackets. The cans tumbled, thumping hollowly on the concrete floor. His dad watched them roll for a moment before his face crumpled and he dropped to his knees, covering his face with his hands as he wept.

"Dad…"

Ben reached out and almost touched his father—but pulled his hand back at the last moment. His dad wouldn't have felt his touch, and Ben didn't want to hear what he was thinking right now. He thought it might break him.

His parents almost never argued, at least not in front of him, and especially not over something so trivial as Snyder's pretzels. Dad was home drinking on a weekday, which either meant he was playing hooky, that he'd taken a sick day—which he never did, not unless he was at death's door—or he'd lost his job. Mom seemed to be doing everything around the house and she'd clearly reached the end of her rope.

He wished he could let them know he was okay. That he was sorry for running away that day, but he was better now. He was *stronger* now. He'd walked three and a half miles from Ghostland back to town and his heart hadn't even skipped a beat, because he no longer had one. They didn't need to worry about his health anymore. All things considered, he actually felt fine.

He left, wishing he'd never come back at all, that his last memories of his parents had remained somewhat pleasant, the three of them sitting around the table at dinner, the news on mute while they shared mundane things about their day.

Dad stopped weeping suddenly, as if he'd flicked a switch. He sniffled and crawled across the garage floor on his hands and knees, then began shoving bags of grass seed and fertilizer and topsoil out of the way until his hands curled around a worn wooden handle. He drew it out and gripped the shovel in both hands, still on his knees as he began to laugh.

Ben left, unable to watch his dad lose his grip on sanity any longer. He found Le Mon out front of his house, watching a fat orange neighborhood cat roll around in the sun at his feet.

"Sometimes I forget these things can sense us," Le Mon said, bending down to scratch the cat's belly. The fur moved with his touch and the cat began to purr contentedly. "So where to now, big fella?" he asked, looking up from the animal.

"You said before you always sniff out the new ones. Does that mean there's more ghosts like us?"

"Au revoir, Minou," Le Mon said to the cat as he stood, leaving it to roll in the grass. "First thing y'oughta know," he told Ben, "the word *ghost* got ugly connotations. Most people I know prefer *ethereal*. Me personally, I feel like ethereal's a bit bougie." He winked, grinning. "As for more—well, I once heard it estimated that one-hundred and eight billion people have crawled on this rock since time began. Seein as there's about seven billion breathers still walking around, yeah, I'd say there's more." His grin widened to a gap-toothed smile. "I guess that means you ready meet th'others?"

GHOSTS BETWEEN US

Stanford University
October 31st

LILIAN RETURNED TO her dorm room tired and depressed after their failure at the cemetery. With all she and Ben had been through that night, she wasn't sure how much more enthusiasm she had left for what they were trying to accomplish. It was rewarding when they worked out, but the trips back and forth were exhausting, particularly since she often still had course work to complete for Monday. When they failed, as they had tonight, it only reminded her of their failure to prevent Garrote from escaping, a fact she already beat herself up over on a regular basis.

Still, they had done some great work over the past few months. She and Ben had freed fifteen ethereals together, not counting those who might have escaped Ghostland when the hatch door had seemingly opened on its own. Thea Petralia had called her personally to commend her a few days after the Ghostland Disaster, and later, she'd offered Lilian the opportunity to work with them.

Even that wouldn't soothe her guilty conscience. She wondered if it would ever be enough.

"There you are," Blake said, watching her from his doorway across the hall. He was dressed as a pirate, with an eyepatch and a fake parrot drooping over his shoulder, a sash with a sheath and a holster for a plastic gun and sword he no longer wore. Lilian had drawn a Jack Sparrow mustache on him after class using her eyebrow pencil. His eyes looked heavy from too much booze or weed.

"Were you watching out the peephole for me all this time?"

He gave her a goofy smile. "Nope. Just listening for your keys. You look tired."

"You look drunk."

He smiled again. "I *am* drunk."

She crossed the hall and sighed heavily, nuzzling into his chest. "And I am tired," she admitted. "I could use a good night's sleep."

He kissed her forehead. "Can I… join you?"

She looked up with mock suspicion. "Sleeping only."

Blake threw up his hands in surrender. "Hey, I'll keep my hands to myself."

She slapped his parrot. "I bet you will. Perv."

He laughed and they crossed the hall together to the room she shared with Abigail, whose parents lived close enough to school she could go home on the weekends. After a few nights with Blake staying over, they'd put up a Japanese screen between their halves of the room, which she drew open now as Blake closed the blinds.

"I messaged you a bunch tonight. How come you never texted back?"

She kicked off her shoes and unbuttoned her jeans. "Honestly, I forgot to take my phone off airplane mode. But it was a super busy night. I would've been rushed and you deserve better." She fell onto the messy bedspread, wearing only her underwear and a sports bra. She could have used a shower but she couldn't muster the energy. "Besides, I knew you'd be here when I got back."

He sat on the bed beside her, looking at his clothes on the floor. "Someday I might not be, though."

With a huff, Lilian rolled over to face the wall. Blake laid a warm, strong hand on her shoulder.

"I'm not saying *that*, Lilian. You know I'll be here for you, whatever you need. I'm right across the hall. But what if I choked on a stale Pop Tart and died? Or what if something happened to you on one of your trips? I know that stuff is important to you, and if it's important to you it's important to me, but do you really want 'text me okay' to be the last thing you say to me?"

She rolled over to face him, lifted his skull and crossbones eyepatch to give him a serious look. "Blake, you know I'd haunt your ass if I died," she said.

He pulled his hand away. "That's not funny."

"Ben would have laughed," she muttered.

"What did you say?"

His voice had an edge to it. She knew Blake didn't like it when she talked about Ben. He thought it was connected to unresolved trauma, triggering repressed memories of what she'd gone through that day. She sometimes wondered if she'd gravitated toward him because of the loss she'd suffered—Allison, her former therapist, in particular—or if it was just a coincidence that she'd fallen in love with a second-year Psych student.

"Nothing," she said.

"No, tell me."

"I didn't say anything. Forget it."

He let out a sharp exhale through his nostrils and laid down, pulling the sheet up over them.

"We can discuss this later," he said.

Can we? she wondered. How could she tell him she'd been seriously considering dropping out of school to take on a more substantial role in GRP2? How could she tell him she stood on the front line in a war between an army of evil ghosts and the rest of the world?

Would he understand? Would he believe her? Or would he leave her behind?

While his breathing grew shallow with sleep, Lilian stared at the blank eggshell wall, her stomach knotted with worry.

Exhausted and anxious, she eventually drifted off to sleep, and she was running from Morton Welles in the hall of mirrors again, like most nights since that day, and when he finally caught up to her it was *her* face with a lobotomy scar above the hospital gown, *her* hand holding the cleaver.

As the blade came down across her throat she'd wake, gasping for breath, praying that Morton Welles was still trapped within the Recurrence Field, that he hadn't escaped Ghostland along with Garrote and the others.

Lilian knew she would have died that day along with Ben if the hatch hadn't opened when it had. She'd promised to hold the door closed, to protect it with her life, and she'd failed.

She'd lived with the weight of that failure for six months and eleven days so far, a secret that often felt unbearable. As the days passed more survivors were brought to safety, several hundred discovered alive. If the door hadn't opened when it had, they might not have survived to be rescued. Even that was cold comfort in light of Garrote's escape.

What happened at Ghostland wasn't just a disaster, Ben had told her. *It was a first strike. Garrote wants a war, Lilian. A war between the living and the dead.*

The bodies recovered over the following weeks were sent back to their loved ones for burial. Rather than join Thea Petralia's fight for compensation, Lilian's parents took the settlement Hedgewood offered, aware that any class-action lawsuit could take years to settle. Her school had offered grief counselling in the final months of that semester, her teachers making awkward statements regarding death and bereavement. Friends who hadn't lost anyone had tried to console her but eventually graduation took center stage, overshadowing even the loss of over two thousand lives not all that far from where they would all soon celebrate.

While her peers chose to put the tragedy behind them, Lilian refused to let herself forget. Six kids from their school had died at Ghostland, including Ben. The others chose to believe the dead would want them to "live twice as hard for the lives they lost," a sentiment valedictorian Billy Turner offered in his commencement speech. Her fellow graduates had cheered, relieved to finally be let off the hook, no longer required to spend their lives in mourning. Billy had survived Ghostland but lost the use of his throwing arm and consequently his football scholarship. If Billy could move past the tragedy, anyone could. Lilian had sat among them, listening to their cheers and applause in utter disbelief, her arms crossed over her gown.

She hadn't attended any of the celebrations, painfully aware she would have just brought everyone down. The following week she'd spent moping, watching Netflix and scanning news items about Ghostland. Wondering how much of the truth people knew. Wondering if she was the only survivor who understood even half of what happened that day. She doubted the Hedgewood Foundation would ever reveal the truth, if they were even aware of what Rex Garrote had done, or how he'd managed to take over the system.

A war is coming.

Ben and his friend Le Mon were recruiting from the ever-growing pool of freed ethereals. But Lilian was sure Garrote would come for them long before they were ready. His army would sweep through Duck Falls, slaughtering everyone she knew and cared for, before moving on to the next town and the next, until the whole world was under his sway.

After that first week of summer, long before Ben returned, her parents had convinced her to get a part-time job. She got hired at the newly opened ice cream parlor beside Ben's mom's realty office, and all day long she'd scoop sweet treats for happy families and kids who lived without the burden of the guilt and grief she carried on their behalf.

When the seemingly endless summer finally ended, her parents drove her all the way across the country to Stanford in their old Chevy. The trip took several days, since her dad had wanted to stop first at Graceland in Tennessee, then Beth Jacob Cemetery in Texas, followed by Monument Valley in Utah.

They'd spent a night in a Memphis motel with her dad doing his very best Elvis impersonation, twisting his hips and curling his upper lip and singing about crying hound dogs. The next night, in a cousin's house in Galveston with her father solemnly reciting the history of one of the first Jewish communities in America, where his own family had first immigrated. The final night they'd spent in a desert campsite, looking up at the endless skyscape of stars while Hiram Roth expounded on philosophy and mysticism and their place in the universe.

When they'd finally arrived at her residence building, her parents revealed their graduation present. "We rarely use it," her dad said, handing her the keys to the family car. "Maybe you'll get some use out of her before the old girl kicks the bucket."

"Hi...." her mother said, using the pet name she'd called him for as long as Lilian could remember. "*It* still has a few good years left. Don't be so dramatic."

"It's in my nature, my dear," Hiram said. "Don't forget, you fell madly in love with me when I played Danny Zuko in our senior year. Imagine it, Lilian, your father, twenty pounds lighter—"

Her mother gave him a dubious glare.

"—*fifty* pounds lighter," he admitted, "under the spotlight with a gorgeous full head of hair in a greased-up pompadour, doing the T-Bird strut."

Lilian had no idea what most of those things meant but she smiled as her father reenacted the scene.

"I love you guys," she said, her heart aching after all she'd put them through over the summer. "How are you getting home?"

"There's this neat little invention called an airplane, maybe you've heard of it?" Hiram laughed and hugged her around the shoulders. "We'll live, my angel. It's us who should be worried. Our little girl is leaving the nest," he said, his voice quavering with sadness.

"Oh, Hi," her mom said, hugging them both. "We'll miss you, honey. You stay safe."

Lilian found herself weeping and wiped her tears

briskly. "I will. Let me drive you to the airport, at least."

"You've put up with us long enough," Hiram said. "We've got a cab coming."

She smiled. "Ooh, big spenders."

"Nothing but luxury from here on out," he said, his belly rolling as he chuckled. "Now let's go get you settled into your new digs."

Getting out of Duck Falls changed her. Living without constant reminders of the tragedy, without the specter of death hanging invisible over the entire town, haunting her wherever she looked, no longer worrying about Rex Garrote returning to finish what he'd started, Lilian finally found herself able to relax and enjoy herself.

Frosh Week was a whirlwind of new faces and new experiences. Living on her own for the first time, both scary and exhilarating. Her classes were all pretty interesting and her profs appeared enthusiastic about the year ahead. As per her guidance counselor's suggestion, she planned to major in Political Science after her junior year. She wanted to make a difference in the world, and she had the aptitude and interests required.

During that first week she'd met Blake Carter, a second-year Psych undergrad. He was good-looking and charming and they'd clicked right away. He was patient with a calm demeanor and he liked to listen, unlike most of the kids in the dorm who seemed to only want to talk about themselves.

Everything was going great.

And then she started seeing ghosts.

On the night Ben returned, she and Blake had gone to see a movie earlier in the evening. *IT Chapter Two* had been her suggestion, but since it had sold out they'd watched the Brad Pitt space movie instead, which they'd both found dull. In the back of the darkened theater, while the THX surround sound boomed, she and Blake spent the final half hour of the film making out.

Blake left her in the hall when they returned to their dorm, even though she wanted him to invite her in or invite himself over so she could jump his bones. All the boys she'd flirted and fooled around with back home had wanted to go further than she'd been willing. The last thing she'd wanted was to end up stuck in Duck Farts the rest of her life with a baby and a crummy job and a husband who drank. She had goals and dreams that were bigger than her small-town upbringing. Bigger than Maryland. Bigger than America. But birth control existed for exactly that reason, and while she found Blake's respectfulness both maddening and endearing, she still fell asleep smiling, her lips tingling and her cheeks still burning from the light scruff on his face.

Even then her happiness didn't prevent the Bright Falls Zombie from visiting in her sleep. That night, instead of turning into a deranged version of her and hacking her to bits with a cleaver, Morton Welles had reached out and grasped her head. The pressure had built behind her eyes like the world's worst migraine, and just like in the funhouse she began to hear his voice in her mind, repeating the strange phrase her maternal grandmother had once said to her in the hospital, from some nursery rhyme or poem: *The spirits are meeting at All Hallows' Close. They're going to decide who stays and who goes.*

When she'd snapped awake, her head still throbbing, Ben had been standing over her bed. She'd thought she must still be dreaming, waking from one nightmare into another, or hallucinating. When he spoke, she'd almost screamed.

Once she'd settled down, they talked for several hours, though mostly she listened to Ben talk about what had happened to him when he discovered he was dead, the things he'd seen in town after she'd left. He seemed embarrassed by the dedication on the memorial, and the weird shrine they'd made for him at school, which Lilian assumed they'd done more out of shame for the way they'd treated him than respect. He told her about the other ghosts he'd met, and all the interesting places he'd traveled to outside of Duck Falls.

She found the timing odd, that he would return to her then of all nights, when she'd finally felt truly happy for the first time in months, even years. It was almost as if he'd sensed her forgetting him, drifting away from him, finally letting him go. She chose not to tell him her concerns, worrying he might take it the wrong way. That he might believe she'd wanted him to stay gone.

"But how?" she asked him. "How can I see you?"

"Some people can see us naturally," he said. "Psychics and spiritual mediums. They seem to have a physical connection to the astral world and no one really understands why. Same with people with epilepsy or schizophrenia." He shrugged. "Maybe they've had a near-death experience or a brain injury, or maybe they were just born with a gift. No one knows for sure."

Lilian felt a stab of anxiety. The same grandmother who'd repeating the nonsense rhyme about "All Hallows' Close" on her deathbed had suffered from schizophrenia. The headaches Lilian sometimes suffered from now, along with the recurring dream, could easily be caused by an untreated brain injury.

"But I've never seen ghosts—*ethereals*—before," she said, absently rubbing her temples.

"I guess maybe it's different when the connection is as strong as ours." Ben smiled. "We'll figure it out. There has to be a reason."

Whatever the reason, the following week, she'd seen a gaunt old man staring at her from the middle of the street. She'd called out as traffic hurtled toward him from either direction, but he passed through the approaching vehicles and his body had vanished like smoke.

Three days later, she'd seen a young girl in the Green Library sitting cross-legged among the stacks. She'd tried to stop the girl from slashing her wrists but the ghost vanished as her blood splashed over the periodicals.

The next day she saw a Native American man in a feathered headdress riding a spotted horse. He'd trotted down the Main Quad as if it was the most natural thing in the world before vanishing among a stand of palm trees, and nobody but Lilian had seemed to notice. She only discovered later that it must have been one of the men who'd played the school's former mascot before they'd swapped him out for the Stanford Tree.

Similar events happened to her every other day from then on, and even though some of her sightings were particularly gruesome, she eventually got used to it.

During that time, Ben visited her frequently. They'd devised a signal to announce his presence if she was in her room so he wouldn't catch her unaware. He would call to her from the hall. If she was in the middle of something or just didn't want to talk, she would shake Whatsit, her teddy bear from when she was little, jingling the bell around its neck. She trusted Ben not to violate her boundaries, otherwise. He'd never been the type to snoop on someone as far as she knew, and he definitely wasn't a peeping tom.

After a while they added video games to their visits, but only when her roommate Abby went home for the weekend. She'd bought the brand-new *Infinite Zombie* game and installed it as a surprise for him. Ben loved it, and found he was able to play surprisingly well. It had taken a fair bit of practice to move even the smallest object, he'd told her. Getting the controller to work was pretty much a small miracle.

"What are you, some kind of Jedi now?" she'd asked him.

Ben had grinned shyly. "Yeah, maybe."

A quick rap on the door had interrupted them, and Ben had winked away, the controller dropping on her bedspread. Lilian got up to answer the door. Blake leaned into the room, looking first at Abbie's messy empty bed and then at the two controllers on Lilian's. Then he smiled. "Hey, boo. Whatcha up to?"

It was a Friday in early October. Lilian had a spare period, and Blake was supposed to have been in class. He'd surprised her, and she replied without thinking.

"Just playing *IZ4K* with Ben—" She stopped herself, immediately regretting her words. She felt like she'd been caught cheating.

Blake gave her a concerned look. "Who's Ben?"

"Nobody," she said, trying to seem nonchalant as she shrugged. "Just a friend online. We team up on *Infinite Zombie* sometimes."

"A friend online." He sounded dubious, looking at the controllers on the bed again.

"Yup. We can hang out later, if you want."

Blake nodded, already backing out the door. He crossed partway to his room, then scowled and turned back, like he'd just remembered something. "Where's your headset?"

"What?"

"I heard you talking to your *online friend*, but I don't see a headset."

"Oh. Yeah, I was just talking to the game." It was such a stupid slip, she felt her cheeks burn with shame the way Ben's used to when he was still alive. "I really get into it."

"Okay," he said, clearly not satisfied. "I guess I'll see you later, then."

He returned to his room, and knocked on her door later that night. His look of concern had deepened since earlier. He was eyeing her clinically, the way Allison had when Lilian was her patient.

"What?" she asked, drawing out the word as he stepped into her room and sat down on the bed.

"Boo. I know about Ben."

Her mind raced. "It's not what you think," she said, which was probably the most guilty-sounding thing she could have chosen to say in that moment.

"So… you're *not* playing video games with your dead best friend," he said. "That's good. Because for a minute there I thought you might need some serious help."

She closed the door gently. "How did you find out?"

"You know, I was supposed to be at Ghostland that day," he said, in lieu of responding. "A bunch of us were driving out there but we got a flat tire outside of Pittsburg. One of my friends, after we found out about what happened, he said it was fate. That we weren't supposed to die there that day."

Lilian sank into her desk chair, feeling the beginnings of another headache. She struggled to keep her breathing normal and her expression blank as her heart thumped rapidly.

"I don't believe in fate," Blake said. "And I don't think some higher power prevented us from going. We busted a tire, that's all. And Renny didn't have a spare. We ended up walking back up the interstate to a gas station, and by the time we got the donut on it was already all over the news. *Something happened at Ghostland.* They weren't letting people in. So we drove back home."

"You were lucky," Lilian said.

"I don't believe in luck, either. Bad things happen all the time. So do good things. That's the randomness of the universe. Renny was driving on that spare for over a month. We hit a rough patch of road and it finally reached its breaking point. It wasn't good luck or bad luck. Renny's a cheap bastard. His car was a piece of crap and he never replaced the tire. That's all."

He paused a moment, gauging her reaction.

"Anyway, the reason I brought it up is, I know what happened to you at Ghostland."

She felt her stomach drop. Nobody had asked her about it since she'd arrived at Stanford. She'd assumed none of them knew she'd been there, despite having been featured on the news. But Blake may have known it all along. She wondered how many others had known.

"I followed the story pretty closely, Lilian. I saw you on the news. You were there with a friend, that kid who died while the two of you tried to get the door open. I didn't remember his name until I looked it up this morning. His name was Benjamin Laramie."

She flinched again, hoping Ben had left. That he wasn't hiding somewhere within earshot, eavesdropping on this conversation.

"I never asked you about it," Blake said, "and I didn't

pry. I figured you would tell me when the time was right. But Lilian, Ben is dead. He's not coming back. There's debate over whether or not it's healthy to talk to dead people as if they're still around. And if that's something you need to do to help get over it, then you do it. But this sneaking around behind my back—I'm not about that. Okay?"

Lilian nodded. She didn't want to lose him. And she supposed as ultimatums went, it could be worse. She hadn't forbidden her to talk to Ben, only asked that she be open with him about it.

"Good," he said, and smiled sadly. "I went to a pretty strict Catholic high school, did I ever tell you that?"

Lilian shook her head.

"We had school dances like every school does, I guess, but they weren't like the dances you see on YouTube, all the kids grinding and twerking and stuff like that. Our teachers would tell us there had to be enough room for the Holy Ghost to stand between us." He chuckled bitterly at the memory. "So when we slow-danced, we'd hold each other at arm's length."

Lilian felt a tear spill down her cheek. She absently wiped it away.

"I don't want to hold you at arm's length, Lilian." He touched her cheek, still damp from her tear. "I don't want a ghost standing between us."

Lying in the dark after midnight on Halloween, still unable to fall asleep, Lilian stared at the back of Blake's head, thinking about the ghost between them as he breathed slowly in and out in a drunken sleep.

What Blake didn't know was that it wasn't Ben he had to worry about. There was more than one ghost between them and Rex Garrote, the *Un*holy Ghost, was amassing an army. If she chose not to help Ben, if she decided it was too much—school and GRP2 and helping Ben gather up an army of his own—Garrote and his ghosts would tear the world to pieces before anyone had the first clue what was happening.

A war is coming.

They'd failed to stop him once. Lilian promised herself they wouldn't fail again.

They *couldn't*. The fate of the world depended on it.

PSEUDOCIDE

Jackson's Auto Wrecking Yard
Seattle—October 30th

THERE WAS NO video of Madame Levanka's death but the traffic cameras at several intersections on her way to the auto yard, and the surveillance camera at the gates painted a picture just clear enough for Sam to see what must have happened but not quite enough to be positive, like an impressionist's painting.

Annika Levanka had left her South Lake Union home at just past noon, driving her BMW 5 Series. A red-light camera caught her speeding through the intersection of Denny Way and Fairview approximately five minutes later, a second camera at Olive and 5th two minutes later, and a third at 5th and Spring not long after that. Eyewitnesses claimed she'd been driving erratically, as evidenced by the videos. The gate camera at Jackson's Auto Wrecking, near the Port of Seattle, caught her driving through at twelve-seventeen.

The wrecking yard was where things got particularly strange. Levanka, a Russian expat, had stopped out front of the gate and sat there a moment, as if deciding whether or not she wanted to go through with it. It was impossible to see her face through the surveillance footage, obscured below the roof of her car, only to see that she was buckled in and that she appeared to be the only occupant. Her expression and her mental state could not be ascertained.

A moment later the gate rolled open and the car passed through the gate and out of the camera's view, into a dead angle.

"And then she…?" Sam asked the owner of the wrecking yard, a man named Jackson Williams.

"Drove on up to the crusher and dropped right in." He spat in the dirt at his feet, wiping engine grease on his coveralls. "Stucky tried to get the damn thing to stop but it was like she had a life of 'er own. The crusher, I mean. Strangest damn thing I ever seen. Then that woman, she come out flat as a pancake. Never woulda known there was someone inside if I didn't see it happen with my own eyes, 'cept for all that blood."

Sam peered across the dusty yard littered with small bits of electronics and crushed metal at the large, loud machine as it flattened a rusty old compact junker. "Thank you for your time, Mr. Williams."

"No trouble. Terrible way to go, ain't it? Barely heard her scream over the sound of them gears. News people says she was psychic, so I figure she musta seen it comin."

He chuckled and spat again, this time directly on his foot. They looked up at each other from the frothy brown spot on his steel-toed boot simultaneously, neither of them acknowledging the error. He scratched his stubbly cheek and shrugged as if to say, *We done?*

"Well, thanks again," Sam said. She stalked off while Williams dug the toe of his boot in the dirt to clean off the tobacco spit. She kicked aside a worn scrap of tire and approached the man operating the wrecker, the man Williams had called Stucky. "You were here when it happened?" she asked, shouting to be heard over the mechanical buzz and grind of the car crusher.

The operator raised one side of his large protective ear muffs. "*What?*" With the car crushed and spat out the other end, Stucky turned the machine off. It rattled and chugged before sputtering out. He took off the ear muffs, letting them rest around his neck at the shoulders. "You're the policewoman?"

"Detective Beadle," Sam said, nodding despite the verbal demotion. "Mr. Williams said you were here when it happened."

"'Mr. Williams,'" the man scoffed, as if he'd never heard such formality. "Yeah, I was here. That lady drove up while we were on lunch, crusher started up all on its own. I ran out to stop it but the motherfucker kept on runnin, like that bird from the Loonie Tunes, you know? *Beep-beep*."

Sam studied the controls. They seemed pretty clear and uncomplicated. There was even a large red button labeled STOP, which she supposed would normally come in handy during emergencies like the one they'd had yesterday.

"Did anyone see her drive in? See her start it?"

He shook his head. "We didn't even know she was there 'til the crusher started up. That's how come I missed lunch. Spilled my Campbell's Chunky all over the table jumpin outta my chair."

"Have you ever had trouble with the stop button before?"

The man looked at the button and shrugged. "Nope. Don't have much cause to use it, 'less somebody forgot to strip a part we can salvage. Or if someone dropped somethin when they was inside one of the vehicles, strippin parts. This was the first I ever seen someone sittin one of em when the crusher was on. An' it was real weird, 'cause she was strugglin the whole time. Like she got in there and only just realized what the heck she was doin, 'cept by then it was too late to stop. But they said on the news she was psychic, so she musta seen that shit comin."

Sam jotted down the word *struggle* in her pad and underlined it. She scrawled *same joke=collaborated story?*

"Did you see anyone else in or around the vehicle? Is it possible someone else was operating the crusher? Overriding the emergency stop somehow?"

"Nah, it doesn't do that. There wasn't nobody around but me and a couple other guys who come runnin from the shed when I started hollerin."

She made a note of it. "Can you start it up for me, please?"

"Want me to run one through?"

"That would great, thank you."

He slipped the ear muffs back on. "No problemo." He made a gesture with his hand to the woman working the crane. The sedan suspended from the large magnet—a similar size and shape to Annika Levanka's BMW—was maneuvered over the conveyor and dropped with a jangle of metal and glass.

Stucky started up the compactor. It jittered and juddered for several seconds as the car rolled into the machine. Sam counted down from when he'd pressed the button until the large metal panels started to close from top to bottom, collapsing the roof. It took a full minute for the panels to finish crushing the vehicle horizontally and vertically and spit it out the other end.

Once it was done the operator gave her a questioning look. Sam nodded. "Thank you for your time."

She returned to her car and reopened her notebook. Jotted down the word *THEORIES* on a fresh page in all-caps and underlined it twice. She wrote the rest of her notes in a flurry:

- Witnesses believe victim drove into machine. No one saw her until it was already running. Approx. 15 seconds from activation until roof crushed. Victim barely had time to start machine and return to vehicle.

- Struggle could indicate indecision, regret. However, if vic went outside car to start machine, likely would not have returned to vehicle, put on seatbelt, THEN doubted her decision.

- Witnesses could be prey to War of Ghosts. Bartlett's memory theory. If aware of Regina Delyse & other psychic suicides, witnesses might have superimposed details of struggle where none occurred, like Marjory Hemming.

- Both men shared same joke, may have hashed out story together, finessing details.

- Other likely possibility for same story is murder. Motive unknown. Reason for M. Levanka driving here, also unknown. Possible scopolamine dose? The zombie drug? Long shot but possible.

- If neither...

Sam paused with her pen hovered over the paper. If neither, then what?

If neither, she thought, *then there's some kind of evil magic at work here. And I truly do not want to imagine who or what could be doing this.*

She left the thought unwritten.

Less than half an hour later, Sam knocked on Captain Brewster's door.

"Come in," Brewster grunted.

She stepped into the captain's neat and meticulous office. Rick Brewster ran a tight ship. His father had been a military man and his mother had worked in a science lab. He'd never considered either profession for himself and Sam couldn't imagine Brewster in any other job. The desk suited him. The uniform suited him, when he wore it. She tried to picture him as a beat cop, a clean-shaven kid with a neat crew-cut shiny with Brylcream, working his way up from the streets around the same time her father had, but even that didn't fit. He was the type of man who looked like he'd been born into his station and would likely die there.

"Any progress on the McKamey investigation, Beadle?" he asked, not looking up from his paperwork, scanning it through the bifocals he held with one hand like a pair of opera glasses.

"Still hunting down a few leads," she said. "I think we might be chasing shadows at this point."

Brewster nodded and gestured toward the chair opposite his, folding his bifocals. She sat.

"What's on your mind, Detective?" he asked, while he stacked the loose paperwork by tapping it against the desk until it was a seamless rectangle, before placing it in a tray labeled ACTIVE. With his office returned to its typically pristine state, he reclined, lacing his calloused fingers behind his head—word around the station was he was building himself a sailboat in his backyard, though Sam couldn't picture that, either—and he held her in his scrutinizing gaze.

She cleared her throat, uncertain how to start. It was too difficult. There was too much history between him and her family. Brewster had been one of her father's peers during the Garrote investigation. He knew all about Stan's hunches, the leaps in logic that had caused guys in the station talk.

"I need a few days off," she said hurriedly, feeling embarrassed and anxious and sick to her stomach at the mere thought of taking vacation time. She was in the weeds with so many other investigations. Brewster knew it as well as she did. Now was not the time to go off on a wild goose chase.

Would there ever be a right time?

Four psychics dead in two weeks—it was far too many to be coincidence. She needed the time off to dig a little deeper, and if Brewster wouldn't give it to her—

"Fine," he said.

"That's it? Just fine?"

"What did you want me to say, Sam? You didn't take any time off when your father passed, despite my suggestion that you should, for your mental health at the least. And you can't carry those days forward forever."

"It's not about Stan—"

Captain Brewster raised a hand. "Ah-ah. I don't need to know. What you do on your personal time is nobody's business but yours."

"Well, great." She'd expected to have to explain herself and had practiced her spiel in the car on the way from the auto yard. "That's great, thank you."

"De nada. Your father was a good man, Sam. And a damned good detective, no matter what some people might have to say about him."

She stood. "Thank you, sir. And thanks for the time off."

"Thank your union. Oh, by the way…"

"Yes?" she said, turning back at the door.

He was leaning forward now, his hands folded on his desk, still fixing her with that studious gaze. She imagined him planing boards in his backyard with that same gaze while his wife Brenda brought him out a glass of lemonade, and she tried not to grin. "The Ringo thing," he said. "Does that bother you?"

The question had caught her unawares. She'd almost reacted. "No, sir."

He nodded. "Good. It's like that old anti-perspirant ad used to say: *Never let em see you sweat.*"

Sam left his office, heading out through the bullpen to her desk. She set up call-forwarding, Detective Borden watching her fingers the whole time, then flashing her a grin when she cradled the receiver, as if he knew it would fail her yet again.

"Anyways, I'll let you get back to it," she said to him, apropos of nothing. It only occurred to her as she reached the lobby that it was exactly what her father used to say. *Anyways, I'll let you get back to it*, whether whomever he'd been speaking to had been up to anything or not.

"Hey, Ringo," Detective Lewis called after her, leaning out from the bullpen as she put an arm in her jacket. "Phone's ringing again."

"You gotta be kidding me."

Sam raced back to her desk, praying it wasn't her mother. This time she managed to grab the receiver before the caller hung up. "Detective Beadle," she said, out of breath.

"Sam. It's Gun," the grizzled voice said. "Your pop's partner. You been ignoring my calls?"

"Hey, Mr. Edelweiss." Detective Borden raised his eyebrows at her from over his librarian's desk lamp. "I haven't been avoiding you, I've just been in the weeds, that's all."

"On the McKamey case?"

"How do you know about—?" Borden was watching her keenly. She turned away and lowered her voice. "What do you want, Gunnar?"

"I need to see you, kiddo. It's about that case. The one your pop was stuck on. The Garrote case."

She sighed inwardly, readying herself for a lecture about following her father's "gut feelings." She needed that like she needed another hole in the head, as Stan used to say. "What about it?" she said, wishing she hadn't hurried back to catch the call.

"I've had a lot of time to think about it, not much else to do these days, what with Rita gone. And with all that's been in the news lately about that place, and this lawsuit, I started to think…" She heard the leather of his Lay-Z-Boy grumble, the coils twanging as he reclined. "Well, I come to think your father might have been right. That he wasn't dead, like we thought. Those remains we found, no matter how it might have looked, that it wasn't him. That he faked his death and went into hiding."

Sam's hand felt slick with sweat. She gripped the receiver hard against her ear. "What makes you say that, Mr. Edelweiss?"

"Call it a hunch."

"A hunch," she repeated, locking eyes with Borden. The other detective shrugged.

"Uh huh. Listen, can you swing by? We really need to

talk."

Gunnar Edelweiss pulled the lever on his Lay-Z-Boy and reclined, holding a large plastic cup of crushed ice and vodka. The Stoli bottle stood on the end table beside him. Ice rattled as he shook his cup. "Care to join?"

"I don't drink," Sam told him.

"No, of course you don't."

The comment didn't appear to be smug or sarcastic. It was matter of fact. Her father drank. He'd only quit just prior to losing custody during the divorce. Sam and her mother had figured he'd go right back to drinking but he never had. Sam often wondered if he kept off the sauce just to spite her mom.

Gunnar's hair had been soft and white for as long as she could remember, his eyes ice blue like an Alsatian's. Their shape and color had always given him a sad look, though he'd always seemed mirthful at Stan's backyard barbecues. He was currently tanned despite the Seattle weather—she supposed he must spend time in Arizona or Florida, as retirees often seemed to—and his skin looked like the leather of his recliner.

They sat in the small living room of the houseboat he'd bought in the '60s, a dock away from the one made famous by *Sleepless in Seattle*. The room was dismal and dim. Sunlight filtered in between the thick curtains, illuminating the haze of Gunnar's last cigarette. Sam couldn't tell if it was the sickly-sweet smell of Lake Union, the cigarette smoke or the clotted litterbox just inside the kitchen doorway that made her feel vaguely nauseated, but all of that combined with the light sway of the houseboat made it difficult to hold down her gorge.

Aside from the recliner, an old tube TV rested on a

collapsible TV tray that didn't seem very stable, a coffee table littered with old *TV Guides* and an overstuffed ashtray, and the tartan loveseat Sam herself sat on. The cat, a Maine coon, had rubbed up against her legs as she stepped in and curled up on the floor at Gunnar's feet once he'd settled.

"Mind if I smoke?" he asked, pulling out a pack from his tattered jogging pants.

"I'd prefer if you didn't."

The man nodded, slipping the pack of menthol Kools he'd smoked for as long as Sam had known him back in his pocket. "To the point then," he said. "When your pop and me were partners, we had a case that troubled him more than the rest. Two actually, but one more than the other."

"The Garrote case," she said.

"Rex Garrote. Pulp horror writer extraordinaire. Never cared for the genre, nor did Stan prior to the day we stepped into that house. I'm more of a biography fan. Your pop, he used to read mysteries. Liked to solve em before the end. He'd write down his prediction and tuck em in an envelope like Carson doing his psychic schtick." Gunnar mimed placing an envelope against his forehead the way Johnny Carson had on the old *Tonight Show*. "Mrs. Peacock with the lead pipe in the conservatory," he said, doing a fairly decent impression of the late comedian. "Then he'd stick em in his desk and forget about em. No idea why he even kept em. Maybe they helped him live with the cases he knew he'd never solve, when he got stuck in the weeds. I asked about em, couple times, but all he'd do is smile the way he did. That *I've-got-a-secret* smile of his."

Sam remembered the smile as well as his envelopes. She'd found them tucked in his drawer at work when she cleaned it out. Dozens of little envelopes like wedding invitations with the names of the books scrawled on their faces. She'd opened several of them in her car that same afternoon and puzzled over their contents:

THEY'RE THE SAME GUY.

EVERYONE ON TRAIN IS GUILTY.

SUSPECTS INNOCENT, WRITER DID IT.

WIFE ALIVE, FAKED DEATH TO IMPLICATE JERK HUSBAND.

She'd dumped them in the hall closet at home, strange mementoes of a peculiar father she barely knew, and had only brought them out again recently, troubled by Regina Delyse's suicide, a superstitious part of her certain that rereading them might jog something loose. That maybe Stan had been trying to tell her something. Whatever that might have been, she still had no idea, no matter how many times she'd read them.

"Anyways," Gunnar said, "the stories your pop loved most were those locked room mysteries. You know: vic in a room with no signs of forced entry, all the clues in there somewhere just waiting to be interpreted by the World's Greatest Detective. I guess they were some of the hardest ones to figure out 'cause of the way they stretched logic, like it was an undetectable poison pumped in through the vents or the baboon did it." The old detective grinned, gazing at her over the rim of his cup as he sipped his vodka through a straw. "Made you think outside the box."

Sam nodded. She'd read Poe's "Murders in the Rue Morgue" in high school English, the story in which an orangutan—not a baboon—had murdered two women, and recalled feeling ripped off. Like the mystery was unfair. No matter how much an orangutan aped its master, it wouldn't have stuck around after the murder to clean up the evidence.

"You've read the Garrote case files, I guess," Gunnar said.

Sam nodded. "I have."

"Then you know about the hidden tunnels in that house of his—the, uh, the secret hatches, all that stuff. How it was basically an amusement park ride of its own."

She did, and said so.

"Still, only way in or out of that house were the doors or windows, all locked from the inside. If it wasn't suicide, the killer would have needed a key. But Stan, he was obsessed with that room with the corpse, this private library. Every detail: the matches, the gas can, the burnt remains of the chair, even the goddamn books on the shelves. Convinced everything was a potential clue, that Garrote faked his own death. The dead man in the library was somebody else, his gut told him, and every time he went back to that house, everything he found deepened his belief. *That was not Rex Garrote*."

"But you had a different opinion," Sam said. "Dental records matched. You followed the evidence—"

Gunnar shook his head bleakly. "I *suppressed* the evidence."

Sam flinched. She felt her gorge rise until she was sure she might vomit. What he'd said was something she'd never even considered. Could Stan have been right all along? "What do you mean, 'suppressed?'"

The old man rankled, shrugging, his light, sad eyes wandering off as he shook the remaining ice in his cup. Out on the lake a tugboat's horn sounded. The cat purred on the floor beside the recliner.

"Look, I was green when that case came up," he said. "I didn't want to be caught in the same spotlight as your pop. This conspiracy bullshit, it taints you. It marks your career, no matter how many cases you solve, no matter how many bad guys you lock up. Look at your father. I bet they still talk about him like he was a kook down at the station. No matter how good a detective he was. And for that, you probably have to work twice as hard to get out from under his shadow. Follow the evidence, not hunches. No matter where it leads."

He paused. Her instinct was to assault him with questions but she reigned them in. Best to let him speak at his own pace. It was one tactic she'd learned from Stan that she still retained. She sat back and tried not to let the smell of cat piss make her eyes water. The wave of nausea had fortunately passed.

"The day it happened," Gunnar said, "we were leaving the library where the body was found. Your pop went first. He was already stewing on it. I could see those gears working. That secret smile of his." Gunnar shook his head amiably. "The way he stood there scratching his head—mostly bald already, I should add—with his crumpled hat in his hand."

Sam could picture it. The image made her suddenly very sad, more than she'd been when she'd first heard about his death.

"Anyways, I was hunkered down to look at the scorch marks on the floor. Thought maybe I saw a streak in them that could prove what your pop said was right. That it *was* murder, and maybe not Garrote's. Then I saw this curly little blond hair on my slacks. Coarse, like horse hair or something. And I thought of that story your pop told me, the one with the baboon, and how the detective realizes it must have been the animal that killed those women because of that inhuman hair he finds."

Gunnar sipped the remains of his drink, slush swishing against plastic, letting the suspense build until Sam just about cried out *What was it?*

"So on a lark," he finally said, "I got it analyzed. Didn't tell your pop, didn't want to get his hopes up. Because in that moment I thought he might be right. By the time I got the results back, my man Stan—he was already obsessed. Only by then we had the dentals confirmed. He already had it in his mind it wasn't Garrote, and nobody could prove otherwise no matter how hard they tried. It was a dead end. Your pop was chasing a ghost."

"And the hair?"

"Turns out it was rope."

"And you never told him?"

Gunnar reached down with a grunt and softly scratched the cat at his feet. "How could I? I sat on that lie for decades. He was a laughing stock, and I could have changed all that with that one word: *rope*. Why would a guy need rope in a library? There was only one explanation I could think of. But how could a man burn himself to death if he was tied to a chair?"

"Could it have been twine? For binding books?"

"It was coarse hemp. A bit long for twine, but I s'pose it could've been, sure. That said, in retrospect, I very much doubt it was."

"What makes you say that?"

"Isn't it obvious? It was Garrote's silent partner that clued me in. The Hedgewood Foundation. Cutting edge tech and development company proves the existence of some kind of afterlife then invents a device that lets people literally see the dead. And for what? To build an amusement park." He chuckled bitterly. "Doesn't that seem odd to you? Does that strike you as the sort of thing a multibillion-dollar tech company would be interested in? Makes me wonder what other kinds of things they might develop with that kind of money. And what type of money it is, exactly. Government money? *Foreign* government?"

"Mr. Edelweiss—" He was getting off track, falling into the same sort of conspiracy junk Stan had in that last message he'd left on her answering machine. "You said you wanted to talk about Stan," she reminded him.

Gunnar regarded the booze in his cup. "Right. Your father, he was a good man. A smart man. Don't let anyone ever convince you he wasn't. He hunted Rex Garrote down to the ends of the earth. He was U.S. Marshall Sam Gerard to Garrote's Dr. Kimble."

"He called himself Ahab," Sam said, remembering their last face-to-face conversation. Stan peering down into the empty foundation of Garrote House.

"That works too. Better, even. 'Cause Moby Dick killed Ahab in the end, didn't he?"

"You're saying Rex Garrote killed Stan?"

"Honey—are you gonna sit there and tell me you think it's a coincidence he was crushed under that house, of all places? Things like that happen for a reason. And the fact that Fischer, that scumbag fuck who walked on the Doll's Head murders, that he was found right there with your pop, the cop who tried to put him away… If that happened in a movie, you'd call it poetic justice. I mean, you couldn't make that stuff up if you tried."

Sam had to admit she'd considered the possibility. What were the odds, otherwise? Someone had to have brought all the players to the board, some Machiavellian mastermind—but to what end? Did that someone have to be a man presumed dead for twenty years, the very man her father had been obsessed with?

And where was Rex Garrote now, if Stan and Gunnar were right?

"Brewster tells me you've been looking into this sudden rash of suicides?"

Sam felt herself flush. Captain Brewster knew what she was up to? He'd felt the need to tell her father's old partner about it?

"Don't get upset," Gunnar said. "Look, I know all about chasing ghosts. Your father did it for twenty years, fifteen of those while we were partnered-up. Can I offer my theory?"

She gestured for him to go on.

"The perp you're looking for, the one connecting all of these so-called suicides together? You're never gonna find him."

"What makes you think that?"

"Because he's *literally* a ghost. Maybe more than one. That thing I said about government money? What do you think the NSA thought when they found out people retain their memories after death? Do you think they sat on that knowledge, like I did with the rope? Or do you think they went straight to Hedgewood out in the Nevada desert, demanding to be let in on his special little secret?" His bright, sad eyes widened. "Imagine what a soldier could do without the burden of his body. Imagine what a *dozen* could do. *Hundreds*.

"You think a ghost is killing these people."

Gunnar shook his head. "I think this is a test. Call it the First Wave. The human trials. The CIA never let ethics stop them from testing on the American public before. The NSA wouldn't either. Right now, they're probably only using a handful of soldiers, most likely Black Ops guys. People with no earthly ties. Guys that are already dead on paper. Just seeing what they can do in a clandestine manner. Feeling around, under the radar. A murder here, a suicide there. Why not? And I tell ya, I think you're gonna see a whole hell of a lot more suicides before this is over."

"But why psychics? If that is what's happening here, wouldn't it be smarter to pick people at random? And why two in one city? That seems sloppy."

"Maybe because they'd potentially make the most difficult targets—people who can commune with the astral plane, or whatever. As for two in one city, maybe they know you're getting close, and this was a not-so-gentle way of telling you to back off."

Sam laughed. "How could they possibly know…?" she started to ask, but stopped short. It was absurd, even slightly entertaining the idea Gunnar was proposing.

But she'd already started down this road, the same road Stan had followed to his death. Those last words of his were still on her machine: *I think he's alive—or maybe not alive, but something like it. I know it sounds crazy, Samantha, but I feel it in my bones. Garrote's out there, at Ghostland. And I think he's waiting for me to find him. So I'm driving out there. And if I don't come back, if you don't hear from me tomorrow… that means I was right.*

After the incident, she'd waited on his call, her unease growing as the days went on. It was a week before they found her father's body under the crumbled remains of Garrote House, leaving Sam to wonder if he been right, or if his death had been a cruel coincidence.

As to Gunnar's psyops theory, whatever clandestine government body was responsible could feasibly have been watching her since she'd started looking into Regina Delyse's suicide.

And if Garrote really was still alive, somehow, he

might have kept tabs on the daughter of the one detective who'd known the truth from the very beginning, a daughter who also happened to be a detective.

"You know," Gunnar said, his sad eyes trained on the red curtains, "they're saying a portable version of that Recurrence thing could be used to solve murders now." Metal rigging clanged on a sailboat mast, tolling like a bell as the room swayed drunkenly on the surf. "Take detective work out of the equation. Put people like us out of a job."

He gulped the rest of his drink and sat the perspiring cup beside the half-empty bottle. "I'm thinking maybe that's a good thing," he said with finality.

Sam set down the musty old paperback novel she'd picked up from the Capitol Hill library and rubbed her eyes. It had been ages since she'd read anything that wasn't non-fiction—probably since Stan left home with his collection of mysteries and thrillers—but she found herself diving headfirst into Agatha Christie's *The Murder of Roger Ackroyd*, the book in which Stan had indicated the "WRITER DID IT."

She didn't read much of anything for pleasure these days, finding it too difficult to concentrate. Her thoughts would often gravitate toward work. Considering this book "research" helped get her out of the slump, keeping her butt planted in the chair when her subconscious mind was eager to get back on the road, to figure out who or what was causing these people to kill themselves.

After meeting with Gunnar, she decided to put the mystery in the hands of fate—a concept she had less faith in than ghosts or the Tooth Fairy—and gave her father's self-styled "freeform jazz" method of solving cases a try.

Hence, the book in her lap. The novel began with a

woman's suicide and her distraught wealthy husband murdered after revealing his wife was being blackmailed. The great detective Hercule Poirot emerges from retirement to solve the case.

Sam found it pretty riveting for an old book, but so far there was no writer character, and she was already about halfway through reading it. A quick internet search had told her this was the book with the "twist" Stan had written down in his drawer full of envelopes. It was beginning to concern her that she hadn't been able to figure it out herself by now.

Stan had been a competent detective. He'd closed a fair share of cases in his day, probably more than average for the precinct. Sam liked to think she was good at her job. Captain Brewster and her colleagues had praised her work on several occasions. But she just couldn't figure out how the writer figured into—

"You gotta be kidding me," she groaned.

It was the *narrator* Stan meant. The doctor—who'd been helping Poirot, who was told about the blackmail and the suicide note in the beginning of the story—*he* was the murderer. It had only taken seventy-some pages and her father literally spelling it out for her to get it. She wondered how long it had taken Stan.

"All right, so the narrator did it. Now what?"

She didn't know. She had no idea how this fact fit into her current mystery, or if it did at all.

Maybe the entire exercise was pointless. So what if she'd picked the same card up over and over, as if an invisible presence were guiding her hands? She could easily have picked up the same card from the box by chance. The odds were… well, however many cards there were in the box to one. Not exactly astronomical.

But Stan didn't write NARRATOR, she reminded herself. *He wrote WRITER.*

Which writer then? Dr. Sheppard, the murderer from the book? Agatha Christie?

"Or Rex Garrote?" she said aloud.

SUSPECTS INNOCENT, WRITER DID IT.

She chuckled contemptuously. It was a huge stretch, a Herculean leap of logic—the mythical being, not the great French detective. But the fact remained that both Gunnar and her father had believed Rex Garrote was still alive. Was it possible he really was still out there, using some kind of psychic-driving or mind-control technique to force these people into kill themselves?

And if so, to what purpose?

Sam had once solved a case where a killer with no memory of the murder was found to be an innocent victim of someone who'd used over-the-counter motion sickness patches, enough for the scopolamine—a drug with similar properties to GHB or Rohypnol, the so-called "date-rape drugs"—to make her unaware of what she was doing and unable to control herself. She'd been manipulated like a voodoo zombie. Scope patches were easy enough to obtain. But none of the suicides had been found to have large amounts of any drugs in their systems, which ruled out scopolamine.

Sam tossed the Christie book on the side table. "This is ridiculous. Use your head, Sam! You're just not cut out for gut thinking."

She got up and went to the fridge, grabbed an ice-cold Jones Soda and brought it back to the living room, to Stan's threadbare recliner. The old thing smelled like cigars but she had to admit it was incredibly comfortable. She could see why Stan had spent so much time sitting in it after he retired, at least according to Gunnar and her mom.

Speaking of Mom. I should give her a call. Not now though. Gotta get out of the weeds first if I'm gonna deal with her.

She flicked on the television, savoring the crisp bubblegum-flavored pop. CNN was airing the traffic cam footage of Annika Levanka's car again. The talking heads on the screen discussed the possibility that if the afterlife was a scientific fact—as "recent evidence suggested," according to one of the current guests—and if these victims had regular contact with the "other side," it followed that these spirits might somehow be "reaching out" and causing these deaths, either deliberately or by accident.

"It's also entirely possible this is a pathogen that attacks the mind," one of the panel's psychology experts said, "as we saw occur at Ghostland in April. The idea that it seems to only be infecting alleged psychics at this time might only be that we have yet to see a pattern in the outlying population."

"That theory is patently absurd," the man who'd just proposed killer ghosts said. "If there was a shred of evidence—"

"How is this news?" Sam grumbled, flicking off the TV and tossing the remote on the couch. "I gotta get out of this apartment."

Here she was, wasting her only vacation time in a year sitting around in Stan's smelly old recliner, reading fluff and watching sensationalist TV. She got up, threw on her jacket and headed out to the car.

It was drizzling again. She had no idea where she was going. It only occurred to her once she was on the road again that driving around aimlessly while mulling over a case was exactly what Stan would have done.

aStral Connections

ANDY PARK HURRIED into his apartment, snapped the lock and the deadbolt, and drew the chain. He pushed a chair under the door handle and set the feet against the stoppers he'd nailed into the floor. Only then did he feel safe enough to relax. Somehow, the goons from the Palais Royale had tracked him down to this address. Two men in suits had been pummeling on his door about an hour ago, according to Ms. Hernandez the landlady, who took the opportunity to remind him rent was due tomorrow.

Hallowe'en already, he thought. *No treats this year. And the trick's on me.*

He crossed the messy floor, strewn with pizza boxes and dirty clothes, to the sofa. He pushed aside his laptop and a heap of junk mail and flopped down, flicked on the television, and lit a roach from the overstuffed ashtray.

The Palais Royale's thugs would get him soon, no question. Meet a nice girl to run away with just in time to get fitted with a pair of concrete sneakers. Never mind trying to sleep with Lamb Curtis—within twenty-four hours he'd be sleeping with the fishes. After all these years, it looked like his lucky streak had finally run out.

"Ghosts," he muttered, exhaling a cloud of fragrant

smoke. "Yeah, right. Casper is my homeboy."

If not for his rotten luck he wouldn't be in this current predicament. Then again, he likely would've died the day the pizza palette nearly fell on his head when he was little, or when he almost got hit by the Humvee while scratching his scratch tickets, or any of the numerous times his "lucky streak" had saved his ass by a hair. The truth was, it was his own damn fault.

Andy's parents had worked themselves into an early grave. His grandparents, too. They'd always tried to instill in him the value of labor, the value of a dollar, of paying your own way. He grew up Methodist. His folks had believed gambling was a sin. When they found out he'd quit his job delivering pizza—of all things—and had been playing professional poker to pay his way through college, they'd kicked him out of the house. Didn't even give him a chance to explain himself.

After that, there didn't seem to be any reason to continue with school, either.

In those days, he'd made a fair amount of money playing cards. He'd even been on TV a few times, in the tournaments with big-time celebrity players. He'd sat at tables with Kevin Hart and Jennifer Tilly and Tobey Frigging Spider-Man McGuire. In his best days, it seemed as if those guardian angels or *gwisin* had been shuffling the cards to come out in his favor.

Until they stopped.

And that was the thing Andy had discovered about luck, best expressed by a fellow High Roller who once told him: "Feels like you're on top of the world when you're ridin Lady Luck, but when she's ridin you… boy, you better lube up."

Inevitably, luck ran out. And when that happened,

things got rough.

This morning, after three small paydays apiece on the loose machines on the mezzanine at the opulent Palais Royale, then hitting the progressive jackpot on the Big Bertha by the fountain in the lobby, Andy had felt a Nudge urging him to leave. Just a little tug on the back of his head, like an invisible string connected to his cerebral cortex. He'd ignored the feeling, eager to hit the machine again, to take it for all it had.

A moment later, with his hand gripping the arm, ready to pull and take his chances, he'd felt the strong, thick fingers of the pit boss squeeze his shoulder.

He'd whipped around, splashing his beer in the pit boss's face. Even now he wasn't sure whether it had been an accident or intentional. While the big man in the suit reacted to that, Andy had grabbed his cup of coins from beside the machine. Somehow, it slipped from his fingers and the coins tumbled out at their feet, and when the pit boss came after him, pissed, his face glistening with cheap beer, his eyes red and bulging, the big man in the suit stepped down on the heap of coins and slipped and fell back against the arm of the machine, then slumped down flat on the red carpet, blood streaming from a gash on his bald head.

Andy's mind had raced as he dashed down the marble steps into the street, two goons in suits already barreling after him. He'd run out onto the Strip, into the crowd of Forever People—always walking, always drinking, always gawking—and lost himself among them for as long as a minute. When he'd looked back a block further, the goons were on him again, like heat-seeking assholes.

Killed the pit boss, he'd thought, running and out of breath. *Ticket's punched in this town, Andy, my man.*

He'd run until he'd found the psychic's shop. When he got back to his apartment, still broke but brimming with good cheer after Lamb had taken his phone number, he'd discovered the goons had already come and gone.

He had to get back inside that casino. If he didn't go back soon, he wouldn't be able to eat, let alone pay his rent and his weed dealer. He'd won on the Big Bertha progressive, and three smaller winnings from the other slots. It was enough to cover it all, but the money was out of his reach. It might as well have been on Mars.

Andy laughed bitterly, taking the voucher out of his pocket. Six-thousand and eighty-three dollars. Utterly useless to him if he wasn't able to cash out.

He stuck a frozen pasta in the microwave and shoveled handfuls of dry Cap'n Crunch from the box into his mouth, watching the Michelina's box rotate. When it was done, he brought it back to the couch to eat. The middle was still frozen so he mixed the scalding hot portion with the cold while his stomach growled, until the entire dish was just warm enough to eat. As he shoveled it into his mouth, he tried to recall the taste of his mother's kimchi and grilled pork belly and bean paste cookies. The spices and tangy sauce. It had been so long since he'd eaten home cooking, he'd almost forgotten what real food tasted like.

His phone rang as he washed down a lukewarm mouthful of pasta with an ice-cold guzzle of Xyience Mango Guava. He swallowed hard and picked it up on the third ring. "Uh-huh?"

"Andy?" The woman's voice sounded frantic. He didn't recognize her right away, even from the slight drawl, though she sounded vaguely familiar. He'd had no close female friends since he quit school and his last few Tindr dates back in the summer hadn't ended well. He'd much preferred Kismet, where he could actually get to know someone before meeting them. Tindr was the *Pokemon Go* of dating apps, as far as he was concerned.

"This is him," he said, slightly suspicious.

"Hi, it—it's Lamb." Her voice trembled. "From this morning?"

Andy put down his fork. He stared at the glob of beef and tomato sauce he'd splattered on the table, looking a lot like gore. He hadn't expected to hear from Lamb for a couple of days if at all, and via text if anything. Who even called people these days?

"Lamb," he said. "You sound weird. Are you okay?"

"No." She sobbed.

"What's the matter?"

"It's my mom. She's dead."

"*Dead?*"

Buzzards of fear circled Andy's paranoid mind. He'd just spoken to her less than three hours ago. Other than Lamb, he was probably one of the last people to see Psychic Sonya alive. He'd be a suspect in her death. On the heels of the accident at the Palais Royale, he'd go straight to jail. He was slender and had never won a fight in his life. The last time he'd gotten in a physical altercation was in middle school when another boy called him Bruce Lee before karate chopping him in the neck, and he'd only scraped by with few injuries by kneeing the kid in the balls. He wouldn't survive a single day in jail.

"Have you talked to the cops yet? The police? Did you tell them about me?"

"Andy, no. They came, yeah, but I didn't tell them about you."

"Okay, good. Can you tell me what happened?"

She told him, her scattered recollection starting at the

end and backtracking to catch him up, leaping from the police questioning her to her trip to the crepe shop, to her mother smashing her own face into the front desk.

"Jesus," he said.

"I was just so scared when the cops left," she said frantically, "I didn't know who else to call, and then I thought about you and what she said to me after you left this mornin… Andy, can you come over?"

"Come over?"

At least she doesn't want to come here, he thought, looking over the mess.

He'd need to shower and put on a change of clothes before leaving the apartment. Not in the hope of getting lucky—his luck had officially run out, this last bit of news was proof if it was anything—but because of the run from the Royale, then sneaking through garbage-choked alleys back home. He doubted he'd be much comfort to Lamb smelling like a fresh corpse. "Sure, I can be there in about an hour. Will you be okay?"

She sniffled. "I think so."

"Okay, I'll be over in a bit. Don't talk to anybody, okay?"

"I won't."

She sniffed again and ended the call.

Andy stood under the hot shower in a downward spiral of paranoia. First the pit boss and now Lamb's mother. If they had him on camera for both incidents—he knew the Royale had eyes in the sky, but not if Psychic Sonya's had a camera—it would be easy enough to link him to both incidents. Though he still wasn't sure if the pit boss was actually dead. He could have just been badly injured.

Better call José, he thought.

José Ortega was a croupier at the Royale. He did a

spot-on French accent, which gave players and colleagues a kick. He was friendly with just about everybody who worked there and knew many repeat players by name. If anyone knew whether any of the pit managers had been in an accident or killed, it would be José.

Andy toweled off and got changed. He had no clean shirts—he'd spilled the last quarters he'd been saving for laundry on the Royale's rug this morning—but he found a hoodie in the hamper that had only been worn once, applied a liberal amount of Axe Phoenix body spray and pulled it on over his bare chest. Vegas was much cooler in the fall, and it was already a day away from November. The summer had come and gone in a blink. He couldn't remember much of it at all.

He called José on his way to Lamb's.

"Bro, are you crazy?" José asked the second he picked up. "You almost killed Mr. Mack."

Andy sighed, relaxing slightly at the word *almost*. He looked both ways before jogging across East Flamingo to the median. "Oh, thank God," he said. "It was a total accident, man. He's okay then?"

"He's in the hospital with a concussion, but yeah, he's okay, cuz. They on the lookout for you now, though. You better not come back any time soon. The Big Boss is pissed."

"Shit." He dashed across the eastbound lane. "I got a winning ticket. Six-grand."

"Six-grand? Damn, son. Cut me in for a piece and I'll cash in for you."

Andy considered it. "Okay, deal. I got some business to take care of first."

"Okay. Just don't be tryna kill no more pit bosses, cuz."

Andy laughed, ending the call as he crossed Howard

Hughes Parkway. He was glad the pit boss had lived—Mr. Mack was the perfect name for the broad-shouldered goon—but the Royale had likely put Andy's name and face out to all the other major casinos.

Might have to bail on the Strip, he thought. *Head up to Reno, maybe Atlantic City. See the east coast. Greener pastures.*

The notion wasn't all that appealing. He'd lived in the Vegas area his whole life, born and raised in Spring Valley. After his parents passed away and the bank reclaimed the land their house had stood on, he'd gotten an apartment in a small building on the northeast edge of downtown.

Vegas was his home. One stroke of bad luck—two now, counting the death of Lamb's mother—and he may as well consider himself banished.

Whatever had attached itself to him—his mother's *gwisin*, or guardian angels, or some kind of supernatural power—it was clear Lady Luck was about to bend him over and go in dry.

Sam drove in the rain for half an hour, from her house to the wrecking yard to Regina Delyse's neighborhood. She still had no idea what she was doing. She could only hope the act of driving, of clearing her mind and focusing entirely on the road would rattle something loose.

When Stan had been obsessing over a case, he'd go for long drives after dinner in the dark, in the rain. When Sam was much younger, her mom thought he'd been cheating on her. In a way, he had. Even when he was home with his family, his mind had been on the job, solving cases.

Sam hadn't understood it then but as she worked her way toward the rank she currently held, she'd begun to realize it wasn't possible to leave police work at the door, at least for the Beadles. The homicides, missing persons, human traffickers, drug addicts and domestic abusers had followed Stan home, as they followed her now. She couldn't imagine a spouse in her life, let alone a child.

Even now, nearly in her mid-forties, she still hadn't been able to forgive Stan's aloofness and neglect, for leaving them when she'd needed him most. Forgiveness was too difficult, even after he'd passed. It was why she'd brought his chair home with her when she and her mom sorted through his house in Centralia. She'd hoped that taking something of his and keeping it close would help her let go of her anger, while the envelopes from his desk had only added more mystery to a father she'd hardly known.

She parked out front of the Delyse house again. She'd been in the house several times and found nothing to indicate foul play. There was no use going in again. Besides, an off-duty detective making an unsanctioned visit to a crime scene, even one that was no longer active, wouldn't look good on her record.

So what now? she thought, peering out through the raindrops streaking the windshield, caught in the yellow glow of the streetlamps. *What would Stan do?*

The drizzle had stopped, and the silence and heat within the car felt suddenly oppressive. She rolled down the window and flicked on the radio. Commercials buzzed in her ears, corny jingles that had no business existing in the modern world and stilted conversations so corny they could've been parodies. At ten after the hour, the news came on.

After a few local news stories, the announcer said: "The first episode of the Ghost Brothers' two-night *Return to Ghostland* special is expected to draw a record number of viewers tonight. The brothers stated on their social media they're hoping to show viewers at home proof of 'real-life ghosts' when they tune in to the second episode on Saturday. And in other spooky Hallowe'en news, the sudden rash of psychic suicides has added another victim, this latest in Las Vegas. The victim's name has yet to be released but police say it is being treated as a suicide. For those counting, this is the fifth suicide of a psychic in the past two weeks. Officials for the Las Vegas Psychic Expo this weekend have yet to make a statement, but as of this afternoon are pushing forward with the event undeterred. I'm Connie Chase and this is your KCBM news update. Weather on the five, news on the ten."

Another announcer came on with the traffic report. Sam stared dumbfounded at the radio, as the voice droned on.

A death in Vegas meant the psychic suicides had branched out toward the east—like an infectious disease sweeping over the mountains, across the plains and the desert.

This wasn't just a pattern anymore. It was the work of a serial murderer. But how? And why? Was Gunnar right? Were the CIA or the NSA testing some new high-tech military gear? Using a psyops weapon of some sort on psychics to see if they could be detected?

Or were the so-called "experts" on the news right and it was ghosts doing this? If Rex Garrote had somehow orchestrated the incident at Ghostland as many people on the internet seemed to believe, was it possible he was behind these deaths as well?

Sam laughed at herself. It was absolutely absurd, far beyond any rational sense of logic and reasoning. For all she knew, every single one of these psychics had looked into the future and seen something so traumatic, so terrible they'd committed suicide to spare themselves an agony worse than death.

Sam laughed at herself. She didn't believe in psychics or telekinesis or any of that Stephen King crap. If not for the Rock N' Roll Psychic's video, she would never have ventured down this road to begin with. She'd still be plugging away at the McKamey murders, weeds or no weeds.

There were only two options left now: throw in the towel, or take this investigation on the road.

She'd already made up her mind by the time the news came on again, repeating the same stories as before.

With any luck, she'd break the case in Las Vegas. If there was ever a place for luck, good or bad, it was Vegas. But it was already Thursday, which gave her two days to put this case to bed before the psychic convention, not including today.

It didn't leave her a lot of time to work with, but she supposed she'd have plenty of time to consider all the angles on the flight ahead.

OUT OF THE LOOP

BEN AND LE MON gaped at the ethereal in front of them. Since the late 1970s, Alan Sparrow had been haunting the Chesterfield Theater, pacing its stage, lingering in his old dressing room, wandering the halls. "He's looping big time," Le Mon said as they entered the abandoned off-Broadway theater. "Stubborn too, or so I heard. Not much worse than a know-it-all ethereal."

Ben and Le Mon had been watching Sparrow run through lines from various productions for the past ten minutes. When they'd introduced themselves, he seemed to believe they were producers. He was looping, just like Le Mon said. Repeating the same things over and over without even realizing it. And overall, it seemed to be a pretty standard haunting, aside from his choice of attire.

"What are we gonna do?" Ben whispered.

"Even if we bust his loop, I ain't about to take him back to the Temple wearing… *that*," Le Mon said, giving the ethereal a sour look. "People are gon' get mad."

Visitors to the theater who'd seen Sparrow claimed he'd been wearing a white sheet, which made stories of the "Chesterfield Theater Ghost" all the more farfetched. But here he was, pacing the stage in a white sheet with holes crudely cut out for his eyes, no better than a child's

Hallowe'en costume. It was how the actor presented himself in death. Le Mon guessed it might be because Sparrow believed he was playing *the role* of a spirit, not realizing he was actually dead. Like the ghost of Hamlet's father in a low-budget, postmodern production.

"It's so dumb," Ben muttered.

"I ain't arguing." Le Mon approached the stage. "Look, Alan. We can't take you with us looking like… like a bag of bones out of a haunted hay ride."

"I beg your pardon?" the man said, fabric muffling the classically trained thespian's voice. "You assume I *chose* this? Take it up with wardrobe!"

Le Mon sighed and returned to one of the remaining front row seats. He shrugged at Ben. "Your turn."

Okay, fine, Ben thought as he approached Sparrow. "Alan," he said, "uh… Mr. Moncrief and I would like to run through some of your lines again, please. As we said, uh… we've taken over the production and we'd like to get a taste of what our audiences will be paying for tonight."

"Expect me to sing for my supper, do you?"

"I guess so, yeah."

"Well, then," the actor said. He swept out his right arm in a dramatic gesture, the sheet flapping. Strutting across the stage, he began his lines with exaggerated loudness to be heard in the decrepit balconies: "'I have heard but not believed the spirits of the dead may walk again. If such thing be, thy mother appeared to me last night, for ne'er was dream so like a waking. To me comes a creature, sometimes her head on one side, some another. I never saw a vessel of like sorrow, so filled and so becoming. In pure white robes like very sanctity, she did approach my cabin where I lay. Thrice bowed before me, and gasping to begin some speech, her eyes became two spouts: the fury spent, anon.'"

He ended his speech and bowed deeply, sweeping out an arm with a flourish that sounded like someone flicking out their laundry to hang on a line. Le Mon gave the actor a standing ovation. "That was terrific, Mr. Sparrow. Truly riveting."

The sheeted ghost turned to Ben, as if seeking his approval.

"That was great, Mr. Sparrow, but uh… there's just something missing. Could we try it again from the top, only this time without the sheet?"

"*Sheet! Sheet, he says! I trained at The Julliard! I've played Richard III and Hamlet with the Shakespeare Theater Company! Don't presume to chasten me for my WARDROBE!*"

The actor flung his arms wide, thrashing the sheet. Long-dead spotlights shone so brightly the bulbs popped, raining bits of glass on the floor and the remaining threadbare seats. Sandbags dropped from the rafters and exploded in puffs of brown dust. Sparrow was so angry he didn't notice he'd flung the sheet off his head. As it fluttered to the stage the actor stood staring daggers at Ben, nostrils flaring above his van dyke beard.

"*There!*" Sparrow bellowed. "*Are you happy now, you despicable devils?*"

Ben and Le Mon gave each other sly grins.

An hour later they returned to Ducks Falls with Alan Sparrow in tow. Le Mon spent a brief time counseling him, assuring him he wasn't experiencing a "bad trip," that his death wasn't the end of the world and his afterlife could actually be very fulfilling, given time and effort. Afterwards, he let the man mingle in with the others at the abandoned church on Kubler Road. Its occupants called it The Temple.

"How did it go?" Ben asked as Le Mon met up with him on the church balcony, overlooking the pews where the living GRP2 members ate dinner.

"Real good," Le Mon said. "When you think about it, stage acting is kinda like looping. Do and say the same things night after night, most times you might even get the same reaction. I guess it makes sense it'd be easier for somebody like him to let all of that go."

"You think he'll join us?"

Le Mon gave him a sidelong look. "Against you-know-who? That man is living rent-free in your head, you know that? You still think he's out there, huh?"

Ben scowled. "I *know* he is."

They'd been through this several times: his faith in a war that seemed inevitable and Le Mon expressing his doubt. Still, they recruited and trained. Le Mon believed it was better to be safe than sorry, and teaching ethereals to take charge of their afterlives and control their individual powers gave him a sense of purpose.

"That thing Sparrow did with the spotlights and the sandbags," Le Mon said. "I think we can mold that into something special if he doesn't let his ego get in the way."

Ben agreed.

"Hey, I meant to ask how you and Lilian did with the Woman in White last night."

"Not good," Ben admitted. "She's still looping pretty hard. But she's powerful. She cracked a whole bunch of headstones just with her voice. If Rex Garrote turns her…"

"Then we best hope he doesn't."

They stood a moment in silence, watching the people below them eat and mingle and chat. Ben would have killed for a burger and fries, but it wasn't really an option for him. Yet another thing the afterlife lacked, despite what he'd gained.

"Guess you heard another one of them psychic folk booked a flight to the Great Beyond," Le Mon said finally. "First this Miss Delyse, and now some woman who calls herself Madame Levanka."

"The Rock N' Roll Psychic, too," Ben said. "And two others, I forget their names."

Le Mon folded his arms across his chest. "Startin to sound like an epidemic."

"It's *weird*. It can't be a coincidence, right?"

"Think maybe someone's guiding their hands?"

"Maybe." Ben shrugged. "Did you see that Facebook video? If something wasn't forcing him, he's a pretty good faker."

"Well, it *ain't* one of us." Le Mon nodded toward the other ethereals gathered among the pews while the living ate. "We know these people. None of them would do something like that. This has got to be a rogue agent. A serial killer, maybe even an assassin. I don't think any of these folks have the mind or the strength it'd take to do what he done. Except for you or me, and I'm one-hundred percent sure I didn't do it."

"What about me?"

"'Bout fifty."

Ben laughed. "Thanks."

"What's worse, whoever's doing it doesn't look like they're using possession or psychic manipulation," Le Mon said. "Looks like sheer force to me. Most of our people couldn't even push a pencil 'cross a table let alone make a grown-ass man pick up a sword and gut himself."

"You're probably right," Ben said, looking over their

peers.

A few of them could control localized pockets of minor weather phenomena, like fog or cold, and one could possess people for short bursts, make them hiccup or flap their arms like a chicken. One woman had telekinetic powers like Ben but only seemed to be able to use it to move dishes and chairs, and one man could manipulate small pockets of water. Another had the ability to cause auditory and visual hallucinations and perform other minor mental tricks, and two others could blow out flames or turn lights and gadgets on and off. Not a single one of them had the raw power displayed in the Rock N' Roll Psychic's suicide video, or could do what had been done to Miss Delyse and Madame Levanka.

"So it's not one of us," Ben said, deep in thought. "Could it be something from the Dark Rift?"

Le Mon grunted. "We gon' talk about this again, huh?"

"We never talk about the Dark Rift. Every time I bring it up you say, 'You don't wanna know,' and I drop the subject."

Le Mon gave him a hard look. "Look I only ever heard about… *things*… coming out of the Dark Rift in stories. They say the ethereals who come back aren't the same as when they went in. You know how cancer works? How old cells don't die off and shed like a normal cell, they just fester and expand? These things that come back from the Dark Rift, I heard they're like cancerous tumors of their former selves."

"Like doppelgangers?"

"Not really. More like… malignant shadows."

"We saw something like that at Ghostland," Ben said. "Me and Lilian called them the Swarm. They're kind of like this smoke that floats around killing people."

"You serious?"

Ben shuddered at the thought of it slamming Ms. Amblin up against the control room monitor wall. "Dead serious," he said.

"I wasn't gonna say this," Le Mon said, giving him a sidelong look, "but is that gonna be your new thing? This 'dead serious' thing ya'll are doing?"

Ben shrugged. "I thought maybe it could be."

Le Mon sucked his teeth.

"It's no good?"

"Nah. It's gotta go, man."

Ben nodded pensively.

"So, you think this Swarm thing could've offed those psychics then?"

"I dunno. Maybe. But it didn't need a reason to kill, it just seemed like instinct. I don't think they have enough brain power to plot something like this."

"Not even if somebody else was tuggin on their strings?"

This gave Ben pause. If Garrote was able to control the Swarm, he supposed it would be easy enough to direct their fury toward a specific target. "I guess so," he said. "But the Swarm didn't really act like that. They were more like… like a *frenzy*. Smashing and squeezing and tearing the life out of people."

"How 'bout orbs?" Le Mon suggested.

"Have you ever seen an orb do something like that to a person?"

"No. But I never seen an imago eat an ethereal for a snack, and I still know it happens."

"Could imagoes do what we saw in that video?"

Le Mon bobbed his head from side to side as he considered it. "Imagoes hunt ethereals. They're like big fish feeding on the little ones the second they hatch. I've never heard of an imago going after a living person. But I guess since psychics sometimes project their astral selves into our side of the world, it might be possible. Like dipping their toes into shark-infested water."

Down below, Thea Petralia emerged from her office and rose the steps to the pulpit to the roar of applause and cheers from the living and dead. She'd been on a business trip the past few days, and had postponed their evening meetings. As usual, she wore all black, from her cropped jean jacket and Blondie T-shirt to her cargos and Doc Martens, her eye makeup in cat's-eye curls. She picked up the microphone, turned the laptop on the pulpit toward her for groups in other cities watching the live stream. The perpetually scowling Bram Merritt, Thea's second-in-command, crossed the stage to the sound system. The tribal tattoo on his neck stretched as he bent to stop the music, scalp shining through his thinning black buzzcut.

"Welcome, everyone," Thea said. "It's so great to see you all, and especially to see so many new faces. I'm told the pews are full tonight—which means we've got a lot of new faces I *can't* see, as well."

This elicited chuckles from nearly everyone and she smiled. Her smile lit up the room. She radiated positivity, as infectious as an airborne disease.

"That makes me feel extremely grateful and excited about the work we're doing here. When we first started GRP2 it was just a small group of us in a DTLA loft, handmaking signs and taking our message to the streets. Now, I'm happy to say we have over one-thousand corporeal members from all across the country, and nearly four-hundred ethereals."

The applause reached the rafters.

"Ben Laramie, I'm told you're here with us. If you could come up to the pulpit, we can start."

Ben winked out from beside Le Mon on the balcony and reappeared in the aisle. The hope, the expectation on the faces in the pews made his heart hurt, a phantom pain that never seemed to go away for good. One hard lesson he'd learned about death: you carry your baggage with you. It was easy enough giving up his body but chronic pain and fear were so wrapped up in his psychological makeup that even now that he no longer had a heart the pain still came back to haunt him.

He floated up the aisle, looking down at the faces of fellow ethereals sitting in the pews, watching him, proud and grateful. The living watched the stage expectantly, waiting for Ben to communicate with them.

Thea stepped back from the pulpit as he rose onto the stage. She always did, as if she could sense his presence, though he knew she couldn't. They'd never had a face-to-face conversation, only ever spoken via text on a screen. To most of the living his presence was as light and invisible as air. Only a handful could sense the ethereals among them and even less could see or communicate with them. For most, the pews appeared barely half full.

Ben approached the laptop and he began to type in the text-to-speech program. The sound of the keys always made the living members raise up in their seats, perking their ears, as if they might be able to tell what he was typing by listening to the clatter.

It was much like magic to them. Ancient cultures had attempted to communicate with the dead, and though some may have made contact, none had fully succeeded in conversing. Modern technology was the Great Unifier. Sara Jane Amblin's discovery had ultimately brought the worlds of the living and the dead together. If only she'd been alive to see her work used for good.

Ben dragged the cursor to SPEAK and clicked it. The astoundingly lifelike British voice Thea sometimes called Benedict Cumberbatch spoke his words aloud: *"We were able to free Mr. Sparrow from the Chesterfield Theater. He's here with us now. But Jessica Kissimon was a no-go. Her death loop is deeply rooted in guilt. She fought us pretty hard. Won't be moved. I'm sorry to disappoint you all."*

Dozens of comments popped up in the livestream chat window, one after another:

—oh no

—I thought for sure she was one of us

—Good work anyway, Ben! Thanks for trying!!!

—does he still wear the sheet?

—u did what you could, its nobody fault don't let it get to you, my friend!

—we love you Ben!

"I'm sorry to hear that, Ben," Thea said, giving the laptop a sympathetic look meant for him.

He could have told them all the truth: that Jessica Kissimon had been complicit in the deaths that held her prisoner. But he'd found it was sometimes better to lie. To let people accept the myths. To let them believe in goodness, honesty, innocence and forgiveness when the world was really just a spectrum of grays, growing darker and darker all the way down.

All the way to the Dark Rift, he thought.

"There's always a chance the individuals we're trying to help won't allow themselves to be liberated, for some reason or another," Thea said. "Jessica Kissimon is still hanging on to a lot of guilt. We can all empathize with that, can't we?"

Nods throughout, from the living and the dead.

"That doesn't mean we have to stop trying. Maybe someday she'll give in, allow one of us to reach her." She smiled in Ben's general direction, and he moved into the line of it, to feel its light, her positivity in the face of adversity. "Thank you for trying, Ben. I know it's daunting—for you, especially. After what you and your friends went through at that…"

She bit her lip. He could tell she needed to curse but didn't want to tarnish her image. She only swore behind closed doors. She was a guardian angel to many of these people. Their Mother Teresa. It was important for all of them that she maintain a good public image.

"…that *terrible place*," she said finally, meaning Ghostland. "I just wish someday I could see your face to thank you in person."

As the entire church filled with applause, Ben felt the sting of guilt. He'd kept all of them out of the loop, lying since the very beginning about why he and Le Mon had joined them. The two of them recruited in secret, passing a word here and there, among the shadows. Thea and her people had no idea a hard line of defense and retaliation was being plotted right under their noses.

Ben knew Garrote wouldn't have invested so much time and effort—not to mention cash—into the construction of Ghostland without a plan for what would happen after he escaped. That plan had been laid out in his 1984 novel *Shōki*, based on the Chinese legend of the Chung Kwei. In it an ordinary man, a veteran of the Vietnam War, rose to lead a legion of ghosts to world domination. Ben was convinced the character was an idealized version of Garrote himself, self-inserting his own ideologies and aspirations into the narrative.

"—and if we're unable to break them free of their loops," Thea continued from behind the pulpit, "we can petition their local government for squatters rights. Moving forward, GRP2 policy will be *No Ethereal Left Behind*."

While Thea Petralia and the others freed ethereals, fought for advocacy and advancement of rights, Ben and Le Mon prepared those willing to fight at their side for war.

Rex Garrote was coming.

Soon, the world would be forced to make a desperate choice: stand against Rex Garrote, join him, or die—and worse, for those who were dead already.

For them, only the Dark Rift awaited.

After briefing the group on new policies, Thea led a vote for which ethereals should be liberated next from their master list, and announced which teams would take lead in each operation. They discussed sweeps for new ethereals to free, a process which had to be done by other ethereals, since the group didn't have the necessary tech for most living members to find them. They discussed the protest of the live *Return to Ghostland* TV special featuring the Ghost Brothers, Jake and Eric Gallagher, and tabled a discussion of when they might risk sending their own people into Ghostland to liberate ethereals who hadn't been freed when Ben opened the hatch. He knew they would attempt it sooner or later, no matter how strongly he would advise against it.

"Ben, I need a word with you," Thea said after the meeting had ended and most of the living had returned to their encampment, or various hotels and motels in the area. "Would you step into my office with me?"

She gave a slightly embarrassed smile in his vague direction. He supposed someone must have pointed him out to her or she wouldn't have known he was there in the first place. "Step, hover—all this time and I still forget to use non-corporeal language."

Ben felt like a kid pulled into the principal's office. Had someone told her he was recruiting? Did she already know?

He followed her down the hall, past the meeting room where fledgling members without homes or tents had already gathered among the mattresses on the floor, taking off their shoes and socks, folding clothes, removing glasses and contact lenses and makeup, flossing their teeth and getting ready for bed. All the trappings of life Ben rarely missed, aside from the routine. Routine felt good. Like how he used to go down to the 86 Diner on Fridays to chat with Lilian's mom and catch up on town gossip. He still sometimes went there but it wasn't the same without being able to talk to Maddy. Still, it was comforting to watch her work, smiling as she offered a "fresh top-up" and small-talked with customers, to see her smile and blush when Mr. Roth came in to surprise her with flowers or chocolates as he sometimes did these days.

When she smiled, she looked like what he imagined Lilian would look like when she was older. It made him sad to know he'd never grow old alongside Lilian, that he'd stay eighteen forever, while eventually she would wither away and die. The young woman he knew now would someday drift away from him again, would get a job and marry and have children she would rather spend her afterlife with than him.

While Maddy and Hiram Roth grew closer together in their daughter's absence, Ben's house became haunted.

His parents fought constantly. After the argument about the pretzels his dad had started digging a hole in the backyard while his mom continued trying to sell houses to pay the mounting bills in a town where the real estate market suffered from the aftermath of a mass tragedy. The hole in the yard had grown bigger and deeper over time, and neither Ben nor his mother had any idea what Michael Laramie was planning. The few times Ben had heard her ask, Dad would tell her, "You'll see," streaking sweat and dirt across his forehead with the back of his hand.

The last time Ben had visited, a week after his reunion with Lilian in her dorm room, he'd tried to give his parents a sign that he was okay. In the early morning while they still slept, he'd gone up to his room. The door had stayed closed since he died, and a thick layer of dust had accrued on his books, his old toys and furniture. He'd taken his Bela Lugosi Dracula collectible figure off his headboard shelf and set it down on the kitchen table for his mom to find. But his dad had woken up early that morning and frowned at it for several minutes. Finally, his dad had muttered, "How drunk was I last night?" and brought it back to Ben's room, returning it to the dustless spot on the shelf.

When his mom found his dad in Ben's room she'd calmly and quietly told him to leave. His dad had gotten upset and the two of them had begun to yell. In the chaos, Ben tipped the whole shelf of toys over and both of his parents stared at the mess on the mattress for several moments.

"Guess I put it back wrong," his dad finally said.

When Ben left, the hole in the backyard was at least fifteen feet deep and just as wide. Again, he considered reaching into his father's mind to find out what the hell it was for, but with the obsessive way his dad had been acting, Ben worried he might be losing his mind. Better to assume he was digging to put in a pool than to find out he was trying to dig for buried treasure or something equally bizarre.

Whatever reason Michael Laramie had for digging that hole, the fights between his parents seemed to be less frequent with his mother always at work and his dad spending most of his time up to his shoulders in dirt.

Ben had always disliked confrontation as a general rule. It was why he hadn't been back home in weeks, and it was the reason he hesitated at the door to the church office where Thea Petralia had set up shop. She hadn't looked pleased when she'd called him in. He expected the worst.

She sat on the edge of her desk and laid the laptop beside her. Ben entered, hovering just inside the door. The room still contained everything the preacher left behind, stuff that meant nothing to any of them. The only things Thea had brought in of her own was a photo of her family at the Grand Canyon and a pink stuffed unicorn she called Taffy, which was ratty and old. Ben made it dance, a trick Thea usually found amusing. Tonight, she just gave him a tight-lipped smile.

She knows.

"Ben, I've been talking with some of the others…."

He typed in a flurry. The British voice spoke for him: *"Thea, I know you're upset but I can explain everything."*

She folded her arms across her chest. "I don't need an explanation, Ben. I know you and Lilian Roth are close, and I know she was there for you at Ghostland, that without her you might still be trapped there with the rest of them, but she hasn't been pulling her weight. You've got to come to terms with that. We have multiple teams now who are drawing in more individuals than the two of you on a daily basis. At first, it was great. You were the Dynamic Duo. But now—let's face it, she's lost her focus. Her head's just not in the game. Whether it's this boyfriend of hers or school, she's overextending herself. She's gonna flame out. I'm worried she might have already."

"*I need Lilian,*" the voice spoke for him. "*We're a team, a good team, you know that. The Woman in White overpowered us, that's all. She's not innocent. Her boyfriend was there, he told us everything. How she turned the wheel on him, how that song she sings was on the radio, how she laughed.*"

Thea shook her head. "Ben," she said over the voice on the computer. "Ben, you know it's true. You've counseled traumatized ethereals before. *You.* On your own. Lilian is dragging you down. You worry too much when she's with you. You're unfocused. And you are so much more capable than you think. You could be a *leader.*" She gave him a serious look. "Isn't that what you want?"

He considered the question. "*Yes,*" he typed finally.

"Good. Because we need you, Ben. *I* need you. We don't need Lilian."

"*But I need her,*" the computer voice said. He let his next thought go unspoken: *She can see me. She's the only one I care about who can see me and I need to hold on to that. What we do here is the only thing still holding us together. I can't lose her again, please don't take her away from me.*

Thea sighed. She let her arms fall from her chest and eased off the edge of the desk. "Look, I know your heart's in the right place. I'm going to give the two of you another chance. I want her on the Ghostland extraction team, once this stupid fucking TV special is finished."

The comment surprised him. He had no idea she was planning to go in so soon, especially after they'd just tabled a vote on it. "*Thea, I really don't think it's wise to go in there yet. We need more intel. We still don't know how many ethereals are left in there, or if any of them are still infected by the Garrote code.*"

Thea shook her head. "That's why we *need* to get them out. And since ethereals aren't able to pass through the Recurrence Field, Bram and I will lead a team of all-living members."

More lambs for the slaughter, Ben thought. He didn't reply.

"There are people trapped inside there who need our help," she said. "They're suffering. You know it's true. You've felt it."

It was true. Every ethereal in the Temple felt their pain, radiating from that place like the victims of nuclear fallout, suffering through every moment. His friends were likely in there, too: Niko and Leonard, Allison and Stan. Innocents trapped among lunatics and monsters.

He knew she was right…. but now was definitely not the time.

"We can do this, Ben. We *have* to do this. It's why I brought my people to Duck Falls in the first place. It's why you and Leon came to me."

"*But you know I can't help you with the Recurrence Field still running. And we can't shut it off. It's the only thing keeping us safe from whatever evil entities might still be in there.*"

"That's your opinion."

"*Not just mine. Why do you think the Hedgewood Foundation hasn't just shut it off themselves? Why do you think they had so many protocols and such heavy security*" *to keep those things from getting out?"*

Thea scowled, giving him a look of disappointment. "They're not *things*, Ben. They're people, like you and me. They're confused and frightened, and maybe that makes them dangerous right now. Like caged lions. But if we *free* them—"

"I want to free them, too, Thea. I do. But we need to come up with a game plan. We can't just Naruto run through the front gate and hope for the best."

"What's a Naruto? Was that a typo?" Thea said. She shook her head in frustration. "Never mind. Bram and I are still hammering out the details for the mission. When we're ready, we'll fill you in."

Ben couldn't help but feel a stab of resentment. Before Bram Merritt showed up, Thea and Ben had shared ideas. It was Thea's idea to start liberating other ethereals, but Ben had suggested they work in teams of ethereals and the living. The ethereals at the Temple had wanted to be put to work. They wanted to feel useful. They wanted to help others like them.

Lately, Thea had been running her ideas past Bram. Ben understood it. Having to use the laptop as a go-between when she could just pull Bram aside and ask for his opinion added unnecessary complications. And Ben was often elsewhere. On missions. With Lilian or either of their families. Recruiting. Training.

Still, it hurt. And it made him wonder if maybe he shouldn't be watching the two of them a little more closely, without their knowledge.

You mean spying, he thought.

Yes, he answered himself. *I mean spying.*

"Oh," Thea said, "and you really burned us tonight not coming to me about the Woman in White before we started. I'd appreciate it if you kept me in the loop from now on."

With no further comment, Thea grabbed Taffy the unicorn, dropped it into the desk drawer and closed it: meeting adjourned.

tHE BEREAVED

Ducks Falls
November 1st

WENDY LARAMIE APPLIED lipstick in the rearview mirror at the intersection of Main Street and Kubler Road, waiting for the red light to change.

The old church up the street was bustling again today. Still strange to see so much life in it after the parish left, when that holy-roller pastor proclaimed in front of the mayor, the town council and several dozen Duck Falls citizens—Wendy included—that the deal they'd made with Hedgewood for Burt Bucklebee's one-hundred some-odd acres of farmland had been a deal with the Devil. Everyone in the council chambers had laughed him out of the room, Wendy included.

"Nobody's laughing now," she muttered bitterly.

She still felt a certain amount of responsibility for having brokered the deal with Hedgewood, blame she supposed could also be applied to Ben's death. Her hands certainly weren't clean. But how could anyone have ever predicted what happened? They'd been building a *theme park*, for Pete's sake. Nobody could have imagined the *type* of theme park it would be, nor that it might turn out to be dangerous. And by the time they learned the truth, it was already far too late to back out.

It turned out they *had* signed a deal with the Devil: a devil by the name of Oliver Hedgewood III.

Everyone involved in the park's construction had signed strict NDAs preventing them from speaking about what they were working on and what they saw. After the tragedy, those documents were null and void. What these people revealed had been damning.

Now that GRP2 group was living in tents and caravans on Burt's old farm, and in the old church Wendy herself had sold to their leader, the Petralia woman. Some people believed Wendy had sold the whole town down the river— first to Hedgewood, then to the Gurpies, as kids around town called them.

They were a strange bunch, though Wendy believed their hearts were in the right place. Thea Petralia seemed to have a good head on her shoulders, even if she was maybe a bit of a spoiled rich princess, and naïve in her ideals. After what happened, to think that any rational-minded person could muster up an iota of sympathy for those monsters beggared belief. Then again, Wendy couldn't fathom women who wrote love letters to men on death row either.

Thea Petralia tried her damnedest, though. Wendy had to give her that. She played to people's sympathies well, and many people in town whose family members died that day had joined her class-action lawsuit against Hedgewood. She'd swept them up in an ideological furor. It wasn't the *ghosts* who were at fault—it was *Corporate America.*

To an extent, she was right.

The Hedgewood Foundation had offered settlement checks, and many in town had accepted them. Hiram and Maddy Roth had taken their check—which some called "blood money"—and Wendy certainly couldn't fault them for it. They weren't in the same financial situation as herself and Michael. Though with Michael out of work, she wondered if they hadn't been wrong to refuse the settlement and join the lawsuit.

Still, Wendy didn't like Thea's *absolute* shifting of the blame, particularly since Wendy wasn't sure she believed in ghosts at all. It was more convenient to her sanity to blame what happened on a chemical attack, or a hallucinogenic substance in the water. But the things she'd heard, the things people had told her in confidence after the fact—if ghosts weren't real, how could they be explained?

Maybe those holy rollers were right, she thought, and barked a laugh.

Maybe this *was* all her fault.

Michael certainly seemed to believe it. He'd barely talked to her since Ben died, and even less since his layoff. He spent much of his free time tinkering on his "project" in the back yard, and why he always had to call it that she had no idea. Why not call it what it was? A big, ugly hole in the ground with no permit. He'd refused to tell her what he was doing out there so often she'd finally given up asking.

Lost his mind, she thought. *At least he finally quit drinking. Can't have it all, Wen.*

A horn honked behind her. The lipstick bounded over her lower lip and left a red slash across her cheek. She looked in the rearview mirror. A pickup truck on large wheels had pulled up behind her. She couldn't see the driver. The lights had turned green.

She pulled through the intersection and continued through town to the west end, where the new houses were still going up. Frankly, Wendy was surprised the developer hadn't walked away after the tragedy. Most of the units had already sold, but nearly half of the buyers had backed out of the deal. She was working with the developer to resell those units while work continued on the last block of houses.

The development was fifty homes, most of them three-bedroom, two-bath brick two-stories spread over three interconnected cul-de-sacs. Wendy found them all pretty tacky, lacking any sort of bold aesthetic or creativity. But they'd broken ground on the development a year before Ghostland was scheduled to open, and the developer had high hopes that with a brand-new theme park opening nearby, real estate in Duck Falls was bound to become a hot commodity. At the time, the mayor and town council had agreed. So had Wendy. More properties meant more opportunities for everyone involved, no matter what the busybodies in town might have thought about expansion. More families would lead to school upgrades, more amenities, a thriving economy.

Sometimes Wendy thought these people wanted Duck Falls to go back to what it was when the paper mill shut down. She remembered those hardscrabble days when her father lost his job along with nearly a hundred other men, when he'd drifted from one odd job to the next, never settling on any one thing, from roofing to lawn maintenance to stripping copper wiring and asbestos from abandoned buildings.

Wendy had vowed at a young age she would never end up like her father, to never let herself become dependent on someone else for security.

A month out of college she'd started working for local realtor Tip Withers—*Ask for Tip!* his signs declared in brush script, with him winking exaggeratedly in the photo like a character in the credits of a cheesy '80s sitcom, his blond toupee always slightly askew. She'd earned a bachelor's degree in business and had wowed Tip during her interview with her candor, her quick wit and, though he would never admit to it in public, her physical attributes. It was the late-Nineties, and though the residential real estate industry was already dominated by women, men had still run the majority of the companies. It was easier to leverage her "assets" than to make waves.

In her first month Wendy had sold three "problem" properties—one a so-called "sick building" on the outskirts of Hagerstown—and Tip had promoted her to partner within the year. After she'd spent ten years in the business, Tip had decided to retire. She'd convinced him to sell to her for less than he might have gotten from one of the major brokers that had been feeling him out, by promising him a share of her commissions. The deal had suited her, since he'd had no spouse and no heirs, and Wendy hadn't expected him to live much longer than another five to ten years—by then he'd already looked like tea-stained parchment stretched over an anatomy skeleton, topped with a badly fitting toupee. The fact that he was still alive more than ten years later was bothersome, particularly since she'd had to divvy up the small fortune she'd made on the Bucklebee farm, and the lesser but still significant chunk of change she'd made selling the church on Kubler Road to the Gurpies cult.

This was a particular problem since she'd meant to leave Michael before the year's end.

She wanted to make sure he wouldn't financially suffer after they put the house on the market. There was no ill will behind her decision. Michael's hole in the backyard was a perfect metaphor for the chasm Ben's death had created between them. She'd watched with morbid fascination as it grew deeper and wider every day. It wasn't either of their faults. They simply grieved differently, and neither could be blamed for it. But it was time for them to acknowledge the rift was unrepairable. It was time to go their separate ways. Live separate lives.

Wendy glanced in the rearview as she turned onto the dusty development road. The truck she'd seen earlier turned in behind her. She supposed it was probably one of the construction guys or a contractor, and thought nothing further of it.

She parked her red Volvo S60 in front of 9 Domingo Drive and stepped out. For some reason the developer—a holdings company called Broadman Enterprises from Las Vegas, Nevada—had named the streets after the Three Tenors, each with an alliterative street designation. Dust blew across the fresh pavement as she stepped out of the car. The sound of hammering and drills and men shouting carried on the cool autumn breeze from Carrera Crescent or Pavarotti Place, whichever houses they were finishing up now.

Looking back the way she'd come, Wendy saw no sign of the truck that had followed her in. She supposed it must have continued on to one street or the other, leaving her to work in peace. Number 9 was the show house, staged to entice potential buyers. With the tasteful furnishings supplied by Wendy's interior designers, it gave them an idea of what they might aspire to, since the furnishings were all this year's hottest designs, down to the crib in the third bedroom.

Tip had thought of staging as a wasted expense and never would've gone for it when he ran the company. Under Wendy's management, the company had more business than ever.

She unlocked the front door and stepped inside. The house had an aura of emptiness to it, despite the decor. It smelled like no one had lived in it, like sawdust and dirt from the nearby construction, and the pungent chemical odor of new furniture. She lit the scented candles on the fireplace mantel and another on the dining room table, dumped a plastic bag of dough into the bread maker and started it. Then she hurried around the house opening windows to let in some fresh, early autumn air.

Checking the upstairs bathroom to make sure the plumbing still worked, she spotted the streak of lipstick still on her cheek in the mirror above the sink. She tore off a piece of toilet paper, wet it under the tap, and wiped off the smear.

With the sink turned off, she heard boots thudding on the hardwood floor below.

She scowled at her reflection. Her first appointment wasn't for an hour.

Maybe it's the contractor.

Thinking this, she left the bathroom and headed down the stairs. "Hello? Darren, is that you?"

She reached the first floor, her heels clacking. The front door stood open, sunlight streaming in.

"Hello?"

Dust blew in through the doorway, scuttling over the floorboards. She crossed the foyer and shut the door, peering around anxiously. She locked it and drew the chain.

Must've come and gone.

It smelled nicer down here now. Like chocolate chip cookie dough from the candles, and the French bread beginning to rise in the machine. By the time her first appointment arrived the house would feel more lived in. Less like a mausoleum.

She returned to the living room, where the scented candle flickered in the breeze from the opened window.

A shadow burst out from behind the dividing wall.

"You sold us out, you bitch!"

Wendy had half-turned when the blow caught her on the side of the head and stars shot across her vision. She cried out, collapsing over the back of the sofa. Something hard and corrugated struck her at the base of her spine as she tried to roll over to face her attacker. She sprawled further with a gasp of pain, nearly tipping the sofa over, the back of her right hand striking the reclaimed-wood basket of multicolored hydrangeas and knocking it to the floor.

Ragged panting arose from behind her. She didn't dare turn, terrified her attacker might try to rape her. Her purse and the bear spray she carried for protection lay on the kitchen counter. The closest object to defend herself with, the heavy flower basket, had fallen on the far side of the coffee table, just out of reach.

"Bitch," the man said again. She heard him spit and felt it land thickly between her bare shoulder blades, cold droplets spattering on the nape of her neck.

Then the footfalls thudded away. The chain rattled, the lock clicked and the door opened. She turned, the tears stinging her eyes making her attacker too blurry to see as he stormed out into the sunshine.

She rolled over finally, the pain in her pelvis terrible as

she slid to the floor, weeping into her hands. Eventually she forced herself to stand up and wipe her tears. She looked at herself in the full-length mirror by the kitchen. There was a dusty boot-print on her pale dress just below the waistline. She wiped it away, angry at herself for crying, for letting her attacker get away. Already her cheek was splotchy red where he'd struck her. She figured there would be a good-sized goose egg there soon. Maybe even a black eye.

She grabbed her purse, took out her cell phone and called the sheriff's office. She waited until she was able to calm herself before calling her appointments to reschedule.

Deputy Logan Lovett showed up to the smell of cookies and fresh-baked bread and took her statement. Wendy told him everything she remembered about the truck: white F150, large tires with wide wheel wells and running boards, along with what she thought might be the last three digits of the license plate. The deputy said he would look into it but couldn't make any promises, unless someone from the job site was able to add any additional information

"If you'd left the boot print, we would have had more to go on," the deputy told her. Wendy thanked him and drove home cautious and hyper-aware, scouring the streets and parking lots and driveways for the pickup she was sure she would remember if she saw it again.

A huge transport truck was parked out front of the house when she arrived, blocking the driveway. The rumble of heavy machinery alerted her to something strange before she saw the crane tower rise above the back of the house. She hurried down the drive as the machinery beeped. When she reached the backyard, she was out of breath and on edge.

Michael stood on the back porch with a glass of lemonade, watching the work with a satisfied smile. It was the first time she'd seen him smile since the day Ben had passed away. He was watching the crane lower what looked like a steel storage unit into his big, ugly hole in their once-beautiful yard. It thumped down heavily and one of the other workers stepped off the edge of the hole onto the box, his boots clanking as he unhooked cables from the crane and stepped back onto the small ledge of grass.

Wendy looked at the large metal box in absolute horror, certain that whatever this monstrosity was it must have cost a fortune.

We don't have *a fortune*, she thought, taking off her heels and crossing the cool grass to the porch, to where her soon-to-be-ex-husband stood. *It's finally happened. He's completely lost his mind.*

Deputy Logan Lovett found the white pickup with a license plate matching what Wendy Laramie had been able to remember parked outside Jerry Dougan's ugly double-wide at the Duck Falls Trailer Court on the north side of town, exactly where he'd suspected he would.

Jerry Dougan had been a troublemaker ever since he lost his job at Roxbury Correctional shortly after his wife left him. He was the poster child for every classic country song, except Noreen let him keep the truck and he hated dogs. Jerry spent most nights raising hell at the Blind Duck Tavern with former friends who worked at the prison, or former millworkers like Wendy Laramie's dad had been before he passed, most of whom had sacked up and moved on to other paying jobs. Not Jerry Dougan. He'd gotten himself hurt on the next job site he'd stepped onto by falling off a ladder. Most folks figured he did it on purpose for the workman's compensation. Or to kill himself. No one could agree on that part.

What Logan was certain of was that ever since he'd passed along the news that Jerry's son-in-law Dustin had been among the dead at Ghostland, Jerry had been getting into more trouble than usual. Dust ups at the Blind Duck just about once a week. Drunk in public and public urination. One more DUI and Sheriff Brigham swore she'd lock Jerry up and throw away the key. She didn't give a damn if Jerry was just sleeping it off in the driver's seat or not.

This incident with Wendy Laramie seemed a little unlike Jerry—he'd never struck his ex, as far as Logan knew, nor any other woman in town, just a whole lot of unlucky men—particularly since he'd finally gotten himself a new job a few weeks back, working security at Ghostland of all places. Logan was surprised they'd hired him with his background, and assumed someone must have pulled some strings. Still, he wouldn't have put it past the guy to attack Wendy. People in pain could be unpredictable. And the whole town had experienced its share of pain.

Logan's best friend from high school had been at Ghostland with her husband, their two little girls at home with their grandmother. They'd both lost their lives that day, and the girls would grow up without their parents. Logan had found their bodies tangled up in the big top tent on the second search day, circled by flies.

He'd had to pass along the news of so many deaths during that week he'd gone numb from it. And the sight of all those dead bodies they'd recovered in various states of damage and decay… if the local shrink hadn't been among the dead, he might've considered therapy. Instead, he got himself a prescription just to sleep through the night. One of its pleasant side effects was that he no longer dreamed.

He stepped out of his cruiser, a black-and-white Suburban, and navigated the junk on Jerry's patchy lawn to the trailer. A pair of badly scuffed steel-toe boots stood beside the mat. When he banged on the screen door, it bounced and rattled like a snare drum.

"Jerry! It's Logan Lovett. Open the door, we need to talk."

He heard Jerry grumble, followed by the squeal of old springs. "What're you blamin me for this time, Deputy?"

"Not a question of what I'm blaming you for, Jerry. It's what you did."

Jerry pulled open the door and squinted bleary-eyed through the screen at Logan. He was still lobster-red from lying drunk in the kiddie pool behind his trailer all summer long, and he scratched at the salt-and-pepper bristles under his jawline. The Shell gas peak cap he always wore rested loosely on a mess of silver hair.

Logan caught a whiff of a sweet chemical odor he thought might be crack cocaine—he could bust Jerry for possession, though it felt petty—along with stale cigarette smoke, a drugstore cologne and the fresh baby powder smell of a deodorizer meant to mask the stench of his socks, which didn't even come close to working. The combination of smells made him rear back and suck in a deep breath through his nostrils to clear it.

"Well? What'd I do then?"

"You left a boot print on the realtor's ass," he said, and then doubled down on the half-truth. "What d'you bet my forensics team matches it to these boots out on the stoop?"

Jerry's eyes widened briefly, then squeezed shut against the bright sun. "So what if they did?"

"Jerry, you assaulted a woman in broad daylight on an active construction site. Did you really think no one would see you?"

The man's lips twitched. In the next moment he was crying, leaning against the doorjamb with his head on his arm. "She sold us out, Logan! You know goddamn well I just gave that woman what she was owed."

"Jerry," he said. The man kept weeping, looking down at his boots. "Jerry!"

Jerry looked up, his eyes red and wet.

"You can't go around beatin up people just because you feel like they did you wrong. Not in my town. Now come on out, goddammit. I gotta take you in."

Jerry wiped his tears with the back of his arm, sniffling. "All right. Just lemme get a shirt on."

A minute later he came out. Logan cuffed him behind his back, holding his breath against the man's stink, and led him across the crappy lawn to the Suburban. He let the man climb up on his own and sit sullenly in the backseat, then he closed the door and went around the front to the driver's seat.

The worst part of all this, aside from the assault, was that he kind of agreed with Jerry. It wasn't Wendy's fault, what happened. But she *had* brokered the deal, and there were whispers she might even have bribed Mayor Anders to push it through, though Logan didn't believe it. He knew Wendy, mainly through her husband, Mike. He was relatively certain she wasn't the type to offer bribes, though he suspected Mayor Anders might be the type to accept them.

Wendy Laramie wasn't to blame. Neither was the

mayor, nor his council. If anyone deserved a boot in the ass it was that smug son-of-a-bitch Hedgewood.

The very worst part of all of this was that if Ollie Hedgewood showed up in town right now, Logan wasn't sure what he would do to him. He just had to hope he wasn't in uniform, carrying his sidearm, because Lord knows he might just gun the bastard down in the street like a rabid dog.

RETURN TO GHOSTLAND

A FRIGID AUTUMN wind blew through Ghostland's silent, empty promenades. No living soul had ventured beyond its walls for months, not since the last attempt to recover the bodies of the missing. Though the entire park had been searched from top to bottom, there were still fifteen people unaccounted for, thought by relatives or friends to have gone there on that fateful day and never returned.

The Ghost Tram cars swayed on their cables, metal squeaking against metal. Birds and squirrels chittered in the bare branches of an oak in a parkette near the Transportation Museum. A once-white ice cream vendor hat caught in the wind, rolled along the pavement to bounce jauntily up the steps of the Dollop Farmhouse and settle against its splintered door. The Merchant Brothers Big Top tent fluttered and flapped, its painted canvas shredded and torn by months of exposure to the elements. And in the grass-lined pit where Garrote House once stood, a chunk of asphalt caused a small landslide. Machinery hummed in the darkness below, lights still flickering on the few servers that remained operational, keeping the Ghostland program running.

A deer ambled into the ditch to drink from the frigid

Conococheague Creek, which stretched from Bucklebee Woods at Ghostland's north wall to the southwest, barely a trickle now but enough for the animal to slake its thirst. It lapped at the clear running water then raised its head abruptly, wide-eyed and alert.

Something had disturbed it—a slight crackling from close by. The wind howled, pummeling the wooden boards of the Buttermilk Falls covered bridge, causing its rafters to creak.

Silence fell again. Reassured, the deer lowered its head to the crisp water and resumed its drinking.

With no warning the deer's neck snapped and the squawking animal was hurled over the creek. It struck the embankment with a crunch of shattered bones. In the next instant its fur began peeling off in strips, gore erupting from its flesh as an invisible presence tore into the meat below, innards spilling and splashing on the concrete.

When the presence had finished eviscerating its prey, the lifeless animal grew still, and silence returned to Ghostland.

On Saturday afternoon, two days after Hallowe'en, members of Ghosts Are People Too gathered in the front lot to protest the *Return to Ghostland* special, scheduled to air live that night. According to GRP2's scouts, the Ghost Brothers and their crew had been parked in the back lot since early that morning.

Almost twenty people buzzed around by the gates on Saturday morning. By early afternoon, members had arrived from the Temple as well as neighboring groups to join in the protest, pushing the crowd closer to two hundred.

While they chanted and marched with their placards,

separated from the TV people by Logan Lovett and Sheriff Brigham's other deputies, the *Ghost Brothers* crew set up for the evening's production. They ran cables and set up light stands. The producer barked orders to the guy sitting at the switcher in the network remote van. The Ghost Brothers themselves, Jake and Eric Gallagher, sat in their production camper with their editor, watching raw footage from an upcoming episode while eating a late lunch. The primary school teacher who also ran the ghostlandpark.com website, blog and online community, hung around the craft services table shyly, watching everything unfold with wide-eyed wonder. Jake and Eric had brought her along due to her dedication to uncovering the truth about the Ghostland Disaster. Elena Feliz had never been on an authentic ghost hunt before, and as both a huge fan of the Ghost Brothers and an amateur historian of Ghostland lore, she was thrilled to be here.

"We knew this day was coming," Le Mon said, heaving a sigh as he and Ben eavesdropped on the crew. "Thea should have buried this thing months ago."

"What could she do?"

Le Mon shrugged. "Bribed em. Convinced them to rethink it. They're here now, no amount of protestin's gonna stop em from walking right through that gate once it's open. Unless Zeus himself reaches down from the sky and plucks em up like pawns off a chess board, every single one of them is gonna die in there. And they don't have a clue what they're walking into, *specially* her," he added, pointing at Elena Feliz.

"Well, Hedgewood must think it's safe," Ben said. "They wouldn't have agreed to let them in otherwise."

"Hedgewood don't give a damn what happens to em! They're too busy dodging lawsuits. And in case you haven't noticed, they're still sticking to their story: *dead energy is harmless*. If those two chuckleheads survive, Hedgewood can claim it wasn't the park's fault all them folks died on April 20th. Say it was some kind of undetectable hallucinogenic that drove people outta their minds, made em kill themselves and each other like a scene from a fast-zombie movie. He can act like all they're responsible for was the lockdown—but they'll assure us it prevented the pathogen or whatever they decide to call it from spreading to Duck Falls. If the Ghost Brothers survive the night it proves they can reopen the park, start bringin in payin customers again."

"They wouldn't."

"Sure, they would. This is free advertising for them. And there ain't a damn thing we can do about it, either. We could try to stop em from going in right now, I guess. Spook em. Mess with their equipment. But they'll go in anyway. I'm half-convinced those two have a death wish. Who else would be stupid enough to go in there after all that's gone down? After all the warnings to keep people out?"

It was true, they couldn't stop this. It was far too late, and maybe it wasn't their business to try. These people knew the risks and chose to ignore them.

Ben was well aware he couldn't protect them beyond the wall. Ethereals who'd gone in to free those trapped inside had never returned. The Recurrence Field made it impossible to escape. It could even be that the main Ghostland program was still running, still warped by Garrote's virus. Their energy would have simply been absorbed into the program the way others had been on April 20th.

But the show would go on, protests or not.

And everyone who passed through that gate would die.

The Hallowe'en episode of the Ghost Brothers' two-night special had been a recap and investigation into the disaster. Ben had deliberately sat it out, opting to take on the cemetery mission instead. He'd wanted nothing to do with what would almost certainly be a misrepresentation of facts based on speculation and rumors.

No one but Ben and Lilian knew exactly what had happened that day. Those who'd survived told stories of bravery and tragedy, but their versions were tainted by low to no information. They saw the ethereal exodus as a murderous rampage, a slaughter of friends, family and strangers with no remorse. In many cases, it was exactly how it looked. Most of the violence had likely been caused by the Garrote Code. But many ethereals were simply angry and vicious, poisoned by their own lust for revenge. Others, like the Swarm, didn't appear to know any better. All they understood was chaos.

The crew set up a large screen for the crowd, and eventually people from Duck Falls and the surrounding area arrived with lawn chairs and snacks to watch the show. The network people had said it was the least they could do for the community, though many residents had opted to stay home or come out to join the protest.

The guy in charge of the LCD projector flicked on the satellite and changed the channel, flipping through ads, crime shows, reality television, and a news clip showing the toppled and cracked headstones at Placid Oaks Cemetery with the caption "HATE-CRIME MOTIVATED VANDALISM?" Finally, it settled on a clothing commercial featuring a multiracial family in bland, samey outfits dancing ecstatically.

Worship at the altar of advertising, Ben thought. *The Great God TV welcomes one and all.*

He snorted, thinking how weird it was that thoughts like this popped up in his head from time to time, like something Rex Garrote might have written. He'd steeped himself in the man's writing for so long it was hard not to think like his enemy—or at least, how the man wrote.

The Hallowe'en episode had been pre-taped. Tonight would be almost entirely live. In the introduction and promos for the episode, Jake Gallagher kept stressing that "literally anything can happen." Both he and Eric had their own head-mounted cameras, along with plenty of impressive-looking but essentially useless gear, which they showcased at the beginning of the episode in a flashy quick-cut montage like something out of an Edgar Wright movie.

The one aspect of their gear that was truly innovative were the filters on their cameras, designed by the Hedgewood Foundation for the Ghostland security cameras. These would allow both the crew and viewers at home to see ethereals as they would have looked on Ghostland's opening day.

"One thing you have to understand, the Recurrence Field has never been turned off," Eric told the viewers as they moved toward the gate, looking directly into his handheld camera. "For your safety and the safety of the remaining haunts, it's been running twenty-four-seven since the tragedy. There's just too much dead energy left in here to let it all spill out into the surrounding community."

"Literally anything could happen in there," Jake said again, leaning over his brother's shoulder. Eric gave the camera a tight smile.

The shot cut to the same blonde news correspondent who'd covered the Ghostland Memorial story back in August. Now she stood in front of the blinding camera light, dressed in a puffy winter jacket with a faux-fur hood, with the Ghostland front gates in the background. She remained silent a moment, holding her left ear as she listened for her cue. Then she nodded and gave the camera a toothy smile.

"Thank you, boys," she said. "Now, before they head through the gates, I'd just like to show you the women and men who are with us tonight. This is a small crew, you might say a *skeleton* crew—" She flashed a grin at the phrase. "—who are dedicated to bringing you the best television experience possible tonight. Let's head on up into the production van."

The camera followed her to a large white network van with a satellite transmitter on the roof, linking them to the Ghost Brothers' cameras and sound equipment and also to the network, sending the signal to affiliates and other broadcasters all over the world.

The correspondent led the camera into a small control room within the van, cramped with monitors and equipment with hundreds of lights and buttons for which Ben had no names. There were only two people inside: a middle-aged woman the correspondent introduced as Paula, the producer, and a man in a backwards Red Sox cap named Lee, sitting at the equipment. He was the "switcher," a job the correspondent explained was "basically editing for live TV," to which Lee shrugged and nodded.

Lee pressed a button and the production cut to one of the shaky head-mounted cameras as the Ghost Brothers and their team neared the gates with their gear. It held for a moment before cutting to a piece introducing the crew members: the two camera operators, a sound mixer, a production assistant who lugged much of the gear, and Elena Feliz, who apparently lived with a big fluffy dog named Fluffer.

As the sun sank behind Ghostland's western wall, the thick metal plates preventing entry drew up into the archway with a loud rumble and clatter. Once the gate had opened, Elena and the Ghost Brothers hopped the turnstiles, escorted by Sheriff Brigham and Deputy Lovett. The deputy looked anxious. The rest of the crew had a bit of difficulty climbing over the turnstiles but finally managed it. The two law officers left them at the gate and returned to the protest as the heavy door rolled back down, closing the team inside.

"Why aren't they wearing keeper suits?" Ben said.

"Death wish," Le Mon said. "Told ya."

On the screen, one of the handheld cameras pointed to Elena. "How do you feel, Elena?" Jake asked from off-camera. She was plump and round-faced, with dark curls and vibrant green eyes. She gave the camera a nervous smile, hugging herself to stay warm in her red hooded parka.

"I'm excited," she said. "But I'm also scared out of my mind. Is it okay if I say hi to my kids?"

"Say whatever you like," Jake told her. "It's your show, too."

Elena waved cheerily. "Hi, kids! I'm on TV!"

Chuckles rippled throughout the audience. If they were scared or anxious for the team, none of them showed it.

"If they're watching: moms and dads, it's past their bedtime," Eric joked.

The chuckles grew into laughter.

Headlights swept across the crowd as another vehicle arrived. It was Thea, in her sporty little electric car. She got out and immediately joined the protesters, picking up a megaphone from Bram, who'd been leading the chant, and starting one of her own personal favorites.

"WHO ARE WE?"

"*Ghosts Are People Too!*"

"WHAT DO WE WANT?"

"*The rights that ghosts are due!*"

It was a clumsy rhyme and made them sound slightly foolish, but it got the point across better than some of the sillier antics the protesters got up to while Thea wasn't there, the interpretive dancing and "tactical frivolity" popular among millennials and aged hippies. When Thea was in charge, GRP2 was all business. Ben respected her all the more for it.

"Shut the hell up!" a man shouted from the lawn chairs. Others laughed. Someone threw a pop can and it clattered on the pavement near the protestors. One of the deputies flicked on their flashlight and scanned the crowd with a scowl.

"This could get ugly," Le Mon said.

On the big screen, the camera lights and headlamps illuminated the park map just beyond the gates, causing a sudden hush to fall over the crowd. Even the protestors quieted. The team was *inside*. The first visitors since the search and rescue crew. The moment received the reverence it deserved.

Eric Gallagher turned his camera toward himself, his face ghostly white in the lamplight. "We're hoping to make it all the way to the pit where Garrote House collapsed," he whispered. "Remember, this used to be the most haunted house in America. If we're gonna see any ghosts here tonight, I'm sure it's gonna be there."

"*What was that?*" Jake hissed. The cameras whipped toward him. "Did you hear it?"

"What was it?" Elena said, clearly frightened. Her handheld camera struggled to focus on her face.

"It sounded like… someone whistling, maybe. I'm not sure."

The cameras scoured the darkness. A sudden gust of wind against the microphones penetrated the otherwise deathly silence.

"Here they go," Ben whispered to Le Mon. "They always have to pretend there's a noise or a cold spot to ramp up the creep factor. Then they'll play it back in slow-mo. Watch."

The cast discussed the sound for a moment before Jake said, "Can we get playback on that?"

Le Mon turned to Ben with an impressed look. Ben merely smiled knowingly.

The program cut to a slowed-down shot from Jake's camera, hovering over the swishing flashlight arcs on the map ahead of them. Even slowed down, the sound was clearly a squeal of metal on metal. Ben thought it was probably one of the tram cars further into the park.

"It sounds like a little girl crying," Elena said. The three of them were huddled over a small replay monitor.

"I definitely heard that," Jake agreed.

Only Eric, often the Scully to his brother's Mulder, seemed skeptical. "It could be anything. Come on, guys. Let's keep going. Long walk ahead of us."

The group paused a moment in front of the park map while Eric pointed out their route. Beyond it, a crumbled structure stood against the darkening sky like something out of a post-apocalypse movie. Ben remembered it as the remnants of the Roanoke Tower, where a gunman had shot several people gathered below before turning it on himself.

Elena screamed. At what, Ben hadn't seen. Some in the audience gasped and cried out. A few laughed at their own terror. The protestors were fully engaged with the show now, placards and chants forgotten. Even Thea was absorbed by what she saw.

The Ghost Brothers hurried over to Elena, chased by the crew. They huddled around her, asking if she was okay and what she saw.

Elena pointed. Several feet from them, Rex Garrote's glowing hologram stood jittery and flickering against the dark.

People in the audience gasped again, then fell into nervous laughter.

As the team approached, the writer spoke his greeting in silence, wearing his trademark smirk. It wasn't audible but Ben knew the phrase by heart: *Tell me... what are you afraid of?*

Eric reached out and passed his hand through it. "I thought they turned off this part of the program."

Jake shrugged. "I guess we got lucky." He shadow-boxed Garrote's hologram until he realized the others had moved on, then he followed.

The production cut to the network correspondent, who threw to the first commercial break. For the next four minutes they were subjected to ads for HIV medication, an insurance company, a medicated hand lotion, heartburn pills, deodorant and a promo for the latest reality mashup series, a dating elimination show crossed with *Survivor* called *Love to Death*.

When the program returned, the Ghost Brothers and Elena Feliz spent the next segment exploring the Visitor

Center. The building looked eerie at night, empty and filled with menacing shadows. The mannequins in the displays spooked Elena. Eric and Jake had been through the building before and seemed unfazed as they pointed out exhibits and gave a brief history of some of the more famous ones. Eventually they reached Legion House, where their holograms had hosted the "tutourial."

They spent a few minutes standing in front of the creepy old Victorian home talking about its history and how much fun they'd had creating what Eric called the Ghostland "minigame." Jake said he was sad more people didn't get a chance to see it. "But obviously the tragedy outweighs our loss," he added hastily.

They decided against going inside, despite Eric's eagerness to reunite with his holographic twin. With a two-hour special they would need all the time they had to reach Garrote House.

They left the Visitor Center and began their trek through the east side of the park. Trash fluttered by their feet, park maps and food wrappers and empty plastic water bottles. Garrote's hologram appeared with suspiciously scary timing to introduce exhibits, and the Ghost Brothers reminisced about the exhibits they'd gotten to visit on their show.

They didn't see any ethereals.

Every now and then one of them would hear "a sound" or see "something" and the production van would wind it back for them to watch, huddled together in the blue light of the replay monitor. One "shadow" Elena pointed out did look somewhat like a person dashing between one exhibit and the next. They saw a similar shadow later, but couldn't decide if it was a person or just some trash that had fluttered past.

Jake joked that it seemed like someone was following them. His subsequent chuckle sounded anxious.

Eventually they reached the deserted midway, the ride structures silhouetted against the night sky like the desiccated bones of old, dead gods. It was fully dark now, the exhibits spaced much closer. Jake and Eric seemed far more wary than out in the promenade.

"Maybe we should've gone around the long way," Eric suggested nervously.

"Too late now," his brother said, scanning the darkness ahead and around them.

They heard footsteps.

The audience heard footsteps.

Running footsteps.

Elena gasped, wheeling toward the sound. Cut to her helmet camera, which struggled to focus in the darkness between a roller coaster and Rocky's Funhouse. In the next shot, from one of the handhelds, the giant gorilla atop the funhouse was visible, a monstrous shadow against the starry autumn sky, one fist outstretched toward a moonlit scud of clouds.

Back to Elena's helmet-cam. Her breath coming heavily. The shot shaky as she took another step toward the alley.

"Did you see something?" Jake asked.

"The same shadow, I swear." She pointed, just her hand and arm visible like a character from a first-person shooter. "It was right there, between these two—"

One of the men close to her screamed.

The audience in the parking lot gasped as her helmet-cam whipped around. It caught a quick glimpse of the camera guy dragged into the darkness by a shadow. His camera tumbled from his hands as his terrified scream was carried away.

Eric and Jake pointed their handhelds at each other with near-identical expressions of terror.

"Did you see it?" Jake said. "What the hell was—"

Darkness consumed him from the shoulders up, swallowing even the light on his helmet. His scream was muffled as the shadow tore him away from his brother.

The audience screamed.

Ben felt a prickle of terror for them. He was likely the only survivor among the people watching this unfold, and the only one who'd experienced anything remotely like this firsthand.

He knew exactly what he was seeing, and he knew Le Mon was right.

This was a live snuff film. Ghostland's international television debut. It would leave no survivors. Not this time.

The park was alive. Tonight, it would *feed*.

"Jake!" Eric ran in the direction his brother had been pulled. "*Jaaaake!*"

Elena chased after him, whispering hoarsely: "What's happening, I don't know what's happening—"

She let out a horrendous scream and the angle of her helmet-cam suddenly canted, legs kicking madly as something lifted her off the ground. In moments she was far above the others, the lights from the crew in the dark midway below growing further and further away. Voices cried out in the dark. She flew over low buildings, now the roller coaster, now the midway entrance—all the while whispering a panicked prayer.

Panicked voices rose in the crowd, genuinely fearing for the team.

Elena's helmet came off and its camera caught her briefly—a shadow holding her by the hood, pitch black against the moon—as she reached out for it. She missed. The helmet hurtled away from her, plummeting, her scream slipping away. It fell in the darkness for maybe five seconds before smashing on the pavement, the image going black.

Eric turned his own camera on himself, his face ashen in its light. "I'm alone," he said. "I'm terrified. Something happened here, I couldn't see what it was. They were all just standing right here." His helmet-cam swung around, taking in the scattered equipment. "*They were all just right here*—"

The handheld went black. His scream was muffled, like his brother's, as if something had smothered the mic. There was a terrible sound, something like a chorus of monkeys all gibbering and shrieking at once amid a squall of tearing metal and breaking glass.

In the next moment, the helmet-cam dragged and bounded along the pavement between two carnival games, then came to an abrupt stop.

Out of shot, Eric groaned in pain. For a moment his lower half was visible, the right leg broken, a scarlet bone jutting out from his cargo pants. Gasping, he reached with bloody fingers for something just out of shot—

The image broke up in a blocky jumble of digital artifacts and garbled sound before cutting to blue.

The network cut to the blonde correspondent whose look of shell-shock, holding her microphone in one hand and her earpiece with the other, lasted several moments before she addressed the camera. "Folks, I am truly sorry for what you've just witnessed. I'm not sure what just happened there but it seems—"

As the correspondent continued her apology on behalf of the network, Ben turned to Le Mon, who was shaking his head in dismay.

"I wish I'd been wrong," he said. "You were in there. Any thoughts on what that was?"

Ben considered telling him what he thought—what he *knew*—had attacked them, had killed every one of them. After a long moment he decided against it. It would only cause panic. "I have no idea," he said.

But he knew. It had been in there all this time, waiting for fresh blood.

It was the Swarm.

INTERLUDE:
AVATAR

Hedgewood Facility
Nevada Desert—June 2014

HARRISON GREELY PLACED the neural mesh over Garrote's thick, dark hair and flattened it down. The writer scowled. He didn't like to be touched. But the Pandora was delicate. Harrison wouldn't allow anyone else to touch it, even the man whose money had made it a reality.

The trials with mice and Sully the rhesus monkey had proven successful, as had experiments Harrison had done using the device personally. Now it was time to put Garrote's money to task. This would be the true test: whether or not his benefactor approved.

"And you're sure this is safe?" Garrote asked. He was seated in a chair near the computers in Harrison's small, white-walled personal lab. With the cages removed it felt barren. Lonely. Harrison wished he could have kept Sully but after months of repeated use of the Pandora the monkey had passed away suddenly. Now it was just Harrison and his computers, which he supposed was fitting. It had only ever been him and his computers, from the very beginning.

He waffled in answering Garrote as he returned to his terminal and started typing.

"You don't look convinced," the writer said.

"It's safe. I've tried it myself. I just don't want you to be disappointed."

Garrote looked at him plainly. "I've followed your work closely while you've been with us, Harry, my boy. I have no doubt your Pandora, as you perhaps fittingly call it, will be a genuine miracle of mind over matter."

Harrison paused with his fingers over the keys, lapping up the praise. Everything the others had said about Garrote, the rumors, the jealousy, none of it matched what he'd seen of the man.

Rex Garrote ran a tight ship. He despised sloppy work, laziness and excuses. But true genius was often misunderstood, requiring diligence and loyalty of those hovering within its sphere. Those who feared it, those who *envied* it, would never understand the self-sacrifice it required. The pain. The hunger and loneliness. All in the name of *inspiration*.

Soon they would all understand.

"All right, Mr. Garrote, I'm just going to sync the program with your brainwaves. Close your eyes, please."

Garrote did.

"Picture a tortoise," Harrison said.

Garrote opened one eye. "Why a tortoise?"

Harrison snorted. "Just a little cyberpunk humor."

Garrote closed both eyes. "All right then. A tortoise, it is."

The Pandora began mapping the writer's superior parietal lobule, which lit up in red on a 3D image of his brain. The basal ganglia and cerebellum lit up as well.

Concerned, Harrison peered over the monitor and saw Garrote was tapping his right index finger on the arm of the chair.

"Don't move, please."

Garrote stopped tapping. The activity in his motor control areas ceased.

"Okay, now just try to make the screen in your mind go blank."

"All right."

The activity in the superior parietal lobule gradually dissipated.

"You can tap your fingers again," he said. "Wiggle your toes, head, any sort of movement."

Garrote pinwheeled his feet, waggled his eyebrows and drummed the armrests with his fingers. "Good?"

The proper areas lit up, in the premotor cortex and supplementary motor area as well as the basal ganglia and cerebellum.

"Say, 'Unfortunately, no one can tell you what the Matrix is.'"

"Excuse me?"

"'Unfortunately—'"

As Garrote repeated the phrase with vague irritation, the Broca's and Wernick's areas in his brain became active. Harrison finished the quote from his second-favorite movie along with him.

"This'll just take a bit," he said. They sat in silence while the data processed. A few minutes later, the words MAPPING COMPLETE flashed on the screen below Garrote's brain image.

"Okay, I've got a pretty good map of your brain here. This should get you a good range of motion. I'm still working on haptic feedback for tactile stimulation. And visual is still slightly limited. I hope to have the kinks worked out by the beginning of next quarter."

"Wonderful."

Garrote's smile didn't reach his eyes. It never did. Harrison suspected the man lived with profound sadness, possibly from trauma, and wondered if it was from his time in Vietnam. He'd never attempted to broach the subject. If curiosity ever got the better of him, he could pluck out the individual traumas from Garrote's brain scan when the Pandora was fully operational.

"Shall we then?" Garrote asked.

Harrison pushed the EXECUTE button.

The first time he'd used the Pandora himself, the visual feedback had been in black and white and slightly wavering, like a scrambled satellite channel swimming in and out of focus. It took a moment to get over the sudden queasiness he'd felt, then he'd stood up from his own body, still sitting limply in the chair. Movement had felt even more strange, a disconnect between his sensations and what he saw. He knew he'd still been seated but he could also feel the movement as he twiddled his fingers in front of his eyes. It was almost like virtual reality without the headset and controllers, or lucid dreaming while still awake. Truthfully, it was unlike anything he'd ever experienced and he found it extremely difficult to put into words.

While he'd stood there, having his first out-of-body experience, Sully had started to whimper. Harrison had moved toward him, hoping to soothe the monkey. Sully hadn't seemed to be able to see him but had become immediately wary, pacing the perimeter of his cage and slapping his fingers against the bars.

As Harrison stepped—*floated*—away from the cage,

the monkey had stopped pacing and sat quietly by his water dish. Harrison had returned to the cage and moved away several more times. Each time the monkey had grown agitated and calmed alternately, though it still hadn't appeared to see him.

I'm like a ghost, he'd thought.

He'd left the lab a moment later. As he passed easily through the wall, he'd marveled a moment at the cables and pipes and insulation, like a cross-section of an architectural image. This wasn't just his mind conjuring up some fantasy. It was real. He'd actually done it. With a sense of elation, he'd passed through into the hallway. A young woman dressed in a lab coat, her brown hair in a tight bun, had hurried down the hall toward him.

He'd held out a hand to stop her but the woman had passed right through him. She hadn't stopped, hadn't shivered, hadn't made a sound or appeared to react to his presence at all. Her heels had clicked away brusquely until Harrison no longer heard them.

When he'd opened his eyes, he was sitting in the chair in his lab again.

It was the most intense rush he'd ever experienced but it was also very disorienting. He'd had to decompress for several hours before attempting it again.

Sully had died later that week. Harrison had found him curled up in the far corner of his cage, stiff with rigor mortis.

The autopsy had confirmed his suspicions: Sully had died of a stroke. His little rhesus brain had no longer been able to handle the overstimulation of the Pandora.

After dozens of attempts, Harrison himself still felt fine. Better than fine. He felt more alive than ever. With the Pandora, his working life was like living inside a dream. He was able to do things he'd never imagined possible.

Over the following weeks he'd covered every inch of the Hedgewood facility, learning as much about the other projects going on around him as possible. He'd watched people chat and eat in the cafeteria, discussing frivolous things. He'd watched people alone in their rooms. He'd found it distressing to see what people did when they thought no one was looking. Wiping boogers, masturbation with various implements—he'd even seen one man put his finger in his mouth after scratching his own anus. The man had seemed pleased by the taste, though not enough to go back for seconds.

When Harrison discovered the women's locker room, he'd spent an inordinate amount of time watching them. Eventually he'd found the courage to virtually caress their soap-slicked bodies while they washed themselves, unaware of his presence. Without haptic feedback it had felt like nothing to him, though when he returned to his body he'd discovered he'd had an erection, and had scurried back to quarters to fap until he was too chafed to continue.

His experiments weren't all pointless, selfish acts. Every morning from his virtual world, he'd walked from where he left off the previous day, his virtual feet eventually clocking over a thousand miles from the facility in the Nevada desert to the Rockies, through Yosemite to San Jose and San Francisco, then up the West Coast through the Coastal range, and into Oregon and Washington.

Each day improvements to the Pandora system gave him further functionality in the real world. He'd crushed scorpions in the desert hardpan and stopped the hearts of jackrabbits scurrying across deserted blacktop. He'd started landslides in the mountains and hitched rides in the backs of cars while their drivers shifted and peered around uncomfortably, feeling a vague sense of unease, as if someone might be watching them.

He'd sat for hours in a hospital intensive care room, watching an old man die. He'd been the only one to hear the old man's dying words.

"Oh," Garrote said with the Pandora secured on his crown, unintentionally mimicking the old dead man's swan song.

Harrison looked at the screen. Garrote's brain was lit up like Christmas morning.

"Where are you right now?"

"I'm standing in my house," Garrote said. "It appears to be moving."

"That could be an issue with the Pandora. I'll take a look under the hood once we're done here—"

"No, it *is* moving. I'm in my office. It's exactly the same as I left it. I'm looking out through the window now. It appears we're traveling through a small town." The writer paused, scowling. "Could it be…?"

It wasn't possible Garrote was in a moving house, which meant there was likely something wrong with the system. The synaptic feedback must have gotten screwed up somehow. Maybe he *was* in his house in Seattle—the two of them had spoken about it several times, and Garrote had seemed overly fond of it, like a lost lover—while simultaneously in a moving vehicle of some kind. A sort of cross-contaminated stimulus.

It had happened to Harrison a few times already. Once, he'd been climbing El Capitan in Yosemite and suddenly he'd found himself *flying over* the mountain, peering out through the eyes of a soaring eagle. He thought of it like "glitching" in a video game, using the program's flaws as advantages, unintentionally and temporarily surpassing the Pandora's capabilities. When he'd returned to his lab, he'd exploited those glitches to further his design.

"I can *feel* the windowsill," Garrote said. "Oh, this is splendid work you've done, Harry! Magnificent. I'm spinning my globe. It's actually moving—hang on… what is that *sound*?"

"Mr. Garrote, I think you're experiencing a glitch. There's no way your house could be moving—"

"*Shhh!* I hear something. It sounds like… bleating." Garrote jumped. "Oh! The door just slammed." He chuckled nervously. "Oh yes, my house is still very much alive. Very, *very* much. This should be delicious."

Harrison didn't like the tone of Garrote's voice, filled with sadistic glee.

"Don't you see, Harry, my boy? They're *moving* it. Remember I told you about my dream?"

"The park? The ghost thingy?"

That joyless smile. "Yes, exactly that. They must be moving my house. Taking my beauty to her final resting place."

The thought didn't please Harrison. He was hoping to exploit this potential glitch once the writer had finished his test run.

"There are children chasing us on bicycles," Garrote said, clearly delighted. "People watching from the street. This must be Duck Falls, in Maryland. This—oh! What was that flash of light? It came from a window on the hill. Flashed right in my eyes."

"Why don't you go and find out?"

Garrote licked his lips. "I can do that?"

"You can do whatever you want. It's your quarter."

"Hmm," Garrote said, thoughtful. "There's a boy in a window, high up on the hill. He's watching the house through binoculars."

Harrison grinned, the prankster in him pondering a million possibilities. "He's alone?"

"He appears to be, yes. He has one of my books. *The House Feeds*. He's looking at the back of it. At my photo. Is it possible he's *seen me*?"

Harrison shook his head. "I haven't given you an avatar yet."

Garrote licked his lips again. "But he *does* see me. Somehow he does."

Another glitch. This one would prove useful, once Harrison had a chance to sift through the data from the writer's synapses. He was still in the early stages of dev with avatar projection, incorporating work from other labs he'd been spying on over the past several months.

"If he can see you," Harrison said, which he still doubted, "why don't you give him a little scare?"

"Yessss, I think that's a fine idea." The writer smiled darkly. On the screen, his brain lit up like Vegas at night. "A little scare would be *fun*."

PART 2
THE PSYCHIC SUICIDES

Some people are more prone to hauntings than the rest of us. Empaths, spiritualists, mediums, psychics, their minds are more in tune with the astral world, which makes them easy prey for psychic attacks.

— comment on the GRP2 message boards

Reluctantly, the writer drew his visitor into the foyer. "I should warn you," he said. "I don't believe in psychics."

The strange, little woman fixed him with a sagacious grin. "And yet, you called me to your home," she replied.

"I wasn't given much of a choice, I'm afraid. You see, the house was very adamant that I call a psychic."

"The *house* was?"

"Yes. It's very hungry, you see. It feeds upon spiritual energy. The others I've brought here before you..." For an instant he seemed apologetic. "...it seems they were merely snacks," he said.

— Rex Garrote, *The House Feeds*

LOW SPIRITS

LILIAN AND BLAKE had picked up dinner from the dining hall and brought it back to her room. The live episode of *Return to Ghostland* was starting in a half an hour and they planned to watch it, despite her reservations. She had no idea whether any of the spirits were still active or if they were all docile after Garrote's escape, but she had a bad feeling it wouldn't end well.

"Did you know Stanford was founded because of a séance?" Lilian asked as they ate, waiting for the show to start. After her ethereal sightings on campus, she'd been looking into the haunted history of her alma mater, hoping to quell her current disinterest in her courses with her keen interest in the astral world. It hadn't helped, but she had learned a fair bit about Stanford's ghostly past.

Blake looked up from his pasta. "Huh?"

"The Stanfords, Jane and Leland, they had this son who died when he was fourteen or fifteen. About six years later they held a séance with this medium—"

"Medium what?"

"A psychic," she said, somewhat impatiently. She often forgot how clueless he was about this stuff. "Her name was Maud Lord-Drake. So the Stanfords had a bunch of séances in their house after their son died. Leland Stanford's brother was like a major spiritualist in Austria— or Australia. I can't remember which. Anyways his brother, Thomas Welton Stanford, he left seven-hundred and fifty thousand dollars for the university to teach 'Psychical Research and Related Phenomena.' I think that's how your psychology program got started." She licked a daub of sriracha off her thumb. "There's also this collection of these things called *apports*—basically stuff that's supposed to have magically appeared during these séances the Stanfords had, materializing from the astral world—"

"Wait," Blake said, looking confused. "What's the astral world?"

"You know how some scientists believe there's like overlapping worlds and ours is just one of them?"

"Sure," he said, and took a bite of his vegetarian ravioli. "The Many Worlds theory."

"Right. Well, the astral world is where ghosts live. Or exist. I guess they don't technically *live*. Whatever. Anyways, astral beings exist in this astral world. And these apports in the Stanford collection, they magically appeared in our world from the astral plane. Allegedly. There's like bits of tile, a shark's tooth, a turtle shell, rocks and arrowheads… and they're all collected in these little blue boxes."

"You've seen them?" Blake asked, skeptical.

"They're in the archives but I haven't gone. I probably should."

His eyes narrowed. "I don't think that's a good idea."

"Why not?"

"It just seems like you're obsessing a bit, that's all." He shrugged. "Considering what you went through, it makes sense. But I'm not sure it's healthy."

Lilian scowled. She hated it when he tried to analyze her. "You know you're just a sophomore and not an *actual* psychologist, right? If you don't think it's healthy, why are we even watching this?"

He looked at her for a moment, clearly trying to think of an answer that would fit. He wanted to watch this more than she did, probably out of the same sort of alleged "professional curiosity" Allison had claimed to possess.

"Exposure therapy?" he finally suggested.

"That's what my therapist called it," Lilian reminded him. "And you know what happened to her."

They didn't talk for a few minutes after that, eating in silence. When the show came on, they both watched with rapt attention, until Jake and Eric Gallagher and Elena Feliz hopped the turnstiles, when Lilian had to speak up.

"Why aren't they wearing keeper suits?" She'd asked it in almost the same moment Ben had twenty-seven hundred miles to the east.

"Like for bees?" Blake shoveled pasta into his mouth, his eyes on the TV. He was so clueless.

Apparently, so were the intrepid ghost hunters. They stood in front of Ghostland's park map, plotting out their route to Garrote House as she and Ben had all those months ago, and not a single one of them wore any sort of protective gear.

As if they thought it was safe.

As if it was dormant.

Lilian knew better.

Even after almost thirty-five years, visitors wouldn't stay for extended periods at Chernobyl. Too much radiation remained in the contamination exclusion zones.

Ghostland was a nuclear meltdown of dead energy.

Even if the deadliest ghosts had escaped along with Rex Garrote—the Swarm, the Behemoth, Morton Welles—enough scattered pockets of the stuff likely still remained to make a casual visit extremely hazardous.

"You okay?" Blake asked, eyeing her strangely. She hadn't realized until just then that she was practically hyperventilating.

Blake set down his tray and shifted on the bed, turning to her, putting one hand on her shoulder, one over her heart. "Relax, boo. Breathe in through your nose, out through your mouth—"

She shrugged off his hands. "I told you not to call me that."

Blake clucked his tongue. "I knew we shouldn't watch this. I knew it was too soon."

"It's not me," she told him, her heart thrumming. "I'm worried for *them*."

"Lilian. It's just an abandoned theme park."

Lilian quietly seethed, certain he was about to go on another anti-paranormal rant.

"All this ghost stuff," he said, chewing absently, "it's just pseudoscience. Professor Saito said what happened was mass hysteria. Shared psychosis."

"Yeah, well, Professor Saito's a know-it-all asshole."

"C'mon, Lilian, just hear me out a second. You were *told* ghosts exist. For a while there, most people believed it, even though we didn't really have any real proof. No peer-reviewed articles in scientific journals. Just heavily-CGI-ed promos for the park, with some behind the scenes stuff at the Hedgewood labs. Nothing else but the word of this Amblin woman, who wasn't even a real scientist. So you saw ghosts with these special glasses they gave you—but everything you saw and heard was through those headsets. Through the literal lens *they* provided. You saw what they wanted you to see, right? They had complete control over the narrative. Not only that, nobody really knows the long-term effect of augmented or virtual reality on the mind. It's much too new to be properly studied."

Lilian waited until he was done, then started packing up her dinner to eat in her own room. "*You* don't know, either. *You* weren't there."

"Aw, come on. Just… I'm just talking hypothetically here, boo."

"I said don't call me that!" she shouted, whipping her yogurt at the wall, where it splattered across Blake's Imagine Dragons poster.

He stooped to pick up the container, oozing pink goop on the rug as he tossed it in the trash. When he was frustrated or upset, he became Busy Blake, straightening and cleaning things up even if they didn't require it.

"You don't know what we went through in that place," she said, her voice almost a growl. "*Nobody* does. I'm sick of hearing people's stupid theories and all this devil's advocate bullshit. I was there. I saw what happened with my own eyes—"

Blake looked up at her. "Through the parameters that Hedgewood designed—"

"I've *seen* ghosts, Blake! Without the glasses." She turned away from him, facing the door. "I still see them," she muttered.

"What?"

"I said *I still see them*. What do you think I've been doing with GRP2 all this time?"

"Wait. Do you see them right now?" He sounded suspicious.

"Not right now. But around campus, and in town, and

on Hallowe'en, me and Ben—"

Blake flicked a handful of yogurt into the trash with a splat. "We talked about this, Lilian. Ben is dead."

She turned from the door, defiantly meeting his gaze until he looked away at the pink smear on his poster. "You're right," she said. "He is dead. And I've been working with him every weekend since the end of August. Freeing ghosts from their death loops."

"Freeing…?" Blake shook his head, not even willing to try wrapping his mind around it. "So what, you're *ghostbusters* now? Lilian, do you have any idea how…" His voice had risen to a high timbre and he stopped speaking abruptly, taking a few breaths to calm down. "…how illogical that sounds?"

He means crazy, she thought. *He won't say it because he's not supposed to, because that's how he's been trained, just like Allison wouldn't ever say crazy, but that's what they mean. Morton Welles was right, it's in my blood, my DNA. My grandma had it now I do too. The ghosts are meeting at All Hallows' Close, they're going to decide who stays and who goes…*

"This is why I didn't tell you," she said, pushing the image of her grandmother in the hospital bed away. "I knew you'd react exactly like this. You're so analytical sometimes it drives me fucking crazy!"

"I drive *you* crazy? Jesus, why don't you tell me how you really feel?"

"You want me to tell you how I feel? Fine!" She slapped her palm against the door. "I'm *terrified* because this is the first time in my life I've ever felt good about someone and you don't even know who I really am! I'm stressed to hell and exhausted all the time, and school is fucking pointless because we're all gonna die, so why should any of us even *bother*?"

Blake waited a moment, then spoke calmly: "Lilian, why didn't you tell me all this before?"

"Because I knew you'd just try to psychoanalyze me! I don't need help. I just need you to *listen*."

"I'm listening now. I hear you. Everyone gets scared, hon. The environment and everything that's going on politically all over the world right now—"

"It's not that." She wasn't sure she could bring herself to tell him the truth. Once she'd said it, there would be no taking it back. "There's..." She sniffled. "...there's a *war* coming, Blake—"

"With North Korea?"

"No."

"Who then? Russia?"

"*Just listen to me*," she cried, grabbing him by the shoulders. He closed his mouth hard and stared at her. "There is a war coming. It's hard to explain how I know, I just do. You have to trust me. We have to be ready. It could happen at any time."

He jostled as she let him go, but he didn't move and he didn't react until she opened the door.

"Where are you going?" he called as she stepped out into the hall.

"I have to get something."

She returned less than a minute later with the folded silver garment in her hands. It crinkled as she held it out to Blake.

"What is this?" he asked. He looked dazed, like he'd been through a recent trauma.

"This," she said, letting it unfold in front of him, "is a keeper suit."

Blake looked at the shiny silver-lined fabric, its hood

and limbs, the powerpack and switch on its lapel. "Like, for bees?" he asked again.

"Not for *bees*," she said, beyond aggravated. "For *ghosts*. It's what the keepers wore when they entered the exhibits to tend to the ghosts."

"What do you mean 'tend to'?"

"It emits a static charge when a ghost touches it. It'll protect you if me or Ben aren't around. I told the police it was mine so I got to keep it. The second things start getting weird, please… just promise me you'll put it on."

Blake took it. He folded it up carefully and set it on the TV table. "Lilian." He sat on the bed, patted beside himself on the comforter. She sat beside him, wary of his reaction. "Lilian, I know you're stressed right now—"

"That's not what this is about."

"Bae. Seriously, I think you need to consider talking to someone—"

"I don't need a therapist!"

"Hon. You were seeing a therapist before this all happened. You watched her die at Ghostland. You were at *Ground Zero* of the 9/11 of our generation. You need to talk to somebody, whether it's me or—"

She opened her mouth to reply, then turned and went to the door.

"Aw, c'mon. Don't be like that."

She grabbed the handle and wrenched it open. Blake stood and crossed to her, barring the doorway, waiting for her to look at him.

"Lilian, you're being unreasonable."

She refused to look at him. "You mean crazy."

"I *don't* mean—" Finally, he huffed. "Fine, go. I'll be here if you need anything. Or whatever."

She stepped out and slammed the door.

The tears came before she made it back to her own room, full-body wracking sobs. No matter how much she wanted to feel strong right now, she couldn't hold them back. She might have just severed the strongest bond she had at school, the only person keeping her tethered to this part of her life. She feared there was nothing left to stop her from walking out right now and never coming back, from putting her work with GRP2 front and center. But what if Thea didn't need her?

She needed to talk to someone. Anybody but Blake. She closed the door behind her and picked up Whatsit the bear, jingling the bell on his necklace and weeping openly, calling for Ben.

She jingled the bell for a full minute before giving up and chucking Whatsit across the room, then flopped down onto her mattress.

Her cell lay beside her. After a moment of hesitation, she rose on her elbows, picked up her phone and called home. On the second ring her dad's smiling, bristly face filled the screen. He twiddled his fingers in a wave. "Hi, honey!"

"Hi, Dad. How are you guys?"

"We're good. What's wrong? Are you crying?"

"Why is she crying?" her mom asked off camera.

"I'm okay. It's nothing."

"It's not nothing. My angel doesn't cry over nothing."

"Good lord, Hiram. Don't *baby* her."

He turned to defend himself. "I'm not babying her."

"You baby her. She's a capable young woman. She doesn't need to be babied."

He turned back to the camera. "Am I babying you, honey?"

Lilian sniffed, smiling through her tears. "Maybe a

little, Dad."

"Well, then. For the duration of this call I am no longer your father. Consider me your cool, older male friend."

"That's weird, Dad."

Hiram looked off to where her mother clearly stood. "Apparently your mother agrees with you. At least we have a consensus. So, what's on your mind, hon?"

"I just miss you guys, is all. It's been a long month."

"Well, Thanksgiving is only a few weeks away. Your mother and I could fly down for a visit on Hedgewood's dime."

"That'd be nice, Dad." She wiped her tears. "I love you guys."

"Aw, honey," her mom said, planting her chin on Dad's shoulder. "We love you, too."

"Things are weird here lately," her father said. "Not around the house. In town. Lots of new people. The diner's been swamped with business. Lots of catering, delivered to the old Holy Roller church on Kubler Road."

"It's those ghost protestors," her mother said. "Those whackos."

"They're not whackos, Mom."

"Well, whatever they are they've overrun the town." She sighed, shrugging. "Still better than the looky-loos, I suppose. Those ghouls are always hovering around, snapping photos, asking about that awful place out on Burt Bucklebee's old farm."

"It'll blow over," her dad said. "Mark my words. A year from now after some other tragedy strikes, nobody will remember Duck Falls even exists. It'll be ancient history, and we'll all be able to get on with our lives."

"I hope so, Dad." She sniffled again. "I gotta go. Talk to you guys soon, okay?"

"Stay safe!" her dad said, and blew her a kiss.

"Bye, love," her mother said.

The screen went black. She stared at her reflection in the glass for several moments. Her eyes looked tired. She felt like she could sleep for a week.

How much longer can I keep this up?

School and Blake. Ben and GRP2. Something had to give, and she knew which one it was likely to be.

After the network cut from the live show back to regular programming, the protestors gathered in Ghostland's front lot returned to the Temple. Spirits were low, Thea and the others acutely aware of the optics. What happened tonight didn't look good for any of them.

"Is it possible this was a publicity stunt?" Thea asked, turning to Bram. He was crammed into the passenger seat of Thea's Chevy Volt, his knees perpendicular to his chest, his scowl and tight, square jaw lit by his phone. "Or a hoax? What if it was special effects, not ghosts?"

"We can't bank on that," Bram said, glancing at her behind the wheel, her eyes on the dark road ahead. "Unless they're all Oscar-worthy actors, what happened in there was one-hundred percent real. Which means you and I need to get ahead of this. We need to make a statement before people start speculating and this all gets out of hand."

"You think people will turn against us?"

He held his phone up to her. She glanced at it, then returned her gaze to the line of vehicles ahead of them, streaming back toward town.

"'Cancel GRP2' is already trending," he said. "As if it was our fault, just for being there. Like we weren't just protesting the damn thing to stop it from happening."

Thea let out a long sigh, gripping the wheel tightly. "We're the face of the faceless, and we're already fighting an uphill battle. Ghosts have always had bad PR. Most people are already scared of them. We don't want people losing their minds with fear when the vast majority of ethereals are docile."

Bram nodded thoughtfully. "I'll whip something up," he said, and began typing on his phone.

She thanked him. The line of vehicles behind them stretched all the way back to Ghostland's lot, where the network people were likely dealing with their own issues. She suspected this would be more than a tap on the wrist for them. People had died, live on air. They should have cut away earlier, before the carnage, but they were still a network news production. *If it bleeds it leads* wasn't an expression for no reason.

Thea had a decision to make. This was a major crisis, not just for GRP2 but for her conscience. She'd dedicated her life to speaking for those who couldn't speak for themselves. A voice for the voiceless, and face for the faceless. Now those people she'd sworn to protect would be even more unfairly maligned because of the actions of one or two rogue ethereals.

Evil entities, she thought, shaking her head bitterly. Maybe Ben was right. The question now became whether she would let those few bad apples spoil the sauce, or go through with the plan she and Bram had devised regardless of what just happened.

There were still good people in there. Ethereals who needed her help, trapped among monsters. Innocent souls doomed to spend eternity in a cage simply because of who they were and what they represented. Because they were feared by the living.

Even Ben, an ethereal himself, feared them.

Thea Petralia had never been scared of ghosts. Even when she was little she'd been curious about them, praying for them to show themselves to her, to make their presence indisputable.

The Petralias had lived in a haunted house when she was five—the first home her parents had bought, years before Kismet became a trending dating app. Every night the closet door in her bedroom had creaked open, and the light in the basement had come on by itself at odd times of the day. Her parents didn't believe in ghosts, so they'd dismissed the basement light as bad wiring and the closet door as a crooked frame.

Thea hadn't believed their theories. She'd never seen anything tangible but over the year and a half they'd lived in the tiny Bakersfield bungalow, she'd convinced herself they'd been living with ghosts.

When the Kismet app had gone public, the Petralias moved to a mansion in the Hollywood Hills, where Thea had become even more obsessed with the idea of the afterlife. The home had been too new to be haunted, although it had allegedly been built on an ancient Native American burial ground—as cliché as that sounded, the history of the area proved it true. Over the years, Thea had consulted with many spiritual mediums and ghost hunters. If there had been any ethereals in that house, they apparently didn't want to communicate with the teenaged heir to a dating app fortune. Not to be discouraged, she'd begun exploring haunted hotspots throughout the Greater Los Angeles area.

Her parents had made it clear she was wasting her time and their money. Throughout her many hunts and explorations over the intervening years, she'd begun to wonder if they were right. She'd never felt more than a chill on the back of her neck, nor heard anything beyond a strange sound in the dark that couldn't be easily explained when she'd listened to her recordings.

Just once, she'd wished she could communicate with a spectral being from the Other Side. To touch and be touched by one. To see some sort of evidence that what she'd believed since childhood was true.

That ghosts *did* exist.

After eight years of fruitless searching, Thea had finally given up, reluctantly falling into her expected role as a Wealthy Heiress, consuming only the best of everything: champagne, men, cocaine. She'd attended all the right galas, the raddest parties, the craziest after-parties.

Then, rehab.

She'd left the clinic three months later stone sober but lacking any sense of purpose or motivation. The parties were tedious without drugs. The five-hundred-dollar-a-plate galas had no longer held her interest. Even the food tasted bland. She'd worried she would never settle on anything to fulfill her the way her quest to discover proof of life after death once had.

She'd taught herself to paint. She'd learned how to cook. She'd tried sailing and riding horses and skeet shooting. Anything to fill her days, to prevent the crushing weight of boredom from turning her mind back to drugs and alcohol, to the parties she'd never wanted to be a part of in the first place but which had eventually, with enough stimulants, become a pattern.

When the late, visionary inventor Sara Jane Amblin had begun announcing that ghosts existed in the form of "dead energy" on a string of talk shows and interviews in

2018, Thea Petralia's interest in the afterlife was revived.

She'd seen her passion reflected in the eyes of the woman on TV. The only difference between them was that what Amblin believed was an opportunity to bring history to life, Thea saw as a massive for-profit prison: a metaphorical plantation where ghosts would toil for the amusement of the living. She saw her own addiction patterns repeated in the "loop" of every ghost trapped inside Amblin's sadistic invention.

Once Thea had gotten this idea in her mind, nothing had been able to convince her the Recurrence Field was "harmless," as Amblin and the Hedgewood Foundation claimed. She'd persuaded her parents to cash in their Hedgewood stock and let her use the money to start a foundation of her own, a fund for the protection and welfare of ethereals.

The way she'd explained it to her extremely skeptical parents, if what Amblin said was true, if the science corroborated it, literally everyone stood to benefit from her work, since everyone would eventually become a "ghost."

Adonis Petralia had once told his daughter that most people had a "watershed moment" at some point over the course of their lives. If they chose to see it for what it was and take advantage of it, to grab it by the reigns, this was what created the legends, the moguls.

Thea had presented her parents with a solid business plan in the form of a thirty-minute presentation, including a summary of everything she'd learned about ghosts over the years, her research on Ghostland itself, and comparable charities and foundations. She'd told them this foundation would be her watershed moment. Her father had smiled.

That same week, GRP2 was born.

When she'd organized the first rally, Thea had no idea

what her small group of likeminded individuals would eventually grow into. A dozen people just showing up to protest anything in those first few months had become a hundred people in a pop-up protest at Hedgewood's L.A. complex, then grown to a full-fledged rally held out front of the White House.

The website and Facebook group had expanded into multiple groups and sites all across the country. There were groups spreading throughout the world now: in Canada, Western Europe, Asia and South America. What happened at Ghostland had propelled GRP2 onto the world stage. And for the first time since she'd left rehab, Stacy and Adonis Petralia had told their daughter they were proud of her.

The missions—the liberation of ghosts—had started after she'd met Ben Laramie and Leon Moncrief. It had taken the incident in April to wake ethereals to her cause, but it wasn't until late-August that they'd decided she could be trusted, which had finally led to her first communion with the spirit world.

Thea and a few dozen of her closest followers had already set up camp in the old Evangelical church on Kubler Road by then. The memorial out front had been unveiled, and the people of Duck Falls had reluctantly accepted their presence—though she'd known some of them thought she was leading some sort of cult—with the class-action lawsuit unifying them.

She'd been typing out an email to groups in other areas about an upcoming mass protest when the text-to-speech app on her computer popped open. At first, she'd thought someone had been remotely accessing her computer: the FBI, or a hacker from Hedgewood, trying to access her files. She'd flicked on Airplane Mode and waited for the cursor to stop moving.

It had stopped. Then letters had appeared in the app. The letters had become words.

After rehab she'd set up the text-to-speech program in her Macbook Air to have what she considered a "proper" British accent. The motivational pep talks she gave herself had felt much more inspiring when they sounded like Benedict Cumberbatch.

When the voice spoke to her that night in the back office of the church, the rest of the place silent, she'd scooched back in her chair so sharply it had fallen out from under her and she'd landed on her butt on the cold hardwood floor.

"*Hello*," the British voice had said. "*Sorry if I scared you*," it had added, after she'd gotten up from the floor. "*My name is Ben Laramie. I died during the Ghostland Disaster. I'd like to speak with you, if you'll listen.*"

Her gaze had shot toward the closed office door. She'd doubted anyone else in the church had heard. It was the proof she'd been looking for at last, with no one around to corroborate it, to tell her if it was real, if she was being punked, or if she was losing her mind. She'd remembered watching her closet door creak open when she was a little girl and thinking, *They won't believe me.*

"Ben? Can you hear me?" she'd asked the empty room, tentatively.

"*Yes, we can hear you*," the voice had replied. "*We're right here with you. We've been waiting a long time to speak to you.*"

"We?" She looked around herself, slightly anxious.

"*Don't be afraid*," Ben had said in the computer's British voice. "*There are twelve of us. Two of us escaped from Ghostland, including me. The others came after what happened. Loads more elsewhere. We wanted to thank you for looking out for us."*

"You're real," she'd said, her breathing tremulous from excitement and the twinge of fear she still hadn't been able to quell. "You really do exist."

"We exist," Ben had said. *"And we want to help you, if we can. Will you let us?"*

Thea's answer had been an emphatic yes.

As she drove back to the Temple, she thought back to their first meeting and couldn't help but feel conflicted about what she'd put into motion. Those first ethereals—her twelve "apostles"—had come to her so eager to help her cause. But Ben and Leon had betrayed her trust. The betrayal couldn't go unchallenged. She was her father's daughter, after all. Adonis Petralia had a zero-tolerance policy for insubordination among his team.

In the days since she'd made the deal, she realized it might well be a Faustian bargain. She'd seen it as a purely strategic decision at the time. After tonight, she had to wonder if the man was being entirely honest with her. Still, he had hordes of equipment GRP2 required and Thea had something he needed, as well.

She just had to hope she wouldn't come to regret it.

At three a.m., Oliver Hedgewood sat in his armored limousine waiting for the authorities to arrive, and he began to suspect he may have to wait until first light. He didn't mind. He was a patient man. His father had always told him, "Good things come to those who wait, Ollie." He'd waited patiently for the old man to die, and when the business was handed to his brother instead of him, he'd waited for one or another of Christopher's fleeting passions to catch up with him.

Ollie derived as much pleasure abstaining from pleasureful things as his brother had derived consuming them. He'd never touched drugs, aside from his pain pills. He abstained from alcohol. He took care of his sexual appetites only when the urge would become so insistent nothing else would suffice, and only then with the service of professionals. He didn't eat sweets and he rarely cursed.

The limousine idled just outside the maintenance hatch, among the mechanical buildings housing the Recurrence Field and backup generators, along with a small security office. He was staring out his window at the hatch he'd had reinforced with lead shielding, after the boy had opened it using a code of which by all logic, he should have had no knowledge.

Local and federal government officials had advised shutting off the Recurrence Field after "The Incident," but Ollie had fought adamantly against it. The field must stay running day-in and day-out, he'd told them. Unless they wanted what had happened *in there* to recur *out here*. Frankly, he wasn't sure how many of Garrote's toys remained within the field, but after what had happened with the Ghost Brothers—*canaries in the coal mine*—it wouldn't be difficult to drum up support from the people in power to do what needed to be done.

From now on, the park would need to remain sealed until Project TANDY was complete. Then, he and his team would stroll right in through the front gate and wipe them all out, scrubbing every last byte of data from the remaining servers.

It was bad enough the boy had somehow managed to breach the security system, letting out God knew how many of those abhorrent things into the surrounding area. Far worse, if any further incidents occurred that could be traced back to the Foundation and its subsidiaries.

Class-action lawsuits had them tied up in years of legal red tape, though the settlements they'd reached with many of the people in Duck Falls had hardly made a dent in his fortune. The Foundation had enough government contracts—some American, some foreign—to keep him from coming within spitting distance of bankruptcy. No matter the losses, no matter the cost, to prevent the remaining entities from escaping until he had the wherewithal to destroy them the Recurrence Field had to keep running. As long as he was in charge, the security protocols would remain in place.

Its exhibits might fall to ruin, succumbing to time and environment, crumbling to rubble, swallowed by forest and foliage… but the equipment would keep running until it was no longer essential.

His cell phone rang, the soothing strings of Bach's "Air" rousing him from thought as he stared at the sealed hatch. He answered it.

"We've found the boy, Ollie," the clipped female voice on the line said. "He's with the GRP2 people. At their church."

"Can you track his signature?"

"Yes."

"Then do it. I want him *unharmed*, Danica. He's our key to finding Garrote."

Ollie ended the call and peered out at the lights flickering atop the Recurrence Field building. He smiled, his reflection in the tinted glass like a man smiling through a great deal of agony. His pills kept it from reaching his pain receptors but not from his eyes. Still, despite the vague opioid fog, he was pleased with the night's progress.

With luck, Danica Jackson, one of his most skilled

contractors, would capture Benjamin Laramie tonight—
and TANDY would have its final test subject.

Cold Comfort

Las Vegas
October 31st

SAM'S PLANE LANDED at McCarran International Airport with the sun a brilliant orange fireball on the horizon, though it was barely five o'clock.

Her hotel just off the Strip was much more opulent than she'd expected, featuring a foyer, a four-poster queen bed and a jacuzzi tub. She'd decided on the Palais Royale since it was holding the Psychic Expo, and she hoped to speak with some of the guests and staff prior to the convention. It was booked solid on the weekend, but there had been a few rooms available tonight and Friday. If she'd need to stick around a bit longer, she would have to work out different accommodations.

Sam dropped her overnight bag on the sofa in the foyer and drew open the French doors to the suite. The carpet, crown molding and antique-looking furniture were a strange, old-world contrast to the glass walls overlooking the twinkling lights of the Strip. From the fourteenth floor she could see the city streets and low buildings give way to desert and mountains beyond, the sunset now just a slight orange glow on the horizon.

It felt strange, flying out here all alone. The last vacation she'd taken was six years ago, with her then-girlfriend, Helena—a Junior D.A. Sam's colleagues often called "Helena Handbasket," though her name was pronounced Hel-*ay*-na and didn't really fit the joke. The trip had been Helena's idea. Sam had no real urge to see France, nor to leave Seattle, really. Their relationship had already been struggling by then and she'd figured Helena had seen it as a last-ditch attempt to salvage what they once had. They'd spent several days in Paris, getting fat on pastries and wine—*Fatter*, Sam thought, though Helena wouldn't have liked to hear Sam thinking of herself that way—then spent several more on the Riviera, with Helena living it up while Sam tried not to feel so out of place. When they returned home, Helena had promptly packed up her things and moved out. Sam hadn't attempted to stop her.

With her shoes kicked off, Sam luxuriated in the feel of the plush carpet on her sock feet a moment, then sat on the edge of the absolutely massive bed. She sighed, allowing herself a moment to relax.

From her rental car, she'd called the Vegas police in the vain hope of getting a name and address for the latest suicide victim. The detective she'd spoken to had been surly and standoffish. He'd wanted nothing to do with Sam and her "off the books" investigation. He'd suggested she head back to Seattle at the earliest opportunity.

The lack of cooperation left her with a long night of phone calls and legwork ahead. She decided to grab a quick shower and dinner first.

The showerhead was large and felt like a warm rain. It reminded her of home, and she stood under it much longer than she needed to, releasing the stress of an already long week. She dried off and dressed to the smooth jazz stylings of the hotel guest info channel, feeling somewhat burlesque as she eyed her reflection in the dark windows, with an impossibly plush towel around her thicker-than-she'd-like waistline and a smaller one twisted on her head. Once she was fully dressed, it was nearly seven-thirty and the lights of Vegas shone far brighter than the clear dark sky above.

She headed down to the lobby, crossed the array of slots and tables jammed with gamblers and gawkers, older men standing around while their younger wives poured coins into the one-eyed bandits, croupiers dealing cards and scooping chips, shooters throwing dice, men in dark suits playing Baccarat, machines ringing and chiming and beeping everywhere she looked. It was a constant cacophony. Sam wondered how anyone could live in this city year-round. Then again, visitors often asked her the same when referring to Seattle's rain.

The hotel restaurant—*Poème de Terre*, a name that sounded classy but from Sam's ninth grade French she was pretty sure just meant "Earth Poem"—was packed and required reservations. It looked too fancy for her tastes, anyhow. Anything with bechamel and bearnaise was well out of her price range. She decided to hit the Strip instead, find someplace cheap and easy.

Out in the cool evening air there were so many people walking around and drinking, it felt like a carnival. Even with the dip in temperature since the sun went down many people wore shorts and sarongs over bikinis, to go with their beers and mixed drinks, as they strolled the sidewalks, taking selfies and group photos with their cell phones, dipping in and out of shops and casinos, cheering wildly. A group of young women clearly involved in a bachelorette party wore tiaras and sucked on penis-shaped lollipops as they whooped and hollered at passersby. Tourists poured out of buses and stretched limousines idling by the sidewalks. Tropical-colored sports cars rumbled and revved as they cruised up and down Las Vegas Boulevard.

Sam hadn't felt so out of place since the French Riviera. Within the span of three blocks she'd avoided four men handing out cards for strip clubs and escorts, and had spotted at least another two who were likely dealing hardcore drugs. The public drinking made her feel like she was in a whole different universe, even without the flashing lights and fountains and perpetual barrage of sound. It took all of her will not to bust the guy standing by the Bellagio fountain who asked if she was "good," his eyes bloodshot, his demeanor squirrely.

She found a walk-in tiki bar with a dinner menu twenty minutes after leaving the Royale and grabbed a table near the front to watch the crowd walk by. The server homed in on her instantly. Dressed in a coconut bra and grass skirt, the Filipino girl rushed through the dinner specials with a slight Southern twang. She brought Sam a Mai Tai a few minutes later, and put in her order for dinner.

After Sam finished her first drink, the rush of sugar and alcohol made her take a chance. She called the server over again. "Can I ask you something?"

"Sure thing, shug."

"Did you hear about the psychic who killed herself this morning?"

The girl cocked her head, eyeing her suspiciously. "Is this like a knock-knock joke?"

"Never mind," Sam said, feeling foolish.

She ate quickly, tipped the girl generously, and

returned to the streets, hoping to catch a lead soon so she could get the hell out of this town before the weekend.

Lamb was waiting for Andy in the narrow alley beside the shop, as the sun began to dip behind the low slopes of the Spring Mountains on the horizon, the rooftops and palm trees silhouetted against its brilliant, shimmering peach, pink and orange light.

"Hey, Lamb, how are—?" he started to ask, but she grabbed him suddenly in a tight hug, squeezing the breath right out of him.

"Thank you," she said, looking slightly embarrassed as she stepped back from the embrace. "I was so scared I didn't know who else to call."

"Well, I'm, uh… I'm here for you, whenever you need me."

She smiled sadly and led him up the fire escape stairs, quickly ushered him inside her small apartment, and locked the door behind them. The décor was mostly pink and purples—*Or is that indigo?* he wondered, recalling what her mother had told him about his "aura"—either plush or fuzzy or both, aside from the psychedelic '70s rock band posters, and a beaten drum kit squeezed into the corner, between the kitchen counter and the bathroom wall.

Lamb headed for the counter, poured two drinks into plastic tumblers from a bottle of Jack Daniels amid a wide selection of liquor and offered one to Andy.

"No thanks," he said. "I don't drink."

Lamb shrugged. She brought both to the sofa, set them on the coffee table and flopped down against the mound of woven, multicolored pillows. She slurped from her cup. "You in recovery or something?"

"Nah, I just don't like to lose control. Only ever got hammered once and—" He shuddered as the memory tried to resurface. "Well, let's just say things didn't go too well," he finished briskly.

She nodded sympathetically, then patted the cushion beside the one she sat on. "Come. Sit."

He sat at the opposite end, feeling suddenly nervous, wishing he'd had another toke or two before coming here, just to relax. "You play?" he asked, nodding at the drums.

Lamb shrugged. "I ain't any good, but I bash on em every chance I get. Mom lives downstairs behind the shop, but she's an early riser so I usually play in the mornin before we open."

"Cool," Andy said. "Very cool."

Lamb took another sip and eyed him over the lip of her cup. It was obvious she wanted to say something and didn't know how to go about it. Andy couldn't help her. He hadn't felt so nervous since his freshman year at college. Instead he smiled, trying to play it off.

"Okay, I didn't wanna say this, but I gotta ask ya," she said finally. She swallowed the last of her first drink, as if to summon her courage. "Do you think… I mean, is it possible…?"

"Is what possible, Lamb?"

"That your friends might have done it," she said, nodding over his shoulder—at *them*. "Killed my mom."

"Oh, *come on…*."

"Andy, I told you I can sense them. My mom, she said right after you left those guardian angels of yours could turn mean if you didn't have a handle on em. I go to the store for ten minutes and she's…" Her lower lip trembled. She gulped the rest of her drink quickly, wiped her lip and set it down beside the other cup. "I gotta wonder if she might've upset em or something. If maybe they didn't guide her hands."

"Lamb, if what she said is true, if I do have guardian angels, what possible reason would they have to kill your mother if they've only ever brought me good luck?"

It wasn't exactly true. That time he'd gotten way too drunk during college was the exception. Though he supposed what happened this morning with Mr. Mack, the pit boss, couldn't exactly be called "good" either. But he still couldn't be sure either incident wasn't his own damn fault.

"I don't know, Andy. I'm just…" She whimpered, and scooched across the couch to take his hands in hers. "My mom killed herself right in front of me. I just wanna know why."

He felt a stab of pain in his heart as she leaned her head into his shoulder. What reason did she have to be so trusting? His "kind" aura? *I'm just some guy off the street, why choose me?*

"Whatever you need, I'm here," he said, feeling lost, hopelessly in over his head. "We'll figure out what happened, okay?"

She looked up at him, her eyes wide and glistening beneath thick false lashes. "Will you do one thing for me?" she asked, her voice thick with tears.

"Anything," he told her, and he realized in that moment that he meant it. He would do anything for this woman, and he'd only just met her. "What do you need?"

"I think my mom was using her Ouija board when she died."

It took him a moment to understand what she was saying to him. "Isn't it *weegee*?"

She laughed and patted his hands. "When we do this,

just let me do the talkin. Okay, punkin?"

"We're gonna use your mom's Ouija board?" he asked, pronouncing it her way.

He felt her nod against his chest. "Uh-huh," she said. "I wanna speak to those guardian angels of yours."

Lamb unlocked the back door to the shop and slipped underneath the police tape. Andy peered up and down the alley before following her inside.

The narrow hallway was far too dark to see anything aside from Lamb's silhouette a few feet ahead of him. "C'mon," she whispered, as if there might be someone in here to disturb.

Andy followed her through a beaded curtain, past a restroom and another door he guessed led into her mother's apartment, then into the séance room. Only then did she flick on a lamp, brightening the small space. It still smelled like the incense Sonya had burned that morning. The Ouija board lay on the table, surrounded by several melted candles, just as she'd said.

"Are you sure this is a good idea? I mean, what if your mom really did channel some bad juju? You think it's smart to go opening that door again?"

Lamb was already seated in her mother's chair. She glanced around, not paying attention to him. "Where's the dang planchette?"

As Andy crossed the room to look among the scattered mess in the corner, she grabbed him by the wrist, her eyes wide with fear. "What?" he asked, with a trace of paranoia. "What's wrong?"

"I feel something," she said. "Don't you feel it? Like the air after a thunder an' lightnin storm."

"I don't feel anything," he said, though his heart had

started to race the moment they'd stepped through the police tape, as if he'd just run all the way from the Palais Royale again.

"Somethin's not right. And the friggin planchette's missin." She heaved a sigh. "All right, we're gonna hafta make due." She reached under the table and slipped one of the beer coasters out from under a leg. An impression of the table footing was stamped in the middle of the Triple 7 Restaurant and Brewery logo printed on it. Lamb tore off two bits to make it the shape of a badly formed tear drop, and placed it on the board. "That'll do. Now, c'mere and sit down. We got work to do."

Despite everything screaming at him to leave—aside from the Nudges, which seemed conspicuously absent at the moment—Andy sat across from her, in the same seat he'd sat in that morning across from her mother.

"Put your fingers on it. Gentle, like mine."

She put the first two fingers from each hand lightly on the coaster. Andy did the same, so they each held two corners.

"Oh, shoot, I almost forgot the incense. You got a lighter?"

Andy shook his head. He never smoked weed outside of his apartment, and otherwise had no use for a lighter.

Lamb got up in a huff and crossed to the heap of objects in the corner. "Ah, there you are." She came up with a barbecue lighter and lit the incense sticks in the corners of the room. "For protection," she said. "Though I s'pose it didn't work for my mom, did it?"

Andy thought it best not to reply.

Lamb returned to her seat and placed her fingers back on the coaster. "We wish to speak with the presence or presences in this room," she said, moving the coaster in concentric circles.

Andy followed along with his fingers lightly on the coaster, watching her closely. Even with her mascara streaked and her eyes still glistening with tears she was gorgeous, maybe more so. It fit her "black T-shirt, cut-off jeans and cowboy boots" aesthetic perfectly. She looked up from the board, catching his eye. He quickly looked down at the circling coaster.

"Speak to us with the board," she said with a ghost of a smile. He could still feel her eyes on him. "Tell us why you've chosen this man, Andrew Park, as your vessel."

"No one calls me Andrew—"

"Will you shut it?"

Andy closed his mouth. It was obvious from her death glare that she needed him to take this more seriously than he felt. Fortunately, he hadn't smoked any weed before leaving the house or he would've been giggling despite the graveness of the circumstances.

He startled as the coaster jittered under his fingertips. Lamb seemed equally surprised by the movement. There was no time to question it. The makeshift planchette suddenly began swishing across the board from one letter to the next, and even though Andy couldn't be one-hundred percent certain Lamb wasn't pushing it, he didn't believe she was.

Whatever was making the coaster move, it spelled out *PROTECT*.

"You're here to protect him?"

The coaster moved to *NO*.

"What then? What do you mean by 'protect?'"

The coaster spelled out *US*.

"He protects you?"

YES.

"That doesn't make any sense," Andy said. "*I* protect *them*? Who are they? And why me?"

Lamb looked flustered. "Those are hard questions. Try asking them yeses or nos."

"Fine. Did you kill Lamb's mother?"

NO.

"Do you know who did?"

YES.

Lamb's eyebrows rose in excitement and fear. "Can you help us communicate with him?"

NO.

"Why not?"

The coaster didn't move.

"Is my mother here with us?"

YES.

Lamb gasped. "Will she speak to us?"

NO.

"Why not?" Andy asked.

It swished across the board: *N-O-T-A-B-L-E.*

The response confused Andy. "No table?"

"*Not able,*" Lamb corrected him.

The coaster moved to *YES.*

"Did my mother kill herself?"

NO.

"Was she killed by a ghost?"

It didn't move.

"Was she killed by a ghost?" she repeated.

The coaster jerked rapidly and returned to *NO.*

"Can you tell us who murdered her?"

Andy expected a repeat of the last movement, back to *NO.* Instead, it moved swiftly across the board: *L-V-P-E.*

"What does that mean?" he asked.

The coaster repeated the movement more forcefully, as

if in annoyance, dragging their hands across the board with it: *L-V-P-E*.

"Maybe it's initials," Andy suggested. "Las Vegas something?"

"The only PE I know is Phys Ed. Unless my mom's murderer was a gym teacher, what the heck is PE?" She thought a moment. "Oh crap," she said.

"What?"

"I just figured it out. The LVPE is this Saturday—the Las Vegas Psychic Expo? My mom usually does a booth but this year she bowed out, said it wasn't worth the expense."

"Is that it?" Andy asked the board. "The Las Vegas Psychic Expo?"

They both stared at the coaster between their fingers, waiting for it to move. It remained still.

"Well, I guess they're done talking to us," Lamb said finally.

Andy could feel it, too. The room felt drained. Dead. Even the smell of incense had dulled. He still had so many questions. He couldn't fool himself into believing they weren't with him anymore, his mother's *gwisin*, but why would they need him for protection? And from what? Was something preventing Lamb's mother from communicating with them? And what had caused her death, if it wasn't a ghost?

They removed their fingers from the coaster at the same time. Lamb smiled cautiously at him.

"You know, I never spoke to ghosts before," she said. "All my life with a house full of ghosts, I never once tried. I guess I was scared of what they might say."

Andy smiled back. "You don't have to be scared anymore."

"Why not?"

He laid his hands on hers. Her smile grew wider. Warmer.

"Because I'm here to protect you," he said.

She turned her hands over and squeezed his. "You're sweet."

After what happened to her mother, Andy knew his offer would be seen as cold comfort. Still, Lamb brought him back upstairs and led him into her bed. The lights of Vegas barely penetrated the bedsheet strung up over the blinds they explored each other's bodies in the semi-dark.

It had been so long since he'd been intimate with anyone, he was overwhelmed by the sensation of her hands on his chest and hips, her lips on his skin, their bodies entwined, enough that he was able to temporarily forget the ghosts in the room with them, and what possible manner of evil force they might need to be protected against.

Lamb woke in the middle of the night. The tradeoff with good sex was that it left her so physically drained she would fall asleep within a few minutes but also have to pee, which meant she'd wake an hour or so later. Andy was curled in the fetal position, breathing deeply as she crept out of bed and crossed to the bathroom. When she came back in the room, he was lying on his back with his hands behind his head, looking up at the ceiling.

"Can't sleep?"

"Thinking," he said.

"Yeah." She climbed back into bed. "Guess you can't pretend there's nothin strange in your neighborhood anymore, huh?"

He chuckled. "No, not so much. And Bill Murray's 1-

800 number won't answer the call."

She gave him a consoling smile and rolled onto her side, propping her head up with an elbow on her pillow. "You know, this all might not be such a bad thing."

"How so?"

"Well, what if your ghosts brought you here because they knew something bad was gonna happen to my mom? They said you're a protector. What if you were meant to protect my mom?"

"I sure bunged that up, didn't I?"

"You didn't know. It's not like anyone told you."

Andy exhaled sharply through his nose. He *had* known—he just hadn't listened. It was the same thing that had happened with his parents, or same enough to be considered a pattern. The Nudges he'd felt his entire life had pushed him here, to her mother's door. "If I'd just listened to her in the first place..." he said, working himself up to reveal his darkest secret, the thing he'd told no living soul. No dead soul, either, though the dead already knew.

I'm gonna do it this time. I have to tell her. She needs to know.

"Andy," she said, before he could broach the subject. She stretched an arm over his chest. "I'm sayin, what if we can make this right? Make it so she didn't have to die in vain."

He watched her fingers stroke the hairs around his left nipple, both glad that he'd prevented her from revealing his Terrible Secret and ashamed that he'd given up yet again.

"What do you mean?"

"Well, if we go to the expo, maybe we can stop whatever your ghost friends think is about to happen. If they could predict what happened to my mom, then maybe they're right about this, too."

He considered it a moment. The idea made him nervous. His chest rose and fell a little faster beneath her arm. "Okay," he said finally. "We'll go." After a moment, he added, "Which casino's it at?"

"The Palais Royale," Lamb said. "They hold it there every year."

LUCKY BREAK

THE OBITUARY OF "Psychic" Sonya Curtis was in the paper on Friday morning. After calling the local papers and news channels the previous day with no luck, and with no one from the LVMPD willing to talk to her, Sam spent several hours calling various psychics from the hotel phonebook in the hope of finding one who was no longer accepting new clients because said palmist, card reader, or tea-leaf prognosticator had killed themself.

The obituary listed Curtis's name and profession, and that she was survived by her daughter, Lamb. She found a listing for Sonya's Psychic Readings quickly on the internet. After picking up a coffee and croissant from the continental breakfast room, she checked out of the Royale and drove across town to the address.

The office was in a strip mall on the west side of town, housing a cheap electronics shop, a nail boutique, a crepe shoppe—Sam never understood the popularity of crepes, particularly when there were IHOPs and Cracker Barrels and Denny's in the dingy corners of every major city—and Sonya's Psychic Readings, nestled between a convenience store and a pawn shop, with what looked like apartments above. The door was crisscrossed with police tape, which meant they likely had yet to officially rule it a suicide, probably due to all the buzz on the news about the other cases.

Sam left her coffee and laptop in the rental car and approached the door. The beaded curtains had been pulled, making it impossible to see inside even with her face pressed up against the glass. She'd have to find some other way in.

She crossed to the convenience store, waited for a few people lined up to get their smokes and pay their "idiot tax"—Stan's pet phrase for buying lottery tickets—then she asked the friendly Middle Eastern proprietor if he knew anything about the psychic next door.

"Oh yes," he said, his accent very pronounced. "Quite a nice lady. Pays her rent on time, in cash. Bit weird, but quite nice."

"You own the mall then?"

"Yes. My wife and I, we bought the building in 2010. Stores may come and go, but Ms. Curtis has been here since before we bought. Always pays her rent on time. Quite a nice lady," he said again. "A terrible shame what became of her."

"It is," Sam said. "Were you the one to find her?"

"No, no. Her daughter lives upstairs, above the shop. The girl is very loud. She plays the drums in the early morning, but she is quite nice as well."

"Does her daughter work with her?"

The man nodded. "She runs the front of the store. Keeps the place nice and clean. I believe she also does the taxes. Very nice, but loud, as I say. "

"Could you tell me which apartment?"

Moments later Sam stood in the entryway and rang the buzzer for L. Curtis in 201. A male voice greeted her over the crackly speaker, sounding sleepy. It threw her off. She'd expected to hear Ms. Curtis herself.

"Hello?" he said.

"Hi there, I'm hoping to speak with Ms. Curtis. Is she at home?"

"Can I ask who this is?"

"Detective Sam Beadle," she said, stepping closer to the mic. "Seattle P.D."

He paused long enough for Sam to assume the man, whoever he was to Ms. Curtis, was attempting to assess the situation.

"What's this about?" he said finally.

"I'd just like to ask her a few questions regarding her mother's passing. Nothing serious."

"Well, she's out getting breakfast. If you leave your card…"

A little late for breakfast, Sam thought but didn't say. "I'd really rather speak to her in person," she told him. "This isn't an official investigation," she added, hoping to win some points by being honest. "I'm actually looking into several recent suicides in the Seattle area, where I'm located. I think there might be a connec—"

The door lock buzzed. She grabbed the handle and drew the open door quickly, before the man, whoever he was, could change his mind.

"Give me a minute to get dressed," he said.

Andy threw on a T-shirt and pants and answered the door at the first knock while Lamb's Sammy Davis Jr. record played "Mr. Bojangles" on her crummy speakers. The detective was a short, stocky woman with sad eyes and downturned lips, dressed in a blue work shirt with a dark blazer and pants, her long, sleek dark hair tied back in a low ponytail.

"I'm Andy. Lamb's… friend," he said, not sure what to call himself. It was far too early for *boyfriend*. "She's just picking up some breakfast."

"You mentioned that. Thank you for letting me up." The detective's sad eyes lingered over the posters, the drums. "How long have you known Ms. Curtis?"

He poured himself a glass of water from the tap. "Not long," he said. "Something to drink?"

"I'm fine."

Andy nodded and sipped the water casually, trying to appear calm. Cops made him nervous—an out-of-town cop, even more so. He was sure she'd try to connect him with Sonya's suicide somehow. A new man in the picture at the same time her mother kills herself in a suspicious manner was a classic setup for murder. It didn't help either that he had cottonmouth and mild paranoia from the bowl he'd smoked when Lamb left for the restaurant.

"You're from Seattle?"

"That's right."

"You came all this way because of Sonya?"

"Actually, I came for the convention. The LVPE. Did you know her mother?"

He flopped down on the couch, trying his best to look calm and act normal. "We met once," he said. "She did a reading for me. That's when I met Lamb."

Can she tell that I'm stoned?

"And when was that, exactly?"

Don't tell her yesterday.

"A couple weeks ago."

The detective nodded.

Can she tell I'm lying? Wait, did I just say that out loud?

"So, uh…" He swallowed hard. "What makes you think her suicide is connected with these others?"

"I guess you haven't been watching the news?"

"Not if I can help it."

"Well, if you had been you'd have heard Ms. Curtis isn't the first psychic to die in a manner made to look like suicide."

Andy choked on a sip of water. It took him a moment to recover. "You think she was murdered?" he said, with tears in his eyes.

"In a manner of speaking, yes."

"What does 'in a manner of speaking' mean?"

"I'm not sure about that part yet, actually. I'm just kind of…" She grinned. It gave her dimples, making her seem suddenly kinder, less sad. "I guess I'm following my gut at the moment." She nodded toward the record player. "Riffing. My father loved Sammy Davis Jr.," she said.

"Mine, too," Andy said, warming to her. "He loved anything to do with Vegas. Sammy, Sinatra, Siegfried & Roy. He always said Las Vegas was the apotheosis of America."

The door opened and Lamb stepped in with a bag full of Styrofoam boxes. She startled, then looked from Andy to the detective and back to Andy.

"Who's this?" she said.

Even before the detective finished introducing herself, Andy knew he was in for it. "She just wants to talk about your mom," he said. The apartment smelled like bacon and greasy fries. He could barely concentrate on anything else.

"Did you ever stop to think maybe I don't *wanna* talk about my mom?"

"I'm really sorry to intrude, Ms. Curtis—"

"Now is not a good time, okay? We were just about to have breakfast."

"I see that. If you'd just allow me a minute of your time—"

"Detective… Beetle? That right?"

"Beadle with a D."

"Well, Detective Beadle with a D, I've gone over and over what happened with the police already, and in all honesty, I don't want to talk about it anymore. So if you don't mind, I'd like you to go."

"Lamb," Andy said. "It's not what you think—"

"Don't you start," she said, clenching her jaw. She turned to the detective. "Please leave."

The sadness returned to her eyes. "I'm sorry to have bothered you both. I'll let you get back to it."

The detective scowled briefly before lumbering out. Lamb slammed and locked the door behind her.

"Are you *crazy*? Why would you let a *cop* in here?"

Andy was already taking the Styrofoam boxes out of the bag and laying them out on the counter. The home fries were calling his name. "What? She said she doesn't think it was suicide."

"Exactly. Which means she probably thinks it was murder and *you're* a suspect."

He licked ketchup off his fingers. "You think?"

"Can you stop eating for a second? Jeez. This is our first argument, and I'd like for you to take it seriously."

"Wait… this is an argument?"

"*Yeah*." She smacked his arm. "You jackass."

He laughed. "Honestly, I'm just glad she didn't notice how high I am."

"Don't know how she couldn't, it smells like the alley

behind a dispensary in here. You know that's what the incense is for, right?"

"Damn, didn't think of that."

As they laid out the food and tableware on the coffee table, Andy said, "She said there's been a bunch of suicides out west. Other psychics."

Lamb froze, holding a fork beside her plate. "There's others?"

Andy shrugged and sat. "That's what she said." He started scooping scrambled eggs onto his plate.

"And you're just gonna eat like nothing's wrong?"

"Honestly, I've got the munchies so bad I could eat even if the world was ending," he said, tucking in.

Lamb stood and hurried around the room, searching for something. "Who's to say it ain't?" she said, picking up the remote and aiming it at the TV. She flicked through the channels while Andy piled home fries and bacon beside the eggs. "*Oh my God!*" she gasped as he squeezed out a packet of ketchup on the potatoes.

"What?" he said, his mouth already full.

"Andy, this is *way* bigger than we thought."

She pointed at the screen. He grabbed a piece of bacon and ate it on his way to the TV. The news crawl said PATTERN EMERGING: COULD FIFTH PSYCHIC DEATH BE LINKED TO OTHERS?

"We gotta go to the Royale tomorrow," she said, staring in shock at the screen. "Whatever it was that killed my mom, it's gonna be shootin psychics in a barrel at that convention."

Andy scarfed down the last bit of bacon in his hand, though he didn't feel so hungry anymore.

Sitting in the silver Ford Focus parked outside Sonya's

Psychic Readings, Sam mulled over what she'd just learned from her impromptu visit with Ms. Curtis and her new beau.

The fact that this Andy fellow seemed eager to hear about her theory despite knowing nothing about the other suicides told her he'd likely suspected foul play himself. Sure, he may have entered Ms. Curtis's life at just about the same time her mother was murdered, which stood to reason he should be the most likely suspect in her death. But Sam had a good feeling about him. Even though he was obviously as high as a kite at nine a.m. on a weekday, he didn't strike her as someone capable of cold-blooded murder, even if the daughter had somehow put him up to it. And Ms. Curtis's evasiveness struck Sam not as guilt but genuine grief.

As the landlord had said, the two of them seemed "quite nice."

Sam picked up her cell phone. It looked like she'd need to book another room tonight, after all.

BETRAYAL

Duck Falls
November 2nd

BACK AT THE Temple the mood was dire. The heavy front doors groaned open and Thea Petralia entered alongside Bram Merritt, with some of the other protestors in tow.

"People, can I have your attention, please?"

The members gathered there, both ethereals and the living, fell silent. Thea didn't wait to continue as she strode up the aisle.

"We're in crisis mode," she told them. "As you may already know, the Ghost Brothers were attacked by some kind of… *presence* inside the park. As of this moment they are missing and presumably dead." She leaped onto the altar with a double-clomp of her boots to stand behind the pulpit. The speakers thumped as she tapped the microphone. "I spoke to one of the deputies at the scene who was also a first responder on the day of the Disaster. He told me any search and rescue missions would likely be put off until morning. We all remember what happened to some of the first wave of officers and firefighters who went in after what happened. They're unlikely to risk that loss again."

Murmurs of agreement rippled throughout the crowd.

"Now we're going to need to get ahead of this. We don't want people to turn against us. I'm thinking we should ramp up our extractions, offer free services to those in dire need. Many people are already frightened of ethereals who may be in their own homes and businesses. If we offer to liberate these ethereals, if we show these people the vast majority of them mean no harm, it should help us win over the hearts and minds of the public. We need people to know we're the good guys. That we won't be painted with the same brush as the rogue element we saw on TV tonight."

She gripped the pulpit, looking over her people with an almost religious fervor. "With that in mind, Bram has just sent out a statement on our social media accounts. They've already gotten over two hundred replies and nearly a thousand retweets. We'll sort through them all over the next couple of days, to determine authenticity and necessity. Then we'll start sending out extraction teams. This could be our shining hour, people," she said. "Thank you all for your strength, your determination and for sticking with us through this difficult time."

In the thunderous applause that followed, Ben turned to Le Mon, the two of them lingering in the balcony above the pews. "If we don't flush out Rex Garrote soon and deal with him, none of this stuff will matter."

Le Mon agreed with a solemn nod.

As Thea left the altar, Bram took her aside to speak in hushed voices.

"Ben, Thea wants to speak to you in her office."

One of the few living members who could converse with ethereals stood behind them—a bald woman who wore a headwrap of a different color each day. From her blank expression it was impossible to tell if Thea was upset with him or merely needed to talk. Le Mon gave him a wary look as Ben followed the woman down the stairs and the aisle to the church office. Once there, she rapped loudly on the door two times, gave him another indecipherable look, and left him there.

"Come in, Ben," Thea said from behind the door.

He passed through the door. Thea opened the top drawer of her desk and took out Taffy the unicorn. She set in front of her and looked at it as she spoke. "It's come to my attention you've been using my resistance group as a recruitment service."

Ben began to type. Thea closed the laptop before the program could begin speaking what he'd typed.

"I don't want to hear it," she said. "Whatever reason you have, it's not enough to violate my trust. I thought we were friends. More than friends—I thought we were *partners*."

"We *are* partners," he said. But Thea couldn't hear him and she kept speaking, his words futile.

"You just don't leave your partner in the dark with something this big. I understand it's important to you. This war you're so certain is coming—"

"It *is* coming, Thea."

"—but it's just not what our work is about," she said. "We are *liberating* and *empowering* ethereals here, Ben. We're *not* putting them at further risk."

"We're putting them further at risk by not preparing them!" Ben cried. Angry and frustrated, feeling unheard and completely powerless, he smacked the stuffed pink unicorn off the desk. It struck the far wall and landed feet-up on the floor.

Thea closed her eyes. She took a deep, meditative breath in and out through her nostrils. Listening to her pause and breathe a moment calmed him down. Feeling foolish, he picked up the unicorn, dusted it off and put it back on the desk in front of her.

"I understand you're upset," she said finally. "But you have to look at this from my perspective. You think Rex Garrote is still out there? I get that. I understand why you believe he might be dangerous. But if you want to amass an army to fight against a threat that may or may not exist, you do it elsewhere. I can't—*I won't*—have you compromising the work I've done to build GRP2 into what it is now."

"It wouldn't *be* what it is without me."

"I know what you're saying right now," she said. "And you're right, what we're doing here now is partly because of you and Le Mon. But I didn't *ask* you to be a part of this. You came to me. You said you wanted to help me. This war of yours is not helpful. It's not what we're about. The Temple is a place of peace and coexistence."

"Some of us disagree with that," he said. "Not just ethereals, either."

Even if Thea could, he doubted she would listen to reason. He knew her too well. He knew her mind was already made up. GRP2 was her life's work. She wouldn't turn her back on her principles over a hunch.

"You do not have my permission to pursue this under my roof," she told him. "If you truly feel you have to do this… you do it elsewhere, without my resources. Are we clear?"

She waited a moment for her words to sink in, then opened up the laptop. Ben looked at the speech-to-text window. The decision was obvious. They would have to go on without her.

As he reached for the keyboard a quick rap on the door startled him. Bram Merritt barged in without waiting for her reply. "We're a go at the shed—"

Thea held up a hand. "Give us a moment, Bram. Ben is here."

Bram's hard face brightened, though it seemed fake to Ben. "Oh. Hey, Ben." The man glanced in his general direction. "How are ya?"

Ben typed a friendly reply. Unsure if Bram was privy to her concerns or her ultimatum, he told Thea he would think about what she'd said. Then he returned to the balcony, where Le Mon waited for news.

"She knows," he said.

"Dammit."

"She said we can't keep recruiting here. If I want to keep doing it, I should leave."

"Well, we can't give up. Not now."

"You'll stick with me?"

Le Mon gave him an offended look. "Man, when that beaucoup ugly, horror-loving freak comes for us, you can bet your ass I'll be right by your side."

Ben smiled. He patted Le Mon's shoulder and the big man smiled back.

Ben saw the office door swing open down below. He watched Thea and Bram step out and head down the back hall together with looks of determination. It reminded him about what Bram had been in the middle of saying before Thea had interrupted him.

"Is there a shed here somewhere?"

Le Mon gave him a puzzled look. "A shed? No shed here, far as I know. How come?"

Ben shook his head. "No reason. I'm gonna go see how

Lilian is doing. She was planning to watch the Ghost Brothers show—she's probably freaking out right now."

Le Mon tapped his nose. "I'll give our people the 4-1-1. We'll parlay when you get back."

"Thanks. Back in a bit."

Ben winked out, reappearing in the back hall as Thea and Bram stepped out the back door, throwing a suspicious look behind them. In the darkened dirt lot on the edge of a small cemetery, Bram's white Econoline van was already rumbling, spewing exhaust into the night. Its headlights illuminated the bright white siding on the back of the church.

Ben followed along behind the van as they drove across town and eventually pulled up to the locked gates of a storage facility. He knew so little about Bram, and now he wondered why he hadn't thought to learn more about him earlier, hadn't questioned the man's relationship with Thea. Where had she met him? Why had they grown so close so quickly? He'd let his trust in her outweigh his instinct for self-preservation.

Bram got out of the driver's seat and unlocked the gate. He pulled the van through, got out again, locked the gates behind them and returned the key to the zipper pocket of his bomber jacket. He drove through a maze of storage units, parked in front of one, and turned off the engine.

For a moment there was only darkness as the headlights dimmed and went out. Bram and Thea got out of the van and met each other at the big orange door. Bram unlocked it and rolled it up. Once inside, he flicked on the unit's light. It was full of plastic tubs, stacked one on top of the other.

Ben hovered in the darkness between two storage units across from them, watching.

"How much were you able to get?" Thea asked.

Bram lifted one of the lids to peer inside. "Enough to do some serious damage."

Thea rose on the toes of her boots and looked inside. She whistled. "And you're sure we can get it all loaded and get out of there without being caught?"

"I've got one of the night watchmen on our payroll." Bram said. "He'll make sure his partner's all the way on the other side of the park when our guys show up to unload it. We should have it wired up and ready to blow by sundown Wednesday."

Ready to blow? Ben thought. *What the hell are they planning?*

Bram reached into his pocket and passed a flip phone to Thea. She looked it over.

"This won't be traceable?"

"It's a burner," he told her. "Just text it and boom— bye-bye, Recurrence Field."

Oh, God... They'll kill us all....

With everything he knew about Thea Petralia, the plan made perfect sense. He'd known she would never drop the idea of going into Ghostland, even after what happened tonight. She believed ethereals were entirely blameless on April 20th, victims of a computer virus that had used them to murder innocent people. The only thing preventing them from freedom was the very thing protecting the outside world from what lay within, the only thing keeping the Swarm and whatever ethereals remained from killing everyone in Duck Falls and beyond.

They were about to doom them all for her beliefs, for what she considered the Greater Good. Her altruism would be the end of every living and ethereal soul who refused to bend the knee and worship at Rex Garrote's feet.

"We'll need someone to pin it on," Thea was saying. "In case this goes south."

"Way ahead of you," Bram said.

Ben couldn't wait around to find out who Bram had in mind. He needed to warn the others. Everyone at the Temple needed to know their plans, even those not yet turned to his cause. He needed to tell Le Mon, to rally the others to stop Thea and Bram from doing this before it was too late for all of them.

Sundown Wednesday.

Bye-bye Recurrence Field.

Boom.

As he turned, ready to wink out back to Le Mon's side at the Temple, a woman dressed head to toe in black emerged from the darkness between the sheds. She wore a large headset over her eyes, and held up some sort of device wired to a heavy-looking case in her other hand.

Before Ben could blink the world around him began to ripple like the air above hot asphalt. He tried to pull away but whatever the woman in black had pointed at him seemed to be holding him in place like a tractor beam.

He tried to call for help—*Who would help me?*—but his voice vanished the moment it left his lips.

The rippling of the air around him grew so intense he could see individual molecules of multicolored steam or vapor rising from him. In the same moment he realized the substance wasn't rising *from* him but were *pieces of him*— that the thing in the woman's hand was tearing him apart bit by bit, quicker by the second—the world winked away, leaving nothing but a deep and soundless void.

CHASING GHOSTS PT. 2

Las Vegas
November 2nd

THE PALAIS ROYALE stood majestic and luxurious on a patch of what was once dry scrubland on the north side of East Tropicana, right across from the airport. Its gold-and-silver fountains had been modeled after the Neptune Fountain at the foot of the Palace of Versailles, though unlike the famous monument this replica constantly spewed white spray to the dulcet tones of Debussy and Ravel and other French composers. Andy had always felt the show was more extravagant than the Bellagio's, but because the Royale was a slight distance off the Strip it received much less attention.

He stood hand-in-hand with Lamb on the virtually empty sidewalk as cars zipped by on Tropicana and a tour helicopter thundered high above them, headed for the desert. The expo didn't start for another hour or so. Lamb had thought it was wise to get here early, and Andy still hadn't summoned up the courage to tell her about his own recent history with the place. When she'd asked what the big deal was with the Palais Royale last night, he'd told her the place was "bad luck," which wasn't even remotely true.

It had been extremely good luck for him over the years, until he'd ignored that final Nudge in favor of greed.

Lamb started toward it, and her hand slipped from his as Andy remained fixed in place. She turned back with a look of concern. "You comin, or what?"

"Yeah," he said. "I'm just nervous, that's all."

"I am too. I haven't been this nervous since I had to make a speech in the twelfth grade." She smiled, nodding back toward the casino. "Let's be nervous together, huh?"

"It's just," he started, unsure where to begin, what failing to admit to first. "What if we can't stop whatever's gonna happen in there? Or what if the ghosts were lying to us? What if going in there *causes* it?"

He didn't want to use his trump card, but if anything would convince her what they were about to do was wrong, he knew this would be it. "What if my ghosts really did kill your mom?" he said quietly.

Lamb shook her head, returning to where he stood on the sidewalk. "Uh-uh. I don't buy that. First of all, you ever been to Seattle?"

"No."

"You been to L.A.? San Diego?"

"The only time I left Vegas was on a trip to Hoover Dam in high school."

"Exactly. If it was just my mom it'd be different. But there's *four other suicides* this—" She shook her head in frustration. "—whatever the heck it is… is responsible for. If it was your ghosts, they'd all have happened right here, wouldn't they have?"

He couldn't disagree with her logic. Now the only thing keeping him from going in there was the Truth. If he told her now, where she could see his face in the sun, in bright detail, he would cry and Lamb would leave him.

You're just making another excuse, Andy. You gotta tell her, man.

"Lamb, if I go in there," he said, and swallowed hard, "those guys who were chasing me the other day? They'll get me. And they're not just gonna kick me out. I nearly killed a pit boss. *That's* why I was running. It was a total accident, Lamb, you gotta believe me. But they'll look at the security footage, and maybe they already have, and they'll start to notice how I always seem to win every time I go in there. Little amounts here and there, that's how you avoid getting caught. Couple hundred at one machine, couple hundred at the next. But I got greedy the other day. I hit the progressive for a few thousand bucks and instead of cashing in like I should have, I ignored the Nudge telling me to go, just like I did—"

He almost just revealed the Truth unintentionally. He swallowed again and covered his slip.

"—just like I did with your mom. I ignored it and the pit boss came after me and he almost ended up dead, Lamb. *Because of me.* He's in the hospital with a concussion, this guy. So if I go in there," he said, his voice rising to a frantic high pitch as he pointed in the direction of the Royale's lavish fountains. "If I go in there, they aren't gonna kick me out on my ass. They're gonna dig a hole out in the desert and put me in it. *That's* why I'm nervous, Lamb. This isn't just speech-day jitters. I could *lose my life* in there."

Bravo, he thought miserably. *A-plus speechifying, Andy, my man.*

"Aw, punkin," Lamb said, pooching out her lip and holding her arms open to hug him. He stepped into her embrace, and as she patted his back the shame poured over him, smothering the pain and guilt he'd felt over the death of his parents, dumping another shovelful of dirt on their pauper's graves.

They'd lost everything they had worked for in that fire, when the successful clothing store they'd run and their apartment above it had burned to the ground.

Shame had killed his parents. The only son of the respected Korean business owners was nothing but a lowly gambler. They'd been ashamed of him and he'd been too ashamed to face them, so he'd drowned the Nudges pushing him back toward home in cheap whiskey and had passed out drunk on the sofa watching cartoons on Adult Swim.

The following morning, he was told by the somber detective that their smoke detector had likely stopped working. They'd unplugged it and left it on the kitchen counter, where it had melted and fused with the tile.

They had likely gone peacefully, the detective said. Died of smoke inhalation in their sleep before the fire had ever reached them. It was cold comfort. His parents were dead and the store had burned to the foundation. Since they'd still owed on the mortgage, the bank took back the property, leaving him with nothing.

Andy felt the same Nudge toward the Palais Royale now, that invisible string tugging him forward. He knew he had to go in there, no matter what might happen if those goons caught him. If he could prevent even a single psychic from dying today… it might not allow him to fully forgive himself for letting his parents burn to death in his childhood home, but maybe he would find a small amount of redemption.

"Okay," he said, slipping on his dad's old black baseball cap with the South Korean Wyverns' stylized W logo. "I guess we'd better get this over with."

Lamb looked up at him with a grin and tucked a few stray hairs behind his ear. "Let's go get em, tiger," she said, and smacked him on the ass to get him moving.

Sam stepped into the Palais Royale's convention center, feeling as out of place among the faux opulence as she had when she'd stayed here the other day. At least most of the people today looked more like Vegas natives than rich tourists and high rollers. She felt like she fit in more with these people, aside from their tans.

She mingled in with the large crowd as they shuffled from table to table. Psychics read palms, Tarot and astrological charts. Vendors sold "precious" gemstones, healing crystals and love potions. A man bent spoons to the delight of a small audience. Empaths offered love and life advice. Healers used touching techniques, bells and various other sonic and olfactory methods to supposedly heal wounds both psychic and physical.

Sam passed a booth called The Psychic Tattoo, where a man drew permanent portraits of the dead on the skin of grieving loved ones, with the promise it would "help their spirits move on" to the next world. A woman in a long, flowing white robe communed with dead pets by looking at their photos. "Tubby says 'I love you, mummy," the Eastern European woman told her client, who promptly broke down in tears. A British man in a somber gray suit and bow tie claimed to be able to speak to living animals, and told the woman whose jittery parrot he held in his lap that her bird suffered from "post-traumatic stress due to an incident with an especially fierce chihuahua."

Sam stopped for a moment at a booth where an older bald man with a white soul-patch beard rubbed his hands together in concentric circles, the swish of skin barely audible above the noise of the crowd, before placing them on the back of a purple-haired girl lying face down on a massage table. "Oh, wow," the girl said. "It's like I feel it loosening up already. All of the tension—"

And then the girl began to weep.

Sam chuckled to herself as she moved on to the next booth, uncertain what she was looking for, only aware that this was where she needed to be. All of the signs had led her here. Whether she was meant to prevent the next suicide or bear witness to it, she had no idea. All she knew was that she'd come halfway across the country with nothing to show for it so far.

This had to be the place.

As she wandered the aisles, she considered the fact that she was pretty much buying into a similar sort of woo-woo thinking as the rest of the crowd. She wondered how many skeptics like her were among them. Probably not many. They all seemed to be fascinated with the goings-on in the booths. Many carried bags full of purchased items. Some were absently rubbing the free crystals they'd been given at the door. Sam's own crystals lay in the front right pocket of her cargo pants, jabbing into her thigh, about as useful as lint.

Then she spotted him.

She saw his face for an instant as he moved between a white-haired woman wearing a bank teller's visor and a sunburnt bald man with a fanny pack, just long enough to recognize him as Ms. Curtis's not-quite-boyfriend, Andy Something.

What's he doing here? she wondered.

She pushed through the crowd, eager to catch up and find out, certain now that she was right, and wondering if she hadn't been wrong about Andy Something, if he hadn't been involved in Psychic Sonya's death, after all.

This is it, she thought. She'd followed her gut all the way to Vegas and had finally found her luck.

Andy fidgeted as they stood in line for tickets. They'd taken the line closest the wall, blocked from view of the rest of the casino by two outer queues. Still, he worried about the surveillance cameras in the ceiling. With just the right angle they could get a computer scan on his face and all would be lost. He tilted his head or turned or pretended to need to tie his sneakers as they neared each one on their way into the convention center.

Security itself was surprisingly lax, considering how heavily conventions and concerts had beefed up security after the concert shooting. Andy suspected most of them were trolling the slots and tables, more concerned with potential theft than any possible physical danger.

"Doin all right?" Lamb asked, holding his gaze.

He nodded. "Yup."

But he wasn't doing all right at all. The slot machines were playing their sweet siren song, and he had the cashout voucher in his wallet, the one worth over six-thousand dollars. He hadn't called José back after he met up with Lamb, and he wasn't even sure if his friend was on shift. But just as every nerve screamed at him to get the hell out of this place before someone spotted him, a persistent voice in his head told him to step out of the line and stride calmly through the casino, walk right up to the closest cashier and slap the voucher down. Get his money. It was enough to last him two months, several more if he was lucky—and he *would* be lucky, if he played. The reels would fall perfectly into alignment—*Cherries, sevens and bars, oh my! The House always pays and may the odds forever be in your favor, Andy, my man*—and the machines would be looser than they had ever been before, paying out much bigger than he could ever imagine.

He'd never felt the urge this strongly and been able to ignore it, but as they moved closer to the entrance of the convention center and further from the chimes and music, he felt it slowly diminish. He chewed on a thumbnail, drumming the fingers of his free hand on his wallet, dodging cameras, lowering his eyes.

Fidget itch scratch fidget, I probably look like a meth addict.

That was the truth of it. At least before he could blame his obsession on the Nudges, pushing him toward the right machine, the perfect table. With the invisible string—*They're ghosts, Eomma's gwisin, you can say it now, Andy, why won't you just say it?*—with the ghosts currently tugging him in the opposite direction it was clear he had a genuine problem. He was a compulsive gambler. An addict. Even if he only played to win.

Lamb grabbed his tapping fingers and entwined them with hers. She smiled at him. "Keep it together, hon. We're almost at the finish line."

Three small groups later they stood at a desk draped with red sheets, bearing the Las Vegas Psychic Expo logo of an eye within a turban. Lamb paid cash for two adult tickets. She could have played a hand of poker or blackjack with that cash. She could have pulled the slots forty times, a hundred and sixty times on the quarter slots, four thousand times on the pennies.

The woman eyed him as she handed over the tickets and two free healing crystals in plastic envelopes. "Enjoy the expo," she said curtly. "Next customer, please."

They were inside. Andy breathed a sigh of relief, the

sound of the crowd within completely overtaking the bright, happy chimes of the casino. The ghosts nudged him forward. He fought one final urge to let go of Lamb's hand and go running back to the floor, find a loose machine and pull the lever. Scratch the itch.

"You made it," Lamb said, squeezing his hand.

"We made it," he said, forcing a smile. "Now what?"

"Now? I guess you just let the spirits guide you, and I'll follow along."

Let the spirits guide me, he thought. *Okay, that should be easy.* Only now that they were leading him toward danger instead of a potential payoff, it didn't feel easy at all.

What if I screw it up? What if I can't stop it from happening?

These were questions he should have been asking Lamb, who held on to his hand so tightly for courage he couldn't pull away even if he tried. It wasn't just his ghost friends who were counting on him now. Lamb was, too.

After everything she'd been through, he couldn't let her down.

The Nudge drew them down another aisle, where someone sold silver trinkets and "precious" gemstones, according to the signage, opposite a guy who looked like Mr. Clean with a white soul patch, doing "spiritual touch healings," whatever that was.

Andy wondered how much of this was real and how many were scammers, preying on the bereaved and the gullible. Lamb's mother had been the real deal. This guy reading the mind of a dour-looking miniature schnauzer had to be a fraud, though. This head-wrapped woman swinging a crystal in the eyes of a girl with purple—*indigo?*—hair sure looked the part, but was it cosplay or was she really able to regress her clients into so-called "past lives"?

Andy felt another Nudge, this time on his hand, which was going numb from Lamb squeezing it so hard. He turned to her. She nodded toward the intersecting aisle ahead of them.

A tall man in a black suit caught his eye, disappearing and reappearing within the moving sea of people like a shark's fin above the surf. He recognized the man immediately, with his slicked-back hair and sunglasses, and the coiled wire trailing down from his earpiece.

"Is that one of em?" Lamb whispered.

Andy nodded and turned on his heels, ignoring the Nudge in the opposite direction, leading Lamb back the way they'd come. They would take the next aisle. Let them lead him from there, like a spiritual GPS.

Recalculating route, he thought, and snorted. Lamb gave him a look of concern.

They slipped through the crowd and Andy just about walked into José Ortega, standing at the precious gemstone booth in his white dress shirt, black pants and red croupier vest, paying for a small velvet bag.

"Dude!" José said, his eyes wide in surprise. "Are you crazy? What are you doing in here?"

"Long story. What are *you* doing?" Andy asked, nodding at the velvet bag.

"Mi madre's big into crystals and shit." José tucked the bag into the pocket of his vest, looking slightly embarrassed. "Lay off, man, she's a very powerful bruja, only she can't get out of bed with her thrombosis. Hey, is this your lady?"

Lamb stuck out a hand, smiling and flicking back her hair. "Lamb," she said. "Nice to meet you."

José took her hand and kissed it. "The pleasure is all mine, mademoiselle," he said, affecting his famous faux French accent.

Lamb blushed. "Ain't he a charmer?"

"Yeah, he's a real catch," Andy said. "Listen, José, you got a second?"

"For you, cuz? Yeah, I got like ten more minutes on my break."

"Wait right here," Andy told Lamb. "If you see that guy again, whistle."

She frowned. "I can't whistle."

"Then clap." He smiled curtly and took José aside, pulling out his wallet. "I need you to cash this. Take ten percent off the top—"

"That's what? Sixty bucks? I could lose my job over this."

"Six-*hundred*," Andy said, handing him the creased and crumpled voucher. "But take a grand."

"You serious?"

"Do I look serious?"

"Honestly, bro? You look like you seen a ghost."

"Yes, I'm serious. A thousand dollars. Please, man."

José grinned, taking the voucher and slipping it into his vest pocket alongside the crystals. "Hell yeah, dude. Where can I find you?"

"I'm not sticking around here any longer than I have to. Come to my place tonight, okay? I'll smoke you up."

José raised a fist. Andy bumped it.

"Thanks, brother."

"Ze pleasure is, how you say, all mine, monsieur," José said, and laughed to himself as he disappeared into the crowd.

Clapping caught Andy's attention. He spun on his

heels, expecting to see Lamb clamoring for his attention. But she was still peering around on her tiptoes for the security goon. The applause came from a small stage where a man appeared to be bending spoons.

He returned to her side and took her hand. "Ready?"

"What was that about?"

"Nothing. I'll tell you later."

He led her down the next aisle, which seemed to be clear of security. They passed astrologists and palmists and a man wearing a jeweler's loupe, painting Chinese characters on a grain of rice he displayed in extreme close-up on a small television. The Nudges pulled Andy along more urgently the further they went, Andy in turn pulling Lamb behind him.

Whatever the ghosts wanted him to see or prevent, he was sure it would happen soon.

"Feels like my hair's standin on end," Lamb said.

Andy felt it too.

A loud squawk arose from the next aisle, and a colorful bird flew into the air above the booths to circle below the exposed pipes and fans along the ceiling.

"Is this it?" Lamb asked, her big eyes fearful.

"I think so," Andy said.

Sam watched as the pet psychic shot to his feet and the parrot took off from his shoulder with a squawk. He stood straight as an arrow, his eyes wide with terror.

The crowd around his booth startled. The owner of the parrot called its name, clapping madly to get it to come down from the ceiling. "Beatrix! Beatrix, come down this instant!"

Sam had already lost Andy in the crowd and now she elbowed back through the surge of people to the pet psychic's booth. The psychic grabbed a hand mirror from his table and studied his reflection a moment, his eyes widening into cartoonish depictions of fear. Then he brought his arm down with a robotic, forceful gesture, smashing the mirror against the table edge. The crowd gasped. He plucked a curved and jagged shard from the table and twisted it back and forth in his hand, peering down in terror without moving his head, his eyes mostly whites.

Sam ran for him.

She spotted a man in a black suit and sunglasses, a security guard closer than her to the booth. He had a taser out but he didn't look like he knew what to do with it. He said, "Sir, put down the glass."

"Tase him!" Sam shouted over the heads of the crowd, holding up her badge. It was a longshot, but she couldn't trust that tackling the psychic wouldn't cause the presence or entity or whatever it was to lash out at the guard or himself. "Do it now!"

The guard pulled the trigger and the electrodes shot out, hitting the psychic with a jolt of electricity. The psychic's body went even more rigid and hit the floor. His table tipped over, spilling business cards and signed posters.

The crowd between her and the booth cried out, stumbling out of the way as if someone had pushed them. A tableful of trinkets at the precious gemstones vendor two booths down went flying with a tinkling chorus of stones and semi-precious metals.

The pet psychic rose, tossed the shard of glass aside in horror, and began visibly weeping.

"You!" Sam called to the security guard. "Follow me!"

The guard chased her, weaving through the people

who'd come to gawk. "What the hell was that?" he asked.

"I don't know, but I don't think it's over. Good work with the taser."

The man nodded, loading another cartridge.

They pushed through into the intersecting aisle, where the crowd thinned as people herded toward the incident to see what was going on. The parrot squawked above their heads, its colorful wings flapping frantically.

"Beatrix, please!" its owner cried, circling below.

Sam spotted Andy and Lamb stepping out from the next aisle. Andy saw her and blinked comically. He turned to run in the other direction but Lamb held him steady.

"There!" the guard said, pointing.

A Mediterranean astrologist in a colorful headwrap screamed. She launched out of her seat and bent sharply at the waist, her upper body slamming down on her table. When she rose again two rivers of blood spilled from her nostrils, dripping on the scattered items.

Sam turned to the guard, who looked back at her, lowering his sunglasses, his glassy green eyes shaded by a thick black unibrow and a look of deep concern.

"Come on," she said, heading for the booth.

Andy heard the shouts and pulled Lamb along, following the Nudges into the intersecting aisle, toward the sound. He spotted the detective first. She saw him. Then he noticed she was with one of the black-suited goons from the other day, the one with the unibrow he'd safely avoided a few minutes earlier. The guard was armed with a taser.

Andy tried to head back into the aisle they'd just emerged from but the ghosts pulled him forward and Lamb wouldn't let him move.

"*This is it*, Andy." She nodded at him, holding his gaze.

"It's your time to shine."

She was right. Whatever the consequences, his *gwisin* had brought him here for a reason. He had to see this through.

The detective and security guard approached from the other side of the thinning crowd, weaving through people as Andy and Lamb reached the booth where the woman in a turban had just rose from the table, her nostrils streaming blood, her eyes wide with terror.

It was just like that video of the Rock N' Roll Psychic Lamb had made him watch yesterday. Something was *forcing* her to commit self-harm. Her upper body bent and her face slammed against the table a second time. She gasped as she rose once more, blood pouring from her mouth, several shattered teeth pattering on the blood-streaked star maps and birth charts strewn across the table.

"I can't look!" Lamb said, squeezing her eyes shut and turning away. After what had happened to her mother, Andy couldn't blame her.

Face to face with the presence his ghosts had brought him here to stand against, he suddenly realized he didn't have a clue what to do. He reached across the table and touched the astrologist. Two fingers on his right hand grazed the silky fabric of her multicolored robes at her elbow as he tried to take her hand.

The astrologist staggered back, as if pushed.

The detective and the guard reached the table as the woman began to stumble back and forth, pushed from one side and the other.

The guard locked eyes with Andy. His jaw clenched. "Motherfu—"

"Do it!" the detective barked at him.

The guard glanced at her, to the jittering astrologist,

bouncing back and forth between invisible forces like a pinball, then back to Andy. He raised the taser and discharged the electrodes.

They struck Andy in the shoulder. Every muscle went rigid like an excruciating charley horse spread throughout his entire body. Lamb called out his name as he dropped to the floor, his every nerve suffering an agony so overpowering he was only able to scream through gritted teeth.

Then Lamb was kneeling over him and his muscles went slack. He felt like he might shit himself for one awful, frightening moment, but the feeling passed as suddenly as it came.

Still circling the ceiling, the parrot squawked. A flurry of feathers burst from its body as if something had struck it, and its wings tucked under its belly. It dropped to the floor with an audible thud.

"Beatrix!" a woman cried. "My Beatrix!"

"Are you okay?" Lamb asked.

Andy couldn't make his limbs move. They felt like wet spaghetti. "Is *she* okay?"

Lamb looked up. A smile crossed her face and she nodded. "It's gone. Whatever it was, it's gone now."

Andy sighed and let his head fall back against the gritty carpet.

"What did you do that for?" the detective shouted at the unibrowed security guard. "You were supposed to tase *her*, not *him*."

The goon got down on one knee beside Andy, bending so his face was almost close enough to kiss him. "I *got* you, you motherfucker."

"Leave him alone!" Lamb said. "What'd you tase him for?"

The guard grabbed Andy by the hand and jerked him roughly to his feet. "Mr. Broadman wants to see you, Andy Park."

Andy staggered woozily as the security goon pushed him ahead. They passed the owner of the parrot who sat cross-legged on the floor, rocking back and forth as she cradled her bird and wept. The evil presence, whatever it was, must have shot right up to the ceiling and struck the bird as it fled.

The astrologist who'd been attacked had unwrapped her hair and was using the wrap to staunch the bleeding on her face. She was okay. Whatever he'd done had saved her life.

He smiled, tears streaming down his face.

"Let him go, you big ugly bastard!" Lamb cried desperately, grabbing the guard's arm. He shrugged it off and pushed Andy forward. His limbs still loose, Andy staggered along.

The detective approached them. Something metallic rattled as she dug a hand into the pocket of her cargo pants. When it came out, she was holding a pair of handcuffs. She stepped in front of them, barring their way, and slapped a cuff around Andy's right wrist, the hand the guard was holding.

"What the hell do you think you're doing?" the guard snapped.

"Andy Park, you're under arrest for the murder of Sonya Curtis," the detective said, jerking him roughly from the guard's grip and snapping the other cuff over his left wrist, behind his back. "Anything you say can and will be used against you in a court of law."

Sam led them right out the front door, the girl trailing

behind them, cursing her every step of the way. "This is unfair! Can't you see he saved that woman's life in there? He didn't kill my mom! Why don't you arrest that big mean bastard in there? Andy didn't hurt nobody!"

Andy himself said nothing, allowing Sam to push him along, stumbling every so often, which she assumed was probably an aftereffect of the tasing. She'd had to undergo a tasing herself during a training session and it hadn't been the most pleasant experience of her life. In fact, it had hurt like a bitch.

Once they were back out in the cool sunshine, Sam took the keys out of her pocket and unlocked the cuffs, one by one. She slipped them both back into her pocket as Andy rubbed his wrists.

"It's about goddamn time," Lamb said, squinting at her angrily.

"Seemed to me he could use a little help," Sam said. "I may be new to Vegas, but I doubt this Broadman guy just wanted to talk."

Andy nodded. "Thanks for that."

"No trouble. All I want in return is for the three of us to have a little chat. You're gonna tell me everything you know, and just how you were able to prevent that woman in there from smashing her own skull like a watermelon at a Gallagher show."

"So he's not under arrest?"

Sam shook her head. "I don't even have jurisdiction, even if I did think he was guilty." She nodded toward the lot. "Come on, my rental's this way. Now spill it."

As they walked, Andy and Lamb told her everything they'd been through in the past few days since her mother died. They told her about the séance and Andy's ghosts, how they'd been lead through the convention toward the victims, and how they'd just missed the first attack—at which point, Sam told them the guard had prevented it with his taser.

"Now what?" Andy said. "It's not like whatever it is will just stop killing because we figured it out."

"Maybe not," Sam said. "But we need to figure out what's happening here, and I think I know some people who might be able to help us."

"Who?" Lamb asked eagerly.

Sam squinted into the sun glaring off her windshield. "Have either of you heard of those activists, Ghosts Are People Too?"

INTERLUDE: PANDORA'S BOX

Hedgewood Facility
Nevada Desert—August 2014

THE PANDORA SYSTEM has more possibilities than you might imagine," Harrison told Garrote as the two of them ate Chinese food in the crowded cafeteria. The programmer was pleased with himself and eager to share his progress with his benefactor—but he'd suddenly found himself overwhelmed by the smattering of muted conversation and clattering utensils, the sound of the industrial dishwasher running in the kitchen, even the hum of the overhead lighting, making it difficult to decide where to begin.

He plucked a perfectly crisp spring roll off the mound of fried rice on his plate and dipped it leisurely into a dish of plum sauce. The muscle memory reminded him he was in full control. He'd made a significant breakthrough over the past several weeks while working in solitude, and he'd brought Garrote here to share it with him.

"First of all," he said, "it has its own 3D virtual space. Kind of like that PlayStation Home thing they had for a while back in 2010."

Garrote blinked at him, the fork in his left hand stuck into the saucy chow mein on his plate. He set the fork down. "Of course, I have no idea what that is, Harry, but please. Go on."

"Okay." Harrison took in a quick breath and spoke in a rush. "Have you ever heard of the Mind Palace concept of memory allocation and recall? This ancient Roman philosopher dude, Cicero, came up with it. It's called the 'method of loci,' which means *location* or *place* in Latin. It's not a physical place, but by creating an imaginary location in your mind and allocating whatever memories you want to recall to those places, the theory is that you could remember far more than by regular recall alone."

"Like mnemonics," Garrote said. The writer picked up his fork again, seeming to finally relax. He twisted noodles onto it, brought them to his mouth and chewed pleasurably.

"Exactly," Harrison said, watching the man eat. "Never Eat Shredded Wheat. Or Please Excuse My Dear Aunt Sally."

"Every Good Boy Deserves Fun," Garrote added with a grin, twirling more noodles around the fork.

"Right. So the Pandora uses virtual spaces to store the memories from your brain map."

"You haven't been traipsing around in my gray matter, have you, Harry?"

"Only as much as I had to. My own virtual space is a recreation of the Nebuchadnezzar."

"The Babylonian king?"

"Morpheus's hovership from *The Matrix*," Harrison said, giving Garrote a dumbfounded look as he squeezed more plum sauce onto his plate.

Garrote rolled his eyes. "Naturally. How silly of me."

"Anyways," Harrison said. He took a bite of the crunchy, juicy spring roll and chewed it while he spoke. The food tasted as delicious as it looked. "After your first experience with the Pandora, I created a virtual space specifically for you. I bet you'll never guess what it is."

Garrote thought for a moment. Then his lips curled upward in a smile. "You've recreated my home," he said. "Haven't you?"

Harrison pointed at him with the stub of his spring roll. "Bingo. I collated all the visual, spatial and textural data your glitch created, and overlaid it with technical blueprints of your house from the Ghostland project, to make what I hope is an exact replica of Garrote House."

The writer's smile widened. He clapped, then patted the programmer on the shoulder. "Harry, my boy, you are a true miracle worker."

Harrison smiled bashfully and plopped the rest of the spring roll into his mouth. "I thought you'd appreciate that. It'll act as your home or *hub* while you're inside the Pandora. You'll be able to interact with anything just like you usually would: eat, drink, read, even piss and shit if you want to, just to feel like normal. Of course, I had to do a bit of pirating and replication for the books in your library and the movies in your theater room. I hope you're all right with that. But I really think you're going to be comfortable there."

"And it will feel like I'm really there? Like it did last time?"

"The only difference is the view. Look out any of the windows and you'll see whatever your eyes—your *real* eyes—happen to be looking at. Otherwise, everything you experience should feel as real as right now."

Garrote twirled up another forkful of noodles and

brought it to his mouth. "Food will taste as good?" He savored the mouthful, chewing pleasurably.

"Everything you've eaten before, any flavor you can imagine, it'll taste exactly like it does in your memory. I've recreated your mindspace from the map of your brain, so anything you've ever experienced will feel as real as ever."

"You've tried it? You know this for sure?"

Harrison grinned. "How's the chow mein?"

Garrote looked down at his plate. He dropped the forkful of noodles and it clattered against the plate. He leaped out of his chair, peering around himself wildly. The other people in the cafeteria ate and continued their muted conversations as if nothing was wrong.

Then every single moving thing in the wide space flickered, resetting ever so slightly.

On a loop.

"This is the Pandora? We're in it now?"

"Bingo," Harrison said again.

Garrote touched the table and withdrew his finger as if it had burned him. "But I don't remember going in," he said.

"I cheated a little," Harrison told him, chuckling as he scooped up a fork full of rice. "Removed the last few minutes of memory prior to entry. I almost forgot we were in the system too, when we first got in."

Garrote grabbed him by the collar and yanked him out of his chair, off of his feet, knocking the fork out of his hand and his full plate of food off the table.

"*YOU PIPSQUEAK MOTHERFUCKER!*" he roared, pulling Harrison right over the table with strength only possible in the virtual world. Harrison's feet dangling off the edge of the table, he found himself face-to-face with a monster. Garrote's eyes had turned yellow and the pupils themselves had narrowed to rectangular slits. His jaws opened impossibly wide, like a lizard's mouth, revealing rows upon rows of needle-sharp teeth and a wet, black tongue that curled inward, dripping saliva, as if it longed to taste human meat.

"P-please!" Harrison cried in genuine terror. "I h-had to do it! I had p-prove it to you!"

Garrote's black tongue licked the sharp edges of his teeth and his mouth stretched wider as he drew Harrison's face closer to him. Harrison tried to calm his nerves, remembering that he was in control here. This was *his* mindspace, not Garrote's. The writer's dark imagination might have been able to generate this grotesque new avatar, but it didn't mean the man could harm him in any physical sense.

"Actually…" Harrison said, drawing out the word in his struggle to sound calm. "I'd be c-curious to see what would happen if a user died in the Pandora. It's a variable I never considered. We could really learn a lot from the g-glitch."

Mr. Garrote's goat eyes blinked. His teeth drew back into his gums and his mouth shrank into human size. The pupils regained their spherical shape, though they kept their disconcerting yellow-gold hue. He let Harrison drop to the table, and while the programmer returned to his chair, wiping rice and julienned carrots off his pants, the writer began to laugh.

"Harry, you truly are a card," he said, his voice and body returned to normal. "You didn't actually believe I'd *harm* you, did you?"

Actually, I know *you would,* Harrison thought.

"Of course not," he said aloud. "We're partners."

* * *

Harrison and Garrote had spent the following months working together closely, stretching the limits of the Pandora's system. Garrote required limitless control over his environment. He'd intended to be isolated within his mindspace for several months, which meant he'd also require a life-support system not only to keep his mind limber, but to prevent atrophy in his muscles. Harrison had memorized the blueprints for such a machine in one of the other Hedgewood projects while sneaking through the facility using the Pandora, and with Garrote's assistance he'd recreated the device in his own lab.

The best thing about working with Garrote was that the bigwigs left them pretty much alone. Harrison had only come into contact with Oliver Hedgewood a handful of times. The man hadn't seemed overly interested in what they'd been working on. His visits felt perfunctory, even an inconvenience. Harrison preferred it to when the younger brother, Christopher, had been in charge. Garrote and Christopher had butted heads a few times, and the outcome was always the same for Harrison: *Fix it, change it, get it done*.

Harrison didn't know much about Mr. Garrote's final plans for Ghostland, but the writer wanted to have full access to the completed park and all of its amenities from within his mindspace. The idea was to be a sort of holographic carnival barker. While guests and even its administrators would believe it was a preprogrammed AI—and in many instances it would be, as it wouldn't be possible for Garrote to be everywhere at once, even within the Pandora—Mr. Garrote wanted the ability to jump to any one of his holograms throughout the park at any given moment. Within his mindspace, his theater room would contain image feeds from each potential avatar.

Eventually, Garrote put in Harrison's name to Sara Jane Amblin to assist with the programming of the park system itself. By then they had already winded down work on the Pandora, anyhow. It was as good as it could get without an operational theme park to test it in. And while Harrison still believed it was the Great Work he'd been born to design, he had to admit he'd gotten a little bored of the project. Even spying on people had grown tedious, like he was just going through the motions. He'd needed something new to focus on, and Ms. Amblin's project provided it.

At first, he found Sara Jane Amblin to be a deeply curious, intelligent and thought-provoking woman. But he soon came to realize how much those characteristics made her a tyrant to work with. She'd never turned into a monster and threatened to bite off his head the way Mr. Garrote had, but she'd also never stroked his ego. He was never made to feel as though he was a partner in her work, more a peon. Another cog in the wheel.

Others on the team told him Sara Jane had been close friends with Christopher Hedgewood, the dead brother. She'd allegedly gone from warm and genuine to cold and controlling within the span of a weekend—the weekend she'd spent prepping Garrote House for travel, during which Christopher had apparently perished somewhere within the house.

Harrison, who'd never had friends other than his big brother Tom, let alone one who'd passed away, could only somewhat sympathize. Even so, it didn't make her any easier to work with.

By the time he'd started with them, the team had been stumped not only with how to affix the holographic avatars to their "dead energy" hosts, but also how to interpret signals from the dead energy itself. Harrison couldn't believe how far behind his own work Ms. Amblin's team was—though, granted, none of them had the advantage of the Pandora. Many of his advancements had come from pillaging the other projects for concepts, tech and actual data.

They'd been working with three pockets of dead energy, each corresponding to a specific "ghost," a term only used when Ms. Amblin wasn't within earshot. The lab was quite large, allowing each ghost to be contained within its own "recurrence field" chamber. Each device appeared to work like a Faraday cage turned inside out, capturing electromagnetic fields *within* the chambers rather than keeping them out.

Harrison had quickly learned what Ms. Amblin called "dead energy" wasn't quite the same as a standard electromagnetic field. Though they were both discernible using EMF meters, in some cases Ms. Amblin's ghosts appeared to be able to manipulate physical matter in a way a "normal" electromagnetic field couldn't. Dead energy seemed to have more in common with black holes, in that their central cores—whether that happened to be "gravity" or the "soul"—were so powerful that its consciousness, its memories and personality and tics, could not escape. The atoms that made a person who they were in life may have dispersed, but like a strand of DNA the things that made them who they were in life remained encoded *within the energy* itself. Harrison compared it to an aquarium whose ecosystem was held in a semi-constant state even though the tank itself had been shattered.

He'd seen the problem in their work quite easily: though consciousness remained within dead energy, it appeared to be scrambled. Like a computer's hard drive, it seemed that without the physical media to contain it—the brain, in this case—various elements of stored "data" existed in a scattered state within the dead energy. In essence, the consciousness itself had to be *defragmented*.

Harrison's solution was to create a deep learning algorithm which pinpointed similarities among the three test subjects and decoded them, like a cipher. Overlaying his own brain scan and eventually the scans of several volunteers from the lab, his algorithm was able to piece together a simulated consciousness for each entity that was about as close to the real thing as possible. And with the work of a small team of historians and digital artists, the first ghosts to ever be studied under laboratory conditions materialized before their eyes.

Gamma Entity was a young girl in Victorian dress, her blonde hair in ringlets, tucked under a bonnet. Her name was Bonnie McCrea. She'd apparently worked as a scavenger in a cotton mill in 1907, and had died collecting bits of loose cotton that had fallen under the spinning mule when it pulled her up by the hair and into the working machinery.

Beta Entity was a Civil War soldier, his intestines a thick soup that constantly spilled from his midsection. He'd defected from the Confederate Army, become a spy for the Union and was gutted by his own compatriots for his efforts against the Confederacy.

Alpha Entity made Harrison and the rest of the team nervous. The algorithm couldn't seem to piece together a single consciousness from the dark, swirling mass of dead energy, no matter how deeply the AI probed. It was as though Alpha was a mass of several pockets of dead energy coexisting within the same entity. This was what Ben and Lilian had called "the Swarm."

With Ms. Amblin's blessing, the digital artists chose to render Alpha as a thick black smoke, something like how Harrison imagined a nano cloud might look. Unlike the other two entities, which interacted with their limited environment and the people surrounding them, Alpha Entity roiled within its recurrence field chamber like a hurricane in a bottle, hurtling itself repeatedly against the reinforced glass as if to escape this prison it couldn't possibly comprehend.

Harrison and the other team members often noted how it seemed likely that Alpha would smash through the capsule and run amok within the compound if not for the recurrence field, killing anyone within reach. Harrison secretly suspected it would start its spree with Ms. Amblin, who seemed to delight in toying with it.

They had given it a simulacrum, a "face"—such as it was—and a hunger for revenge. Whatever Alpha was, it had no business being in a theme park admitting children, let alone adults.

When Harrison wasn't in his own lab, tweaking the Pandora to fully integrate with Ghostland's various subsystems, he often found himself the last in the Ghostland lab, coding well into the night. During these quiet moments he would try to ignore the presence of the Alpha, the constant motion in its enclosure like a lion on the savannah: the apex predator.

Late one night, while staring blankly at the entity as he worked over a difficult problem in his head, slurping electric-blue Gatorade through a curly straw, Ms. Amblin's voice startled him.

"It's captivating, isn't it?"

Harrison choked on his drink. He hadn't known anyone

was in the room with him, let alone Ms. Amblin. She must have come in while he'd been zoned out. When the fit of coughing subsided, he turned to her. She stood in the doorway, looking elegant in a pencil skirt and matching jacket. He often found it difficult to look her in the eye, as much because she was his superior as because of her attractiveness—even when she was dressed more appropriately for the lab, in her drab white lab coat.

"Huh?" he asked, feeling incredibly awkward and insignificant.

She came forward, the caps of her high heels clicking on the hard floor tiles. "Do you ever wonder about the nature of the soul?" she asked, her eyes on the Alpha as she approached it between the workstations. The entities in their chambers cast a cool blue glow over the room, shimmering on her dark skin like moonlight.

"The soul?"

She turned her gaze toward him, and Harrison looked away deferentially. "Is it the dead energy?" she asked. "Or is consciousness itself the soul, and the dead energy just another shell? A different housing?"

She looked up at Alpha again. This time Harrison followed her gaze. The dark mass rippled beyond her contorted reflection on the glass as she reached out to touch it. Her index finger paused barely an inch from the surface. The bulk of the Alpha immediately hurtled itself toward her, swarming close to where her manicured nail just about met the glass, as if it could sense her presence or possibly even see her finger. The entity had shaped itself into a point, making Harrison think of the meme of God creating Adam.

When she pulled her finger away the Alpha darted at the glass. For a brief moment he worried it would break, but the entity struck the enclosure and retreated without even causing a sound.

"I try not to think about that kind of stuff," Harrison said.

Ms. Amblin turned with a slight smile. "It's all just code to you, isn't it?"

"What is it to you?" he shot back, feeling defensive.

"It's *everything* to me," she said, her dark eyes beginning to dazzle. "It's this world's last enduring mystery."

"The soul?" he asked.

"The soul," she agreed with a nod. "Rex sends his regards, by the way."

Harrison felt a twinge of jealousy. He hadn't spoken with Garrote for weeks. Hadn't even seen him around the facility. "You were with Garrote?"

"I just came from dinner. We were discussing the final plans for our project." She looked up at Alpha again. "We'll be wrapping up here soon, I suspect. Shipping out." She turned back to him, her smile entirely gone. "Is it odd that I'll miss them?" she asked.

After the Ghostland project wrapped up, it was a year before the Hedgewood Foundation required his services again, during which time Harrison was furloughed with pay. He'd returned to his mother's house where his big brother, who'd lost his job and his wife and son within the span of six months, had also unhappily returned. Mom's house had become the Greely brothers' very own Recurrence Field, one Harrison hoped he would someday escape. He'd quickly realized he no longer felt any connection to these people he'd once called "family." Their systems no longer functioned with his own. Integration failure. Tech support required.

Though his salary helped pay down his mother's mortgage, he felt useless without the Pandora. It had become second nature to travel outside of himself, to wander the empty desert and streets at night. Being without it made him feel trapped. Confined within his weak, pathetic body. Even escape into video games brought little solace.

He'd found himself thinking a lot about Ms. Amblin, and the question she'd posed about the nature of the soul.

Could he exist entirely outside of his body? Could the human soul truly be condensed to a series of ones and zeroes? Or did the soul transcend beyond death, leaving only dead energy, complex tangles of leftover thoughts and memories—as separate from the soul as sugar to water?

After months of quiet desperation, filling seemingly endless days with *Call of Duty* and Top Ramen noodles, while trying hopelessly to ignore his brother's constant litany of self-deprecation and his mother's urges to "get out more, find someone nice to play with," he'd packed a bag and caught a flight back to Las Vegas. He'd taken a Lyft to the Hedgewood Facility in the middle of the desert, its single-story dome lighting the black of night like an alien spacecraft, the bulk of the facility spanning several hundred feet below the earth.

"I'm sorry, sir, your pass is no longer valid," the well-armed guard said at the gate, handing it back through the car window while the Lyft driver spoke in Arabic to his friend or family member on the phone.

"I just want to speak to Mr. Garrote," Harrison said, trying desperately not to whine. He leaned his head out the window. "Please, just let me speak to Mr. Garrote!"

The guard's jaw clenched. With a resigned sigh, he seemed to come to a decision. "Please stay inside the vehicle." He stepped away, speaking quietly into the walkie hanging from his uniform. A moment later a tinny voice responded and the guard returned to the car, holding the walkie toward him.

"Harrison?" the voice said. It wasn't Garrote, but he recognized the man's deep, booming voice even over the walkie.

"Y-yes, this is Harrison."

"Grand," the man on the walkie said. "This is Ollie Hedgewood. I understand you're eager to get back to work."

"Y-yes, of course. I'll do anything you need me to, Mr. Hedgewood."

"That's very good to hear," Hedgewood said. "How quickly can you get to Maryland?"

PART 3
SILENT PARTNERS

"A house is a living organism, Carruthers," the writer said to his critic. "It stretches. It breathes. It grumbles and groans. And this house, in particular… *this house must feed*."

Carruthers turned, but it was too late. The mud-streaked blade of the shovel came down upon his head and in an instant of skull-shattering agony his world went entirely black.

When he awakened, it was to the sound of the spade piercing the earth. The first load of soil landed upon his chest. He didn't feel it. He couldn't move. Couldn't breathe. Couldn't even groan.

It was only then that Edwin Carruthers realized he was already dead.

— Rex Garrote,
The House Feeds Again
(unpublished manuscript)

THE IN-BETWEEN

B EN AWOKE TO a repetitive beeping near his head. With his eyes open, the world was a white haze around him. He blinked until his surroundings came into focus.

He was lying in a hospital bed. To his left was a window, the swaying leaves of a large tree creating patterns of sunlight that streamed into the room. To his right, machines beeped and buzzed between himself and a pale curtain providing slight privacy from the next bed over. He was covered in a pale blue-green sheet from his neck to his feet. A TV on a swivel mount about six feet above the floor played some old black and white movie he vaguely recognized.

How did I get here?

The last thing he remembered was playing the new *Infinite Zombie* game with Lil over headset. Lil had seen something out her window and… everything after that was a blur. Something bad must have happened for him to have ended up in the hospital bed, but he couldn't for the life of him remember what.

He tried to sit up but his chest felt incredibly heavy, throbbing and itchy. He found the sheet tucked too tightly for him to raise his arms. His hands made dull little thuds on the underside of the fabric. He supposed it was to prevent him from scratching the wound. Whatever had happened to cause such intense pain would likely be prone to infection. Stitches splitting. Something like that.

An intense feeling of déjà vu suddenly struck him, though he wasn't sure what caused it. He'd never been in a hospital bed before, as far as he could recall. Maybe it was the movie. Three scientists watched over a brain in an aquarium. The main character's dialogue appeared in the captioning: A BRAIN WITHOUT A BODY—ALIVE!

Ben remembered it: an obscure movie from the '50s called *Donovan's Brain*. Dad had watched it every time it came on Turner Classic Movies.

Dad!

Ben stirred in the bed, certain something bad had happened to his father. Maybe Mom, too. He had a terrible feeling they were in danger or hurt, but the reason for it lingered just beyond his reach. The more he tried to remember, the more the pain radiated out from his chest, shooting through his limbs and up into his skull, making all but surface-level thought painful and disorienting.

BOTH LEGS COMPLETELY GONE, HIS CHEST IS CRUSHED, the captioning read.

Ben collapsed against the pillow with a strained gasp. Something was wrong and he couldn't do a thing about it stuck in this bed, whether he remembered it or not.

"Y'all right over there, lad?" a disembodied voice grunted. The man had an accent, Irish or Scottish. Ben couldn't quite tell which from the few words he'd spoken.

He made to reply and found he couldn't speak. He licked his dry lips, swallowed painfully and tried again. "I'm… fine," he croaked. It hurt to talk, like needles tearing at the back of his throat.

"Aye," the man said, chuckling. "Sounds as though."

Still unable to focus, Ben lay back and watched the movie. The scientists were removing Donovan's brain. Ben felt like someone had removed his brain, or at least scooped out a good portion of it, leaving him with wide gaps in his memory. He wished his mom and dad had been here when he woke up. Or Lil. Even a doctor would do—*someone* to tell him what had happened to him. Tell him he'd be okay.

THIS BRAIN CONTAINS ALL THE KNOWLEDGE AND EXPERIENCE OF WARREN DONOVAN'S ENTIRE LIFE, the main character said on the screen.

Time seemed to draw out. A nurse entered the room a minute or ten minutes later, he wasn't sure which. The room had no clock—at least on his side—and he couldn't tell if his watch was on his wrist. The movie didn't even have commercial breaks to gauge the passage of time.

"Well, hello, Nurse," the man in the other bed said, clearly flirting.

"Good morning, Mr. Cruikshank," the nurse replied cheerily. Her shadow fell on the fabric of the curtain as she reached the foot of the man's bed. She wore a cap, which seemed strangely archaic. Like something out of an old movie itself.

"How are you today?" she asked her patient.

"Well, seeing as I'm still crippled from my heid to my wee piggly-wigglies, I'd say I'm doing just about the same as last you asked. How 'bout you?"

"Oh, I suppose I can't complain. I'm just going to check your vitals."

"Pretty much SNAFU, I reckon. Situation Normal, All Fucked Up."

The nurse chuckled softly. Ben heard the blood

pressure cuff begin to *hiss-hiss-hiss* as she pumped the bulb, inflating the cuff with air.

"Am I supposed to feel that?"

"I'm afraid not. With the injuries you've sustained, you may not be able to feel anything from the neck down for some time. You may never feel anything again."

"Aye," he said sullenly.

"Of course, after you have the procedure it's possible you may return to normal. Feed yourself. Use the toilet. Bathe yourself."

"Then I wouldn't have your pleasant bedside manner to look forward to, would I?"

She chuckled again. The blood pressure cuff hissed as it deflated. "Situation Normal," she said cheerfully. "The doctor will be in to see you shortly."

"Thank ya, hen."

Ben waited for the nurse to step around the curtain to his side, but her shadow disappeared from the fabric and the door squeaked shut a moment later. He'd left it too late call out for her now.

How long are they just gonna leave me here?

"Excuse me," he said. The man in the other bed didn't answer. "Excuse me, sir?"

"Talkin to me, lad?"

"Yeah. Do you know when I got here?"

The man took a moment to answer. "Don't know, to be honest. Suppose I musta dozed off watching the film when you arrived."

Dozed off? It seemed unlikely. He would have been wheeled in on the bed or brought in on a stretcher and transferred to it. That amount of noise and commotion would have woken the dead.

Then again, the man—Cruikshank, the nurse had

called him—was apparently paralyzed from the neck down. He must have been in some sort of accident, and his doctor had probably dosed him up on painkillers.

Give me some of those, Ben thought. His chest was still throbbing from the last time he tried to move.

"My name's Ben," he told the man.

"Jeremy," the man said. "Jeremy Cruikshank."

"What happened to you?"

Again, the man took a moment to answer. "Can't say I recall. Last I remember, I was down the pub enjoying a pint with a couple o' mates after work. Woke up here, can't even summon a pinky to scratch my bollocks. Suppose something musta happened to me on the walk home. Accident or the like."

"That's weird."

"What's weird?"

"Well, if you got hit by a car or fell or whatever, don't you think you'd remember something like that?"

Another pause. "I reckon you're right. The doctor fella did happen to mention some shite about short-term memory loss but."

"But what?"

"But what, what?"

"Never mind," Ben said, supposing it was just a figure of speech. "I don't remember what happened to me, either. I was playing video games with my friend Lil—Lilian," he corrected himself. Hearing her full name spoken from his lips brought the memories flooding back and he tried to sit up again. The pain was enormous. He dropped back to the pillow with a groan.

"The house!" he cried.

"House? What house, lad?"

"Garrote House."

"Carrot? As in Bugs Bunny?"

"It came through town," Ben said, ignoring him. "*Floated* through town."

"A floating house," Cruikshank said. "You sure you weren't havin a nightmare, lad?"

"No, it really happened. Lil—Lilian—she told me to get my binoculars. She said I had to look out the window. And when I did, Garrote House was floating down Main Street. Only it wasn't really floating, it was on the back of this trailer. They were *carrying* it somewhere…"

He trailed off, trying to recall where they were taking it, certain he knew somehow. "Anyway, that doesn't matter. I was looking through the binoculars my parents got me for Christmas and I saw the house, it was the same one from *The House Feeds*, from the cover, and there was a man in the window. It was *him*. I *know* it was him."

"Know it was who, lad?" Cruikshank said after a moment.

"It was Rex Garrote. He's my… my favorite horror writer," he finished flatly. Something about the statement felt off, even though he had every single paperback Rex Garrote had ever published. He even owned the Blu-ray rerelease of the short-lived TV series, *Ghost World*. "It was him in the window," he said. "Only it *couldn't* have been him, because Rex Garrote's been dead since 1999."

Garrote had been standing in the window, watching him. It was impossible, but undeniable. He remembered trying to articulate this to Lil—*Lilian*, he corrected himself again—over the gaming headset, but something had prevented him from speaking. That was everything he could remember about what had happened before he woke in the hospital.

Like Cruikshank, the in-between was missing. It felt

like a mound of fresh dirt had been heaped over the missing memories and if he dug deep enough, he might find much more buried with it. But each time he tried to dig a little deeper a wave of pain washed over him and he ended up right where he started, standing at his bedroom window as Garrote House rolled through downtown Duck Falls.

Digging, he thought. *What does that mean? Why is that important?*

Lil would know—*Lilian*, he reminded himself a third time, and wondered why he was so adamant all of a sudden to call her by her full name when she'd always gone by Lil.

Is she okay? What if what happened to me happened to her, too? What if Rex Garrote did something to me somehow?

"Has…" he began. His throat was too dry to continue. He swallowed hard again. "Has a girl come in here to visit me?"

"A girl?"

"Yeah. She has, um… long, shiny black hair, usually it's in a ponytail…"

"Fancy her, do ya?"

Ben could hear the smile in the man's voice and felt a blush rising in his neck and cheeks. "Did she come in or not?"

"Nah, lad," Cruikshank said. "I didn't see a girl."

It didn't surprise Ben she hadn't come to visit. She didn't like hospitals. Still, he wished he could see her now. She would make him feel better. Crack a joke about his condition and get him laughing, rather than feeling sorry for himself, like he was now.

What happened to me? he wondered. *One minute I'm watching a house roll down Main Street and the next—I'm stuck in this place. Where's Mom and Dad? Where's the doctor? Why won't someone tell me why I'm here?*

"Did I lose you, lad?"

The man's voice pulled Ben from his wallowing. "Sorry. I was just thinking. It's kinda strange we both can't remember what happened to us, don't you think? Why we're here?"

"Now you mention it, it does seem a bit unco. Maybe they stick the amnesia patients together. Someone to help fit the missing pieces back into place with."

"That makes sense."

"Aye. Can you get out of bed, at least?"

"I can't move," Ben grunted, trying again to raise himself into a sitting position. He fell back against the pillow. "My chest… hurts too much."

"What about your hands? Is the gizmo on your side?"

"The what?"

"The remote. For the tellie."

"Oh, the clicker." Ben rolled his head to the side. The bedside table was empty. There didn't even appear to be a call button to press if he'd been able to sit up to reach for it. "I don't see it."

"Shite. Bloody film's been on a loop since I woke. If I've got to watch Mick prance around in the nude one more time, I'll bloody top myself."

"You'll what?"

"Top myself, lad. Commit suicide. Film's doing my nut in."

"Your *nut*?"

"Never you mind," Cruikshank said, a smile in his voice.

"My dad used to watch *Donovan's Brain* all the time," Ben said after a long moment of silence.

"*Donovan's Brain*?"

"On the TV."

"That would be Nicolas Roeg's *Performance*, 1970, starring the venerable Mick Jagger, he of the large lips and spastic hips."

Ben frowned. "I guess we both have TVs. They're playing *Donovan's Brain* on my side," he said, though the television appeared to be placed between them, facing the middle of the room.

"Could do with a change. This shite on mine, first X-rated film I ever specked. Snuck into the theater when I was a wee lad, no older than fourteen. Bastard thing turned out to be an art film."

"That's how old I am," Ben said, though once he'd said it, the statement felt untrue. Weirder still was the idea that the hospital would be playing an X-rated movie, or have access to the pay channels.

Maybe the guy's not all there, Ben thought. It wasn't the first time he'd considered it.

He turned to the window. It was dark. A large, bright moon shone through the tree, its bare branches creating long shadows on the wall.

Wasn't it just daytime? And leaves on the tree? Maybe I'm the one who's losing it.

He was starting to second guess himself. Everything about this place felt wrong. The nurse's cap, the movies, the man in the other bed he could hear but couldn't see, the amnesia, both of them being unable to move.

The beep of his heart monitor increased. He could feel the blood thumping in his neck, thudding dully in his ears.

"What is this place?" he said aloud, suddenly very afraid.

"Come again?"

"I don't think this is a proper hospital," he said. "Something really weird is happening here. Something bad."

"Never had morphine before, have ya, lad?"

Ben ignored the question, turning his head from side to side, peering around the room. The television, the window, the monitors and IV drip stand. And on the side table, his beaten-up library copy of *The House Feeds*.

Was that there before?

Cruikshank was still talking, "Are you experiencing any of the following symptoms: nausea, lightheadedness, dizziness, increased sweating or dry mouth?"

Ben snapped back to reality. He hadn't even seen the other bed's shadow against the curtain. For all he knew, there was no bed on the other side of the curtain at all. Cruikshank's voice could have been coming from a speaker, hidden somewhere on the opposite wall.

That doesn't make any sense, he told himself. *You really are losing it.*

"You know that feeling when put your shirt on backwards," he said, "and even though it looks the same you can tell it's not right? That's how I feel. Like my head's on backwards. Or the world is."

"Aye, that's the morphine but. Bastard drug. Heroin's made from morphine. Oxy and hydro, too. Dreadful shite."

"No," Ben said, suddenly angry, at Cruikshank for confusing him and at himself for not trusting his senses. "It's not a bad trip or something. I know what I'm seeing. It was a bright sunny day just a few minutes ago and now the moon's out. There's no leaves on the tree anymore. The season changed while we were lying here talking about movies." He stared at the Garrote book on the table. "And that book wasn't there. I know it wasn't there!"

Nearly a minute passed before Cruikshank replied, defeat in his tone. "I cannae see the window, lad. Maybe you passed out. You know, fell asleep."

"I… maybe," Ben said, feeling defeated himself. He didn't think he had fallen asleep, but it didn't seem like he'd be able to convince Cruikshank any differently, and he didn't have the strength to try. He needed to reserve what little energy and mental fortitude he had to find a way out of this place.

Wherever this was, he was sure it was no normal hospital.

The sound of the door opening pricked his ears. Hard-soled shoes clicked slowly into the room.

"You?" Cruikshank said, a razor of fear in his voice. A dark shadow like a stain spread over the curtain, long and broad-shouldered. "I've seen you before… *Who are you?*"

"Calm down, Mr. Cruikshank," said a man with a deep, resonant voice. "I'm not here for you."

The shadow flitted off the edge of the curtain and a very tall man stepped out from behind it. He had pale skin that almost washed away under the florescent lights against his baby-blue three-piece suit. He stopped at the foot of Ben's bed, blocking the television, and smiled down at him. The smile looked at once sad and vicious. Almost sickly.

"Come back here, you gobshite!" Cruikshank cried from behind the curtain, his voice risen to a frantic pitch. "I wannae know why I'm here! *Tell me why I'm here!*"

The tall man's smile grew sicklier and he gazed up at the ceiling tiles. "Do something about him, please."

Cruikshank's cries ceased immediately.

"Hello, Ben," the man with the sickly smile said.

Ben said nothing. He couldn't speak. His lungs felt like

empty sacks. Desiccated husks. No breath remained to allow words to pass through his throat.

"I understand you're feeling quite a bit of confusion at the moment. That's to be expected. This procedure has certain—" The point of the man's tongue came out to wet his thin, purplish lips as he considered his choice of words. "—side effects, let's say, one of which is a difficulty in processing sensory input. Your memory may appear fragmented. You may also lose the ability to speak." The strange smile broadened. "I assure you, it's all very normal for someone in your condition to feel confused, agitated, even frightened."

Ben found his voice. It was almost as though a switch had been flicked, allowing his vocal cords to suddenly function again. "What did you do to him?" he croaked.

The tall man gave him a disappointed glower. "He's perfectly fine, I assure you. He's just been given a mild… sedative, let's say."

Ben didn't believe the man, but his own predicament was more pressing. "You said my 'condition.' What's my condition?"

"That's unimportant, for the moment. You'll be told everything, in time. For now, let me assure you that you are very safe. You are being cared for. Our people are monitoring you around the clock, and will be checking in on you periodically."

A sudden wave of pain radiated out from his chest. "What's wrong with me?" he moaned, the desperation finally overwhelming him, causing tears to roll down his cheeks. "Why can't I move?"

"Ah, yes. Another unfortunate side effect, I'm afraid. The next time we meet, perhaps we can discuss making you a little more comfortable. Until then, let me be the first to welcome you to Hedgewood's state-of-the-art medical facility," the man with the awful smile said. He peered over his shoulder at the television. "Relax. Get cozy. And enjoy the rest of the movie."

The man stepped back behind the curtain, humming an indistinct song. His shadow followed him to the door.

The moment the door clicked shut, Ben thrust his fists against the sheet, thrashing his head back and forth despite the pain, trying to get his shoulders moving, to loosen the sheet and break free. It was no use. He was stuck here, imprisoned by a thin layer of mint-green fabric.

"You all right over there, lad?"

Cruikshank's voice startled him. He'd forgotten the man was there. "Who was that?" he asked. "Do you know him?"

"Who was who?"

"The man who was just here. The man in the blue suit? You said you knew him."

"I didn't see a man. The wee nurse hen stepped in a moment ago, but she's far too lovely to be mistaken for a fella."

"You didn't see—" Ben fell back against the pillow. He didn't have the energy to help the man remember, nor to convince him this place wasn't what it seemed.

"Is the gizmo on your side, lad?"

He didn't reply. Whatever had happened to the two of them, it wasn't amnesia. The fear Cruikshank had experienced when the man in the blue suit entered the room, the confusion, the questions. All gone. They'd deleted the man from Cruikshank's memory, as if he'd never entered the room at all.

As if he didn't exist.

Maybe that's how it starts, Ben thought. *Maybe that's*

what'll happen to me.

Whatever was going on here, he couldn't get out and could hardly think coherently. Until he could manage both, he didn't think he'd be leaving this "Hedgewood" place anytime soon.

LIFTED SPIRITS

LILIAN DIDN'T TALK to Blake for several days after their argument. Even though it hurt every time she passed him in the halls or the stairwell or the Quad and he'd cast his eyes downward, looking away, she'd never attempted to push him. If not speaking to the only boy she'd ever loved was the cost of saving his life, she would gladly pay it.

As for Ben, she hadn't seen him since that night at the cemetery. Usually he'd drop by every couple of days just to check in on her, even when they weren't on a mission. The fact that she hadn't seen him in almost a week was troubling. Several times she'd considered calling Thea Petralia or messaging her on the GRP2 boards, but the woman intimidated her. The less she had to deal with her, the better.

Classes over the following days felt more ponderous than normal. She found herself drifting off during her lectures multiple times, even when her instructors spoke about subjects that would normally hold her interest. Her mind would wander to the Woman in White, to their failure at Ghostland, to Garrote and the impending war— *When would he strike? Are these psychic suicides connected? Would there even be a warning? He could mobilize a million ghosts and hit everyone at once before anyone even knew they were there*—and she would suddenly realize she hadn't thought about Blake even once. She wondered what that said about her. What it said about *them*. What was she even doing sitting here thinking about why she wasn't thinking about Blake when the whole fucking world was about to end?

"Ugh!" she said aloud, slapping her textbook closed.

The students around her chuckled cautiously. Several rows below, the professor looked up from the lectern. "Something the matter, Ms. Roth?" she asked.

Lilian wasn't even aware Professor Angstrom knew her name. She fumbled for a lame excuse but came up empty. "What's the point?" she said, shrugging as she collected her things. "I mean really, what's the point?" she asked the students watching her with sly grins. Some stared at their desks, embarrassed by the outburst. A few agreed with shrugs and nods, muttered *Yeah*s and *Preach it*s.

The professor waited for her students to quiet down before replying. "What's the point *is* the point, Ms. Roth. Perseverance in the face of adversity and indifference. That's the *essence* of political discourse."

Lilian paused, her bookbag clutched at her chest. "But what *is* the point? Why even bother?"

The professor sighed. "Nevertheless, she persisted."

The class chuckled. Lilian fumed.

"Ms. Roth, while I do appreciate your philosophical query," Professor Angstrom said, "I believe this is a question best left for after the lecture." She nodded with finality and turned to the slide on the screen. "Now, if we could return for a moment to Kierkegaard…"

While the professor resumed her sermon, Lilian sidled down the row, bumping knees and textbooks until she reached the aisle. She left the class, stepped out into the bright morning sunshine, and walked across campus at a brisk pace. The days were getting cooler in Stanford, California, though nowhere near as cool as home. Blake had told her it rarely went below forty-five degrees, even in the winter. Duck Falls would likely get its first overnight snowfall soon, when the temperature often dropped below forty in the coming weeks. When she'd first arrived in California, Lilian thought she'd never tire of the sunshine and warmth. Here it was not even three months in and she already wished she could go back to Duck Falls, where the weather was unpredictable and life was simpler. Where her old friends had probably long forgotten about her. Where her life as a teenager had ended and her new life as an adult had yet to begin.

She ignored a lonely ethereal kicking a soccer ball across Manzanita Field and another studying quietly in the quad. She encountered one or two nearly every day now, and the few she'd tried to help hadn't seemed all that interested in her. They didn't appear to be suffering, so she hadn't pushed them. It was as though the university grounds were a safe space for them to while away their afterlives. She suspected it wouldn't remain this way once Rex Garrote returned.

Blake was out front of the dorm playing hacky sack with a couple of his friends when she arrived. He caught her eye for a moment and looked away, missing the bag. His friends laughed at the fumble. Embarrassed, he bent to pick it up from the grass. As he rose, he caught her eye again. This time she gave him a brief, awkward smile and entered the dorm.

She'd reached the second-floor landing when the door opened below. "Lilian, wait!" Blake called up. She paused with the toe of her sneaker on the next riser, caught between ignoring him and continuing up the stairs or waiting for him, not sure if he would try to apologize or just dig himself deeper.

He ran up the stairs, slightly out of breath when he met her. "Can we talk?"

"What about?"

He looked trapped, like he didn't want to have a frank conversation about their relationship in the stairwell. "Lilian, I'm sorry," he said finally.

The door to the second floor opened and two girls entered the stairwell. One of them Lilian recognized as the floor senior. Both gave a hungry look to Blake's bare, tanned arms, then a dismissive glance in Lilian's direction, before giggling to each other as they hurried down the stairs. Blake looked at the floor until the door closed behind them.

"I'm sorry," he said again. "I should have taken you seriously, and I'm sorry."

"Blake—" she started, uncertain what she meant to say, only wanting him to look at her again, instead of at the floor between his feet.

His chin titled toward her. His sad, puppy dog eyes and crooked smile so sweet and awkward it made her heart ache. "I know all this ghost stuff means a lot to you. It's just hard for me. I've always been a skeptic. When they started talking about ghosts, I wasn't sure what to believe. That's why I wanted to go on opening day. To Ghostland. But what happened there the other night—"

"You watched the rest of it?" she asked, eyeing him. She'd turned off the TV once she'd ended the call to her parents and had spent the rest of the night listening to music, wondering what the hell to do with her life. She'd only found out what happened the following day, when she overheard a couple of boys talking in the cafeteria about how the Ghost Brothers had "died on live TV" and "can you believe they *showed* it?"

She'd looked it up on her phone immediately, worried about the woman who'd gone with them, Elena Feliz. The news just said the Ghost Brothers and their crew were considered "missing." The authorities hadn't found any bodies yet.

"It's on YouTube," Blake said with a morose look. "I just can't get over it. And I know it's not even close to what must've happened to you that day, and that—" He shook his head, shaken up by it all. "I feel awful about what I said to you. About all of it. And I know that's no reason to forgive me, because it took seeing it with my own eyes to believe you, but I just want you to know that I'm okay with you seeing Ben—"

"Blake…"

"No, I'm serious. He was your *best friend*. It would have been one thing if it was just that but the fact that he's a ghost—I guess with me being weirdly jealous and my disbelief… I was an asshole to you, Lilian. And it wasn't fair. I'm sorry."

Lilian felt the tears coming. She held out her arms to him. Blake stepped up to her and let her embrace him. He hugged her back fiercely and she smiled through her tears.

Le Mon reached out again with his mind, searching for any sign of Ben. It was no use. Wherever he was, it couldn't have been within a thousand-mile radius. He hadn't felt the kid's presence since the night the Ghost Brothers died. At first, he was mildly concerned. A few days passed here and there while Ben explored the larger world and his own powers, or merely winked out to California to visit Lilian. But Le Mon could no longer pretend he wasn't deeply troubled. He couldn't get over the idea that something bad might have happened to him. The *what* was anyone's guess.

"Where the hell are you, Ben?" he muttered, hovering in the lotus position in the middle of a wheat field on the outskirts of Duck Falls, just far enough away to clear his head of the buzzing thoughts and feelings of a town full of the living and the dead.

Complete radio silence was as close to impossible as anything, particularly so close to Ghostland. There was always interference, mental "static" doubling up over the stations. He had to carefully attune his mind to find the exact consciousness he was looking for—and sometimes even then Le Mon found he'd come up with nothing. A whisper of thought would turn out to be a psychic transmission from the physical world. A misheard call for help would be nothing more than a snatch of dialogue from a particularly loud television.

Still, he should have picked up a trace of Ben by now. Wherever the kid had gotten himself to, it was far away from here.

Le Mon had always had an aptitude for scouting. As a boy it had led him to believe he might want to be a bounty hunter or a detective when he grew up. He'd imagined himself as a mix of Sydney Poitier's Detective Virgil Tibbs, a silently brooding Boba Fett (for all he knew, there was a black man under that helmet, since James Earl Jones's had played Darth Vader), and a dash of "bad mother" John Shaft. Though he'd been too young to watch the *Shaft* movies until much later, his older brother Clem had the posters on his side of the room, along with *Action*

Jackson and *Superfly*.

In the end, he'd turned out not much like any of his early heroes. Experience and circumstance had led him down a different path. Growing up in the Lafitte Projects in Tremé during the 1970s and early '80s, he'd seen too many friends and relatives lose their lives to drugs and violence. Teenage Le Mon—then known as either Lee or Leon, depending on who it was calling on him—had escaped into the fictional world of comic books, where evil and misdeeds received swift and often brutal punishment. His first taste of this exciting world was when he'd found a worn copy of *Green Lantern* #87 at the Lafitte Branch of the Jefferson Parish Library. The edition featured the first appearance of John Stewart bearing the magic lantern and ring—a character his creator had based on Sidney Poitier, Mister Tibbs himself.

Sitting in that cramped library nook devouring the vibrant pages of artwork and story, absorbing every frame, every nuance of expression and movement, every thought and dialogue bubble, the hours had passed by so quickly young Leon hadn't even noticed he'd missed dinner. Over the following days and weeks, he'd taught himself to draw by tracing the images from comics he'd found in BSI Comics and various bookstores, from *Black Panther* to *Falcon, Luke Cage* to *Blade*. He'd followed his favorite characters throughout various storylines in the Marvel and DC universes, scrounging up enough change each week to buy them, and would eventually create several characters of his own: most prominently The Fearing, a black superhero from New Orleans whose powers were the ability to become invisible at will, to travel anywhere within the blink of an eye, to see the evil within men's hearts and laugh in the face of fear. Of course, none of these powers would have been useful without incredible strength, but Le Mon had decided this would need to be honed through exercise and a balanced diet, which he'd thought would be a good lesson for kids.

His brother Clem had left home to join the Army in the following years, and Le Mon had been left to help his father get clean from an addiction to prescription painkillers alone, after an accident at work had left the man bedridden. Clem had sent money home monthly, and their father's disability checks covered the rest of the rent, but Le Mon had needed to get a job to pay for food on the table among other things. He hadn't put down the pen and paper completely during that time, but his comics became secondary. When it finally came time to choose a direction in life, becoming a social worker—a drug counselor in particular—had just seemed to fit. Comic books, especially his own creation, *The Fearing*, were missed but never forgotten.

As a late-bloomer among his friends—which he attributed to caring for his bedridden father, rather than his childish obsessions—Le Mon lost his virginity to a girl named Kizzy Smith in his first year of college. They'd married soon after graduation, shared several passionate years, and divorced a few years later. Kizzy had complained that he was never happy. Le Mon had felt happy enough in their marriage and in life and couldn't understand her complaint. It had seemed to him *she* was the unhappy one.

For almost a decade after the divorce he'd remained what his friends used to call a "playa" or "mack daddy," though in truth he'd never felt quite like either. He supposed women gravitated toward him because of his sensitivity, strength and intelligence, and because he genuinely liked to listen. He'd enjoyed their company for as long as they'd wanted it, though none had ever moved him quite like Kizzy had. During that time in his life, his father had passed away and Bush Sr. shipped Clem out to Kuwait. His brother had returned in a body bag.

A few months later, Shawna Gaines had swept across his scene and Le Mon's life found new meaning for just over a decade. Their love had burned brightly and ended too soon. He'd expected to live the rest of his life with her, but God or whoever was behind the driver's seat had different plans for them. Cancer took her life just a few days before Katrina tore through New Orleans, leaving so much death and devastation in its wake. He'd swapped one force of nature for another, and with the disaster effecting so much and so many he'd barely had time to grieve.

He'd lived another thirteen years in virtual solitude. But his personal loss and the injustices he saw every day following the disaster had given him a rejuvenated interest in his first love: comic books. He'd sold *The Fearing* to an indie comics distributor, with an initial eight-issue run, in which the titular character, John Fier, uncovers a corporate conspiracy in the wake of Katrina that left the people of New Orleans at the mercy of a faulty dam, and punishes those responsible with his newfound powers. The series was renewed for two more runs, in which The Fearing tackled first the mob and street crime, then a ring of child traffickers. But his fans' interest and his own began to wane. Le Mon had still felt the anger necessary to empathize with John Fier's brand of justice, but his passion for it was gone. The line was cancelled shortly after, and Le Mon returned to social work.

In the afterlife, he'd found the skills he acquired during his eighteen years in social work could be applied to death loops. What the living called "hauntings" could be treated like any addiction, just as addictions were often treated as illnesses by the medical community. Every one of the wounded ethereals he'd met over the past decade had been trapped in a mental prison of their own design, endlessly perpetuating the guilt, sadness and despair they'd carried with them when they passed. It was an obsession, a physical *need*, as much as any form of substance abuse. Le Mon discovered he found immense pleasure in helping others release their burdens. Helping them to let go and move on.

Several ethereals he'd helped over the past few years had referred to him as a "travel agent" or "concierge for the dead." Le Mon preferred to think of himself more as an ambassador to the ethereal world. Most newly awakened spirits shouldered heavy baggage. Not quite as heavy as his own had been in most cases, but pain—*emotional* pain in particular—was relative. He'd helped many people carry that weight until they were able to give it up on their own, though many had turned away from him, choosing to succumb to their "addiction," returning to the places and people they refused to leave behind.

Ben Laramie was the first ethereal Le Mon had met who'd seemed to be a cohesive consciousness from the get-go, emerging from the cocoon of death fully formed, almost as if he'd been *born* into the afterlife. As it turned out, he was different in another very important regard, as the first ghost to escape Rex Garrote's house of horrors.

Ben was Ghostland's Firstborn Son.

His only real issue appeared to be the lingering feelings he had for his high school best friend, Lilian, and the guilt with which he constantly struggled. The whole town and everyone at GRP2 had adopted him as a de facto hero, yet

Ben seemed to feel he was somehow responsible for what happened at Ghostland. As if he was the one who'd let all of those shellshocked ethereals out of their cages and personally sicced them on the living.

Though he'd entered his afterlife fully aware, the burden Ben carried was heavier than any Le Mon had encountered before. He'd arrived with the warning of a war between good and evil, the living and the dead. He'd spent the past two months helping Le Mon release fellow ethereals from their death loops, only to burden many of them with the knowledge of the impending apocalypse, the War to End All Wars. They could either join in the fight or punch their ticket for the Dark Rift.

And now the poor kid was gone.

The last time Le Mon had seen him was late Saturday night, after what went down at Ghostland and the post-protest meeting. Ben had told him about what Thea said, that they couldn't continue to recruit under her roof. He'd asked him about some kind of shed, told him he was going to check on Lilian, and left.

It was the shed Le Mon's thoughts kept circling back to—was that where Ben went? What was this shed? And where was it? No kind of shed he could think of would be fortified enough to hide him away from the physical and astral world the way he seemed to be.

When he'd brought his concerns to Thea, she'd told him not to worry. She hadn't seemed much concerned at all, assuring him Ben was likely just trying to "work things out" and "find himself." Le Mon thought she'd seemed distracted. Even during their evening meetings, she'd lost her train of thought mid-speech several times and Bram had leaned over and whispered in her ear. That hardass partner of hers was always right at her side, ready with a whispered word or a nod of encouragement. He was like her hype man, the Flavor Flav to her Chuck D, only he rarely said a word aloud.

Rasputin to her Emperor Romanov might be more like it, Le Mon thought now, hovering in the whispering wheat.

He didn't trust Bram. Ben hadn't either. Something about him was shady. For one thing, where the hell had he come from? And where had Bram been when Le Mon and Ben had helped Thea grow GRP2 from a ragtag bunch of burnouts, hippies and hipsters into a nationwide network of ethereals and the living, using their individual talents to free their brothers and sisters and educate the world?

It seemed like nobody knew. Maybe not even Thea herself. And worse, no one seemed to care.

The days following the Ghostland broadcast had been difficult at the Temple, so Le Mon supposed he could excuse them a little apathy. It felt like everyone was beating themselves up over things beyond their control. What they needed was a win, now more than ever. As he lowered himself from the lotus position into the sweet golden straw in the middle of the field, Le Mon thought he had just the thing.

He approached Thea again that evening, a few hours before the meeting. "Any word from Ben?" she asked, after he made his presence known.

As usual, she'd taken the stuffed animal out of her top drawer and set it on the desk. Le Mon suspected there was some deeper meaning to the affectation, but he'd never bothered to ask. Thea Petralia was the biggest ally to their cause and if she'd needed to pretend like she was talking to a stuffed pink unicorn to make their exchanges palatable—well, that was her deal.

He typed slowly, searching for each key and pecking

them out one by one. He'd never liked computers, even in college when they were really just starting to become pervasive. He couldn't quite comprehend the reliance on them. Sure, it was nice to be able to find the answer to just about anything with the click of a few keys, but it couldn't equal the satisfaction of looking something up in a library or an encyclopedia. And for all the good that computers had helped humanity achieve there was a lot of bad to answer for: besides Ghostland, there were the Nazi punch cards, the negative effect of social media on empathy, governments broadening the ability to spy on their citizens, gene editing, the dark web. The list was practically endless.

Still, he had to admit it, as slow as his typing might be it was better than having to use a Ouija board. With all the skills he'd acquired in the afterlife, penmanship wasn't one of them. The words always looked more like squiggles and scratches, completely illegible. Even when he was still alive, he'd never been much of a letterer.

He typed out the last word, then slowly dragged the mouse-clicker thing to Speak. The bougie British voice spoke the words he'd typed: "*I've put out some feelers but he's style not responding—*"

"Shit," Le Mon said. He'd missed the second L in "still," and the robot had mispronounced it.

"*—I'm going to keep trying though. In the meantime, I was thinking we need to lift spirits up around here so to speak ha ha. I have an idea for that, if you have a minute.*"

Thea nodded, though she ran a hand through her loose hair, seemingly stressed. "I'm listening."

"Here we go," Le Mon said to himself, and started pecking at the keys again. After about a minute he clicked Speak and the voice read his proposition, with no misspellings to stumble over this time.

Thea began smiling halfway through. When the proper BBC-English voice finished speaking, she said, "I think that's a wonderful idea, Leon. Thank you."

Smiling himself, Le Mon typed again. A moment later, the voice said, "*You're welcome, Thea.*"

"We'll go tomorrow," she said.

Le Mon typed. "*We?*"

"I'd like for Bram and me to tag along with the two of you, if you don't mind. Not to chaperone. Just to see how you do in the field together, without Ben."

"*Of course,*" the British voice said, while Le Mon chewed on his suspicions. "*It's your carnival.*"

"Excellent. Bram and I will fly out there first thing tomorrow morning. Why don't you go on ahead and make sure Lilian is up for joining us?"

"*Will do,*" the computer voice said.

Le Mon was just about to leave when he remembered the shed. He typed up his question and press Speak. A brief scowl flashed on Thea's face when the computer said the word "shed," but he couldn't be sure if it was because she was confused or something else.

"A shed?" she asked. "At the Temple? Not that I know of."

"*Forget I asked,*" the voice said for him.

"All right then," she said, tucking the plushie into the desk. "Thanks for coming in."

Le Mon considered asking her about the unicorn, but the thought of typing more made him reconsider it. Now wasn't the time, anyhow. There were more important things to worry about and he suspected she'd evade the question.

Half an hour later, he stood out front of Lilian's

dormitory. It was already dark in Duck Falls but the sun was still bright in Stanford, California. He had an ulterior motive for coming out here. He realized now he should have ventured out a couple of days ago when he first noticed he couldn't sense Ben's presence, rather than letting himself get wound up about it.

Ben had probably come out to see Lilian the night he disappeared, as he'd said he would. She might have been the last person to see him. But he'd still needed to tread lightly. If she hadn't seen Ben, if she didn't know where he was, she was likely to be upset by the news.

"Here we go," he said again.

In a blink he was on the third floor, standing in front of Lilian's door. "Lilian," he called out.

He waited. From behind the door, he heard muffled voices. Bare footsteps padded across the floor. Then the small bell's jingle. Meaning she was with someone and didn't want to be interrupted. Probably messing around with that kid with the yuppy name.

"Lilian, it's Le Mon. It's urgent," he added. She needed to know he wasn't bothering her just for the sake of it.

Her muffled voice came from behind the door: "I'll be right back, I'm just gonna go pee."

The door opened a moment later. Lilian stepped out briskly and closed the door, wearing nothing but socks and a red men's Stanford jersey that reached down to her mid-thighs. She was skinny as a baby deer but she had a mean look that made Le Mon's smile quickly fade. Her annoyance softened when she saw his face. "What's wrong, Le Mon?"

No use beating around the bush, he thought. "Lilian, Ben is gone."

"*What?*" She glanced back at the door, worried she'd

spoken too loudly, and crossed to the stairwell door. He followed her through. "What do you mean, Ben is gone?" she asked once the door was closed behind them, her voice echoing hollowly in the stairwell.

"I can't feel him out there and I'm worried…" It hurt to say it, but he had to. He'd become fast friends with Ben, and the thought of having to stand against Garrote without him was genuinely troubling. "I don't know, maybe he's gone off on some sort of spiritual quest, a walkabout or something. I never just felt *nothin* like this. I'm worried he got himself into beaucoup trouble. Lilian… I'm worried maybe he's gone to the Dark Rift."

"*No*," Lilian said. She tugged at the hem of the jersey as she paced in a tight circle on the landing. "No, he has to be out there somewhere. Why would he go to the Dark Rift? *How?*"

"He was askin about it again on Saturday. After the show. Said he was gon' come out here to see you, and that was the last I heard from him."

Her brow creased. "He never came here."

"That's what I figured. That's why I think he musta got himself into trouble somehow. Whatever happened, this is bad gris-gris."

"You don't think…?" She stopped herself, placing a hand over her heart.

"Our mutual friend got to him? Nah, I don't think it's that. One of us would have sensed it, if Garrote came back." He scowled. "But I suppose there is a slim chance."

"What are we gonna do, Le Mon? We can't go up against him without Ben."

"We can," he said, though he wasn't sure he believed it. "There's less of us than we'll need but we've been trainin. We'll fight to the bitter end. Whatever it takes. First things first, you and I need to do somethin for Thea. An act of good faith. Somethin to boost morale."

"What?"

"You and me, we're gon' drag that Woman in White out of her death loop—kickin and screamin, if we have to. And we're gon' use all the good will that earns us with Thea and her people to gather up as many souls as we can. We're gon' find Ben and we're gon' get him back, Lilian. Wherever the hell he is."

FRAGMENTED

B EN WOKE AGAIN to the sound of his heart monitor beeping. He had no clue what time it was, what day it was, what season. Aside from his limited view through the window, he was entirely out of touch with the outside. His entire world was this hospital room, even then only one side of it. For all he knew everything beyond the window, the walls and the curtain didn't exist.

"You awake, lad?"

"Yeah," Ben croaked. His throat was dry again. He couldn't remember the last time he'd had a drink of water. He couldn't remember the last time he'd eaten or gone to the bathroom. He couldn't remember dreaming either, but he definitely felt as though he'd been asleep since the man with the terrible smile had left the room.

"Is the gizmo on your side?"

"You already asked me that."

After a pregnant pause, Cruikshank said, "I did?"

"Yeah. You said if you had to watch Mick Jagger jiggle his hips one more time you'd 'top yourself.'"

The man in the other bed laughed. "Aye, musta done then. Spoken like a true Scotsman, by the way. Good on ya, lad."

Ben groaned. He'd grown weary of his roommate's

cluelessness. Maybe he could do something about it. Put the man to work. "Jeremy, can you see the door on your side? Can you see into the hall?"

"Why?"

"Because we have to find a way to get out of here."

"Leave? In five and twenty, the lovely nurse Miss Danica shall return to provide me with the warmest, soppiest sponge bath I've ever had. Why would I leave when Heaven awaits?"

Ben groaned. Even if they were both able-bodied, he didn't think he could convince Cruikshank to help him escape. And what would be the point? At least he wasn't in pain anymore. He wasn't hungry or uncomfortable. All of that seemed to have passed some time ago. In the in-between.

Just let it go. Try to relax. Nobody likes being in the hospital. Recovery is always tough.

He'd almost convinced himself. Then he remembered the tall man in the pale-blue suit whose twisted smile made him want to be as far away as possible when the man returned.

"This place," he said to Cruikshank, "it isn't what you think it is. I'm dead serious." He flinched. The phrase *dead serious* struck him as important, though he couldn't place why. "Have you ever heard of something called Hedgewood?"

"Not that I reckon. Should I have?"

"I don't know. Something about it seems familiar. It seems—" *Dead serious*, he thought. "—bad," he finished aloud.

"Sounds like a wee cottage on the seaside to me, lad. Besides, I cannae move from the neck down. And in case you've forgotten, your sheet is pulled too tight."

"How did you remember that?"

"What d'ya mean?"

"You couldn't remember when you asked about the remote the first time, why would you remember that?"

"I dunno. I suppose I feel… sort of discombobulated, if that makes any sense. Fragmented. I remember bits and bobs. But I still haven't got a scooby how I got here or how long I've been here."

"Doesn't that seem strange to you?"

"Aye, surely. We're in hospital but. It's the morphine. Dreadful shite."

"What if it's not the morphine? What if…" The fuzz in his brain lifted for a moment. "I dunno… what if we're being *experimented* on?"

"Experimented?" Ben heard the humor in the man's voice. "Well then, if the experiment is to see how many times ol' Jeremy Cruikshank can climax using nothing but a damp sponge, consider me a diminutive rodent from Guinea."

Cruikshank laughed at his joke and Ben sighed. It was no use trying to convince him. The man was too far gone. Apparently, all he needed to sell himself to medical science or whatever torture Hedgewood had in store for them was the possibility of an unintended handjob. There had to be some other way to get out of here without him.

Ben turned to the window. The end of a bare branch was scratching against the glass. It was day out again, an impossibly clear blue sky shining through the dead branches. He tried raising his arms. Once again, his hands thumped feebly against the sheet.

The door opened. "Well, hello, Nurse," Cruikshank said saucily. Her shadow fell over the curtain as her heels clicked briskly into the room. She rolled a large object into the room, then approached with something smaller held in both hands.

"Wait—what are you—?" Cruikshank gasped. "*Hang on, I—*"

Hard-soled footsteps entered the room. Cruikshank fell instantly silent as the tall man's shadow quickly approached the nurse. "Is he stable, Danica?" the tall man said.

"He is."

"Excellent. Please ready the machine to administer at two-point-one hertz."

"Sir, that's far lower than he's ever—"

"*Do it,*" the tall man hissed.

The curtain drew open with a screech of plastic rings against metal. The man in the pale blue suit gripped its frilled edge in one large hand and grimaced down at Ben. The nurse stood on the opposite side of the bed, reaching for a sleek-looking machine with various dials and a digital readout. There was something familiar about her dark hair pulled back from her soap-white forehead, making her already severe features even more extreme.

On the bed, a middle-aged man with a few day's growth of ginger stubble and wavy auburn hair lay with the mint-green sheet pulled up to his neck. A large pair of muffled headphones rested over Jeremy Cruikshank's ears. His brown eyes darted wildly from one thing to the next. When they finally settled on Ben, the fear softened to a look of sympathy.

"I want you to watch this closely, Ben," the man with the sickly smile said. "According to NASA, the human eye has a resonant frequency of eighteen hertz. Those same tests showed that infrasound in the range of seventeen to nineteen hertz can cause hallucinations. A researcher named Vic Tandy believed sounds in this range—*infrasound*—may in fact be the cause of many ghost sightings." The sickly smile spread across his face. "Though of course, you and I know that to be false. Don't we, Ben?"

"I don't know what you're—"

"Then allow me to explain," the man interjected. "You see, it's our contention that infrasound doesn't cause people to *hallucinate* ghosts, but rather causes ghosts to *materialize* within that range of sound, to some extent, thus rendering them visible to the human eye."

"What does that have to do with—"

"You? Everything. You see, Ben, *you* are a ghost. An *ethereal being*, I believe you call each other."

Ben felt the world literally drop out from beneath him, and he gripped the fabric clinging to the mattress to maintain his hold on sanity, reality—or whatever this was he was currently experiencing. His head shook seemingly of its own volition. It was as close as he'd come to an out of body experience, though he could still feel the prickle of tears in his eyes, a thickness in the back of his throat. It seemed like these sensations belonged to someone else, or to a body that no longer belonged to him.

I'm not dead, he told himself. *That's not possible.*

"I assure you, you very much are," the man said, as if reading his mind. "Another fascinating thing we've learned about frequencies is that infrasound *below* a certain level can cause an extreme amount of pain to your kind. What you're about to see might be disturbing, but I urge you to keep your eyes open." The man behind the curtain glanced up at the ceiling tiles, smiling again. "Or perhaps we should keep them open for you?" He nodded toward the nurse. "Danica, if you will."

The nurse twisted the dial and Cruikshank began seizing beneath the sheet. His eyes and jaw clenched shut as he began to thrash, screaming through his teeth, tears streaming down his temples as his head swung back and forth against the pillow.

Ben tried not to look but his eyes refused to close. He tried to turn his head and found he couldn't move at all. His face was aimed at the other bed, and his gaze locked on the horror of Cruikshank's torture.

And suddenly the man in the bed began to fade. The headphones remained solid on Cruikshank's almost fully transparent head as the agony still tore through him, his translucent head jerking, his arms and legs, paralyzed until just moments ago, kicking futilely below the sheet.

A rancid, powerful stench worse than anything Ben had smelled before in his life caused his eyes to water. Like raw sewage and burnt hair, scorched rubber and diesel fuel all mixed into one repulsive, pungent odor. As Cruikshank faded away to almost nothing, Ben felt the urge to gag.

Just when he thought he couldn't stand it anymore, the man with the sickly smile said, "That's enough for now, Danica."

The nurse returned the large black dial to the off position and Cruikshank's body instantly regained its solidity, twitching from the infrasound until he became still. His eyes, wide and glassy, stared catatonically at the ceiling. A runner of white froth spilled down his cheek from the corner of his lips.

The nurse removed the headphones. She placed them on the cart beside the sleek machine and rolled it out of the room. The tall man sat on the edge of Cruikshank's bed, gripping the lowered safety rail. He locked eyes with Ben, and Ben still couldn't blink, couldn't turn his eyes nor move his head.

"Now," the tall man said, once the nurse had left the room, "tell me what you know about Rex Garrote."

"I—" Ben swallowed, the phantom stench still prickling his nostrils, lingering in his olfactory memory. "What did you do to Jeremy? Is he okay?"

"Tell me," the man repeated, "what you know about Garrote."

The look in the tall man's eyes told Ben he'd better answer the question, and fast. "He's a horror writer," he said. "His first novel was published in 1977. He was a Vietnam veteran and a high school English teacher—"

"We *know* about his biography. Tell me what *you* know about him."

"What… what do you mean?"

"When did you first meet? Was it at Ghostland, or before?"

"*Ghostland*….? What do you mean *at* Ghostland? I read about it in an interview once, I think—but that was from the Eighties." The confusion returned, the feeling of his mind being in fragments. The discombobulation. The backwards shirt. He felt the mound of dirt heaped over his memories crumble and spill into the hole. It was dark down there, like a haunted basement. Like a hole in the earth where a house had collapsed. "It's not… it's not a real place," he said. "Is it?"

"Ben, I trust you understand what I will do to you if you evade my questions, do you not? I'm sure you wouldn't like to see what two-point-one hertz will do to a ghost with such a delicate frame as yours."

"Why do you keep *saying* that? *I'm not dead!*"

"Oh no? Then how is it you're unable to close your eyes at the moment? How is it you're unable to move?"

Ben didn't answer. He couldn't. Because he didn't know, and he feared this man was telling him the truth. Another tear scratched a damp track down his cheekbone and soaked into the pillow beside his ear.

"This hospital room," the tall man said, with a broad sweep of his right hand, "is a mental construct. It doesn't exist. In actuality, you're confined—I suppose one might say *entombed*—" he added with a flash of that sickly smile, "within a pocket Recurrence Field. You, myself and your *friend* here—" He patted the bed beside Cruikshank. The comatose man didn't so much as blink. "—are merely avatars. Though I assure you, the agony you've just witnessed was quite real."

Ben looked away, facing the window. Relief washed over him as he realized he was able to move his head again, but the respite was brief. It was dark out there. The leaves on the tree were heavy with snow. Soon it would be day again. He had no idea how much time was actually passing in the real world but he knew what he saw outside his window couldn't possibly be real.

Avatars, he thought. *A mental construct. It's like something out of a movie.*

"I don't believe you," Ben said, turning back with a look of defiance. In truth, he believed everything the tall man had said. He was dead and this was Hell. Hell was a mental construct, a prison of his own making, designed to tempt and torment. And the man in the blue suit with the sickly smile was the Devil himself.

"Very well." The tall man pushed himself up from the bed and approached Ben's bedside. "That's entirely your prerogative. But please believe me when I tell you that when I return, if you haven't changed your mind—" He slapped a flat palm against Cruikshank's chest. The other man didn't even flinch. "—you'll be counting holes in the ceiling tiles for a week, like your friend here. And if you *still* don't tell me what I want to know, well..." Mirth reached the tall man's eyes as he said, "I suppose Danica and I will finally discover how much infrasound an ethereal can handle before it just......*winks out*."

THE NUDGES

ANDY AWOKE WITH a bluish light shining in his eyes and absolutely no idea where he was. His neck strained as he raised his head to look blearily through the car window. It was fully dark. They had parked by the gas pumps and the bluish light came from the convenience store fluorescents, brightening the entire lot. The closest pump ticked away, gas hissing as the detective filled the tank. He smelled it filtering in through the opened front passenger window. Lamb had been sitting there when he'd drifted off in the backseat. Her seat was empty now.

He rolled down his window. The smell of gasoline sharpened, mingling with hot tar, cigarette smoke and a whiff of something skunky, like scalded coffee or burning tires. Sam peered down at him and grinned.

"It's alive," she said.

"Where are we?"

"Just east of Albuquerque. Near Cibola."

"How long have I been out?"

"Lamb said you passed out around Flagstaff. I guess

what happened at the expo took a lot out of you."

He blinked blearily and wiped the crust out of his eyes. "Where is Lamb?"

"Had to pee. Said she'd get some grub for the road, figured we could all use something to eat. I'm so hungry I could eat a gas station hot dog at the moment."

Andy scooted over to the other side of the car, opened the door and stood, stretching out his sore legs and back. "I'm gonna go in," he said, once he felt good enough to walk.

The detective—Sam, she'd told them to call her—nodded and jerked the nozzle free of the tank.

The glass doors slid open as Andy approached. He shaded his eyes against the harsh light and saw Lamb at the Slushie machine, pouring herself an impossibly blue beverage.

"You're awake." She smiled as he sidled up beside her and laid a hand on the small of her back. She grabbed a lid from the stack and squeezed it onto the rim, then jammed a straw through the top and sucked some of the sticky liquid off her thumb. "I love the blue stuff."

He kissed her lips, already tinged blue. "I'm gonna get a soda. You want one?"

"I'm good. What kinda snacks you want?"

"I could use a bite of this," he said, squeezing her left buttock. She flicked blue off the end of the straw at him.

"Quit playin," she said.

"Funyuns, then," he called back, heading down the aisle to the fridges. He found the Dr. Peppers and opened the door to grab one.

He froze with the door partway open.

A young couple lay to his left, blood on their chests, staring at the ceiling, their haunted faces reflected in the glass. Andy turned violently, prepared to bear the full impact of their deaths… but the floor to his left was empty.

His gaze flicked back to the glass, where the dead man and woman lay. The man was dressed in a black suit with heavy shoulder-padding, blood staining his dress shirt. The woman wore a slightly more modern style of hanbok, the floral-patterned blouse splashed with blood, and a high-waisted, ankle-length skirt.

"Lamb…?"

She was near the front counter, looking at the chips. "Huh?" she said. His call had been so quiet—as if he didn't want to disturb the entities in the reflection—that he was surprised she'd heard him at all.

"Come here for a sec."

She approached down the aisle with a cautious look. As she neared, her smile faltered. She must have seen the horror in his expression. "You okay?"

"Look at the glass and tell me what you see."

She came up behind him, peering over his shoulder. Her gaze roamed for several seconds before returning to his face. "What am I looking for?"

"You don't see them?" He opened the door slightly wider, angling it so she could see what he still saw.

"What do *you* see?"

"I think I see… well, *dead people*," he finished.

Her lashes fluttered as she blinked rapidly in shock. "Your ghosts?"

"I guess so. A man and a woman. Lying right there, holding hands. I guess they must be a couple."

She followed his gesture. "What do they look like?"

"They're about my age, maybe younger. Korean. It looks like they were shot or stabbed or something on their way to a formal event. I don't recognize them, whoever they are."

"Wonder why now?"

"What do you mean?"

"I mean, you never seen 'em before. You think they're trying to tell you something?"

He looked closer, hoping to discover something he may not have noticed before. "I dunno," he said with a shake of his head. "They're just lying there."

Lamb reached past him, grabbed a cold Dr. Pepper and closed the door, the ghosts disappearing from sight. "Then you don't need to focus on that right now," she said. "Let's get some snacks and get back on the road. You up for drivin?"

"Sure, I could drive for a bit."

She led him to the front of the store. They paid for their snacks and drinks, barely registering the man in the knit winter cap standing behind them in line. The doors slid open on the cool New Mexico night and Lamb stepped out first.

Something caused Andy to stop and turn.

The man in the knit cap stood at the counter, head twitching, absently scratching his arm. His face was gaunt and gray under the harsh lighting. "Yeah, uh… lemme get a pack of Luckies," he said, his voice low.

Looking at the man got Andy's spider senses tingling. The methamphetamine twitches, the manic look in the man's yellow, bloodshot eyes. Just a typical tweaker. But it was more than that. He felt it *physically*—the same feeling he got when a slot machine was about to pay out. The same he'd felt at the expo, searching for the entity that had murdered those psychics and had been about to kill again.

It was the Nudges, pushing him toward the tweaker.

The murdered man and woman whose reflections he'd seen in the refrigerator glass had been warning him. Were *still* warning him.

His ghosts. The *gwisin*.

"You comin?" Lamb said.

He ignored her, cautiously approaching the counter. The clerk turned to get a pack of Lucky Strikes and the tweaker reached into the pocket of his corduroy jacket.

What now, Andy—what now?

Instinct took over. He didn't even stop to consider he might have made a mistake. He grabbed the sunglasses rack beside the counter and pushed with everything he had. The tweaker struggled with whatever was in his pocket, and the rack toppled over him before he could react. Knockoff Ray Bans and Chanels tumbled off their hooks and clattered to the floor around him.

The man cried out in surprise, causing the clerk to whip around with the pack of cigarettes in his hand. For a moment Andy was sure he'd screwed up, that the guy wasn't reaching for a gun at all, just for his wallet.

"Andy?" Lamb said outside.

The tweaker wrestled the rack off of himself and fixed his yellow-tinged eyes on Andy. He jerked his hand free from his pocket finally, a snub-nosed revolver held in a jittery grip.

Andy's mind raced. He knew this was it, his curtain call—and he was glad at least that he'd gotten Lamb out of the store. At least he'd bought the cashier a moment to hide. At least he helped to save those psychics' lives. Maybe it wasn't the best legacy, but it was something.

This is it, Andy, my man. You had a good run but your luck's finally run out.

The register came down heavily on the tweaker's head

with a rattle of change, and the man slumped to the floor. The gun skittered across the tiles, knocking aside sunglasses like pool balls until it came to a rest at Andy's feet.

"Andy!" Lamb cried, throwing her arms over his shoulders.

"Holy hell, man!" the clerk said, his eyes goggling behind thick glasses. "That guy coulda kilt you!"

Realizing how close to death he'd just come, a shudder of relief passed through Andy's whole body. He let out a gasp, teeth chattering as Lamb hugged him from behind. He glanced down at their feet, saw the gun lying there—what could easily have been the instrument of his death if the clerk hadn't been quick with the register—and he kicked it away, down the aisle.

"Good work with the register," he said.

The clerk blinked. "What do you mean? Dude, I was *hiding*. I thought that was you?"

He turned to Lamb. She was looking at him with tears of awe and relief and shock in her eyes. He cocked his head quizzically and she nodded, answering his question without the need for him to voice it.

It was *them*.

"Call the police," Sam said from the doorway. She was looking at the unconscious tweaker on the floor.

"Damn right, I will," the clerk said. He peered over the counter. "You think he's out for a bit?"

"Couple of minutes, at least. Call them and leave. If they ask, we were never here."

"Yeah, you bet," the clerk said. "No worries."

Back in the car, on the road again with Andy driving, heading east on Interstate 40, Sam said, "You know, you could've gotten yourself killed back there."

Andy considered it, glancing in the rearview at Lamb, who lay across the backseat, her eyes closed. For a moment he watched road signs brightened by the headlights drift by in the dark, trying to decide whether to take this woman he barely knew into his confidence.

"Maybe," he said. "I spent most of my life running away from myself. From my family. From what I let happen to them."

He expected her to ask him to elaborate on that. "Oh?" was all she said, forcing him to push on without prodding.

"All I know is I can't be that guy anymore." He tipped his head toward the backseat, where Lamb slept. "Because she cares about me."

Sam nodded. She peered out her window at the passing telephone poles, the endless flat landscape and scrub brush. She was a quiet woman, for the most part. Andy thought she seemed sad.

"Those ghosts," he said. His palms felt slick on the steering wheel. Confessions always made him anxious and slightly queasy, ever since he was little. "Whoever they are… it seems like they have a higher purpose in mind for me. Maybe they always did. I smoked way too much weed so I wouldn't have to feel it all the time. These Nudges. Like they were pushing me to be better. When I was a kid, I thought it was a curse. The money I won at the slots was payback for dealing with the burden of… whatever the hell it was pushing at me all the time."

He chuckled, remembering the story his mother once told him about the palette of pizza boxes in the grocery store that nearly fell on him as a baby.

"My mom always said they were my guardian angels. My *gwisin*. I don't know where they came from or why they chose me, but if those people in Maryland can help me communicate with them somehow… maybe I can ask them." The reflection of the headlights from the car behind them illuminated his wistful smile in the rearview mirror. "I could *thank* them."

Sam smiled back. "I think that'd be nice. You did good today, Andy." She patted his shoulder briskly. "Try not to beat yourself up so much, huh?"

Andy turned to her, hoping to gauge whether or not she was messing with him. Aside from Lamb, he couldn't remember the last time someone had praised him outside of the casino after a big win.

His parents had been hard people, difficult to love. Though he'd known they had loved him. They'd just been preparing him for a world they no longer understood, if they ever had. Aside from their suppliers and customers at Park Fashion Apparel they'd been fairly insular, their only acquaintances other Korean immigrants, even though his father had been born in America. They'd never traveled much beyond Vegas, except to his mother's hometown of Busan to visit her parents.

Andy wished he could have saved them. He wished he'd responded to the Nudges sooner.

"Thanks," he said. "You should get some rest."

Sam yawned behind a hand. "You're probably right." She folded up her light jacket against the window and rested her head on it, closing her eyes. "Wake me when we hit Oklahoma, huh?"

"Will do."

As she settled in, Andy looked at Lamb sleeping in the backseat again, her fists curled up in the crook of her neck. He wished he'd listened to her mother when he'd had the chance. He had a lot to atone for. The deaths of his parents and her mother weren't his fault, but the fact that he might have prevented them if he'd only followed the Nudges weighed heavily on his conscience. He needed to make good, if only for his own peace of mind.

A few minutes later a large green sign came up on the right, reflected in the brights. *Welcome to Texas. Drive Friendly – The Texas Way*. Andy adjusted his hands on the wheel and put New Mexico in the dust.

DEAD REDEMPTION

Placid Oaks Cemetery
November 5th

A LIGHT RAIN fell on the crypts and headstones, the monuments of weeping angels and cherubic children, each stark white under the half moon. It splashed in puddles and pools left from a harder rain earlier in the evening, and pattered on their heads and shoulders as the three of them—four, if you included Le Mon, the only one of them not effected by the rain—walked the cemetery grounds. Lilian had worn layers against the chill but hadn't expected rain. The cold dampness had already seeped into her bones, making her teeth chatter.

In the limousine ride from the airport in Palo Alto, where Lilian had parked to meet them, Thea had asked what Lilian wondered herself: whether the Woman in White's boyfriend had been driving drunk or not, if Jessica Kissimon had turned the car into oncoming traffic, causing not just her own death but the death of four others, two of them small children, was she really worthy of redemption?

"I was raised Catholic," Le Mon had responded. "I suppose I still consider myself a spiritual person—" He'd chuckled at the unintended double entendre, which Lilian didn't pass along to Thea and Bram. "—but I'm not affiliated with any particular religion. My father," he said, smiling wistfully as he stroked his small beard, "he believed everyone deserves forgiveness, if they seek contrition. From the purest soul to the most evil."

"And what do *you* believe?" Thea had asked, after Lilian repeated his words.

"I believe Jessica has served her time," he'd replied. "She's punished herself enough. From what Ben and Lilian said, the blood on her dress, the anger and fear she displays—these are classic examples of an ethereal acting out her guilt. Yes, I believe she can be redeemed."

"What about the family they killed? The mother and father and two little boys," Bram said. "Don't you think they should have a say?"

Until then, Bram hadn't spoken more than two words since they'd met at the airport. Lilian still couldn't get a read on him. He was attractive, yet she wouldn't exactly call him "hot"—more like a third-billed action hero, with a square jaw, a thick neck and broad, muscular shoulders, and the requisite "more on top" hairstyle every generic white reality-TV star seemed to have these days. Despite his looks, his apparent indifference to just about everyone around him made him unattractive, almost repellent. His sudden concern for the deceased family intrigued her.

"Fortunately for her, it's not up to them to decide," Le Mon had said.

Thea and Bram had passed a look as Lilian repeated it, and that had been the end of the discussion.

Thea must have seen something in Bram, though it was pretty obvious they weren't dating. He seemed to be part bodyguard, part confidante. Ben had once said the two of them had grown secretive and almost seemed to have a private language of nods and facial expressions. But Ben had been known to read more into these things than Lilian did herself. When she'd suggested he take a peek inside their brains he'd of course rejected the idea, not wanting to invade their privacy.

"It's such a waste," she'd said. "If I could read minds, I'd be doing it all the time."

"Then it's a good thing for all of us you can't," Ben had said, grinning the way he did when he had something over her.

The familiar ache in her heart returned, a small echo of the pain she'd felt when she'd found him dead at her side, slumped over the hatch doorway. It hadn't even been a week since he'd vanished and she missed him already. But now was no time to wonder where Ben might have run off to, nor to preemptively mourn the loss of him. She was wet and cold and trudging behind Le Mon in the dark cemetery. Thea and Bram walked side by side behind them, their flashlight beams sweeping over headstones and trees. There would be time to worry later, in the comfort and warmth of her dorm room.

She caught up to Le Mon as they passed between the headstones Jessica had cracked in her fear and confusion on Hallowe'en. Le Mon eyed the cracks in the stone and let out an impressed whistle. "Did she do all this?"

Lilian nodded.

"Well, okay. Let's hope she's chilled out a bit in the meanwhile then, huh?"

"This was her?" Thea asked, indicating the same cracks.

Lilian nodded again, wishing there was an easier way for everyone to communicate with each other without having to listen to the same questions and repeat the same words.

"Ben wasn't kidding about powerful," Thea said. "Let's try not to provoke her, get ourselves hurt."

The four of them ascended the small hill surrounding the columbarium, their footwear squelching in the wet grass. Hovering alongside her, Le Mon's gaze vigilantly darted around the trees and gravestones. She knew he was able to sense other ethereals, whether they meant to remain hidden or not. That was what concerned her most about Ben—if Le Mon couldn't find him, no matter how hard he'd tried, Ben really might be lost for good.

She stopped beside the coffin-shaped crypt, engraved with the name UNTERGANG, gobs of wax and a few scattered leaves on its wet surface. Burned down to nubs, the candles she'd brought the last time she was here lay at its foot. The plastic planchette was wedged into the damp grass nearby. She pulled it out and laid it on the cold stone.

"The board's missing," she said.

"Doesn't matter," Le Mon said, his gaze flicking toward a large puddle near her feet. "We won't need it."

"But she only ever responds to the Ouija board."

Le Mon winked. "Then it's a good thing Ouija is my middle name."

"Mine's Esther," Lilian said, tucking the planchette into her bag. She grinned back and he laughed.

"You got a bit of The Fearing in you, Lilian," he said.

"I'm not that scared," she lied.

"I know. It's…" He shook his head. "Maybe another time."

Thea and Bram were watching her. "Le Mon said he can speak to her without the Ouija board," she explained.

Thea jutted her chin toward the columbarium. "*This* is where Jessica loops?" She seemed surprised. "Where they put the family's ashes?"

"We saw her there," Lilian said, pointing to where Ben had caught her in his arms, where Jessica Kissimon's dress had gone from white to crimson, stained not by her own blood, but by the family's she'd had a hand in killing.

"She's here now," Le Mon said, his eyes closed, an ear perked toward the wind. His head twitched. "She's in pain. Her hands. The blood on her hands. It burns like scalding water."

The area brightened as Jessica Kissimon's gauzy white form appeared on the columbarium steps. She was speaking in that slow, dreamlike way again, her voice unheard, like a gothic horror movie with the sound turned off. Her hair and gown flowed as if she were underwater, her hands slick with fresh blood.

"I'm gonna try something," Le Mon said. "Distract her a minute, huh?"

"How?"

"Just talk to her," he said, and vanished.

"What did Le Mon say?" Thea asked.

Lilian ignored her. "Um… hi, Jessica," she said, waving anxiously. "I'm, uh… I'm Lilian. Lilian Roth. And these are my friends Thea and Bram."

It felt strange to call them *friends*, since she didn't particularly like either of them. The two of them tried to acknowledge the ethereal, Thea waving and Bram nodding in her general direction.

"We're here to help you," Lilian said, speaking loud enough to be heard over the rain. "You've already punished yourself enough."

The Woman in White shook her head violently. She clawed at her stomach, and the red stain her bloody hands left on her dress began to spread.

"We met your husband here. Eddie," Lilian said. "On Hallowe'en. That's when you died, seven years ago that night, isn't it? When you turned the wheel into oncoming traffic—"

"Lilian…" Thea whispered hoarsely. "Didn't I say *not* to provoke her?"

Lilian shot a glare over her shoulder, causing Thea to shut her mouth. Bram turned to Thea, clearly surprised by her reaction.

"The two of you killed a family of four in a minivan," Lilian said, deliberately playing into Jessica's guilt. Lying hadn't worked and placating her had made her fly into a rage. She thought Allison might have approved. Blake, too. "The buckle on one of the baby seats snapped and the smallest boy, Declan, they found him dead on the pavement fifty feet from the van."

The hurt on the dead woman's face made Lilian's eyes sting with tears. It was easy to pity her, despite what she'd done. Le Mon was right. She had punished herself long enough. Seven years mourning her victims, night after night, tearing at herself, blood scalding her ethereal flesh.

One of the cracked headstones split further, and the upper half toppled onto the gravemound. It was impossible to tell if Jessica had done it or if it had finally given out and fallen on its own, but Lilian wasn't about to give her another chance to attack.

"'*Hold on loosely*,'" she sang, projecting her voice despite her fear, hoping to distract the ethereal long enough for Le Mon to finish whatever he planned to do. "'*Don't let go.*' That was the song on the radio, wasn't it? You were both drunk and a little high and you thought it was funny. Maybe you didn't see the car in the other lane. Maybe it wasn't deliberate, but both of you killed that family. The

O'Neals. Brian and Michelle, and their little boys Declan and Tyler."

The Woman in White was pleading now, tearing at the red stain on her dress as if she was trying to pull out her guts on the steps.

The clouds above flashed blue with chain lightning, and the rain came down harder, hammering on the roof of the columbarium. In the prolonged rumble of thunder that followed, Le Mon reappeared, hovering near the foot of the steps.

"Jessica!" he shouted. "I've got some folks here who'd very much like to meet you."

A young man and woman appeared at his side. Each cradled a small boy in their arms.

Jessica's fingers dug into her belly, her soft features twisting with remorse.

"Jessica, these are the O'Neals," Le Mon said. "They asked me to say they forgive you."

"What's happening?" Thea whispered.

Lilian ignored her. Another flash of lightning brightened the cemetery. As the thunder rumbled, Jessica cocked her head to one side. Her hands stopped kneading at her stomach and the languid undulation of her dress began to subside. It was like her form was finally catching up to the real world. Becoming whole again.

Le Mon turned to the ethereals he must have coaxed from their ashes within their columbarium urns. "Isn't that right, Brian? Michelle?"

The couple nodded.

"They're fine," Le Mon said. "They're going to join us at a place we call the Temple, where others like you and me—like them—are welcome. They asked me to tell you, they'd like for you to come along."

Lilian couldn't be sure but she thought she saw a tear running down his cheek. Whatever it was, it couldn't have been the rain.

"It's time to forgive yourself, Jessica," he said.

Jessica began to weep. A smile spread across her face. Already the crimson stain in her dress was diminishing, drawing back into itself. But her hands were still bloody. She hadn't completely forgiven herself just yet. She might never. But it was a start.

Will I ever forgive myself? Lilian wondered. Did she even deserve forgiveness for letting Garrote escape? For damning the world to whatever Hell he had in store for them?

A sound like breaking glass startled her. The large puddle at her feet had cracked open—though she was pretty sure it wasn't cold enough to have frozen—and a pale, blurry hand snatched out, grasping at the sharp edges of the puddle that looked more like glass than ice.

"Uh… Le Mon?"

More puddles cracked open with a shattering sound: in the grass, on crypts and burial mounds, on the columbarium steps. Blurs in the shapes of hands and paws and heads emerged from them, both human and animal, drawing themselves up of the standing water.

"What's wrong?" Thea asked, clearly unable to see or hear any of it.

Another hand reached out of the puddle at Lilian's feet. She backed away in horror as a blurry, seemingly nude man pulled himself to his feet.

"Imagoes!" Le Mon cried. He waved her away. "Get out of here, Lilian!"

Without a second thought, she turned and ran, not daring to look back until she'd reached the bottom of the hill. Thea had followed her, her dripping wet hair falling in her face, her leather jacket beaded with rain.

"What's happening up there?"

"Imagoes," Lilian told her, and shivered. "Dozens of them."

Thea's eyes widened. "I thought they were a myth."

"Apparently not. Why didn't Bram run?"

Bram had stayed above, his fingers pressed against his temples as if holding off an intense headache. All around him, the indistinct shapes of humans and wolves and cats—eight of them in all, semi-translucent and blurred like impressionist paintings—approached their prey at the columbarium steps.

Thea hadn't taken her eyes off Bram.

"He's gonna get himself killed," Lilian said.

Thea shook her head. "I don't think so."

Lighting flashed directly above them. The thunder boomed with the sky still electric. Rain poured down as Le Mon stepped in front of the O'Neals, holding out his arms to protect them from the advancing entities. The scene was surreal, rain striking the headstones and grass and soaking Bram to the skin, yet passing directly through the others.

Wide-eyed with fear, Jessica Kissimon cowered in the darkness below the columbarium archway, peering from one imago to the next. Whatever these imagoes were, it was clear they intended to prey on the ethereals.

"You wanna eat the family special, you're gonna have to get through me first," Le Mon shouted. "And this meal bites back!"

A catlike entity slinked toward Le Mon and crouched as if readying to pounce.

Several headstones away, Bram's arms fell to his sides. Suddenly there were two of him. Lilian blinked hard, certain for a moment that the rain in her eyes had doubled her vision. But the Bram approaching the imagoes was a semi-transparent form. The rain still pattered on the body he'd left behind, his head lolling as if he was unconscious, while it fell straight through his—there was no doubting what she saw—ethereal double.

"Is that…? Is Bram…?" She found she couldn't finish the thought, staring dumbfounded at the two Brams.

"What do you see?" Thea asked.

"There's *two* of him."

The woman nodded, her gaze never leaving Bram's corporeal self. "He's astral projecting."

"Astral projecting," Lilian repeated in wonder.

A humanoid imago rounded on Bram's astral form. With a solid right hook the imago went flying, literally hurtling through the air until it disappeared through the columbarium wall.

In the same moment, the cat pounced on Le Mon, latching onto his forearm. He struggled to shake it loose, momentarily distracted. The two wolves darted in from either side. Their vicious teeth tore at the shins of the O'Neal husband and wife.

The human imago Bram had sent flying reemerged from the darkness directly behind the Woman in White.

"Look out, Jessica!" Lilian called out, but the sky was blue with electricity and the thunder smothered her warning.

The imago grabbed Jessica from behind.

The wolves tore at the O'Neal father's pantleg and peeled flesh off the mother's ankle below her dress. One of the humanoids reached for the baby in her arms, which began to silently cry.

Lilian took a single step up the hill, eager to help

despite her fear. Thea clamped down on her shoulder and drew her back fiercely. "*Don't*," she said.

Le Mon grabbed the cat by the throat as two humanoids flanked him. Bram fought off the two other wolves. Struggling against the imago's grip around her waist, Jessica unleashed a shriek so loud and high-pitched even Thea, who shouldn't have been able to hear it at all, had to cover her ears.

Bram's astral form snapped back into his body and he fell to his knees with a wet splash. Le Mon and the other ethereals reacted as though the scream hurt them, while all around them their blurry assailants shattered like carnival glass, raining down into nearby puddles. The survivors recovered from the sound after a moment, peering around themselves to see if they were safe.

"Oh, my Lord," Le Mon said, a smile pursing his lips. He wiggled his fingers in his ears comically. "You ever consider a career in music? You could give Whitney a run for her money."

Jessica Kissimon let out a relieved laugh.

"And you," Le Mon said, turning to Bram as the man staggered to his feet. "You got anymore tricks up your sleeve, big guy?"

Back in his body, Bram couldn't hear him. He wore a ghost of a grin as he turned to face Thea.

The storm had passed. The clouds overhead moved swiftly but had calmed, the rain no more than a drizzle. Lilian and Thea climbed the hill to meet the survivors. Thea threw her arms around Bram, who hugged her back with one arm.

"That was pretty amazing," Lilian said to Le Mon. He was looking at the teeth marks on his arm with mild concern. "How did you find the O'Neals?"

He glanced back at the family and spoke in a hushed voice. "They've been cowering in the dark in there all this time, wondering why they never got to Heaven. Took me a bit of time to convince them what you see is what you get." His lips twisted in a rueful grimace. "But they were quick to forgive Jessica. Turn the other cheek and all that."

"I'd say she redeemed herself pretty well," Lilian said.

"She did a fine job," Le Mon agreed. "She could be a boon for us, if she sticks around."

"You think she will?"

He looked back at her again. Mr. O'Neal stuck out his free hand, holding the baby in the other arm. Jessica took his hand reluctantly, smiling as she shook it. When she moved on to Mrs. O'Neal, her smile looked less forced, more earnest.

"I think she's on a long journey toward healing," Le Mon said. "And maybe that journey starts with us."

Thea approached them. She nodded at Lilian. "Is Le Mon with you?"

"He's standing right here."

Thea looked in the direction Lilian pointed, her gaze falling several inches above Le Mon's head, as though she assumed he was taller. "Bram tells me you may have convinced Jessica to join our cause. Thank you for that. He also said you're hurt. When an imago injures an ethereal, the wound can become tainted. He'd like to perform a ritual to rid you of the infection."

"Thought I got the cat scratch fever," Le Mon said, sneering at the gaping wound. He watched the O'Neals for a moment as they examined each other's wounds with looks of distress. "Mr. and Mrs. O'Neal got bit, too. If Bram thinks he can get rid of it, I'd appreciate him trying."

Lilian repeated what he'd said to Thea.

"We'll head back to the jet and meet you at the Temple in the morning," Thea said. "They should be good until then, right?"

Bram nodded confidently.

"Good." Thea turned to Lilian. "Would you care to join us at the Temple?"

Lilian gave the offer a moment's thought. What value did school have for her anymore? How could she live a normal life knowing things like imagoes were hunting innocent ethereals? With psychics killing themselves en masse and Garrote still out there, raising an army of the dead against the living? There was more rewarding work to be done with GRP2. More ethereals to free. A war to prepare for.

And they still had to find Ben.

The only issue was how she would explain her decision to Blake and her parents.

"Do you think it's okay if my friend comes along?" she asked warily.

Thea looked to Bram. The hard-faced man shrugged.

"Why not?" Thea said. "The more the merrier."

BLUE HELL

BEN WATCHED THE man in the other bed stare at the ceiling for several minutes. Cruikshank remained unblinking and unresponsive to his queries and calls for far too long until Ben finally, reluctantly, gave up trying.

The tall man in the blue suit had told Ben he and Jeremy Cruikshank were dead—that they were ghosts, he'd said, ethereal beings—and that they were trapped in a pocket Recurrence Field. The moment the tall man said the words it had triggered a slow but steady recovery of Ben's lost memories. As the minutes and hours passed, he began to remember the time between the first time he'd seen Garrote House rolling down Main Street in Duck Falls and how he'd come to be in this place, which he assumed must be the Hedgewood Foundation's headquarters, somewhere in the desert.

He *was* dead but this wasn't Hell. It was *Nevada*.

He remembered the years between his heart attack and the day he and Lilian had reunited at Ghostland, a time that had often felt like purgatory. He remembered each and every one of the deaths they'd witnessed, the friends they had made and lost that day.

He remembered convincing Lilian to stand with him

against Garrote, to give up her life to prevent him from escaping, only to turn his back on her in his final moments, opening the hatch door despite what he'd asked of her.

He also remembered waking several months later in the very same place he'd died, discovering Thea and GRP2 and probably half of the world believed he was a hero. The shame he'd felt knowing they were wrong about him returned, too. The knowledge that he'd failed them.

He remembered meeting Leon Moncrieff and learning what to expect from his new life as an ethereal. Their fast friendship and common goals. Freeing other ethereals from their loops while hiding their secret from Thea and the others. Thea finally confronting him, in his last minutes of freedom before waking here, with the revelation that she'd known he'd been recruiting ethereals for his war under her nose. That she wouldn't stand for it.

Finally, he remembered discovering Bram and Thea's plan to destroy Ghostland's Recurrence Field, the only thing preventing the Swarm and all of the other potentially dangerous ethereals from running amok on the streets of Duck Falls.

Then he'd woken up here, in this hospital bed which may or may not be real... and he was lying here staring at a man named Jeremy Cruikshank, who'd been put through an excruciating torture that the tall man—who was likely Oliver Hedgewood III himself—had promised would befall him next, if Ben didn't tell him what he wanted to hear. Had promised he would twist the dial on his infrasound machine until Ben "winked out."

He remembered the awful stench as Cruikshank faded from reality, and knew of only one thing that could possibly make a terrible smell like that.

The Dark Rift, he thought. *That's where I'll end up if*

Hedgewood makes me disappear. I'll end up in the Dark Rift and no one ever comes back from there.

He'd spent the last who knew how long trying to wake Cruikshank from his coma. Hoping to pull him back to reality or whatever this place was long enough to find out what he'd seen on the other side. Hoping to wake him before Hedgewood returned with the nurse. Something about her striking features seemed familiar to Ben, as if they had met somewhere before. But that was something he might never recall.

"I guess that about sums it up," he said aloud, and uttered a weak chuckle. "Previously on *The Ghostland Chronicles*."

Cruikshank blinked.

Ben raised his head to get a better look, thinking he might have imagined it. The Scotsman's eyes were glassy and dulled, still directed at the ceiling.

A minute passed. Two.

Cruikshank's eyes remained wide open. Blank.

Ben fell back against the pillow. It took a moment to realize it hadn't just been his head that moved this time. His shoulders had raised from the bed, too.

He sat up, pushing against the covers, the pain in his chest gone, the sheet no longer a dead weight against his limbs.

He could see further out the window now, as well. The sky beyond the trees was empty and blue. When Cruikshank had first blinked, it had been a cloudy, rain-drenched night.

He couldn't see the ground, nor any structures. Just the leafless tree and the sky. It reminded him of the outer edge of the map in an old, open-world video game, an endless expanse of blue with nothing beyond.

Ben eased himself out of bed. His bare feet touched the cool tile floor and he fell back wearily against the mattress, reaching out to grab the metal footrail. Experiencing so many sensations he hadn't felt in so long had overwhelmed him. He stood again, slowly, and ambled cautiously to the window, worried that a fall might be dangerous, as though his body was fragile again, the way it had been when he was still alive.

He stood at the window and peered out, palms pressed flat on the warm glass. Below the hospital room was an empty blue Hell. The tree floated in an azure void, its network of bare roots visible, like clusters of neural pathways. Except for the tree there seemed to be nothing beyond the four walls of his hospital room but endless sky.

He let a desperate moan escape his lips. His hands fell from the glass and he turned back to face the room, his death row prison cell.

But there *was* something out there, he remembered— somewhere beyond the sea of endless blue. There was the Hedgewood Facility. There was the Nevada desert. There was Lilian and Le Mon and all of his new friends. There were his parents and there was Rex Garrote, secretly amassing an army of the dead.

"I have to get out of here," he told himself.

Determined now, he returned to his bed, pausing briefly to regain his strength, leaning against the footrest. From there he moved to the television—there was only one in the room, as he'd suspected—and was about to turn it off when something came to mind. He crossed the curtain area to Cruikshank's side of the room. *Donovan's Brain* became an old color movie with a clean-cut Mick Jagger in a brown suit, singing a song Ben couldn't hear under swinging lamps.

The television was showing two different movies on either side of the room, like one of those optical illusions that changed depending on your relation to the image. He moved back and forth, watching each movie fade into the other as he passed the middle of the room.

Reminding himself why he'd gotten out of bed in the first place, he continued to the door and twisted the handle. It turned and turned without resistance nor the click of a latch. He pushed and pulled but the door didn't budge. It was likely only ever meant to open when Hedgewood or Danica the nurse decided it was necessary to maintain the illusion of entry and exit.

Shoulders slumped in despair, he returned to the TV, reached up and flicked it off.

Cruikshank groaned.

Ben spun around. The man in the bed blinked rapidly. "You found the gizmo," he said, but his head didn't move and his eyes didn't leave the ceiling.

"I got out of bed," Ben told him, excited to finally have his roommate back. If nothing else, he was someone else to talk to again, to work out this dilemma with and potentially escape, even if he wasn't entirely lucid.

"Aye?"

"You probably can, too. This room isn't real. I betcha you're not even paralyzed. What they did to you with that machine, that's the only real thing in this place." He grabbed the footrail of Cruikshank's bed in both hands. "We have to get out of here," he said, feeling suddenly like it might be possible after all.

Cruikshank's gaze fell on him. He looked incredibly tired, eyes bloodshot and dazed. "Feels like my bloody nut's on fire, lad. I'm pure done in."

"If you don't get out of bed, what's to stop them from

doing what they did to you again and again? We have to go before they come back."

"How? I cannae lift a finger."

"Try it."

"It's no gonnae work."

"Would you just *try*? Jesus!"

Cruikshank blinked. He squeezed his eyes shut and the tendons in his neck tightened.

Ben waited, not really expecting anything to happen, certain he'd have to drag Cruikshank out of the room, and wondering if he'd even be able. After nearly a minute watching the man clench his jaw and strain his neck, one of the two slightly pointed bulges in the sheet at the foot of the bed twitched.

"You just moved your toe!" Ben announced.

Cruikshank laughed, surprised himself. "I did it! I fuckin did it, lad!"

"I told you. Now let's see if we can get you out of bed. It might be a little harder, but I'll be right here. You okay if I take off the sheet?"

"Aye, do it."

Ben went around the bed to Cruikshank's side. He tugged on the sheet, pulling it up from its tight tuck under the mattress. Cruikshank turned his head to watch as the sheet came up from the side. Ben yanked it back with a grunt. He had to stifle a cry of fright at what he saw.

Below the sheet, the bed was empty. Cruikshank's head was severed at the base of his neck, a bloody and visceral stump. The snapped tendons wriggled like rat tails as Cruikshank strained to raise his head and peer down at himself. The spinal cord leaked fluid onto the fitted sheet.

"What's wrong, lad?"

"Nothing," Ben said hurriedly, drawing the sheet back,

not sure how to explain what he'd seen. How had Cruikshank managed to wiggle a toe that didn't exist? How had he been able to enjoy the nurse's sponge baths? Why had his body appeared to be intact until the moment the sheet had come off? "Let's just hold off on that for now. You're tired."

"Aye, but I think I can do it." He smiled proudly. "I moved my bloody toe!"

"Get some rest. We'll try again later."

"Aye," Cruikshank said, still smiling as Ben crossed to his own bed, trying to work out what to do next.

He supposed if he could get out of this room, he could carry Cruikshank's head under his arm like that football player at Ghostland. Steamroller? Was that his name? First, he'd need to figure out how to escape when the door didn't work and the window led to an infinite blue abyss.

If he could manage to surprise Hedgewood or Danica the next time they entered the room, hit one of them with something, maybe he could distract them long enough to make a dash for the exit. But to get the upper hand they would have to be unaware he'd gotten out of bed in the first place. Which meant he had to tuck Cruikshank neatly back into bed, turn the TV back on, and get back under the covers himself.

He just had to hope they hadn't already noticed.

They're probably watching me right now, he thought miserably.

With no time left to lose, he tucked the sheet under Cruikshank's mattress as best he could.

"What are ya doing, lad? I thought we were getting out of here."

"We will. The next time they come in, you just stare at the ceiling like nothing happened, okay?"

"Aye. What then?"

"When they come over to my bed, I'm gonna give them a surprise."

"With what?"

Ben looked around the room. He found what he was looking for on Cruikshank's bedside table.

"I found the gizmo," he said.

As he strode around the foot of the bed to pick it up, a plan began to formulate. The type of plan they used to say on TV was *just crazy enough to work.*

WINK OUT

AFTER *DONOVAN'S BRAIN* had played through twice more, and the sky outside had gone from middle-of-the-day blue to midnight black to an overcast afternoon, the door finally opened again. Glancing out the window, Ben saw the tree that was bare twenty minutes ago was shaggy with colorful autumn leaves that wouldn't last half an hour.

Nurse Danica entered, pushing the same cart she had earlier, carrying the same sleek machine.

Cruikshank's face brightened. "Well, hello, Nurse." Ben couldn't tell if he was faking civility or playing along with his plan. He just had to hope the man's memory hadn't reverted to zeroes again.

"Good morning, Mr. Cruikshank," she said with a pleasant smile. Her face had a pale sheen, with high cheekbones and red lips devoid of lipstick, her dark hair pulled back under the nurse's cap. Ben still couldn't remember where he recognized her from but he hoped that soon it would no longer matter. "How's my favorite patient today?"

"Bit of a headache, to be honest."

"The procedure can have that effect on patients." She turned to Ben, her smile fading. "Yours is scheduled for this morning, Mr. Laramie. Is there anything you'd like to say before we proceed?"

Lying still and straight under the sheet, tucked in haphazardly on the window side, Ben shook his head. In his right hand he held the TV remote, hidden under the covers, his grip sweaty.

"Very well," she said curtly. "Mr. Hedgewood will be with us shortly."

"Don't you mean *Doctor* Hedgewood?"

The nurse gazed at him with half-lidded eyes. "*Mister* Hedgewood is the hospital administrator."

"Right," Ben said. "Because this is a hospital. And you're a nurse. Where did you go to school, by the way?"

She blinked leisurely. "Roseman University."

"Have you always worked with paraplegics?"

"No. I used to be in intensive care."

She was a quick liar, he had to give her that.

"And you're not a paraplegic, Mr. Laramie. You've had an emergency coronary bypass. The scar is still healing but if you cooperate with your treatment, you'll be good as new in no time. You might even be allowed to leave."

"Like Jeremy?" Ben nodded toward Cruikshank.

"If his treatment works, he can leave as well, yes."

"The infrasound therapy," Ben said.

The nurse—who wasn't a nurse—smiled slyly for a brief moment. Then the smile faded. "Yes. It's a standard procedure with his type of injury."

"And what injury is that, exactly?"

"This patient's history is none of your business."

"No," Cruikshank said. "Go on. Tell him."

Ben smiled. He'd been playing along, after all.

The nurse hesitated for a split second. "Mr. Cruikshank has suffered a complete spinal cord injury on the cervical spine between the C7 and C8 vertebrae. The nerves are severed, causing complete paralysis and loss of feeling."

Cruikshank frowned at this, and for a moment Ben thought he might break cover, revealing that he'd just moved a toe that didn't exist—a fact that was clearly impossible, because below the C7 vertebrae *he* didn't exist.

"So how will he recover from that, do you think?" Ben asked. The answers no longer concerned him. He merely wanted to keep pressing her until she cracked.

"He'll be chairbound," she said matter-of-factly.

Cruikshank let out a pained breath. "That's a bitter pill to swallae, Nurse."

"If you know so much, then what happened to me?" Ben asked. "My parents must have said something when they brought me in."

She turned to him, with another languid blink before she replied: "From what I understand, you suffered a massive coronary event. Your mother found you lying on your bedroom floor."

How could she know that? How is that possible?

His own voice answered: *Because they're inside my head. All of this, it's like Hedgewood said. A construct. Which means they saw me get out of bed. And they probably know what I'm planning.*

The door opened as if on cue. The nurse turned.

"Ah, here you are already, Danica," Hedgewood said, as if he didn't know. He was wearing a different suit today, in another pale, pastel color. He glanced at Ben before returning his gaze to the chart in his hand. "Is the patient prepped?"

"Right away, sir."

Danica moved to the cart and rolled it around the foot of Ben's bed, positioning it between him and the window.

She picked up the large headphones and approached him. Ben twisted his head away from her as she reached out with the headphones. Her jaw tightened but her bland expression didn't change.

"Are you going to cooperate?"

He sighed through his nose, then nodded with a look he hoped expressed the defeat he no longer felt. Danica leaned over him to place the headphones on his ears.

In the same moment, Ben pushed the Mute button and the blare of the TV filled the room. "LOOK AT MY BRAIN, MY DEAR," the doctor said at full volume. "YOUR LAST LOOK. I PROMISE YOU IT WILL NOT BE A PAINFUL ONE."

Hedgewood and Danica turned to the TV, shocked by the sound. Ben launched up from the bed, throwing off the sheet and swinging the remote at Danica's head.

Her gaze flicked away from the TV. She grabbed his wrist mid-swing and slammed his hand back down on the mattress, pulling him down with his right arm crossed over his body, pinning him to the mattress. He kicked out with his right leg but she blocked it with her knee and the pain of their bones colliding rattled up his shin.

"*Drop it*," she said, her jaw clenched, squeezing his wrist so hard his hand had turned purple. Still, he held on. For how much longer, he didn't know.

"I'll *break* it…"

He could tell she was serious. The strength in her hand, whether it was real or enhanced by the computer construct, made him believe she could snap his wrist like a dry twig.

Ben dropped the remote with a whimper. It slipped off the edge of the bed and clattered on the floor. Danica kicked it across the room without taking her eyes off him, or her hand off his wrist.

"Are you gonna fight me?"

He shook his head angrily.

"Okay, then."

She let go of his wrist. He rolled onto his back and massaged the injury, feeling pathetic but at least the pain had diminished.

Hedgewood reached up and flicked off the television. "Now that wasn't very nice, Ben." The man's expression held genuine disappointment. "Danica has been nothing but pleasant with you. She answered all of your questions to the best of her ability, and this you reward by attacking her with a blunt object."

"Leave the poor lad alone!" Cruikshank said.

A flash of annoyance crossed Hedgewood's features. He looked up at the ceiling and commanded in a booming voice: "*Remove Cruikshank from the construct!*"

"Hang on," the Scotsman said. "What does that—?"

His head disappeared before he could finish the question. The phantom body remained below the sheet a moment longer, before the loose fabric settled back down on the mattress.

"Do you see how easy it is to leave this room, Ben?" Hedgewood said, fixing him with a monstrous gaze. "One moment you're here and the next… you're not."

"Where did he go? Where did you take him?"

"I assure you, he'll be fine. He's safely tucked away in his own pocket Recurrence Field. The next one over from yours, in fact. Now, Ben, I'm going to give you one final chance to cooperate." He spat the words, as if the courtesy caused him discomfort. "Tell us what you know about Rex Garrote and we'll let you leave, too. It's that simple."

"I *told* you what I know," Ben moaned. As much as he tried, he couldn't keep the desperation from his voice.

"You told us what you *knew*. You remember more now. You remember what happened at Ghostland. How you and your friend survived despite the *infinite* odds stacked against you. How you managed to open the hatch door when no one but the highest levels of security would have been privy to the code. Tell us where Garrote is and you can leave here a free man."

"*But I don't know where he is!*"

The sickly smile returned to Hedgewood's face. "Very well." He looked at the ceiling. "Hold him in place."

"*No—*" Ben tried to jump out of bed but his body was frozen again. No head movement. No blinking. "I don't know *anything*," he said, glad that his voice still worked at least, although it didn't surprise him. He suspected a man like Hedgewood would leave him the ability just to hear him scream.

"Please remember, Ben: this is what happens when you cross me." Hedgewood nodded curtly to Danica. "Two-point-one."

She placed the headphones over Ben's ears and turned to face the machine.

The sound started as a low hum, a mild vibration. In a moment his vision began to quiver and his jaw clenched involuntarily, with so much force it made his teeth hurt. He felt the individual hairs on his scalp stand on end while the room around him grew hazy and indistinct, almost as though he was losing his vision.

"Why did Garrote help you escape?" Hedgewood's voice seemed independent of his blurry body standing beside the bed.

"I..." Ben's head began to throb, a dull ache arising from the center of his brain and ebbing swiftly outward. "*...don't know*," he finished through gritted teeth.

"Two, Danica."

"No!" Ben cried. But it was too late. The deep hum oscillated and his blurry vision jumped and jittered, like looking at faraway objects through a pair of binoculars in a bumpy car. The smell of raw sewage and burnt hair and scorched rubber made him nauseous. His head felt like it might explode.

"There was a man!" he shouted to be heard over the sound only he could hear. "The computer programmer! H-Harrison!"

The answer seemed to pique Hedgewood's interest. "Why would he help you?"

"I don't know, he just did!"

An ear-splitting crack drew Ben's attention to the foot of the bed. The stench intensified as the wall beyond split open like the shell of a thousand-year-old egg, and a limb ending with a large, crablike claw emerged from the hole. The first was followed immediately by another, its flesh darker than the hole itself. Impossibly black. Black like the darkest regions of space, devoid of stars, yet radiating a shimmering bioluminescence like a creature from the deepest ocean trench. Its claws pushed against the opening and the drywall peeled back wide enough for the creature to skitter through.

Unable to move, Ben could only stare at it, cringing inwardly. It scrabbled over the wall and then let go, floating toward him devoid of eyes, its carapaced limbs propelling itself forward. The stench oozed off its glistening, vibrant flesh. Somehow it seemed more solid than anything else in the room, as if he'd suddenly shifted into its reality, rather than it into theirs.

"*That's not enough!*" Hedgewood shouted from a thousand miles away, rattling the siderail with clenched fists. "*Why did you help him escape? Why did you open the hatch?*"

The creature's limbs flicked out, thousands of fleshy barbs springing from each one. Where the deadly appendages met its carapace a toothless maw opened, filled with tiny pinpricks of light like an alien galaxy hidden within its belly, and Ben knew that if he didn't tell Hedgewood what he wanted to know immediately and get the infrasound turned off, the Horrible Thing from the wall would lash out at him, the barbs would spear into his flesh, and this eldritch emissary of the Dark Rift would drag him into its infinite mouth and *chew* and he would vanish, just disappear from the world altogether, and no one would ever remember him, not even his own family. Not even Lilian.

"Because I needed to save her!" he cried with all of his remaining strength.

The creature flinched at the sound of his voice, its limbs momentarily withdrawing into its abdomen. Was it afraid of him? Not likely. Maybe it could only dine on what it thought was carrion, and his voice had startled it.

"She was gonna die!" he yelled, as loud as he could. "I couldn't let her die!"

"You did it for love." Hedgewood barked a laugh. "You let the most prolific mass murderer of the twenty-first century out of his cage because of a *girl*?"

Ben sobbed weakly, entirely drained of energy. The entity's barbed limbs emerged again, poised over him, the stench absolutely unbearable now. Ben knew that the endless galaxy within its mouth would *savor* him. His afterlife would not end swiftly. He would suffer within the belly of this beast for centuries. For *eons*.

"Yes!" he said, though he couldn't be sure if he was

speaking aloud or merely crying out in his mind. "Garrote escaped and it's *my* fault! He's raising an army and we're—
"

"What is that?" Hedgewood shouted over him.

"I don't know!" Danica sounded frantic. "Some kind of breach!"

The infrasound and vibration stopped immediately, and all of it vanished: the Dark Rift entity with its terrible mouth and claws, Hedgewood and Danica, even the hospital room itself. Ben looked around, relief replacing terror. He found himself upright in a once sterile lab. Desk items lay scattered across a table and on the floor. Sheets of paper fell like dry autumn leaves. A computer monitor lay face-down on one of the desks, the tower below sizzling with sparks. Other hardware spewed snapped circuits and shredded wires. The smell of ozone and burning plastic were almost strong enough to cover the sharp smell of blood and piss. Even this was a relief compared to the stench of the Dark Rift, still lingering in his memory.

An alarm blared from somewhere beyond the room. A man in a lab coat lay against the security door. The red light in the ceiling flashed over his face, revealing the bloody slash across his throat. In the second flash Ben saw another body in a lab coat. She lay on her front with her head against the far wall at a sharp angle, her neck snapped.

Neither of them looked like Hedgewood or Danica. These were lab drones. Probably the people in charge of the construct, the ones Hedgewood had addressed when he'd spoken to the ceiling. Judging by their reaction to the breach, Hedgewood and Danica probably weren't even in the same building and had likely escaped whatever or whoever had wrought this destruction.

A disaster had happened here, something that had pulled him out of the hospital construct—but what? Had the interdimensional creature with the barbed tentacles caused this? Was it still here, in the room with him?

He stepped forward, intending to flee. His face and hands struck cool glass, so clean he hadn't noticed it. Escaped Hedgewood's mind prison, only to find himself trapped again.

It's a pocket Recurrence Field, just like he said. How am I gonna get out of here?

Another glass capsule stood to his right. Some kind of terrarium or a giant bell jar that reminded him of the tank of red liquid they'd found Rex Garrote floating in beneath Garrote House, but smaller and empty—or so he thought, until he saw Jeremy Cruikshank's severed head hovering at waist height, blinking wildly at the sight in front of them.

"Jeremy! Hey!"

The head tilted up to face him. "What's happening, lad?" He looked down. "What happened to the rest of me?"

"That might take some time to explain," came a man's voice from behind them, very near Ben's ear. He stepped out from behind Ben's capsule, wearing his joyless smile. "Hello, Benjamin," said. "How wonderful it is to see you again."

REX GARROTE LIVES

"**W**HAT DO YOU want with me?" Ben said. There were so many questions he wanted to ask, he found it difficult to choose any single track. He'd spent six months waiting for this day. Six months preparing. Now that the enemy stood before him, all that he'd wanted to say had flittered from his mind.

"You know this fella?" Cruikshank asked.

Garrote favored the floating head with a sneer.

"All this time," Ben said, "all this time we spent arguing about whether or not you were gone, or when you'd come back to kill us all. Why now? Why here?"

"Benjamin, I have no intention of *killing* you. In point of fact, you may have noticed I saved your life a moment ago. The man you've just had the misfortune of meeting," Garrote said with another sneer, "was Ghostland's silent partner, Oliver Hedgewood. Why now, you ask? Because the moment Hedgewood got what he needed he would have eliminated you with his infrasound device."

"Why should I believe you? After all you did to me— to my friends!"

"The loss of their lives was unfortunate but essential collateral damage. If it makes you feel any better," he added with a dark grin, "a few of them have even chosen to forgive me."

Ben scoffed. "Why would they *ever* forgive you?"

"Because there is a war coming, Benjamin. You were right on that point. And you'd be wise to join your friends on the winning side."

"You're starting it!"

The writer gave him a look of disappointment. "Are you still harping on *Shōki*? Benjamin, that book wasn't a play-by-play manual. It's a novel. *Fiction.* I wrote it when I was a very troubled and confused young man, reeling from the horrors of Vietnam. Forget *Shōki*. Forget what you think you know about me. The war that's coming is not of my design. But I do intend to *win* it, no matter the cost."

"Then who?"

"You haven't guessed? Why do you think he tortured you to find me? It's Oliver Hedgewood. That device he used on you and your spineless friend here, that was simply to prove its worth to his military contacts. He'll use a much larger one *without prejudice* to wipe you and me and everyone like us off the face of the planet."

"Why should I believe you?"

"Consider it for a moment," Garrote said. "What I did at my park—which I freely admit may have been a tad melodramatic, even for an old hack like me—that was all the ammunition Hedgewood required to start a full-on, government-sanctioned assault on our kind. *A genocide the likes of which no one has ever seen.* Why do you think he let that film crew inside, knowing full well how dangerous my park still is? He *needs* the public to see for themselves. He wants them to *beg* him. 'Please, oh please spare us from the big, bad Ethereal Menace, Mr. Hedgwood, sir!' He would have killed you simply as a message to me."

"How do you know this?"

"Because I *worked* with him, Benjamin. I know how he feels about us. Oliver Hedgewood believes ethereals are *inherently* evil. His brother, Christopher, was slightly more sympathetic to our kind. We may have turned him around, in the end. Unfortunately, my house had other plans for him." Garrote shrugged. What was one more death among thousands? "I suppose that may have solidified Oliver's beliefs about us, I don't know."

"If all that's true then why did you save me? Why did you show me the code that day? *Why did you let me open the door?*"

"Because I *chose* you, Benjamin. You think I didn't *know* what you intended to do with that gasoline? Do you think I didn't *remember* you watching me from your window?"

"You *did* see me…"

"Ohhh," Cruikshank said, finally clueing in. "You must be the Carrot House fella."

"I did see you," Garrote said, ignoring Cruikshank. "And *you* saw *me*. That's, I believe, the more significant factor. Why don't we get you out of here, hmm? Then we can discuss everything in a bit more detail."

"I'm not going anywhere with you?"

"Oh no? Rather stay to find out what my pets will do with you?"

Ben considered the threat. Whatever "pets" Garrote had brought with him had already wreaked this much havoc among the living. He supposed they could just as easily do the same to him. He'd seen ethereals attack their own before. He'd seen them wipe each other out of existence. For all he knew, Garrote could have been the one to summon the entity from the Dark Rift to lurk over his hospital bed.

"I'm not leaving without Jeremy," he said.

The writer chuckled. "I wouldn't dream of leaving the head behind."

He crossed the room then, walking rather than floating, and stopped in front of a server dotted with blinking lights. He studied the machine just long enough for Ben to think he might actually know what he was doing, then reached through the face of it and tore out a handful of wiring. It sparked and fizzled, burping black smoke.

Garrote turned promptly with a satisfied grin. "I'm a bit of a luddite, but you should be free now."

Ben stepped through the glass. He hovered over the mess on the floor, feeling completely normal again. Completely himself. He was free.

But what's the price of freedom?

Cruikshank's head floated through his own capsule. "Aye, thank ye. Now if only you could do a thing or two about the rest of me."

"That can be arranged," Garrote said. "Let's blow this pop stand first, hmm? The atmosphere is really dead."

Ben and Cruikshank followed Garrote out of the lab. The destruction had carried through into the hallway. The alarm wailed. The red lights flashed. Track lighting popped and fizzled overhead, while employees in lab coats dragged themselves across the floor with blood-slicked hands, gasping for breath. Some were stuck with foreign objects, others slashed or merely battered, dead already or in the process of dying.

Doors had been thrown wide, files and equipment and machinery trashed and strewn across the floor, spilling into the hall. Men and women in street clothes lay sprawled over desks. Services workers hung from torn overhead pipes leaking fluid that mingled with their blood. There were dozens of corpses on this floor alone. Who knew how many were dead on the others?

Around the next corner Ben thought he saw a wisp of thick black smoke curl into an open doorway. He was instantly on his guard, certain of what he'd seen. "Was that…?" he started to say, then left the thought hanging, not wanting to speak its name aloud.

"One of my pets," Garrote said with a proud smile.

As they passed the room Ben thought he'd seen the entity slip into, it was empty aside from the dead and their business scattered across the floor.

"*Why would you do this?*"

Garrote gave him a sidelong glance. "These people would have erased you from the world as if you'd never existed and gone back to their quarters to watch *Bonanza*. As far as I'm concerned, they got what they deserved. I'm just peeved I wasn't able to find the man in charge, or the woman who'd abducted you."

The memory came back as a revelation. From her height and build and the lower half of her face he'd seen below the strange headset she'd been wearing: Danica, the woman who'd played the nurse, was the same person who'd captured him outside the storage sheds where Bram and Thea had been storing the explosives.

"They're going to blow it up," he said.

"Beg pardon?"

"GRP2 has a shed full of C4. They're gonna blow up the Recurrence Field and let out all the ghosts."

A slight smirk crossed Garrote's face. "Yes, I suppose that is a possibility," he said.

Around the next corner, a woman in a lab coat lay half

inside one of the elevators. The door opened as it struck her thigh and drew slowly closed again, pressing her against the jamb. A mechanical pencil had pierced her windpipe and she scrabbled at it with her fingers, unable to grasp it let alone pull it out. Her throat gurgled.

Ben crouched to help her. The woman's glassy eyes rolled toward him, as if she could see the three of them.

"Don't bother," Garrote said. "She's already dead, she just doesn't know it yet. Rather like my misfortunate literary critic, Mr. Carruthers."

The woman gurgled once more, then her hands dropped to her sides. Garrote grabbed the dead woman by the ankles and dragged her out of the elevator, her blood smearing on the tiles. He stepped inside and looked at Ben expectantly. "Aren't you coming?"

"With you? No way."

"Don't you want to see your mother and father? Don't you want to see Lilian?"

"She isn't in Duck Falls. And what makes you think I can't get there myself?"

Garrote made a wishy-washy gesture. "You can try. Go ahead, I'll wait."

Ben squeezed his eyes shut and thought about home. He thought about his mom and dad, the hole in the backyard and the hole he'd left in their hearts. He pictured minute details he never would have had to imagine to wink out here and wink back there before: his shelf of monster memorabilia, his Rex Garrote paperback collection gathering dust in a box in the closet, his dad's chair, his mom's home office. None of it worked.

"What's the matter, lad?"

"It won't work. I can't get home." He turned on Garrote. *"Why can't I go home?"*

"Let me take you there," Garrote said, directing him toward the elevator. "Back to Ms. Petralia and Mr. Moncrief." He reacted to Ben's surprise. "Yes, I know all about you and your friends. You didn't think I'd been on safari all this time, did you? I've been watching you quite closely."

Reluctantly, Ben entered the elevator. Cruikshank floated in behind him.

"Why can't we just float through the ceiling?" Ben said after a moment.

"That would take far too much time to explain," Garrote said. "And as you know, I don't like exposition. Going up."

He pressed G1. The panel displayed twenty floors below ground level, all labeled with the B prefix. There were only a handful above ground. The doors slid closed and the elevator began to rise.

"Have you read *Charlie and the Chocolate Factory*?" Garrote asked as the numbers lit up one after another.

"I'm not your friend, Garrote. I'm not interested in chit chat."

Garrote shrugged. "Suit yourself. It's a very long way to the top. But that's true of most journeys."

They passed a few more floors in silence.

"Just three fellas riding in an elevator," Garrote said.

Cruikshank's head rotated to face Ben. "Does he always talk so much?"

If he wasn't so angry and anxious and confused, Ben might have laughed. Instead, he watched the floors light up, one after another.

When the bell dinged, the elevator doors opened on a brightly lit glass atrium, the low, desert sun shining in. A security guard lay dead in the center of the marble floor at the far end of a wide streak of blood, as if he'd been thrown and slid a distance of about ten feet. Closer to the doors, a number of shell casings were scattered. He must have unloaded a clip on whatever had come through the doors, unaware that guns posed no threat to ethereals. A second guard leaned against the wall behind the security desk, beside his toppled chair, his innards in his lap.

Garrote paid the bodies no mind. "We can swift from here."

Cruikshank frowned. "Swift?"

"Travel," Ben explained. "Wink out here, end up somewhere else."

Garrote gave Ben a grim look. "Unless you want to teach him, I'm afraid we're going to have to leave the head behind."

"I have a name, you numpty."

Cruikshank had a name and likely had memories of a life before his death, and Ben refused to just leave him stranded. The Scotsman was "newly woke," as Le Mon had once said of Ben. Who knew how many of the ethereals Garrote had turned to his side remained within these walls? How many creatures like the Swarm?

Soon the facility would likely be teeming with imagoes, hunting fresh ethereals like Cruikshank. And as curious as Ben was to see what the entities who hid in mirrors and glass and other reflective surfaces looked like, there was nothing he could do for these people to ease their transition. There were far too many of them. If they survived the assault—and Ben had no doubt it would be easy pickings for the imagoes—they would either come and find him and the others at the Temple on their own… or Garrote would reach them first.

He felt a certain responsibility to Cruikshank, though.

After all, Hedgewood had tortured the poor guy just to make a point.

"I'll carry him," he said.

"Good lad. Just don't use me for a footie."

"A what?"

"He means a soccer ball," Garrote said brusquely. "Now could we move, please? Time is of the essence."

Ben held out his hands and Cruikshank floated over, nestling between them. "Let's hope this works," Ben said.

The three of them winked out, leaving just shy of one hundred dead Hedgewood Foundation employees to fend for themselves. As the first ethereals emerged from their physical bodies, vulnerable, confused and afraid—the atrium glass came alive.

AN ULTIMATUM

BEN OPENED HIS eyes, expecting to find himself standing in front of the Temple with Cruikshank cradled in his hands. The last thing he'd wanted to see was what lay before him.

"Where are we, lad?"

Ben let Cruikshank go and wheeled around, taking in his surroundings. Above and around them were towering structures and collapsed tents, colorful facades and empty food stands. A crinkled and torn map fluttered across the dusty promenade. A sign once proclaiming the Magnificent Quentin's magic show hung from one frayed piece of rope, flapping in the desolate wind like a flag at half-mast. The wood-and-steel bones of the children's Ghoster Coaster grumbled and groaned. The tram cars directly above their heads swayed, creaking rhythmically against their cables. In the far distance thin reeds of smoke rose above the northeast wall, near the place where Garrote House had once stood.

"This," Garrote said to Cruikshank, his arms spread wide, "*this* is my crowning achievement. *Welcome to Ghostland.*"

Ben glowered. "If you ask me what I'm afraid of, I swear to God...."

Garrote chuckled. "All right, all right. No need for theatrics."

"Why did you bring us here, Garrote?"

"You mean to ask, why aren't we at the Temple. The reason is simple. I told you I would bring you to your people and I will, if that's what you decide. But first, I really must show you something."

"What's to stop me from—?"

"If you want your friends to die, by all means—*go*. If you want to *save* them, I urge you to come with me. I promise, everything will be explained to you shortly."

The writer held his gaze. Despite everything he'd done to deserve disbelief, his eyes held a sincerity Ben had never seen in him. Before Ben could react one way or the other, Garrote turned on his heels and strode away, heading south along the promenade toward the midway entrance. "You're free to go, Mr. Cruikshank," he said, without even a glance behind him.

"Go? Where the hell would I go?"

The writer pointed, not looking back. "Head three miles that way, as the crow flies. You should find some of Benjamin's people waiting at the big, white church."

"But the Recurrence Field," Ben said.

"That won't be an issue," Garrote said offhandedly. "Oh, and if you'd like your body back, Mr. Cruikshank, you'd be wise to come find me soon. I know some people who should be able to help."

"Don't listen to him," Ben said.

Cruikshank scoffed. "That guy? I'd have to be a total radge to take his word as gospel, wouldn't I?" He bobbed his head in a friendly nod. "Thanks for the lift, lad."

"I'll see you soon. Just follow those directions and you should find my friends."

"Aye. See you then."

Cruikshank floated off. Ben had no idea what he'd do once he reached the edge of the park with the Recurrence Field still running, but he supposed since Garrote had brought them here, he must have also had a plan to get them out.

He caught up to the writer. "Why are we walking?"

Garrote didn't turn. "Because we have things to speak of which don't concern the person I'm bringing you to meet."

"Who?"

"That, you'll have to wait to find out."

"Then talk."

Garrote smiled back at him. "I like you better this way. You were far too timid the last time we met. Brave but frightened. You don't seem at all afraid now."

"You don't scare me anymore. I've seen things…" He shook his head. "…you can't even imagine what I've seen. Things I couldn't even *describe*."

Garrote gave him another sidelong glance. "You've read my books, Benjamin. Tell me I can't imagine what you've seen."

Ben just looked at him. Hard.

The writer laughed. "Well, maybe you have, maybe you haven't. Regardless, we have much to discuss and we can't do it in front of *him*."

"Why are you acting like you care about any of us, all of a sudden? You seemed pretty fine with exploiting ethereals at Ghostland, all the way up until the minute I let you out. You made a computer virus to control their minds."

"Benjamin, you of all people should know, those ethereals you've implied I brainwashed, I only did to them what was required to *free* them."

"But you're the one who *captured* them!"

"They were already *imprisoned*," Garrote seethed. "I did exactly what you and your fellow Gurpies are doing now. You're merely continuing my work."

"We're *helping* people. You *used* them."

"I *empowered* them. I gave them what they needed to help themselves. That's far more valuable. Why give a man legs when you can teach him to walk without them?"

"And all those clones of you? All of those ethereals wearing your face, that's what they were doing? *Helping* themselves? Not just helping *you* escape?"

"*You* helped me escape. *They* were the catalysts I needed them to be."

"For what?" Ben snapped.

"For you to play your part, Benjamin. And you just couldn't help yourself, could you? Even with your mind corrupted by thoughts of revenge, I *knew* you couldn't resist being the White Knight. I *knew* you wouldn't let the girl you love die, even if she was standing right at your side."

Ben's anger boiled over. He launched himself at a tram car parked in the station. The windows shattered and the car crashed against the ticket booth. It swung back like a pendulum as the entire booth collapsed.

As Ben calmed, Garrote applauded. "Wonderful! It's unhealthy to bottle up all that rage. Let me teach you to harness it. Channel it toward a higher purpose."

"Fighting your war? I don't think so."

"You'll change your mind once you've seen what I have to show you."

"Then stop wasting my goddamn time and take me there!"

Garrote raised an eyebrow. "Very well," he said.

In the next instant they stood just inside the heavy door to the control room. The dead were gone but the evidence of destruction remained: the smashed security monitors where Sara Jane Amblin had been crucified, the overturned computers and desk chairs, the loose papers and scattered desk ornaments, from bobblehead movie characters to photos in smashed frames. It smelled putrid in here—not quite as bad as the entity he'd encountered in Hedgewood's construct, but enough to make him uncomfortable. The hum of circulating air and the whir of a lone computer fan were joined only by the incessant buzz of flies.

"I love it when a story comes full circle," Garrote said with a smile. "Don't you?"

Ben ignored him, following the sound of the fan to a workstation row near the middle. A man sat in the ergonomic desk chair, his arms draped over the armrests, fingers dangling. His head was tilted to one side, a latticework of wires and flashing nodules resting on his filthy, matted hair. His clothes were grimy and torn, with a stain that looked suspiciously like vomit smeared across his chest, and a patchwork of scratches on his face and upper arms. He smelled terrible. A smudged pair of glasses lay on the desk as coding on the monitors flashed in his glazed, glassy eyes.

"Harrison." Ben shook him. "Harrison, wake up!"

A fly landed on Harrison's eyelash. He didn't blink as it rubbed its legs together, preparing to dine—but the pupil dilated. He wasn't dead, but his mind must have been elsewhere.

Ben reached for the device on his head.

"I wouldn't do that, if I were you."

He turned to find Garrote watching him cautiously from the next row up.

"I thought he was dead."

"Dead? Whatever gave you that idea?"

Ben thought back to the waves upon waves of ghosts that had swept over them that day. Maybe he hadn't seen Harrison among them. Maybe he'd been mistaken. Or maybe it had been the same hologram that had helped him and Lilian in the first place. Maybe he'd been here the whole time, interacting with them through this mesh on his head.

"What's wrong with him? Why won't he wake up?"

"Because he's not with us right now."

"What do you mean, he's not with us?"

Garrote grinned. "He's in my home. Safe, for the time being."

"Your…" Ben tried to decipher what the writer was saying. "Your house is gone. It's a pile of rubble in a hole."

"In a manner of speaking, yes. But it also exists in the *virtual* world. Harrison is there now. The device on his rather ugly cranium is called the Pandora, named after his favorite film."

"What? *Avatar*?" Ben scoffed. "That movie sucks."

"It didn't sound like something that would appeal to me, either," Garrote said. "I tuned out after a while, to be perfectly frank."

Ben scowled at the programmer's prone body. His blank, dirt-streaked face. The mesh of wires and flashing diodes on his matted hair. "What does it do?"

"The technology is far too complex for me to explain even if I fully understood it myself. Suffice to say it allows a consciousness to relocate anywhere in physical space. It also allows for said consciousness to occupy a *mental* construct, which I believe you experienced in Hedgewood's labs. You may recall I was wearing one of these when you roasted me like a marshmallow over a campfire," the writer added with a sardonic grin.

"Why does he smell so bad?"

"Regrettably, while a consciousness is able to exist within a construct for prolonged periods, the physical body still has certain requirements. While he's been… *indisposed*, for lack of a better word, I've taken it upon myself to take care of those needs for him. Once we ran out of food in the staff fridge, we had to make due with leftovers from elsewhere in my park. Fortunately, some of the fridges are still running at various facilities and food stands. And with my permanent access to the grid, I made it so he's been able to avoid being caught by the security cameras. You see, Harry's been doing some… *covert* work while I've been busy elsewhere."

For a moment, Ben had no idea what Garrote could mean. Then it all fell into place. He'd been right all along. "It *was* you killing those psychics!"

The writer patted Harrison's shoulder. "Technically it was Rip Van Winkle, my foul-smelling somnambulist serial killer. It's really very clever the way he managed it. His brain-mapping chapeau seems to work as a sort of psychic projector, if you will. When you saw me cruising down your main drag that day all those years ago, I wasn't actually inside my house at all. I was at the Hedgewood lab, wearing Harry's fancy little doodad. When I realized you were able to see me, I knew in a heartbeat there must be something special about you, no pun intended. And when I saw that you recognized me—that you were, in fact, my number one fan, I knew it was *destiny* that led me to you. Don't you see that, Benjamin? So I reached out …

and I gave you a little fright."

"You tried to kill me!"

Garrote rocked his head from side to side. "What happened to you wasn't deliberate. I regretted what I did immediately, but frankly in my erstwhile state I wasn't able to help. All I could do was return to my body and hope for the best. Fortunately for all of us, you pulled through."

"I was in recovery for months! Do you even *care* how much pain I was in?"

"Pain? How about the pain of being set on fire, hmm? Did you forget about that?"

"Everyone called me The Dead Kid!" Ben shouted over him. "My parents pulled me out of school! *You ruined my life!*"

"On the contrary," Garrote said calmly. "I gave you a *purpose*. Let's face it, Benjamin: you were never going to do much with your life before I touched your heart. Now, you're an American hero. *You held the door*."

Garrote smiled his dark smile, but Ben had already tuned him out, focused solely on his anger, his burning rage.

"Thank you for that, by the way," the writer droned on. "It's a courtesy you don't often get these days. You know, I find it's the little things like holding a door for someone."

Ben pushed out with all the fury in his body and the wall behind the security monitors split open with a deep rumble. A cloud of dust fell as the monitors tilted and shifted, creating an uneven mosaic of cracked plastic and concrete.

Garrote was eyeing him anxiously. "Whoa, there, kimosabe. Just calm down, would you?"

The workstations all began to tremble. Computers that hadn't already fallen over toppled. Tchotchkes rocketed over their heads. Several cans of Coke Zero heaped in a loose pile exploded in a fountain of beige fizz. The bags of random brands of chips nearby popped like a strand of fireworks, their contents littering the carpet.

Then, one at a time, everything settled as Ben felt himself calm again.

A wide smile spread across Garrote's face. "That felt good, didn't it?"

Ben's gaze flicked toward the writer. "It did," he admitted. "But I'd feel a lot better if I could do what I wanted to."

"And what is that?"

"To kill you for good," Ben said, his eyes narrowed to slits. "Send you to the Dark Rift."

"Well, we can't always get what we want. Speaking of which, my friend Harrison's Great Work here is finally complete. He's claimed the lives of four very prominent psychics and a handful of lesser-known but no less powerful mediums. All in service of my… *grand scheme*."

"Which is what?" Ben said flatly.

"To open the Dark Rift." Before Ben could react, he held up a hand. "Now, now, here me out—"

"You're crazy! That's *death. Forever* death."

"For many, yes. But not for *us*. If you stand with me against Hedgewood, with the unfortunate creatures of the Dark Rift doing my bidding—"

"What makes you think they would listen to you?"

"I'm the Dionne Warwick of my very own little Psychic Friends Network," Garrote said. "Think of it like a satellite array of astral energy. I'm in control of them, for the time being, and with their linked psyches I should be able to harness the entities within the Rift. Of course, this is all theoretical. I could open the Dark Rift and let loose an ocean of noxious dead energy into the world, smothering all life and afterlife as we know it. But you can't get ahead if you don't take risks, I always say."

"You'd risk that? Killing everyone on earth, living and ethereal? *Why?*"

"Because if I don't, *he'll kill us all anyway.*"

Much as Ben didn't want to admit it, he believed Garrote. The cavalier way Hedgewood had treated him and Cruikshank, pushing them so close to the edge of the Dark Rift merely because he thought Ben had been working with Garrote—who knew what a man like that would do with that kind of power? And what Garrote said about Hedgewood's reasoning for allowing the Ghost Brothers and their crew into the park—a decision that hadn't made a whole lot of sense to anyone at the time—did seem to track. He needed to drum up a fervor among the public to get the government's support.

But Garrote had already done worse. He'd murdered thousands of innocent people, all in service of his "grand scheme." As if that wasn't enough, he'd had Harrison murder a bunch of prominent psychics. Now he intended to open the Dark Rift…

It was madness. All of it.

"Maybe that's a good thing," he said aloud, answering Garrote.

"A good thing," Garrote said, taken aback. "To be wiped out? To be *nothing*?"

"Maybe we weren't meant to exist after we die," Ben said. "Maybe the afterlife is a cosmic fluke. A mistake of nature. I mean think about it, there's been *one-hundred and eight billion* people born on this planet since the beginning of time. There's just not enough room for all of us."

"That theory might be fine for you, Benjamin. I happen

to *enjoy* living."

"But *you're not alive.*"

The writer shrugged. "Quibble with semantics, if you like. The reality doesn't change." He held out a hand. "Anything you want, it's yours. You want to be older? I can make you taller, smarter, stronger. I can give that to you, Benjamin. I can give you the girl, if that's what you want. Anyone you choose, you can have. *Stand with me*, Benjamin. This is your last chance."

Ben looked at the programmer, his body wasting away while Garrote abused his mind. This was the price of loyalty. He wondered what Harrison had been promised. What had it taken to bend him to Garrote's will?

"No," Ben said.

The writer's gaze narrowed. "Are you testing me? Would you like a demonstration of my powers?"

"The only thing I want from you is to leave us alone. That's what you don't get. I liked your books, that's all. But you're a terrible human being. A *monster*. Why do you think I set you on fire, you maniac? Because I wanted to be your bestie?"

Garrote barked a laugh. "Well done. I am really going to miss you, Benjamin. And to think, I was going to let you unleash your rage on poor, pathetic Harrison."

Without warning he reached down and snapped the programmer's neck, twisting his head all the way around so Harrison faced Ben with his eyes still wide and his mouth agape, neck bulging where his spine had snapped.

It took a minimal amount of force for Garrote to tear the head right off with a hollow crack and a snap of torn flesh. Twin jets of deep-red blood spurted from Harrison's jugulars as Garrote held up the head to Ben like a macabre carnival prize.

"Would you like to keep him? He and that Cruikshank fellow would make a lovely matching pair."

Ben threw himself at him.

Garrote cast the head aside and threw his hands forward, halting Ben's momentum so forcibly Ben felt it in bones he no longer possessed. He hurtled backward, rolling over and over in the air above the workstations, and though he expected to keep spinning all the way through the back wall he only remembered what Demont had said about the salt in the cinderblocks as he struck it solidly, knocking the sense out of him momentarily, and leaving a spiderweb crack in the concrete as he slumped to the floor.

"*YOU ATTACK ME IN MY HOUSE*," Garrote bellowed, launching across the space between them. His eyes had changed to a strange yellow-gold, the pupils flat and black like a goat's. He struck Ben backhanded, knocking him back to the floor just as Ben began to rise. He waved his hands like a conductor and Ben shot into the air, slamming against the ceiling. Ben struggled to move but he was pinned there, the way the Swarm had pinned Sara Jane Amblin to the security monitors a lifetime ago.

"You can *rot* with your friends, for all I care!"

Garrote threw his hands again, dragging Ben across the ceiling until he struck the wall above the monitors. He fell to the floor once more, entirely drained of energy. This was a fight he would never win, not in the state he was now. He had to surrender.

"Go home," Garrote said, turning away from him. He was hunched over and appeared to be breathing heavily, though he didn't need to breathe. He sounded hurt. Betrayed. "You're not wanted here."

"You're just gonna let me—"

"*GO!* Before I change my fucking mind."

Ben prepared to wink out, doubtful Garrote would ever let him leave. Certain this was just another mind game. Another trick.

"Oh, and just so you're not surprised," the writer said with sudden good cheer. "You might discover a few changes to the Duck Falls you remember."

"What do you mean, *changes*?"

When Garrote finally turned, his dark smile had returned. "Ask your friends," he said.

Then the control room vanished.

Ben winked back in the middle of town, hovering directly in front of the Temple. Several of its windows had been smashed and appeared to be boarded up from the inside, as if the church had been abandoned once again.

He wheeled around to take in the rest of downtown. A sedan had crashed through the exterior wall of town hall, its rear wheels hovering over the steps. A streetlamp lay across the street like a felled tree, and a fire hydrant had been knocked over, creating a small, dammed creek in the gutter. Further along, the road itself looked like it had been torn up, the asphalt cracked and fissured until it reached a massive sinkhole. A fire crackled from the hulk of a burned-out cube van near the hole.

Armageddon was the first word that came to mind.

"What the hell happened here?" he said aloud.

He continued on to Main Street, where a three-car pileup had blocked the intersection below the four-way flashing red lights. The doors hung open, as if the injured parties had all left in a hurry. Each of the surrounding buildings had shattered windows just like the church, some boarded up from the outside with plywood, others blocked from the inside by furniture and whatever else might have been at hand.

Ben hovered in the middle of the road, pondering over a dark stain in the asphalt, wondering if it was engine oil or blood.

"How long was I gone?"

The blinds hung bent and twisted through shattered glass in Lilian's living room window when Ben approached the bulk food store below. He winked out and reappeared in their apartment, calling her mother's and father's names. The kitchen and living room were empty, but relatively clean. Whatever had happened in town must have occurred while the Roths weren't at home.

Maybe they left town.

He wouldn't acknowledge the fact that they might have died out there. That whatever had happened in Duck Falls while he'd been kidnapped by Hedgewood had gotten them killed—and that this, *all of this*, was his fault for opening that goddamned hatch in the first place.

I'm no hero. I got everyone killed.

If he'd been able to cry, he might have. Lacking tears, he simply wallowed in despair as he wandered through the Roths' apartment. He found luggage in Lilian's room. A duffel bag and Lilian's red suitcase on the bed, her suitcase open. Folded neatly inside was clothing he thought he'd seen her wear recently. He pulled some out, smelling her light perfume and fruity-scented shampoo as he looked them over. He was sure she'd worn this exact black top on Hallowe'en.

She's here. I don't know why, but she's here right now. Somewhere in town.

For a moment, his hopes rose. Then he realized Lilian would have been caught up in all this along with her parents. If they were dead, chances are she was dead too.

Beneath the black top was something made from

crinkly silver plastic like a cheap tarp. He recognized it, though he wasn't sure how she would have gotten one, or why she would have brought it to Duck Falls. Maybe it was the same keeper suit she'd worn at Ghostland. Would they have let her keep it?

For whatever reason, it was here. He needed to get it to her. He wasn't sure if it would keep her safe outside of the park—he certainly didn't seem to have any issue holding it, though the power was currently off—but if she was out there somewhere, he would get it to her.

As he entered the hall a chillingly familiar sound arose from the street, like raving laughter from an insane asylum filtered through a tin can. He shot through the living room wall to the window overlooking Main Street, peering down through the cracks in the bent and lopsided blinds just in time to see two entities like tattered black rags flitter down the alley between the ice cream shop and Green's Antiques.

The Swarm. It's here in Duck Falls.

All of the pieces fell into place suddenly: the smoke he'd seen flittering in the distance above Ghostland. Garrote's shrugging dismissal when he'd told him what Thea and Bram had intended. His warning that things in town would be different than he remembered.

"It happened," he said, watching the Swarm vanish down the alley. "*It already happened.*"

While he'd been trapped inside Hedgewood's pocket Recurrence Field at the Hedgewood labs, Thea and Bram had destroyed the only thing protecting Duck Falls and the rest of the world from whatever evil entities had remained within Ghostland.

Now those ethereals were loose in the streets of Duck Falls. His hometown. Terrorizing the lives of his friends.

His family.

No one was safe.

If anyone's still alive, he thought.

Overwhelmed by panic and fear, Ben winked out, heading back home.

INTERLUDE: MIND PRISON

Ghostland
April 20th—April 21st, 2019

NOBODY CAME TO rescue Harrison.

Within six hours of the park going into full meltdown, the main gate finally rolled up and the first responders had charged right through. The monitors—those that hadn't been shattered by the impact of Ms. Amblin's body when the Alpha pinned her to the wall—had showed soldiers and police in keeper suits and riot gear tromping through the park grounds, searching the rubble for survivors, checking the dead for signs of life, all while fending off random ghost attacks. They'd gathered up groups of survivors and brought them back to the parking lot on foot and in vehicles.

Oddly, not a single one of them had approached the control room. Though Harrison supposed they'd assumed it was a mechanical building, judging by its flat, cinderblock exterior, and ignored it, he couldn't help but think they might have been directed to stay away.

While they'd searched, he'd been content to believe he was still needed. He'd convinced himself Garrote would be disappointed if he left, and disappointing Garrote was a surefire way to end up dead like the rest of them.

Now they were gone, and wouldn't be back until first light. He was alone in a park full of ghosts. In the dark.

Except he wasn't truly alone, was he? If he was, he could feasibly deal with that. But his colleagues were still in here with him. Every time he glanced over the tops of his monitors, he caught their glazed eyes watching him, *accusing* him. And very soon, they would start to stink.

"Mr. Garrote?"

Nothing.

He hadn't expected a reply but the rejection still stung. Garrote hadn't spoken to him in hours. The only voice he'd heard was his own anxious muttering as he sifted through pages and pages of code, wondering how exactly Garrote had managed to compromise the system.

"*Mr. Garrote!*" he shouted, one last time.

The monitor wall remained blank. The control room, eerily quiet.

"Fine," he grunted, pushing up from his desk chair. "If that's what I have to do, that's what I have to do. My work isn't done. My work is *never* done."

He spent the next fifteen minutes trying to summon the courage to drag the bodies of his coworkers into the women's washroom. He spent the following twenty-five accomplishing it. Their wrists and legs were cold and their bodies as stiff as dolls as he dragged first Ms. Amblin, then Nia, then "Ace" and Rodney across the glass and plastic-littered carpeting. Rodney was the most difficult, as he weighed much more than Harrison, and his Deadpool hoodie kept bunching up around his jostling breasts so that Harrison had to stop every few feet and pull the sweater back down around Rodney's doughy gut.

When he was done, Harrison stood in the doorway looking at them all, lined up against the stalls like a serial killer's menagerie. Their faces had gone gray and their glassy eyes had sprung open, staring at him accusingly.

"It wasn't my fault," he muttered, but they kept staring at him until he looked down at his feet. Even then he could feel their eyes boring into him. "I didn't know what he was planning. How could I know?"

He slammed the door on them, dragged a desk chair over and tucked it under the handle, telling himself it was just in case.

"Just in case," he repeated, throwing a nervous glance over his shoulder at the washroom door as he hurried back to his desk.

Sitting in front of his terminal, Harrison thought back to the night Ms. Amblin had surprised him in her lab, and her sudden question about the nature of the soul. Was it merely data, he wondered, converted from matter to pure energy? The same, with different housing? If so, would a consciousness that existed solely within the Pandora still retain its human essence? Its—for lack of a better word—*soul*?

More importantly, was the Garrote who'd perished when the kids smashed his capsule and burned him alive the same man as the uploaded consciousness who'd orchestrated this mass tragedy? Why spend so much time and money to create this place only to tear it all down like a child having a tantrum on his toys?

That was the real question Harrison hoped the code would answer. He needed to know if Garrote had planned this from the start, if someone else had tweaked the code without his knowledge, or if existing within the construct had corrupted Garrote's mind.

The problem he was up against was that the virus—or whatever it was—seemed to be a heisenbug. Every time he thought he'd found its source, it disappeared or changed, hiding itself among the countless processes, functions, subroutines and data structures.

I need to know why he did it. And if he won't tell me in person, I'll just have to make him.

He settled the Pandora back on his head, logged in and pulled up Garrote's mindspace. In a blink he found himself in the foyer of Garrote House. The chandelier he'd created from Garrote's memory swayed lightly, its crystals tinkling, and the oil lamps along the staircase alighted one by one with dull *thwoomps* of igniting flame. The fireplace at the far end of the high-ceilinged room rumbled and popped, nestled between Clayton O'Dell's bizarre human-and-machine hybrid sculptures.

As he took a step into the house, the heavy front door creaked shut and slammed. He started, spinning on his heels to face it.

"Mr. Garrote?" he called out, turning back toward the interior of the house. The echo of his voice further disturbed him.

He laughed at himself. There was no need to be afraid. This was a virtual space—nothing in this house could harm him. Still, being here all alone made him nervous. Alone inside the mind of a maniac, while his body sat vulnerable behind his desk in a theme park filled with the dead.

Footsteps thumped on the carpeting above him. He followed their movement along the ceiling. Could it be Mr. Garrote? Harrison had added a host of companions for the writer while he languished here: every ghost that had ever darkened its doorstep, from the hideous human amalgam known as the Behemoth to the cleaning staff of the original owners, Oliver and Desdemona Hedgewood. Each an exact replica of its corresponding ghost within the park. It could be any one of them up there, though Harrison recalled the Behemoth generally signaled its approach with a blast of its makeshift horn.

A moment later, a door opened. The hard-soled shoes pounded down a set of stairs, continued briskly down a hall, clicking on the hardwood. A second door opened and a shadowy figure stepped out onto the landing.

Only one set of arms, judging by the shadow thrown large on the wall behind it. It wasn't the Behemoth. Harrison let out a sigh of relief.

Thick fingers curled over the handrail. They were too pale and hairless to be Garrote's. A rotund man with apple-red cheeks and a thin, waxed mustache appeared over the top of the balcony, peering down. He wore a cinched tuxedo, its buttons stretched to their limit. The fingers clenched, creaking against the wood as he smiled darkly over the railing.

"Good evening, Harry," he said.

Harrison recognized him instantly. It was the man who'd accidentally blown off the top of his own head with a shotgun while trying to assault his maid.

"We're so pleased you've decided to join us," said Oliver Hedgewood, the first of his lineage. The portly man let out a girlish titter. "In fact, you could say we've all been *dying* to meet you."

PART 4
THE FINAL DAYS
OF DUCK FALLS

"The stakes need to be life and death, and not just for the protagonists. It needs to be, 'Such-and-such is going to happen and the fate of the whole world is at stake.' Otherwise what's the point of it all?"

— Rex Garrote, interview excerpt,
Playboy, May 1984

It is our responsibility to lead the charge toward freeing our ethereal brothers and sisters on a global scale. We must continue to speak out for those who cannot speak for themselves, no matter the cost. Our objective is total ethereal liberation. Anything less can no longer be permitted.

— GRP2 manifesto

HOME FREE

Three days ago.

LILIAN AND BLAKE stepped off the private jet together and waited inside the terminal for Thea and Bram to deal with the flight staff. The trip was just about as extra as Lilian had expected. Wide, fully reclining leather seats, hot towels and champagne mimosas—Thea's "absolute fave, *omigod*"—free movies and a three-course meal. Lilian had never experienced so much decadence in her life, and felt a little guilty for enjoying it while Ben was still missing and could've been sucked into the Dark Rift, wherever and whatever that might be.

"I can't believe I'm finally gonna meet your parents," Blake said, hiking his backpack up on one shoulder, sounding both excited and terrified.

Lilian felt the same: excited, terrified, a little dizzy. Her guts churned with anxiety and a lack of proper sleep, her mind buzzing: *Maybe this was too soon. What if they don't get along? What if Mom doesn't like him? What if Dad grills him too hard?*

"I can't believe you're gonna meet *my dad*," she said. "He's such a total doofus."

Blake smiled, exhaling his stress through his nostrils. "Then we'll get along fine."

Lilian smiled back.

"There you are!" Thea burst through the sliding doors into the terminal. "Well, back to the cold weather, huh? Who needs sunshine, anyway? Guess you must be used to this though, right, Lilian?"

"I guess so."

Bram entered behind Thea, who looked relieved by his presence. On the plane, Bram was no less standoffish than before, but after what had happened at the cemetery, Lilian felt a little less wary around him. Knowing what he was capable of, and the struggle he might have dealt with to keep his gift a secret, to hold that power in check, made her feel somewhat sympathetic toward him. It was no wonder he was so reserved. It was also no wonder Thea had wanted him by her side.

The thing she didn't understand was why Thea still used the Benedict Cumberbatch text-to-speech thing to speak to Ben, or why she relied on Lilian for translation, when Bram could interact with ghosts in his "astral" form. She supposed being out-of-body might use far too much energy to do it often. She'd attempted to ask, but Bram had picked up an old-looking paperback after dinner—something called *On the Beach* by a writer named Nevil Shute—and after she'd dozed off for an hour or so in her seat, he'd been still deeply absorbed. He hadn't put the book down to eat when the meal was served, and he didn't put it down until the plane began to descend.

"Well, the car's waiting," Thea said, looking up from her phone. "Let's head back to the Temple."

They all piled into the "car"—a sleek, black stretched Escalade—and were back in Duck Falls within the hour, where Thea dropped Lilian and Blake off on the sidewalk in front of her apartment.

"I'd love to pop in and meet your folks," she said, as if Lilian had suggested it. "But our people are waiting. Swing by the Temple when you get a chance. We need to chat."

"I will."

"It was nice to meet you, Blake. You've got a great girl here. Don't mess it up."

"Yeah, uh… you too, thanks," Blake said, apparently not sure which statement to respond to first. "Later, Bram." He held up a hand.

Bram nodded curtly. Thea chuckled and closed the door. The limo drove off, leaving them alone.

It was early, the sun barely up over the top of the hill to the east. Frost had formed on the shopfront windows and windshields of cars parked in the street. The crisp air, redolent with dead leaves, already edging toward winter. She looked across the street at Green's Antiques, Mrs. Laramie's realtor office and the Fresh Scoop ice cream parlor she'd worked at over the summer. Then to the 86 Diner where her mother's shift would start in an hour or so. Finally, reluctantly, up at her living room window.

"So this is Duck Falls, huh?" Blake said, peering around. "It's nice."

Lilian glared at him.

"What? It's quiet. The streets are clean. You could really put down roots here. Have a whole bunch of kids, neighborhood barbecues. I bet you don't even lock your doors at night."

She smacked him on the shoulder.

He laughed. "Hey, I'm serious."

"Dead serious?"

He shrugged. "I guess so."

Lilian took out her key and twisted it in the lock. She held the door open for Blake, and the two of them stepped into the vestibule, greeted by the familiar scent of dusty carpeting and fried food, the creaky, lopsided stairs, painted thick and sloppily, and the small mailbox unit on the wall with the single door hanging open, its hinge busted for as long as Lilian could remember. It was the landlord's box anyway, and Mr. Deetz asked the mail carrier to drop his mail in front of his door, labeled with a brass SUPERINTENDENT plaque that had fallen off so many times there were strips of torn double-sided tape all around it.

Blake looked around until he noticed Lilian watching him, then he flashed a surprised smile.

"If you say this is nice, I swear," she grumbled.

He laughed. "I definitely wasn't going to say that." He glanced up the stairs. "Well, are we gonna just stand in the hall and hope your parents happen to come down or what?"

"I'm working up to it."

He smiled and took her gently by the shoulders. "Hey. I'll love them. And they'll probably tolerate me. It's gonna be fine."

She sighed and grabbed the banister. "All right, let's do this." She climbed the stairs, Blake following behind her. On the third floor were three apartments. Her door was marked with a black "3B" sticker. She was about to knock when the door opened on its own.

Her father stood silhouetted by the morning light from the windows, like a chubby angel. "Lilian, my darling girl!" He swept her up in his arms and kissed her cheek, his bristles scratching her face. "And this fine young gentleman must be Blane."

He let the mistake hang for a moment, while Blake

turned to Lilian, wondering if he should correct her dad or if she would, or if they should just let it pass.

"I'm *kidding*," Hiram said, relieving the tension. He clasped Blake's right hand in both of his and shook it vigorously. "Of *course*, it's Blake. I'm Hiram. Pleasure to meet you finally. Welcome to casa de Lilian. Otherwise known as the Roths' residence. Come in, come in!"

Lilian stepped in, feeling like she'd been sucked into a whirlwind. Blake followed, a wide smile plastered to his face as he looked around the apartment. He glanced at the shoe mat beside the door. Then at Hiram's slippers. "Should I take off my shoes…?"

"Did you hear that, Maddy?" Hiram called into the hall to the bedrooms and bathroom.

"What?" she called back.

"He asked if he should take off his shoes!"

"That's nice. I'll be out in a minute."

Hiram smiled back at them. "You caught your mother getting ready for work. Take them off, keep them on," he said to Blake. "We're flexible. Speaking of, did Lilian tell you I used to dance?"

"Ohmigod, *Dad*…"

Blake was grinning, taking off his shoes and placing them on the mat. "No, she didn't."

"It's true. It's how I met her mother. I played Danny Zuko in my senior year's production of *Grease*—"

"*Da-a-ad*," she whined.

"Oh," Hiram said, favoring her with a pout. "Oh, my precious angel has heard this story a hundred times." He cupped her behind the head and kissed her forehead. "I'm just excited, that's all. My little girl's first real boyfriend. In our home." He turned to face the kitchen and living room. "Come in, come in. I'll make pancakes. D'you like pancakes, Blane? I'm just kidding, everyone likes pancakes and I know your name is Blake."

"*Oh my God, Dad*," Lilian groaned again.

"Yes. My God. It's wonderful to have my very supportive and loving daughter back. Have a seat, Blake. Take a load off. I'll make pancakes."

"I love pancakes," Blake said dutifully. He waited until Lilian sat on the loveseat before taking a seat beside her.

In the kitchenette, Hiram selected a pan and a mixing bowl, got a spatula and a whisk, got the mix from the cupboard, opened the fridge and took out the eggs and the milk—he'd always added them to the box mixes, assuring Lilian they made the pancakes fluffier—all the while treating them to a running monologue about his high school musical career.

Lilian squeezed Blake's leg and mouthed, *I'm sorry*.

Blake smiled. *It's okay*, he replied silently.

"—the drama teacher's mouth *agape*," Hiram was saying, stirring the milk into the mix, "and that's when I realized *A Chorus Line* probably wasn't the best choice for me to mess with gender norms, especially not by auditioning for the part of Val."

Hiram laughed. Blake joined him, though Lilian wondered if he even knew what he was laughing at.

"Oh Lord, Hi," her mother said, stepping in from the hall. "Are you telling them the tits and ass story?"

"It's called 'Dance: Ten, Looks: Three,' Maddy, but yes, I am *entertaining* them with that story, aren't I, Blake?"

"Yes, sir," Blake said, standing to greet Maddy Roth.

Hiram turned and pointed at Blake with the whisk, dripping batter. "No 'sirs,' in this house, young man. You call me Hiram or Hi, but never sir."

"Honey, you're getting batter on the floor."

"It's nice to meet you, Mrs. Roth," Blake said. He shook her hand.

"Maddy," she said with a smile. "No 'misses' in this house, either. Pleasure's mine. Now, is my lovely daughter going to favor me with a hug or do I have to beg?"

Lilian hugged her mother. She hugged back fiercely.

"We missed you, twinkletoes."

"Twinkletoes?" Blake said.

"Long story," Lilian replied. She held up a finger in her father's direction. "Don't even *think* about it, Dad."

"I wouldn't dream of it," he said, chuckling as he returned to mixing the pancakes, the tines clinking against the inside of the bowl.

"I missed you guys too, Mom," Lilian said, meaning it. "Even though Dad's obviously had too much caffeine."

"Oh, I'll get him out of your hair but I've got to leave right after breakfast," Maddy said. "It really is good to see you, sweetie. But why now? I thought we'd planned for Thanksgiving."

"It couldn't wait, Mom. I'll explain everything, soon. Can I show Blake my room for a minute first?"

Maddy glanced back at her husband, who raised his eyebrows but didn't skip a beat with the pancakes. "Of course," she said. "We'll call when breakfast's on."

She took Blake's hand and dragged him to the hall.

"I'd like to hear the rest of that story sometime, sir, I mean, Hi," Blake said as they left the kitchen.

"Don't worry," Hiram said with a wink. "I've got it bookmarked."

Lilian pulled him into her bedroom and closed the door. He grinned and she kissed him. "Thanks for putting up with them."

"Nah, they're great. I like wacky people. Why do you think I'm dating you?"

Lilian laughed and kissed him again. He kissed her back, then pulled away.

"What *are* we doing here, though? Your mom's right. Why now?"

She hadn't told him when Thea had driven her back to the dorm, just asked him to pack a bag and come along. When he'd asked on the plane, she'd told him she would tell him when they got home. They were here now. She couldn't put it off any longer.

"So you know we've been working with Thea and Bram and the Gurpies—GRP2—right? You remember I told you we've been freeing ghosts?"

"You mean ethereals," he said.

She smiled. "Right, exactly. Well, last night, before we picked you up, we broke an ethereal out of her death loop that Ben and me weren't able to help on Hallowe'en. She's really like, psychically powerful. Like, Carrie, blowing stuff up with her mind powerful."

"Psychically," Blake said. He crossed the room and sat down on the edge of her bed, his brow clouded.

"You don't believe me."

He looked up at her. "No, I believe you. I mean, I'm *trying*. It's just confusing, that's all. So you couldn't break her out before but last night you did?"

"Right." She sat down beside him. "And it's a really big deal, because Ben and Le Mon think she could help our side."

"In the war. Against that dead horror guy."

"Exactly. The Gurpies have been talking about her for ages, on the message boards and at the Temple. She's kind of like a mini celebrity for some reason, and I wasn't really sure why—but now I get it. Anyway, last night we broke her out—"

"Of her… death loop?" Blake said cautiously.

"Right, and Le Mon was able to convince her to join us. Then it turns out Bram, who we all thought was just a dick, is really an astral projector."

Blake's face brightened. He knew this one. "Like from MKUltra?"

"Sure," Lilian said. "I guess. Anyway, we almost died because these weird blurry things Le Mon called imagoes came to attack us. Like people and cats and wolves. It was pretty scary, but Bram astral projected to try and help them and then Jessica—the Woman in White, they call her, she's the ghost we were freeing, the ethereal—she like *screamed* really, really loud and then all these imagoes just kind of broke apart like glass and vanished."

Blake looked confused. "And… that's why we came here?"

"No," she said. "The reason we're here is my friend Le Mon—he's an ethereal too, a ghost—he told me the other day that Ben disappeared after the Ghost Brothers show. He hasn't seen him since and he's worried he's gone—" She shook her head, not wanting to say he'd gone to the Dark Rift, like speaking the words might make it true. "That's why I had to come back. Because we need to find him. He's the only one who knows more about Rex Garrote than me. He's the only one who can lead this war."

Blake gave her a sidelong look. He seemed shy all of a sudden, like he wanted to ask her something but didn't know how to say it.

"Then why am *I* here?" he asked finally.

Lilian smiled, taking his hands and squeezing them in his lap. "You're here because I want you to meet my family and friends. To share these parts of my life with me. I've kept things secret from you and I don't wanna do that anymore. I don't want any more ghosts between us either, because..."

She hesitated, unsure if she could say it. If now was the time.

If not now, when?

"Well, because I love you, you dummy."

It felt nice to say it. Felt *right*, flooding her heart with an intense feeling of joy. Blake smiled, having waited for some time to hear her say it back to him, and kissed her lightly on the lips.

"I love you, too," he said, delicately touching her lower lip with his thumb. "And I can't wait to meet your friends."

She smiled, wondering if she'd ever been this happy in her whole life. Wondering how long Garrote would let that happiness last.

The smile had faded by the time her dad called them for breakfast.

FAMILY LEGACIES

S AM PULLED THE rental car up to the curb outside GRP2's Duck Falls headquarters a few minutes past noon. The three of them got out, stretching their legs, and looked up at the freshly painted white church.

"So this is it, huh?" Andy shaded his eyes to get a better look. "Home of the infamous Thea Petralia and her Gurpies."

In cheap motels along the long stretches of interstate highway through Texas and the Midwest on their way to Duck Falls, Andy had looked up and shared everything he thought they might need to know about GRP2 and the Temple. They knew how the group had started, which celebrities were involved (at least by way of donations), and that they were currently in the process of freeing ghosts—which they called *ethereals*, like Lamb's mother had—from haunted places all over America. By now, Andy felt like he could have written a thesis on Ghosts Are People Too and Thea Petralia, the Kismet heiress.

"Look at this sign," Lamb said, standing in front of a large, gray stone plaque. She wore a fuzzy olive-green jacket over a vintage Billy Idol T-shirt and ridiculously tight jeans, which hiked up far enough for Andy to get a good view as she bent to read the text at the bottom aloud.

"'For Benjamin Laramie, who gave his life to hold the door.'" She pouted. "*Aww*, that's so sad."

"Kid's a national hero," Andy said, slipping an arm around her waist. He ran his fingers over the memorial's smooth granite surface.

Sam squinted at them from the car. "We should head on up."

"No rest for the wicked," Andy said with a sigh.

The three of them ascended the church steps and stopped at the door. Andy passed a look between Lamb and the detective. "Do we knock, or…?"

The door swung open as he said it, squeaking and grumbling on its hinges as it disappeared into the darkness. He had to squint into the vestibule to be certain there was no one standing inside holding open the door for them.

Like who? Benjamin Laramie?

Even though he'd been accompanied by ghosts for as long as he could remember, the idea caused Andy to shudder.

"Well, ain't that creepy?" Lamb said.

Raised voices came from within. A woman shouted to be heard over the noise, her words muted by the inner door and distance.

"Sounds like a sermon in progress," Sam said. "Guess we may as well head in and join the congregation."

Once through the outer doors, the voices were much louder. At least a dozen people argued against whatever had been said. The woman's voice—he supposed it must be Thea Petralia—rose above them again.

"I think we have to treat this issue with the gravitas it deserves," she said. "Every one of us knows ethereals are still suffering in there. Dozens. Maybe *hundreds*. You can sense it. I know I can. And yes, it will be dangerous. That's why we go in during the day. Take the same precautions the authorities did when they went in."

She paused a moment, then continued, seemingly in answer to a question Andy hadn't heard. "Yes, I am aware ethereals haven't been able to pass through the Recurrence Field. That's why it will have to be living members only."

Voices rose in opposition behind the doors.

"I guess we came at a bad time," Andy said.

"No, this needs to be our number-one priority," Thea Petralia said, answering another muffled question. "We can search for him when—"

Sam hiked up her khakis. "Screw it. I'm going in."

Andy grinned at her brashness as she threw open the doors. Thea Petralia stood behind the pulpit, gripping it firmly, her brow furrowed. The sun shone through a cluster of circular stained-glass windows above her. The gatherers were still in an uproar, at least fifty or sixty of them in all. In the multicolored sun dapple, Andy thought he glimpsed more people than there were, sitting in silhouette in the spaces between the others. When his eyes adjusted to the light, they were gone.

"Oh, my Lord," Lamb breathed, her eyes wide with wonder. "There's *so many* of them…"

Before Andy could ask what she'd meant, Thea spoke from the pulpit.

"Well, it looks like we have some visitors."

A muscular, hard-faced man Andy had seen in several photos at Thea's side during his research rose from a chair on the stage and approached her. The two of them conversed a moment, then Thea addressed them again through the microphone. "New recruits? No, you don't look like new recruits."

"Miss Petralia, I'm Detective Sam Beadle—"

Thea seemed to recognize the name. "Beadle? Was your father…?"

Sam shifted uncomfortably from foot to foot, her dress shoes scuffing the hardwood. "Stan Beadle, that's right. How did you—?"

"I know the name of every person who lost their life that day, Detective. Especially the heroes. From what I gather, your father may have been instrumental in helping survivors escape that nightmare."

Sam looked wary. "What makes you believe that?"

The woman at the pulpit smiled patiently. "Your father's remains were discovered under the rubble of Garrote House. Only two other visitors were able to make it that far. He helped Benjamin Laramie and Lilian Roth reach the maintenance hatch."

Sam looked pensive for a moment, then nodded. "Thank you. But that's not why we're here."

"Then why are you here, Detective?"

"I'd like to speak with you alone, if we could."

"You're among friends. We have no secrets here."

A handful of people in the pews seemed to disagree, though only amongst each other, casting wary glances and hiding their reactions behind seemingly innocuous gestures: cleared throats, tugged earlobes, scratched foreheads. Andy caught their tells, as obvious in life as they were in poker.

Sam shrugged. "Fair enough," she said, and moved a few paces up the aisle. "Are you aware of the deaths of Regina Delyse, Drew Agnew and Annika Levanka?"

The crowd reacted to the names, speaking in hushed tones. Some were clearly upset, others simply looked secretive like moments ago, as if they might know something more than just what they'd seen on the news.

"The psychic suicides," Thea said. "Yes, we are aware of those names."

"And do you have an opinion on that?"

Thea grinned at her people. "Well, you know what opinions are like, don't you, Detective?"

Relieved laughter greeted this.

Sam barked a single laugh with them. "They sure are. But I'm curious about yours—your opinion, that is—you being the preeminent expert in this sort of thing. I'm sure you saw the videos. What do you think caused those people to do that?"

"I wouldn't consider myself an *expert* in anything," Thea said. "Though if you're implying what I think you are, I suppose I do know more than most. Do I think an ethereal could be responsible for their deaths?" She tilted her head from side to side. "It's a possibility we've considered. Do I *believe* it?" She paused. "No, I don't believe an ethereal was responsible."

"Why not?"

"Because an ethereal that powerful would have been discovered by one of my people by now. You have to understand, Detective, the ethereal community is very tightly knit. Events like these cause ripples among them. People talk. Gossip, let's be frank." Some chuckles arose from the pews. "And yes, before you ask, we were aware fingers would be pointed in our direction, especially after what the Ghost Brothers did last weekend."

"You mean what *happened* to them," Lamb said angrily. "'Cause I don't know what *you* saw, but I heard they died."

"Yes, what happened to them was terrible," Thea said, looking toward the ceiling with her eyes half lidded. "Of course."

The admission made Lamb relax, but only slightly.

"And you don't think it's possible," Sam said as she surveyed the crowd, "that one or more of your people might be… let's say *withholding the truth* from you?"

Thea chuckled. "It doesn't work that way."

"What do you mean?"

"Ethereals share a… an innate telepathic bond. It would be virtually impossible to keep a secret of that magnitude for this long."

"You mean you have spies," Sam said.

Thea frowned, then covered it with a smile that didn't reach her eyes. "This is a democratic group. We all share responsibilities. We work together and break bread together. What reason could we possibly have for spies?"

"You tell me."

Thea remained expressionless, though Andy noticed her knuckles were bone-white, gripping the edge of the podium. "There's nothing to tell," she said finally. "If you'd like to ask me any more questions, Detective, I'll have to ask you to wait outside until we've finished our business."

Sam shrugged. "I'll let you get back to it," she said, turning and heading for the doors.

"Hang on a minute," Lamb said, taking a few rushed steps toward the pulpit. "We just drove two-thousand miles across the ass crack of America to get here and I have some questions I want answered."

Thea smiled. "What's your name, darling?"

Lamb looked defensive. "Lamb. Lamb Curtis."

"Well, Lamb, I appreciate the effort to reach us. And I'll do my best to answer any questions you might have. But right now, my people are eager to adjourn this meeting and get to lunch."

Andy took Lamb by the elbow, ushering her toward the

door. She jerked her arm away.

"'And I saw the dead, great and small, standin before the throne,'" Lamb said, quoting something Andy didn't recognize. "How many of em are in here?"

"How many what, Ms. Curtis?"

"Ghosts. Ethereals. *Whatever.* How many are here with us right now?"

Andy looked around the room at the concerned faces watching Lamb. He tried to see *between* the faces, as he must have when they'd first walked in—but he couldn't see them or sense them. And though he'd never doubted Lamb's gift, the magnitude of it finally hit home.

"By my estimation," Thea said, "there are sixty-three ethereals in the room with us." She turned to the hard-faced man in the chair. "Would that be about right, Bram?"

The man nodded.

"Are you a psychic or an empath?" Thea asked, her eyebrows raised in curiosity.

Lamb shrugged. "Neither, I guess. I can sense things. Ethereals. My mom was the psychic."

Thea reacted to this. "You're Sonya Curtis's daughter. From Las Vegas. I'm very sorry for your loss."

"You know about her?"

Andy had known Lamb long enough now to see how deeply she cared about her mother's legacy, and that she hoped her mother would be remembered fondly by others. She'd already planned a funeral for the coming Saturday, which she expected many of her mother's clients and other members of the spiritualist community would attend.

"Your mother must have been a powerful medium," Thea said, looking at Lamb directly, without pretense. "Please, you and your friends are more than welcome to stay. But we really must conclude this meeting."

"Come on, Lamb," Andy said.

She came along with a single glance back at the woman on the pulpit. Their shadows stretched long in the light from the stained-glass windows as the three of them left the church.

"That was pretty amazing," Andy said, squeezing Lamb's hand in the dimness of the vestibule.

She startled and gave him a distant smile. "I can't believe she heard about my mom."

"I meant you," he said. "Your power."

She blushed. "I've just never felt so many of them all in one place before, is all."

Andy nodded. He thought she might never think of herself as *powerful* in comparison to her mother—but she possessed an ability few people could claim. So did he. Whether they chose to think of it as a gift or a curse—and what they chose to do with their abilities—was entirely up to them.

He turned to Sam as they reached the sidewalk. "So what now, chief?"

"I was thinking we should split up," Sam said. "Find a place to spend the night. I've got personal business to take care of, and you'll want to speak with Petralia on your own." She squinted, nodding back at the church. "Get some answers. Find some peace."

Andy smiled at the thought. After all this time, he might finally learn the identity of his guardian angels, why they'd chosen him, if they'd known his parents, and if they might even be in contact with them now. Lamb slipped an arm around his waist. He leaned into her, hugging her by the shoulders.

Sam watched them a moment with a slight smile. Then she nodded, the smile leaving her face. "Anyways, I'll leave you to it." She went around the front of the car to the driver's door.

"Hey, Sam," Lamb said. "If you don't have plans tonight, why don't we meet up for dinner? Our treat. Least we can do for all you've done."

Sam squinted off toward the small downtown. When she turned back, she was smiling again. "I'd like that, thanks." She opened the door. "You've got my number."

"Sure do."

The detective nodded once more with finality, and climbed into the driver's seat. She started the car and pulled out from the curb, waving a single finger at them, both hands on the wheel.

It was the last time they saw Sam Beadle alive.

SOLE SURVIVOR

DEPUTY LOGAN LOVETT reached the ICU at Meritus Health in Hagerstown, and asked the desk nurse where the school teacher they'd rescued from Ghostland was being treated.

Following her directions, he found Elena Feliz in a bed near the middle of the large, six-patient unit, spaced by curtain dividers. She was asleep. She hadn't spoken a single word since the broadcast, not even to the first responders who'd discovered her, shivering and badly wounded, in the farthest corner of the park from the site of the incident. The circus tent had apparently broken her fall, but had left her broken and borderline catatonic.

The other folks on the broadcast had been found dead, most of them close to where the incident had occurred, in the midway. Jake and Eric Gallagher, their bodies mangled, had been less than twenty feet from each other when they died. The two camera operators had been dragged off and apparently mauled to death. The sound guy had been found in the funhouse, as if he'd run in there to hide, his arms and chest slashed so badly he'd bled out inside the hall of mirrors. The audio he'd recorded bore the sounds of his panting and screams—along with what had sounded to Logan something like laughter, though none of the police present during playback could be sure it wasn't just static or some other sort of interference.

Deputy Lovett had been the one to find him—Kipling "Kip" Sanderson was the kid's name—and though Logan had loved funhouses when he was a kid, even enjoyed them as an adult from time to time, taking a date to the State Fair, or bringing along his nephew, he knew he would never visit another one for as long as he lived.

He'd had his share of trauma in the days following the tragedy on April 20th. Dead bodies had been nothing new to him even then. Still, he would have hated to reach a point where none of this affected him, where he could look at a dead person, someone who'd just recently been breathing and eating and fucking, with hopes and dreams and possibly even aspirations, and feel the same as he might if he'd been looking at a single-slice toaster.

The survivors made the effort worthwhile. The relief he'd felt when he'd seen the kids open the hatch had made up for countless deaths. To see Lilian Roth and the other survivors reunited with their families.

Elena Feliz lay perfectly still, her dark, wavy hair spilling out over the pillow from the gauze wrapped around her head injury. Her eyes were sallow, her face pallid. She had scratches on her arms but the worst injury seemed to be to her head. The circus tent had broken her fall but she must have struck one of the poles holding it up or something. Whatever the reason, it had left her unable to speak. Mute.

"Miss Feliz," he said, not wanting to wake her. She seemed so peaceful. But he needed answers.

A nurse came in, nodding at him as she crossed the room to check on another patient.

"Elena," he said, moving in closer. This time her eyes

sprang open in terror. The beeping of her heart monitor sped up and she grasped at the sheet with both hands, clawing at it, dragging her chipped and torn fingernails down the fabric toward her then reaching again and repeating the gesture, almost like she was trying to claw her way out of a hole.

The nurse rushed over with a syringe and grabbed the tube on the IV bag.

"I need to speak with her," Logan said.

"And I need to calm her down."

She stuck the needle into the port and emptied the syringe. The liquid mixed with the saline in a translucent cloud, and a moment later Elena Feliz stopped clawing at the sheet. Her eyes dulled and her head fell back onto the pillow. She lay staring at the bedside table as her heartbeat slowed, one arm draped over her stomach. He wondered if she even knew what she was looking at.

"Miss Feliz, can you hear me?"

"She never talks," the nurse said brusquely as she returned to the other patient. "But she can hear you."

Logan took the chair from beside the next bed and carried it over to Elena. He sat, hands on knees, and studied her face. Her eyes looked drugged but he could swear the fear in them remained. As if she was reliving what she'd gone through in her mind, over and over on a loop.

"Miss Feliz, it's Deputy Lovett. Logan. We sorta met the other night at the park."

Her eyes never left the bedside table.

"I'm here to talk about what happened to you that night, but if you don't want to talk about it, or you can't, that's okay, too."

The heart monitor beeped steadily. She blinked.

Logan settled into the chair. "I read your blog, you

know. Actually, I was reading from the start. Well," he corrected himself, "at least after Ellen talked about it. I think it's admirable, what you tried to do. Gathering all that stuff about the tragedy and the park and putting it online, making it available. A lot of folks here would be happy to erase what happened from history. Take their settlement checks and move on. I guess you probably talked to some of them, when you were here—in Duck Falls, I mean—the last time. I guess you probably met a lot of strange people. Town's full of em. Hell, I guess I can't exclude myself."

The nurse passed the bed and Logan quieted, feeling slightly embarrassed for spilling his guts to this barely conscious woman he didn't even know, who probably couldn't even hear him anyway. Once the nurse was gone, he leaned forward again, hands on his knees, his face closer to hers.

"I gotta admit, Elena, I was worried about you when you wrote that you were getting all of those weird calls in the night. And then when you said you were gonna be meeting with the Ghost Brothers to do that TV special." He shook his head. "Guess I felt like I knew you by then, even though I'd only seen you in passing that one day back in September, and I didn't know who you were when I saw you. 'Cause I've seen what can happen to people who go in there. I've only been there in the daytime, and I was scared shitless, to be honest. Excuse my French."

He laughed at himself and leaned back. "I wanted to talk you out of it when me and the sheriff escorted you through the gate, but Sheriff Brigham would've canned my ass faster than StarKist cans tuna. I got a feeling she might be in Hedgewood's back pocket. Nothing concrete, just some things she's said that seem a bit… I dunno. *Off*, I guess."

A voice over the PA system called a Code Blue. Logan waited for it to quiet before speaking again, not wanting to be interrupted.

"I spoke to your sister," he said. "She told me she'll be coming out here just as soon as she's able to take some time off. Boss is giving her grief. I know how that is. Your brother's coming, too. Said they'd bring Fluffer along. She said he's been a good boy while you've been gone. Fluffer, not your brother. I figure if seeing him doesn't make you smile, nothing will."

He waited, having come here just to say these things and saved the best part for last, the part about her dog, because he knew how much she cared about the gray-and-white bearded Collie she'd lived with on her own. He'd figured just hearing about him might draw her out of mind like a magic spell, and realized now how silly that assumption had been. How hopelessly optimistic.

She stared at the bedside table. He shrugged, satisfied that he'd done his best, and he eased out of the chair.

"Anyways," he said, looking down at her with a sad smile. "It was nice to see you again."

He left the hospital and drove back to Duck Falls, stopping by the house briefly to check on Cash. Casius was asleep when he crept in, but the Boxer sprang up from his bed and ran to the door, claws clicking on the linoleum, and leaped up onto Logan's leg. Logan petted the dog and scratched behind his one nicked ear the way Cash liked. He let him out back for a piss, then gave him his lunch: a half a can of wet food mixed with a scoop of the dry stuff. He crept back out to the prowler while Casius crunched away hungrily, his tags jingling against the metal bowl.

Sheriff Brigham was waiting for Logan when he got back to the station. He'd just bitten into the Reuben sandwich he brought from home when she stepped out of her office.

"Lovett!"

He chewed quickly and swallowed hard, taking his feet off his desk. "Yes, ma'am."

"Need you to check in on a bylaw complaint after lunch."

Alice Brigham was a former homicide detective for Baltimore P.D. but she was also an elected official. Her curt and officious manner, her formal attire and stiff-necked posture reflected a combination of those two disparate worlds. She'd been a pain in the ass since two elections prior, when she'd succeeded Dallas Kerr, the chain-smoking, ball-busting sheriff who'd hired Logan eleven years ago and had since moved to Florida with his girlfriend, a nurse ten years his junior.

Logan packed his sandwich back up and brought it with him, annoyed to have had his lunch interrupted for a bylaw call, of all things. On his way back to his cruiser he stopped to check in on Jerry Dougan in the cell, but the cell Jerry had occupied until this morning was empty. Frankly, he was surprised Sheriff Brigham had let him hold Dougan as long as she had, after Wendy Laramie waffled on pressing charges. Still, it riled him up. Especially after she'd interrupted his lunch for a stinking bylaw complaint.

He knocked on her door, calming himself just enough to keep from pounding on it with a fist.

"Come in."

He opened the door but remained just outside the office. Brigham was looking at paperwork with her reading glasses on and only glanced up to confirm her visitor before diving back in.

"You tossed Dougan loose?"

Brigham licked a finger and flipped the page in what he supposed was the official report she'd been typing up about the Ghost Brothers incident. "We couldn't hold him any longer with the Laramie woman refusing to press charges, confession or not," she said, still not looking up from the pages. "You know that. I held out as long as I could, but he has a job to do."

"At the park," Logan said.

She looked up from the report finally, a look in her eyes as if she thought he might be implying something. "That's right," she said. "Anything else you'd like to discuss, Deputy?"

"Guess not."

"Good. Coincidentally, the bylaw complaint is against the Laramies. Apparently, the husband's been doing some major digging without a permit."

"Unpermitted digging," Logan said, keeping the aggravation from his voice. He nodded and closed the door as he left.

When he got to the Laramie house, he parked out front and immediately saw that some major work had been going on. Zig-zagged tracks of mud lead back and forth down the driveway. He heard the rumble of some kind of heavy machinery in the back behind the house.

He went up and rang the bell, aware they probably wouldn't hear it with whatever was going on in the backyard. After two rings and nearly a minute standing on the glassed-in porch, he'd just prepared to head around back when the door opened.

Wendy stood in the doorway, looking tired, lacking her usual business sheen and attire. Her black eye had faded to a yellowish-green with a thin streak of purple directly under the eye, like some new kind of mascara application.

The swelling on her cheek where Jerry had hit her was entirely gone.

"I've already told you, I don't want to press charges," she said.

"I'm not here about that, Wendy. It's about the hole."

She threw a cautious glance inside the house. "Well, I guess you'd better come around back." She stepped out onto the porch, pulling the door shut, then led him down the driveway to the backyard.

"I told Michael it was going to get him into trouble digging without a permit. He just kept telling me he didn't have time. I thought it was late in the season to be worried about putting in a new pool, but apparently that was never what he had in mind."

As they rounded the side of the house Logan said, "How are you two holding up?" He'd meant with the death of their boy. He'd been the first to see Ben sprawled over the maintenance hatch that night. He'd called out over the bullhorn the moment he'd seen them in the doorway: their boy and the Roths' girl, Lilian.

He barely heard Wendy's sigh over the grumble of machinery in the back. "I'm dealing," she said. "I'll let what's in the backyard speak for Michael's state of mind."

Odd thing to say, Logan thought. Unless Michael had built himself a monkey house or something strange like that back there, he couldn't imagine what might speak so definitively to Michael's mental state. He could already see half the body and massive back tires of some kind of construction vehicle, parked partly in the driveway and on the lawn.

Once they got back there, he saw there *was* no more lawn. Most of the yard was covered in dirt, aside from the roots of the large white oak near the back-neighbor's yard, and the small toolshed against the fence. The backhoe was pushing the last of a diminished pile flat over whatever Michael had buried back there.

Michael himself stood over the last of the hole, hands on hips, surveying the job. His knees and arms were streaked with dirt. The day was crisp but he had his sleeves rolled up as if he'd been in there digging with his hands. Logan could see something within a cement alcove that looked like—

"Is that a *hatch*?" he asked Wendy.

She nodded, heaving another sigh.

The backhoe covered the hole with the last small pile of dirt and the driver turned off the machine. Logan recognized the kid, probably on loan from the new suburb out on the west end Wendy herself was still selling units for—though Logan was surprised they were still building, considering what had happened only a few miles from here.

Mike turned around and saw the two of them standing there. At first Logan couldn't tell whether he was shocked or embarrassed. Then he smiled and crossed the packed dirt toward him. "Hey, Deputy. You here about what happened the other day?"

"Nope. Figure your wife and I already talked that one just about to death." Logan immediately regretted his choice of phrasing, considering the wound of their son's death was still somewhat fresh. "Reason I come by is, someone called in a bylaw complaint, said you folks were digging without a permit. Only it looks like you did a bit more than just digging, huh, Mike? Looks like you got yourself a bomb shelter."

"It's not a bomb shelter," both Mike and Wendy said in unison, as if they'd argued over it many times. "It's a tornado shelter," Mike finished solo.

"Tornado? We haven't had one of them in the area since… well, since I dunno how long."

"Nineteen ninety-eight," Wendy scoffed. "It's not *for* tornadoes, though. Tell him what it's for, Michael."

Mike gave her a wary look.

"What's it for then, Mike?"

The man waffled, considering whether or not to tell Logan. He finally said, "It's just a precaution," in a very small voice like an apologetic child.

"A precaution against what?"

"Go on. Tell him, Michael."

"Against ghosts," he practically sighed. "It's a precaution against ghosts."

"Against ghosts," Logan repeated.

Wendy raised her eyebrows at him. "Now ask him what it cost?"

Logan ignored the provocation. "Mike, we've already got the Recurrence Field to protect us against ghosts."

"Sure we do, but what if something happens to it? Don't you think it's better to be safe than sorry?"

"Happens? Happens like what?"

"Well, what if the power goes out?"

"They've a huge power generator and a backup. They say the Recurrence Field is completely off the grid."

"But what if it goes down somehow?"

Michael's voice had risen to a fever pitch. Logan eyed him suspiciously.

"Mike, do you know something I'm not aware of? Have you heard anything?"

"I haven't heard any—" He was upset now, the veins on his neck prominent. "I'm just being safe, goddammit!"

Wendy put a hand on his shoulder, attempting to calm

him, though the gesture looked anything but tender. Michael seemed to sense it and shrugged it off angrily.

"*What is wrong with you two?* Two-thousand people died less than three miles from us and you're just walking around like everything's gonna be fine? There are God knows how many ghosts left behind the walls of that place, just waiting for someone to come along and set them free. The same ghosts that killed *our son*, Wen. Just *waiting*. Why doesn't that *concern* you? Are you telling me you trust that sociopath Hedgewood?"

Logan had to admit, the man had a point. Several points, to be honest. They were like the people of Pompei, living in the shadow of a sleeping monster. But what could he do? Cower in fear with every breath, wondering when the mountain would finally blow its top?

At least Michael was taking ownership of his fear. Putting it into action, albeit not entirely sound.

"I can't deal with this anymore," Wendy said. "I have houses to sell."

"To *who*, Wendy? What kind of moron buys a house next door to Chernobyl?"

Wendy looked like she might bite, but she just shook her head and headed back down the driveway to the front of the house.

"Hey, uh," the driver interrupted. "You don't need me anymore, do you?"

"No," Michael said. He took out a wad of bills—his share of the Hedgewood compensation, Logan figured, since he'd heard Mike had lost his job—and counted out a few hundreds. "Here you go. I appreciate you coming out."

The kid took the money, clearly delighted. "You ever need a hole filled or dug, I'm your man." He hurried back to the machine and climbed up into the rig with the ease of a monkey, then started up the engine.

"Mike, I gotta write you up. I'm sorry."

Michael shrugged, pausing in tucking the billfold away. "How much? Can I pay cash?"

Logan chuckled. The big machine rumbled as the kid turned the shovel around. "You gotta pay at the town hall," he said. "Next business day. Just so you know, they might send me back out, make you tear this all up. I won't want to but those are the rules. Get a permit, next time, huh?"

Michael looked sufficiently chastised, nodding at his dirty shoes.

Logan was about to leave but he turned back. "I don't feel right about any of this either, Mike. What you got here…" He shrugged. "I guess it might not be that bad an idea."

Michael nodded again. "Thanks, Deputy."

Goddamn, what an absolute waste of a day, Logan thought as he headed back to the cruiser behind the excavator. He wanted to have a quick word with Wendy before heading out, but she must have already gone back inside, dolling herself up to sell houses to desperate people with more money than sense.

His phone rang as he opened the driver door and sat behind the wheel. He found it on the passenger seat and picked it up on the third ring. "Yeah?"

"Deputy Lovett?" the caller asked. The woman's voice sounded vaguely familiar.

"This is him."

"Elena Feliz spoke after you left."

"She did?" In his excitement, he nearly dropped the phone. He recognized the voice now. It was the desk nurse at Meritus Health ICU. "What did she say?"

"She said your name. Deputy Lovett. Logan. She kept

repeating it louder and louder until one of the nurses came by to check on her. Then she said *tell him*."

The words gave him an inexplicable chill despite his winter duty jacket. "Tell me what?"

"That's the weird thing," the desk nurse said. "It didn't make a lot of sense. She said she was *shown* something."

"Shown what?"

"Bear in mind, I'm just passing along what she said. Personally, I don't think she was in a lucid state."

"I'll bear that in mind," Logan said with as much patience as he could muster.

"So, she woke up and asked for you, and when the nurse told her you weren't there, Ms. Feliz said she was shown that… well, that the world would end in three days, whatever the heck that means."

"Three days? Would that be the Friday or Saturday?"

The nurse sighed. "I just work here, Deputy."

"Well, can I come in and speak with her? Is she still awake?"

"I'm afraid that's not possible."

"Why not?"

"She's dead, Deputy."

"*Dead?*"

"She said her peace and then her body just… gave up, I guess."

Logan hung up with an uneasy feeling. Elena Feliz, the sole survivor of the Ghostland TV special, was dead. Her last words hadn't been to her family or friends but to him, passing on some sort of vague premonition about the end of the world.

It was silly to even entertain the idea, but for some reason he felt as anxious as he'd been since the day this all started back in April, when he'd watched it all go down from behind the massive park wall, unable to do a damn thing to stop it.

Could Elena really have had a vision of the future? Logan wasn't sure he believed in psychic visions, but he was damn sure three days wasn't a lot of time to work with if she had.

Pompei, he thought, staring at his phone. *Maybe Michael was right.*

LAST MISSION

LILIAN KNOCKED ON the big church door, feeling nervous for some reason, as if this moment was the culmination of everything that had come before it, like graduation day. She remembered Billy Turner's valedictorian speech, telling her and their fellow students to "live twice as hard for the lives that were lost," and how cliché that phrase had felt at the time. She realized now that he was right. Because time had felt endless during high school but she'd learned very quickly that time was fleeting. You had to grab on to the people and the things you loved and squeeze as much happiness out of them while you still had the chance.

"How come they call this place the Temple?" Blake said. "Was it a synagogue or something?"

Lilian snickered. Hers was one of only two Jewish families in town. "In Duck Falls? It'd be a pretty empty house."

The door opened, and Blake dropped the subject.

A guy Lilian recognized peered out. He had long, blond dreadlocks, and wore camo cargo shorts and socks with sandals. They'd been on a mission together a while back and had nearly been killed at the hand of some insane mall security guard. Thea had introduced him as "Coop."

Coop blinked at her with squinty eyes. "Oh, hey, dude," he said, holding up his hand for a high five, which she reciprocated. "Good to see you. Who's your friend?"

"I'm Blake," he said, holding up his hand in greeting, which Coop gave a mid-height five. Blake grinned in amusement at his slapped palm.

"Cool, cool. Is he like, your *friend* friend, or…?"

"He's my boyfriend," Lilian said.

Blake grinned at her.

"Right on," Coop said, tucking a loose dread behind his ear. Cooper was far older than her, probably in his thirties, and didn't appear to have any intentions toward her as far as she could tell. He was just a friendly dude. "Hey, so come on in, my dudes. *Mi casa es su casa*, welcome to our humble abode and all that."

They followed him into the darkened vestibule, where he opened the inner doors to the sun-brightened sanctum. People were milling about, working on things: some were painting protest signage, others folding and stacking colorful GRP2 pamphlets that must have just come from the printers. But something about the Temple seemed off, and she couldn't quite put her finger on it.

"Is he cool?" Coop asked, squinting at Blake.

"Cool how?"

Coop raised his eyebrows suggestively. "You know. *Cool* cool."

"Yeah, he's cool," she said, realizing he was asking if Blake could be trusted. She'd assumed for a moment he was talking about getting high.

"I guess Thea told you we're going in, huh?" Coop said. "Day after tomorrow."

"You're going into *Ghostland*? After what happened on Saturday?"

"The Ghost Brothers didn't have keeper suits."

"Where are you getting keeper suits from?"

"Hedgewood, dude. Thea's got him bringing in a big shipment of supplies. Keeper suits and these boss new glasses to see ethereals with."

"Cool," Blake said.

Lilian shot him a glare. She wondered if he remembered the keeper suit she'd given him, asking him to promise he'd wear it if things got strange and she or Ben weren't around. She'd brought it with them, packed in her own luggage, though she'd hoped it wouldn't be necessary.

"Why?" she said. "Why would you go in there? Why would you risk your lives—?"

"Because that's what we're *here* for, dude. Nobody cares about those people trapped in there but us."

Blake started. "Hold up, there's *people* trapped in Ghostland?"

"Ethereals," Lilian said.

"Ethereals *are* people, dudes."

"Don't you think I know that? My *best friend* is one of them." She felt Blake's eyes on her, but she continued anyway. "Does anybody *know* the people behind those walls? Are they somebody's relatives or best friends?" Her mind flashed on Allison and Stan, on Niko and Leonard. But she couldn't let it phase her. She just had to hope they'd escaped when the hatch was open, or would endure and survive long enough to be rescued eventually. "Like I get that we need to get them out of there," she said. "When it's *safe*. Why do you have to go *now*?"

Coop shrugged. "We voted."

"You voted to die in there, Coop."

Another shrug. "Then we die. That's what I signed up for—Lilian, this is GRP2's entire reason for being here.

This is our *purpose*."

He turned away abruptly, ending the discussion, and walked bowlegged down the aisle. Lilian hurried to follow him, hopefully to Thea's office, where she could plead with the woman to stop this insanity before she got every one of her people killed.

All around her the Gurpies busied themselves. There was a jovialness to the work, people joking and laughing and helping each other. It reminded her of kids getting the gym ready for prom night. They were excited about tomorrow's mission. They wanted nothing more than to help these ethereals they didn't even know.

As she thought this, she realized what had bothered her coming in.

"Where are all the ethereals?

Coop turned back at a door beside the altar. "They're training," he said.

"Training for what?"

He gave her a look, as if he wasn't sure he could trust her anymore, then knocked on the door. "Just training, dude," he said, then walked away, leaving her and Blake at the door.

"Come in," Thea said from inside.

Lilian opened the door. She'd expected to see Bram by Thea's side but it was just Thea, going over some papers wearing a pair of glasses with thick black frames. She took the glasses off. "Hello, Lilian," she said, smiling as she stood. "Hello again, Blake. Have a seat, please."

They both sat in the chairs opposite the desk.

"You said to come by—"

Thea nodded. "I wanted you to hear it from me first. Ben is missing. We're going to put together a small group of ethereals to search for him, and I'd like you and Le Mon to head that team."

"Of course. I'm ready whenever—"

"But first," Thea said, talking over her, "we have to deal with Ghostland. This is the most important thing we can do at this time. I think Ben would agree, if he were here."

"Ben didn't want anything to do with Ghostland."

"I admit it was a touchy subject between us, and that's natural considering what happened to the two of you. But we've spoken about it quite a lot. He agrees there are people in there who need our help, he just believes the risk outweighs the benefit. But that was before. He doesn't know the Hedgewood Foundation is providing us with essential equipment so our teams can survive any sort of defensive attack from the ethereals inside. Oliver Hedgewood himself will be opening the gate for us, first thing tomorrow morning."

"And you trust him all of the sudden?"

"It's a marriage of convenience. We need his equipment to free those ethereals—"

"What does he get in return?"

Thea smiled and blinked. "A cleaned conscience."

Lilian scoffed. "Who are you sending in?"

"We've chosen eight volunteers. We had so many volunteers we had to pick names from a hat. Coop and Bram will head the team."

"If you lose Bram—"

"I'm aware of the consequences, and so is he. But his ability is essential to the mission." Thea rattled off the names of seven other team members Lilian didn't know, and one woman she'd spoken to online who could also communicate with ethereals.

"This is a really, really bad idea," she said when Thea

had finished.

"I appreciate your honesty, Lilian. You can go now. Once the mission is over, we can reconvene and discuss plans to find Ben."

They left the room, Lilian more upset now than she had been when she'd first heard the plan. "I can't believe they're doing this."

"It sounds like they've got it handled," Blake said.

"They think they do."

Le Mon emerged from the pews, looking panicked until he saw them, then relief washed over his features. "Lilian! Glad you made it. I made a case for us, I really tried. But savin Jessica just got everyone excited to head into Ghostland and get the rest of em. I tried talkin them out of it but it's useless. They're gung-ho and rarin to go."

"Still nothing from Ben?"

Le Mon shook his head despondently.

"What are we gonna do, Le Mon?"

"I wish I knew." He squinted off at the front doors, stroking his soul patch in thought. "Some kids came in earlier, during the meeting," he said after a moment. "With this cop, asking all kinds of questions about those dead psychics. Asian kid and blonde chick who can sense ethereals. Daughter of one of the psychics."

"Oh, wow." Lilian considered the development. "Do you think they can help us?"

"I don't know for sure, but the Asian kid had two fancy-dressed spirits kind of attached to him. Like he's some kind of spiritual magnet. If we can find them before Thea talks to em, rope them into our cause…"

Lilian thought she knew where he was leading. "If they can help us find Ben before those teams go in…"

"Exactly. If anyone can convince these people what

they're doing is insanity, it's Ben. They trust him. Maybe more than they trust Thea." He gave Lilian a serious look. "I think that scares her to death."

After Lilian and her boyfriend left, Thea texted Bram. He called her a moment later.

"You don't call anymore," he said.

She could hear the grin in his tone. "Everything's ready to go here," she said. "Lilian just showed up. She thinks going into Ghostland is a terrible idea."

"Just like you thought," Bram said. "This is good. She and Le Mon will round up a few sympathetic minds and go looking for your missing ethereal. Only they won't find him, will they?"

Thea bit her lip. She still felt divided about handing Ben over to Hedgewood, but she'd needed both of them out of her hair for the time being. Ben's influence over GRP2 was too strong. Most of them still considered him a hero. Thea realized she was mostly to blame for that. The inscription on the memorial was a tad over the top, she'd be the first to admit. But she'd needed him to play the hero then. She'd needed someone to inspire the others, and he'd served his purpose well.

Hedgewood could tear down everything she'd built in an instant if he chose to—and for his part of the bargain he'd promised to leave her and the others alone, to let them continue their work unhindered. The equipment he'd offered would be invaluable to their cause, putting them leaps and bounds ahead of where they currently stood.

It was a simple exchange of goods. They'd needed Hedgewood, and Hedgewood had needed Ben. As to the why, Thea could only imagine.

What she did know was that this afternoon, while she

met with Hedgewood to collect what they were owed, she planned to use the burner phone to detonate the explosives, providing a reasonably impenetrable alibi, and a cover story corroborated by everyone present at the Temple, by Lilian's fierce opposition to their plan, even the police detective who'd fortuitously stumbled in during their meeting.

What possible reason would GRP2 have to blow up the Recurrence Field when they were already planning to go in the following day?

And with a patsy to pin it on, with Bram's strategic placement of that drunken imbecile Jerry Dougan onto the security team working Ghostland, and all of the fabricated paperwork for the explosives pointing directly to him, both Thea and Bram would be untouchable.

"No," she said, in answer to Bram's question. "They won't find him."

She just hoped whatever they were doing to Ben, and whatever Hedgewood needed him for, that he hadn't suffered too greatly.

She hoped for his sake the end had been quick.

WILLING SPIRITS

S AM LEFT THE quaint bed and breakfast room she'd rented and got back into the rental car, wondering what Helena would have thought of this place, all doilies and lace and flower-printed everything. She likely would have spent much of the time laughing about the decor while secretly loving it.

It was weird, Sam supposed, the way she sometimes still considered how Helena would feel about certain things in her life. They'd already been apart twice as long as they'd been together. She assumed it was because the two of them had been so unalike and seen the world in entirely different, often opposing ways. When a person spent so much time trying to see through someone else's eyes, it was probably natural they might still attempt it even after that someone else was long gone.

Sam was pretty sure Helena would've hated Duck Falls. It didn't have much if any character. Just another typical small town on the way to somewhere better. The people she'd encountered so far had been kind, though she suspected much of that kindness was due to her job, and that some of them might have been less kind if she'd come here holding hands with Helena. She supposed she could be projecting her own assumptions of small-town folk onto them, which also wasn't fair.

As she neared the sheriff's station, she considered she'd likely been too hard on Stan all these years. Even Helena had told her as much. She'd said it was long past time to forgive him, that her anger was only holding her back. Sam knew as well as anyone how difficult it could be to juggle family with the life of a cop, especially a homicide detective. And eventually she'd pushed Helena out of her life the same way Stan had edged out Sam and her mother.

Three years together, and they never spoke now even if they happened to pass each other in the courthouse. Sam knew much of the blame fell on her shoulders. She'd become an expert at excising people from her life, at hardening her heart toward the people who'd hurt her. Even after all Helena had taught her about accepting love and pushing out hate, she was still adept at cutting herself off from the world before it could shut her out.

I'm trying, Helena. I'm doing my best.

The Washington County sheriff station was a small one-story building dwarfed by a couple of sad-looking pines whose branches hung over its flat roof, leaving a carpet of brown shag on the asphalt lot.

Sam pulled up alongside one of the patrol SUVs and headed inside. It was a pretty small operation. One young woman working the phones at dispatch, a couple of desks and a glassed-in office, a hallway beyond likely leading to the cells.

Sam approached dispatch. The bored-looking young woman behind the desk glanced up from a magazine filled with glossy interior design photos. "Can I help you?"

"Yes, I'm hoping to speak to Sheriff Brigham."

The girl looked surprised, as if nobody ever came in to speak to the sheriff. Then she pointed. "Her office is right over there."

Aside from the missing children and FBI's Most Wanted posters, along with a few other small details, it could have been an insurance office. Sam crossed the small workspace to a door with SHERIFF stenciled on the frosted glass. She knocked.

"Come in," a woman said behind the door, clearly perturbed. The sheriff looked up from her computer when Sam opened the door, reacting as though she'd expected someone else. "Oh. Can I help you?"

"I hope so," Sam said, taking a step in. "I'm Detective Samantha Beadle, Seattle Homicide."

The sheriff stood, smoothed out her uniform and came around the desk, offering her hand and a bright, officious smile. "Alice Brigham. What brings Seattle Homicide all the way to my door?"

Sam shook the offered hand. "Nothing official." She blew out a breath, trying to decide where to start. She'd already come all this way. Giving up now, when she was so close, would be silly. "My father died at Ghostland," she said finally.

A brief scowl passed over Sheriff Brigham's face before she offered Sam a sympathetic smile. "I'm sorry for your loss. It must have been a difficult time for you and your family—"

"Actually, we were estranged when it happened."

The sheriff appeared flummoxed. "What can I do for you, Detective?"

"I know it's a longshot, but I'd like to speak with the first responder who found him. I'd just like to get a little sense of closure, if that makes sense."

"I understand," the sheriff said, clasping her hands below the waist in a slightly officious stance, the way she might at a press conference. "But I'm afraid that's not possible. It's just not likely whoever discovered his remains would even remember. I know that may seem callous, but you have to remember, there were over two-thousand casualties that day."

"I'm aware. And I know it's unlikely someone would remember him over any of the others. But if I could get the names of—"

"Who is it you're asking for?" a man's voice came from behind her.

Sheriff Brigham scowled over Sam's shoulder. "I'm handling this, Deputy."

The deputy, a young-looking man with messy dark hair and sideburns that reached his jawline, tightened his jaw and crossed the room to meet them. "I remember every single man, woman and child I found that day. If who you're asking about was one of em, I'd know it."

"His name is—*was*—Stan Beadle."

The deputy squinted. For a moment, Sam thought he might offer another apology. "Retired detective out of Seattle, right?"

"That's him," Sam said, relieved.

A glance passed between the sheriff and her deputy. There was obvious animosity between them. Rather than relieved, the sheriff looked annoyed that he'd been able to remember.

He nodded. "I remember him. Early to mid-seventies, sport coat and cream fedora."

Sam sighed. "Thank you, Deputy…?"

He stuck out a hand. "Lovett. Logan Lovett."

They shook.

"Well," the sheriff said, retreating to her office, "I'll leave the two of you to speak." She gave her deputy a cautioning look and closed the door behind her.

Deputy Lovett offered a chair and sat behind his messy desk. The chair wobbled as she sat as though it might collapse but held for the moment.

"You're a cop, too?"

Sam nodded. She rhymed off her details.

"Homicide, huh?" He seemed impressed. "Same precinct as your father?"

"That's right."

"Were you close?"

Sam shook her head.

"Didn't think so," the deputy said with a grin. He picked up a pen and began twirling it between his fingers. "Old-school lawman, right? Held you at arm's length."

"He did."

"My dad, too," he said, offering an apologetic smile. "Yours died a hero, if it's any consolation. That's all we can ask for any of us, isn't it?"

"I guess it is. Do you mind if I ask how you know that?"

"What's that?"

"That he died a hero."

Logan set the pen down. "Well, he died on the job, even though he was retired. Once we IDed the fella who he was with, a pair of bracelets hangin off one wrist, I looked into your dad's caseload. Turns out it was the guy he liked for a string of Seattle-area murders. And it also turned out one of the exhibits was one of that bastard's kills." He scratched the sideburn on his right cheekbone. "Two and two together…"

"Fischer walked," Sam said. "His mother was rich and powerful and Stan was never able to definitively link him to the murders."

"Well…" The deputy shrugged again. "I mean what are the odds otherwise? What else would have made the guy your dad liked for the Doll's Head murders go there that day? Like it was coincidence?"

"Doesn't seem likely."

"Right. It wasn't just that, though. It was what the girl said, later on. When I interviewed her."

"Girl?"

"Lilian Roth. She said your father, Stan, that he was with her. That he tried to help get everyone out of there but that the guy, the Doll's Head killer, he was waiting for them. Hiding in the tunnels. Somehow, he found them and he had a knife. Your father died instantly, the coroner said, and that's corroborated by the girl, but I figure with the handcuffs we found on the killer's corpse, he musta given the guy one helluva run for his money. Either way, the scumbag's dead. Fischer, I mean. Not your dad."

Sam nodded. It was good to hear, that Stan hadn't died chasing the same ghost he'd been after for twenty years. Rex Garrote was gone and her father was gone, but at least he'd died bringing a real-life murderer to justice. If what the deputy said was true, he'd also died trying to save those kids, to find a way out and get as many other people to safety as possible.

She supposed it was all the closure she could have ever hoped for—she just wished she could conjure up the old man's ghost so she could talk to him one last time. Hear it from his lips. Forgive him to his face.

Since that wasn't an option, Lovett's testimony would have to do. She stood and held out a hand. "Thank you for your time, Deputy. I'll let you get back to it."

The deputy stood and shook her hand again. "Hey, listen," he said. "You come out all this way, you wanna grab some lunch? I know a place that serves the best burger you'll ever eat."

Sam considered it. With Lamb and Andy likely to spend their afternoon in some motel bed if they weren't already back at the church, what harm was there in accepting?

"Wait, you're not a vegan, are you? If so, I don't mean to offend."

"No, I'm not vegan. And I'd love to."

The deputy grinned. He grabbed his tan jacket and threw it over his shoulder like a varsity football sweater. His phone started ringing the second they stepped away from his desk. The deputy ignored it.

"Aren't you gonna get that?"

He shrugged. "I'll check my messages on the road." He seemed to see her anxiety, and added: "I'm sure it's not the end of the world."

His expression clouded for a moment. Then he shook his head and continued toward the lobby. She followed him.

"After you," he said, holding the door open.

Sam stepped out into the cool sunshine, unable to keep from smiling as the sun warmed her face. For some reason, she'd expected rain.

Andy fell back against the lumpy pillows as Lamb strode around the foot of the small motel room bed toward the bathroom. Her clothes were piled messily on the floor near his own. He pulled the sheet up to his chest—it was chilly without her in the bed—and watched her tiptoe in her bare feet and tan lines across the low-pile carpet until she pulled the bathroom door shut behind her.

Staring up at the ceiling while Lamb ran the tap, Andy

marveled at his luck. Barely a week ago he was a lonely burnout with a dark secret and a thousand-dollar-a-day habit, sometimes up, too often down. Now he had a girl, his secret had been shared and accepted, and the answers to all of his questions and potentially a purpose awaited him at the old church across town. After all this time, he might finally have the opportunity to confront the ghosts who'd been at his side since his birth, his protectors or his curse. He felt genuinely happy, and he wasn't even the least bit stoned.

For a few hours this morning, as they'd driven through town and spoke with the people in the church, he'd even forgotten all about the six-thousand dollars José had waiting for him back home. It was the first time in as long as he could remember that he'd gone so long without thinking about money or gambling. The itch had waned somewhere between New Mexico and Missouri, despite the dozens of Native American casinos dotting the landscape of Oklahoma.

The money didn't bother him anymore, either. He knew he could trust José. They'd been friends for over a decade. Unless something drastic happened, like José's plumbing went to shit and he hadn't gotten paid, or his "powerful bruja" mother got sick and needed to go to the hospital, José would hold the money until Andy said otherwise. As it stood, he had a few hundred bucks he'd socked away in case he ever got too far down on his luck, and Lamb's credit card had a decent limit, which she'd mentioned when they'd stopped at the mall in Columbus to pick up some warmer clothing for the weather. He didn't expect to be in Duck Falls very much longer, anyhow. Couple of days, tops.

Andy swung his legs out from under the sheet and

grabbed his pants, pulling them on and zipping up as Lamb emerged from the bathroom.

"Ready to go?" she asked.

"It's a little cold to go topless," he said.

Lamb chuckled and sat beside him on the edge of the bed. She laid a warm hand on his bare shoulder. She was like a human radiator, especially in bed. In her hot apartment it had been too much to sleep close together. In the cheap motel beds on their trip across America, Andy had welcomed the warmth.

"I know you're worried, but you'll do fine," she said. She kissed his forehead tenderly and stood. "You seen my panties?"

"I think I threw them over there," he said, grinning as he pointed to the other side of the bed.

"Is it called 'throwin'' when you do it with your teeth?"

They laughed and she crouched to pick up the rest of her clothes, setting them on the bed as she hunted for her underwear. She found them hanging over the lampshade. "Nice shot," she said, dangling them for him to see before slipping her feet into them and pulled them up.

"You really think I'll be okay?" he asked, watching her dress in the full-length mirror.

Lamb gave him a stern look, clasping the bra in the front and twisting it around to the back. "They're gonna love you. How couldn't they?"

"But what if they're disappointed in me?" He was already tying his shoes. For some reason he remembered his mother teaching him how, looping the loops and crossing them over, and thinking of how she'd died made him feel ashamed. "*I'm* disappointed in me."

The furrow in her brow deepened. "What you did back in Vegas, you coulda been—" She paused just short of saying *killed*. "—those goons coulda hurt you real bad," she finished. "But you went anyway. That's a selfless act, Andy. You put someone else's life above your own. Whatever you did before then, it doesn't matter. You helped *save lives*. And if that's not enough to please your ethereal pals, then fuck em. We don't need em anymore."

He laughed, and Lamb joined him. Because she was right. Whatever the reason his *gwisin* had for entering his life, they'd served their purpose. It was time for them to move on, to whatever comfort lay beyond this world.

"Okay," he said, rising from the bed with both shoes tied. "I'm ready."

They walked the short distance across town back to the old church. The streets were pretty busy for a town of its size, which Lamb supposed was likely because of what had happened at Ghostland. Duck Falls was the new Salem, Massachusetts. Or Burkitsville, Maryland, where the *Blair Witch* movie took place, which she'd seen was actually about a half hour's drive from here. Lamb had been too young to watch *The Blair Witch Project* when it came out, but she remembered the hype from kids in the grades above her. She also remembered her mother saying it was evil propaganda, that people like her would have been accused of witchcraft in those days and burned at the stake, drowned or hanged.

Even before the movie had come out—she thought she must have been ten or eleven since she was born in '88—Lamb had understood she was different than the other kids. She couldn't remember her age or grade with any clarity, but she'd probably been eight or nine when all the girls had done "Bloody Mary." They'd gone into the bathroom in small groups and Lamb would hear their muffled voices from behind the door, and a moment later they'd come running out screaming and laughing and asking each other if they "saw her."

One day it came time for Lamb to have a go at it. She couldn't recall how she'd gotten in with the girls who were doing it that day but she did remember how eager she'd been to join them—yet also deeply afraid. However it happened, she'd ended up in the bathroom with three girls whose names and faces she no longer remembered. One of them had flicked off the light, plunging them into darkness. It took a while for her eyes to adjust, but by then she was already spinning around and around with her eyes closed like they told her to, chanting Bloody Mary's name.

Even as she spun and chanted it seemed as though there were more people in the bathroom than had come in with her. Like someone had slipped in through the door, even though it would have been impossible without causing a change in the light. A hand fell on her shoulder, stopping her in mid-spin, prickling her flesh with goosebumps. She stood there in terror, her eyes snapped open wide and fully adjusted to the dark.

She supposed they must have said her name thirteen times, because the other girls screamed and she saw their shapes in the dark and heard their shoes squeaking on the tile floor as they ran away. When the door opened, the bathroom brightened just long enough for her to see her own reflection in the wide mirrors, standing beside the wash fountain—*her own reflection and no one else's*, even though the cold hand still rested on her shoulder.

When the hand finally let her go, she'd dashed from the bathroom and ran out into the hall. The other girls were still out there, watching the door, still panting and giggling nervously. "Did you see her?" one of the girls had asked.

"I definitely saw her," one of the other girls said, and her two friends had nodded in agreement.

"I didn't see anything," Lamb had admitted sorely. "But I felt her. She touched my shoulder." She'd still felt the imprint of the cold flesh where it had touched her, the nerves still prickling.

"She *touched* you?"

Lamb had nodded. The other girls had looked at each other and burst out laughing. "There's *no such thing* as Bloody Mary, loser," one of the girls had said. Everyone around them in that moment had pointed and laughed, and Lamb had burst into tears in front of the girl's washroom at Floyd Lamb Elementary.

That hadn't been the first time she'd sensed the presence of ethereals, but it had been the most public. She remembered the first clearly, even though she must have been as young as five or six. Her mother had been mad at her for something—Lamb thought she must have used her hairbrush, which was a no-no, and mom had been able to tell Lamb's blonde hairs apart from her own. She'd run in absolute terror, certain her mom was going to spank her, and had hidden in her mother's closet, closing the door behind her. She'd nestled in the dark among her mother's dresses and shoes, smelling of mustiness and perfume and moth balls. She'd tucked herself into a dark corner with her arms wrapped around her knees, waiting for her mom to give up her search.

When the coast had finally cleared—she'd heard the *Matlock* theme song as her mom turned on the TV in the living room—she'd gotten up to leave when she'd felt the presence of something crouched beside her in the dark. It was like nothing she'd ever felt before and she'd found it impossible to describe to her mother later on, when the two of them finally made amends. All she'd known for certain was that *someone* had been inside the closet with her… but she'd torn open the door and run, slamming it behind her. When she'd finally summoned the courage to open the door again, just to be sure it wasn't still in there, the closet had been empty but for the clothes and shoes and folded linen she'd scattered across the floor.

If it had stopped with these childhood incidents, and if her mother hadn't been blessed with a gift herself, she supposed she might have passed it off as a typical child's overactive imagination. But it had continued, and eventually she'd broken down and told her mother.

Sonya had assured her the ability to sense ethereals was a gift. It wasn't debilitating and it had never been a large part of her life, so Lamb had gotten used to it. It was just another facet to her personality, like the fact that she loved banging on her drums to classic rock, or that for as far back as she could remember she hadn't been able to wear socks without wanting to tear them off her feet the first chance she got.

She supposed her "gift" was why she'd felt an immediate connection to Andy. But it was also the deep sadness she'd felt radiating from him, even when he was smiling. She'd always been attracted to sad men. No idea why, considering she wasn't sad herself. She still felt it from him now, even as he turned to smile at her while they walked hand in hand past the downtown shops. She'd felt the same sadness radiating from Sam: some buried grief smothered by an all-business attitude.

"You good?" she asked Andy.

He nodded, a little too quickly. He was nervous. His palm was sweaty against hers, despite the chill in the air.

As they neared the street with the church, a boy and

girl in their late-teens came around the corner ahead of them. The dark-haired girl with a pale complexion was talking but she wasn't looking at the handsome, fresh-faced boy, even though the boy was watching her. There were enough people in the street that their presence shouldn't have made any impression, but Lamb was sure she recognized the girl from somewhere.

The girl turned to them as if she'd been directed to, and a look of realization flashed in her eyes. "It's you," she said.

The two couples stopped in the sidewalk as other pedestrians weaved around them.

"Do we know you?"

As Andy spoke, Lamb realized there was someone else with them, standing on the opposite side of the girl from the boy. An ethereal. She supposed the girl must have been talking to him or her when they'd approached.

"Wait," she said. "You're her. You're Lilian Roth."

"Yep," the girl said. "You're Sonya Curtis's daughter, right? We were just heading out to look for you two."

"You're with the Gurpies?" Andy asked.

"Yeah," the girl—Lilian—said, though she seemed less than enthusiastic about it. "We're with them." Lilian turned to her side, where Lamb sensed the presence, and looked at Andy briefly before turning away.

"You can *see* them, can't you?" Lamb asked her.

"See what?"

"Ghosts. Ethereals. You're with one right now, ain't you?" Lamb pointed. "Standing right there," she said.

The boy turned to Lilian, scrutinizing her.

"I can see them," Lilian said softly. The boy nodded as if he was just now coming to realize it was true.

"And you can see them with Andy."

Lilian nodded. "I can see them. An Asian man and woman. They're holding hands."

"Can you…" Lamb approached her. "…can you *talk* to them?"

Andy's eyes widened in anticipation. "Wait… what?"

The girl shrugged. "I can try," she said with a sigh, as if she'd played this game so many times before. She held up a hand in greeting. "Hello. Yes, I can see you. Hi. Do you speak English?" She seemed disappointed as she turned back to Lamb. "They don't speak English. The man said 'hello,' and 'thank you' and 'no English," but that's about all I could understand. Sorry."

Andy's shoulders slumped. Lamb squeezed his arm.

"Actually," Lilian said brightly, "my friend said he can translate."

Lamb and Andy turned to the boyfriend. He looked surprised. "Not me. I barely know high school Spanish."

"My *ethereal* friend," Lilian said, turning to her left. "His name's Leon Moncrief, but everyone calls him Le Mon." A look of wonder came over her, reacting to something Le Mon must have said. "That's cool, I didn't know that."

"What?" Lamb asked her.

"Le Mon said language isn't a barrier in the ethereal world. They can understand each other's thoughts."

"Can you please ask them why me?" Andy said.

The girl looked at him as if she didn't understand the question. "Why you?"

"Yeah."

She listened for a moment, following a conversation none of the others could see or hear. Then she nodded. "They said it's because they were there when you were born. They promised your mother they would watch over you and protect you."

"Were they friends with my parents or something?"

Lilian followed the dialogue between the ethereals. "No, they weren't friends," she said after a moment.

Andy frowned toward the church in the distance, contemplating this. He squeezed Lamb's hand. "I guess we should get going. We're supposed to go talk with your boss."

Lilian scowled, looking over her shoulder at the church. "She's *not* my boss. And they really won't have time for you right now."

"Why not?"

"Because they're getting ready to go into Ghostland tomorrow."

Lamb startled. "After what happened on Saturday?"

"Exactly. That's why we need your help to find my friend. He's the only one who can stop them."

"This friend… is he an ethereal?"

"Yeah, he is."

"But we can't see ghosts," Andy reminded her. "What makes you think we can help?"

Lilian turned to her invisible companion, then gave Andy a look of deadly sincerity. "Because your ethereal friends just told us they could."

PREMONITION

BRAM HAMMERED ON the trailer door. This was the last place he wanted to be at the moment. If anyone saw him, it would put him under scrutiny once the authorities discovered all of the evidence he'd planted on Dougan. But the man wouldn't answer his goddamn phone, forcing Bram to violate his own rule. "Dougan! Get your ass up, Jerry!"

"Hell's your problem, man?" the idiot said, answering the door in an undershirt and grungy pair of once-white briefs.

"What's *my* problem? Why did I get a call from your partner telling me you're late for work?"

Jerry guzzled from a can of Pabst contemplatively. "'Cause he's a prick," he said, shrugging up his scrawny shoulders.

"Why aren't you *there*, Jerry?"

The idiot scratched his ass absently. He wouldn't meet Bram's eye, and it only made Bram angrier. "Ain't going to work today," he grunted.

"Do you have any idea how many strings I had to pull to get you that job?"

The man finally looked up, his eyes unfocused. He was three sheets to the wind and the fourth wasn't all that far behind. "Man's entitled to a mental health day every now and then, ain't he?"

"Not today," Bram said. Then his shoulders slumped, and his face went slack.

Jerry's feet came off the floor so suddenly his bladder emptied in his underpants. He whimpered, looking down at his dangling feet in grimy socks. Something—some invisible *thing*—had picked him up under his armpits. His eyes widened in terror as the presence launched him backwards into the dank trailer. He tripped over his Salvation Army coffee table, scattering cigarette butts, beer cans and porn magazines, and went sprawling across the ratty tartan sofa. Beer cans from his collection lined up on the high shelf spanning the trailer's four walls toppled like dominoes. A vintage 12 oz. Billy beer struck him on the back of his head.

"*Get away from me! Don't you touch me!*" Jerry ranted, staring bleary-eyed at the man in the doorway. But Bram hadn't moved an inch. His eyelids fluttered and his dark eyes rolled out from his head, focusing on Jerry.

"I wouldn't dream of touching you," Bram said, eerily calm. "Not without a tetanus shot."

Bram turned, peering out at the other homes in the trailer park, before pulling the door closed behind them. He needed to sober the lazy son of a bitch up. If coffee didn't help, he would have to use brute force—but he definitely wouldn't touch a hair on the idiot's head.

Not physically, at least.

Lilian, Blake and Le Mon crossed town following Andy and Lamb. The ethereals leading Andy by the shoulders had told Le Mon they could help find Ben, but so far they'd been enigmatic about how and where they would find him.

They ended up on Koestler Street, and as they passed the house Lilian had grown up in—where the Edisons now lived, the rose bush and lawn neatly manicured—she turned and looked back the way they'd come. Practically the whole downtown was visible from here, with an even better view from the second floor of the Laramies' house near the end of the road.

"Le Mon already looked for him up here," she said. "He came here first thing."

The man in the dark suit, hovering slightly above Andy, turned and spoke in what Le Mon had said was Korean. Even if Andy had been able to converse with them, he'd said he only remembered a handful of phrases from his childhood. His father had always insisted they speak English at home, even though his mother's English had been very poor.

Le Mon nodded once as the man spoke, then again. "He said this is where he'll be."

"*Will* be?"

"Will be what?" Andy said.

"What do you mean 'will be'?" Le Mon asked the man in the suit.

The woman in the colorful blouse and dress spoke this time. On the walk here, Le Mon had asked them questions and passed on their answers to the others. The couple had known Andy's mother and father, but not well. His mother had been with them when they died. They were murdered and his mother had been shot in the shoulder, which had caused her to give birth to Andy prematurely. This last part had been news to Andy. He'd told them his mother had never mentioned being shot. She'd apparently never mentioned any of this to him.

"Ben's not here now," Le Mon translated. "He's not in

Duck Falls at all, they said. But he *will* be. And when he comes back, we'll find him here."

Lilian tried to parse this. She knew ethereals could sense each other, even across great distances. But this didn't make any sense. "How could they *know* that?"

"Know what?" Andy interrupted. Lamb squeezed his arm, urging him to be patient while Lilian listened.

"I don't know," Le Mon said. "I haven't met any, but I've heard stories about ethereals who can predict things before they happen."

Andy shrugged loose of Lamb's grip and approached them. The ethereals followed him. "What is he saying? Is it about me?"

"He says your ethereal friends… that they might be able to predict the future."

Andy seemed to take this in stride. "Of course, they can," he said. "That's how they knew where the psychic murderer would be."

"This is too much," Blake said, shaking his head.

Lilian ignored him. "What do you mean they knew?"

"We stopped it," Lamb said, "whatever it was, from killing a bunch of people at the psychic convention back in Vegas. Andy's friends told us it would be there and they were right. They chased it away before it could hurt anyone."

"Did they see it? Whatever it was that murdered the psychics?" Le Mon asked. Lilian repeated the question.

"No," Andy said. "But we saw it possess someone."

"Two people, actually," Lamb said.

"Possession," Le Mon said pensively. "More tricks up its sleeves."

Lilian shrugged. "Well, that's great. So if your friends really are psychic I guess that means we'll have to wait for

Ben to come back on his own. In the meantime, they're sending a bunch of innocent people into Ghostland to die tomorrow."

The ethereal couple spoke again.

"They say we need to keep going," Le Mon said.

Lilian didn't see the point in going on with them. But she supposed what they had said proved Ben was still safe, wherever he was. That was something, at least.

"Okay," she said, and they followed what Andy had called his "Nudges," which was actually the ethereals taking him by the shoulders and gently leading them to Ben's house.

They crossed the front lawn at a diagonal. Rather than going directly to the front door, they went up the driveway caked with tracks of dried dirt, and along the side of the house. Lilian couldn't remember the last time she'd been here. She'd passed on her condolences to Mr. and Mrs. Laramie at the funeral. She supposed the last time must have been a week or so before Garrote House had rolled past her window so long ago.

She'd beaten herself up so many times for telling Ben to go to his window that day. He would have found out about Ghostland either way. But things might have ended up differently if Ben hadn't seen Garrote in the window. He might not have died. They might not have gone that day at all.

"You need to stop thinking like that," Le Mon said.

She turned to him, realizing a tear had spilled down her cheek, and wiped it away briskly. "What do you mean?"

"Like this all happened because of something you did, some mistake you made. That's not a road you wanna travel down, believe me. I've been there."

Andy and the others had continued on ahead of them.

They waited at the edge of the backyard, still on the fresh asphalt driveway. "You guys might want to see this," Blake said, staring at whatever was in the yard.

Lilian hurried over, wiping her tear.

"Were you crying?" Blake asked.

"I'm fine," she said absently, looking at the thing in the ground. There was a slight mound, freshly sodded, and a rectangular ledge made of cement. It looked like stairs lead down into the trench. She noticed a metallic glint, the sun winking off something in the dark below. Then it all clicked.

"Is that… a *hatch*?"

Andy nodded. "Why would they bring us to a bomb shelter?"

Le Mon asked the ethereals. The man and woman, who were husband and wife, as Andy had suspected, looked at each other gravely. Finally, the man spoke.

"They said they don't know what's going to happen," Le Mon said after a moment. "But you'll be inside the shelter when Ben comes back, Lilian. Your man, too."

"Why would we be in there?" Blake asked.

Le Mon asked the couple. They shared another dark look before the man spoke. "They said 'bright light, loud sound,'" Le Mon translated.

Lilian passed it on to the others, and the five of them contemplated it in silence for a moment.

"I guess the bright light must be something real bad," Lamb said finally.

"If it means Blake and I have to hide in a bomb shelter with Ben's parents—yeah, I'd say it's pretty bad. But when is this all supposed to happen?"

Le Mon asked them. The man said something that sounded like *God* with a long "O."

"Soon," Le Mon translated.

"So why don't we all just wait here for him together?" Andy suggested. Before anyone could respond to this, the ethereals at his shoulders nudged him forward. He stumbled and almost went sprawling in the fresh sod.

"I guess that's a no," he said, looking annoyed.

"It's a no," Le Mon agreed. "Because the two of you, wherever you are when it happens, you're not here. And I don't think I am, either."

Sam and Logan sat in a booth at the 86, a '50s-style diner downtown, eating the best burgers and fries Sam had ever tasted while Pat Boone's "Love Letters in the Sand" played on the juke.

Logan watched her expectantly, holding his banquet home burger in both hands. "What'd I tell ya?"

She swallowed a bite and wiped her lips with a napkin from the shiny chrome dispenser. "You weren't kidding." She sucked the amazingly thick strawberry milkshake through a straw. "Is this place what keeps you sticking around? Or are you a Duck Falls native?"

Logan grinned. "Not from here, no. Germantown area, near Black Hill. A ways southeast from here."

"Small town?"

He shrugged. "Small city."

"I tell you, Deputy, I don't know that I could do it."

"Do what?"

"This." She swept her gaze across the bustling diner. "The small-town cop thing."

"Not a lot of use for a homicide detective in Duck Falls," Logan said, dipping a fry in his side gravy like he was dunking a tea bag. "Worst we get is a brawl or two at the Blind Duck."

"Is that a bar?"

"That's a bar, yeah. Play on duck blind, I guess."

"It's cute," Sam said, stirring her milkshake with the straw.

"Well, that's Duck Falls in a nutshell. But we've had our share of excitement lately, as you know."

"Right. That must've been difficult."

"It wasn't pretty. You've seen your share of it, I s'pose. Being homicide."

He was deflecting, squinting out the window at the civilians in the street. Most of them tourists, Sam suspected. Looky-loos, eager to take a little piece of the tragedy back home with them. "Sleep Walk" had come on the juke, and some girls from a table of them got up to slow dance, laughing with a sense of detached irony Sam felt teenagers seemed to have about everything, even more than when she was their age.

"Fair share," Sam agreed. "The Capitol Hill massacre happened when I was still a uni. Even that was just six people. Aside from that, I can't imagine it's anything like what you must've seen here back in April. Even just last weekend, with that TV crew. That's more than I typically see in a single incident."

"You jealous?" He grinned. Then his eyes clouded. "Sorry, bad joke."

"It's okay. I appreciate what you said earlier, by the way. About Stan. My father," she clarified. "I can tell you're a good cop with a good heart, and the world needs more of that. If you ever get bored doing the small-town thing, I could put in a word for you with my boss."

"And leave all this behind?" He sputtered. "Nah. But thanks."

Lovett wiped up a splotch of ketchup and mustard with

the last bite of his burger and scarfed it down. He took a healthy gulp of cream soda, then grabbed a couple of napkins from the dispenser and wiped his lips and his hands. He crumpled up the napkins and tossed them on the empty plate. "These are my people," he said, nodding over his shoulder. "Well, the ones that aren't tourists, which isn't much of them at the moment, to be fair." He shrugged. "But while they're here, I guess they're my people, too."

"Got your work cut out for you," Sam said with a slight smile.

"Sure do. How long you in town for? I never did ask."

"Not long. Done all I came for. Might head out to the park site a bit later."

"Well, I'd be happy to escort you. Won't be able to go in, that's against the rules. But I can point out where we found your father, if you like."

She smiled again. "That'd be nice, thanks."

"All right, then." He rose onto one cheek to take out his wallet, counted some bills and set them on the table between their plates. "Thank you kindly, Maddy," he called to their waitress, who was serving pie to the group of teenaged girls who weren't currently dancing.

Maddy looked to be in her early to mid-forties, her dark hair with a single gray streak done up in a bun. She was pretty and talkative and seemed completely natural in her carhop skirt and collared shirt uniform. "Always a pleasure, Logan," she said. "Detective, you come by for breakfast tomorrow. I'll make sure Carl cooks you up something special."

Sam tipped her well. "Thank you, ma'am."

They left the diner as the song ended.

"Wanna head out there now?" the deputy asked. "Should be able to finish up before dark."

"Sounds good."

"Well, great. Follow me then."

"I'll be on your six," Sam said with a grin.

As Logan climbed into his prowler, Sam headed for the silver Ford Focus parked a few spots up the street. He waited for her to pull out, then pulled out into the sparse traffic himself. She stayed close all the way to Ghostland.

THE BREACH

JERRY DOUGAN SHOWED up almost three hours late. His breath reeked of beer, coffee and cigarettes, but still smelled better than normal in general, as far as his shift partner Clive Stephens was concerned. It was definitely a welcome change from the sweaty socks and dank armpits he usually smelled like.

"What's the occasion?" Clive said, leaning back in his chair with his hands clasped behind his head.

"What the hell are you yappin about?"

"You took a shower." Clive grinned. "Got a new lady friend?"

Jerry swung his chair around and sat noisily. He rubbed his neck and winced. He had bruises there, like big purple fingerprints, but this was nothing new. He was always getting into shit at the Blind Duck. If not there it would be some other place stupid enough to take his money and not give him too much grief for getting fall-down drunk, starting shit with locals and tourists alike. Clive wouldn't be surprised one of these days to show up to work and find that his partner had gotten himself laid out in the hospital or even killed. After the new kid had to cover Dougan's shifts a couple of days this past week, Clive kind of hoped tonight was going to be the night he got the good news.

"Yeah, I got a new lady friend," Jerry said, showing his yellow teeth in a smile. "Your mom."

"My mom's dead, Jerry. You know that."

"That's what makes our love so special," Jerry said with a wink.

Fists clenched, Clive stood up so quickly his chair rolled back and slammed against the desk. The hillbilly piece of trailer trash could take a punch, Clive knew, but damned if he'd let him talk about his mother that way.

"You wanna tussle, Clive, just throw the first punch," Jerry said calmly, picking dirt out from under his nails. "See how fast you get your ass shit-canned."

Clive sat back down, fuming, his hands still squeezed into fists. "Speaking of fired, you're lucky I called your buddy and not the boss. I guess he musta sobered you up enough to come in today. Bully for me."

"Guess so."

Clive sat a moment, looking at the monitors. As usual, Jerry didn't even peek at them when he came in, and he was still picking dirt from his fingernails, not looking at them now. Nothing to look at anyhow, but at least he could pretend to give a single shit about the job.

"I got first rounds," Clive said, eager to get out of the room. The smell of beer on Jerry's breath was getting to him. Clive had quit drinking last year when Cynthia moved in with him. What he wouldn't do for an ice-cold Natty Boh right about now, even though he knew the smell on Jerry's breath was probably Pabst or some other crap hillbilly pieces of shit like him drank sitting on their porches at the white trash menagerie called the Duck Falls Trailer Court.

"Fucked if I care," Jerry said with a shrug.

"You gonna at least glance at those monitors once or

twice while I'm gone?"

Jerry looked back over his shoulder at the bank of monitors rotating through various areas in and outside of Ghostland. They weren't supposed to ever go inside the gates, even if they saw somebody trespassing. If they did see someone, there was a speed-dial button Clive was told went directly to the Big Guy's personal phone. For some reason, that big red button made Clive nervous—which was why he called it the Uneasy Button, like the opposite of those commercials. As long as he'd been working there, he'd never seen a single person inside Ghostland who wasn't supposed to be there, so it hadn't much mattered anyway.

He'd been doing his rounds when the Ghost Dudes or whatever they called themselves ended up getting killed. It took over an hour to circle the wall, checking entries and outbuildings. The new kid probably hadn't even been watching the monitors, either. He wasn't much better than Dougan, though rather than just not giving a shit, his problem was his face was always in another screen: his cell phone.

Not that there hadn't been enough witnesses to the Ghost Dudes deaths, anyway. Clive heard on his morning radio show that the live broadcast got something like thirty-six-million viewers, more than the *Seinfeld* finale pulled in and over a third of what the average Super Bowl got, at least according to *Geek and Stu in the Morning*, whom he trusted more than just about anyone in his life, even Cynthia.

Clive stepped outside and fired up a butt. He wasn't supposed to smoke on his rounds, only on lunch, but other than himself and Jerry there was nobody around for miles. If he did it discreetly, with the cigarette hidden in his palm like a magician doing a trick, even the cameras wouldn't catch him.

Inhale. Walk a few steps, holding the smoke in his lungs, really getting his money's worth. Soothing that nic fit. Then exhale, the smoke dissipating behind him as he moved. Hedgewood couldn't begrudge a man a few minor habits, and at least he wasn't drunk on the job like Jerry. Or stoned, like the new kid who mainly worked the midnight to noon shift, doing his weed in one of those vape things so no one could tell it wasn't bubble-gum flavored, as long as they weren't within the radius of its skunky smell.

"Goddamn punk kid," Clive said, blowing out smoke, his nerves calming from the almost-fight in the security station. "And fuck Dougan, that asshole. Make me late for my smoke."

Ever since Alfie Whitehead had a heart attack on the job, Clive had been stuck working with Jerry Fucking Dougan. He'd thought it was a temporary thing, but just like herpes whenever he thought he'd gotten rid of the guy, Jerry came back with a vengeance. His pal who'd gotten him the job—Clive hated cronyism just as much as nepotism—had told Clive to call him if he ever caught Jerry fucking up. He would straighten Dougan out toot sweet.

As much as he would have preferred to get Dougan's ass fired, the guy had been pretty convincing. The thought of Jerry getting his ass kicked and having to come in to work with his tail between his legs was pretty gratifying, Clive had to admit.

But Jerry never felt ashamed or embarrassed. Jerry never apologized. He was a human cockroach. You swat it, you squash it into the ground with the sole of your boot and it just kept scuttling along. Only in Jerry Dougan's case, he'd keep on running his mouth.

"Fuck it," Clive muttered, exhaling smoke. "Next time, I'm calling the boss."

He looked up. The sun was low above the far wall, and the roller coaster and peaked rooves inside the park stood in silhouette against the deep blue sky. Their shadows stretched long and chilly across the tarmac and field to the east of it.

Even though he'd been stationed here since last May, this place still gave Clive the creeps, especially at night. That was why he worked the noon to midnight shift. Sure, it meant he'd be here a few hours after the sun went down—more in the fall and winter, when the days were shorter—but at least he wouldn't have to be here in the wee hours of the night, with no company but the owls and raccoons. Oh, and all the ghosts creeping behind the three-foot-thick wall.

And Dougan, he supposed, who was no company at all.

Clive rounded the east wall to the south, heading into the main parking lot and toward the front gates. It was the part of the rounds Clive disliked the most, passing the front gate. In the dark, it was worse, like everything about this place. But sometimes even in daylight he could swear he heard people whispering or calling his name beyond the gate. Even if he hadn't been strictly prohibited from going inside to find out what the hell was making all that racket, he wouldn't have set foot in there. The voices chilled him to the bones even in high summer, with the sun's rational light reminding him the ghosts were locked up tight so long as that machine in the largest of the outbuildings kept running, even if it seemed like they should just be able to fly out the front gates or through the walls.

He quickened his pace as he passed the gate. No one called his name this time. He made it to the other side and didn't hear anything at all. No whispers. No laughter. None of the crazy shit he'd sometimes hear coming from beyond the turnstiles. A few times he thought he recognized some of the voices, too—coworkers who'd lost their lives on opening day, like Niko and Lenny, calling for him to open the gate and let them out.

Not hearing anything kind of made him suspicious, truth be told. Like they knew something he didn't.

"Goddamn ghosts," he muttered.

Out of sight from the next camera, he lit another smoke and dragged on it a little faster than the last, letting the nicotine calm his nerves even though it made his heartbeat quicker.

The sound of crunching gravel echoed from the far end of the lot. He spotted the vehicles coming from the county road: an SUV and a small car. As they got closer, he noticed the lightbar atop the SUV and realized it must be Sheriff Brigham or one of her deputies.

Come to arrest Jerry Dougan, if I'm lucky. Bully for me.

He paused there, just beyond the gate, waiting with bated breath. He realized his cigarette was still cupped in his palm and dropped it casually, then sidestepped to crush it out on the asphalt.

The two vehicles parked and Deputy Lovett got out first, followed by a short, chubby woman in khaki pants and a heavy coat. Judging strictly by her looks, Clive assumed she preferred the company of women but he didn't much care about those things. It was just a detail he considered and set aside, in case she said something that might annoy him later, so he could call her mean shit behind her back like he did about most people.

"Hey, Logan." He waved, then nodded at the woman. "Miss." Christ, he hoped she wouldn't take issue to him calling her that. He tried his best to be politically correct in public but you never knew these days what would set some people off.

"Hey, Clive. How's Tricks?"

"She's good," Clive said. Tricks was his golden retriever, short for Trixie. He and Logan often met in the street when the deputy walked his Boxer. "How's Cash?"

"Strapped," Logan said, patting his pockets jokily. "My dog is fine, though."

Clive chuckled.

"This is Detective Sam Beadle," Logan said. The woman held up a hand in a not-quite wave. "Drove out all the way from Seattle, wanted to take a look at the place, if that's all right."

Clive shrugged. "Good to meet you, Detective. Long as you don't wanna go in, I'm not gonna stop you from lookin around."

"Thanks," Logan said. "Say, how's that partner of yours doing?"

"Cynthia? She's fine."

Logan grinned darkly. "I meant Jerry. Had him in lockup for a few days over an assault. Seems Brigham got eager to spring him so he could get back to work. Hope he isn't aggravating the shit outta you."

Clive chuckled. "Nah, he's all right. Mean son of a bitch, but nothin I can't handle." He glanced toward the western edge of the wall, eager to get another smoke in before his rounds were done. "Best get back to it," he said. "You two stay safe."

"Will do. Thank you, Clive."

Clive tipped an imaginary cap. "Detective," he said.

She smiled and nodded. "Thank you," she said.

The rest of his rounds were pretty uneventful, most nights. A few times he'd caught kids doing graffiti on the western wall. He supposed they chose that side because it was still in the sun's light longer into the day, and far from the security station. Whatever the reason, that was where most of the graffiti tended to be, and where he'd caught that group of asshole kids doing it, way high up on a ladder one time. It wasn't art, either. Not like those street murals. It was stupid shit, like spray-painting their tagger names or big fat dicks shooting loads.

There was no one out here tonight, which was good for them considering the police presence by the gate. He did see some new graffiti, a phrase he noticed kept getting repeated, either out here or by the hatch:

ReX GARROTe LIVeS

Whoever this Garrote kid was, this wiz with a spray-can, Clive ached to tase his ass to all the way to Kingdom Come. Imagining all the ways he might discreetly abuse his limited power when he got his hands on the kid, he rounded the northwestern corner to the north wall, where the outbuildings stood: the main and backup generators and the Occurrence Field, or whatever they called it.

The generator buildings hummed. The sound always set his teeth on edge. He didn't much like it out here, but inside the Occurrence Field building—or whatever they called it—was much worse. Something about knowing its purpose, he supposed. Electricity he understood, to a point. He still wasn't sure whether hydroelectric towers caused cancer or if 5G waves killed all those birds in Sweden or wherever like Geek and Stu said one time. But he understood the *principle* of it more than the pseudoscientific mumbo-jumbo behind the ghost forcefield in the biggest of the outbuildings.

Clive stood beneath its cold shadow now, the sun hidden behind it. He pulled his keycard on the retractable lanyard and swiped it over the access panel. The light flashed from red to green and the maglock clunked. He pulled the handle before it could lock on him again, and he stepped into the cool building.

The giant coils hummed with an undulating sound. Clive could swear when he came in here the air itself vibrated. If he had microscopic vision, he thought he'd be able to see the dust particles pinging off each other like pool balls after a good break.

Like the generator buildings, the entire structure existed to house a single machine. This one was so tall a set of metal stairs was set along the inside of the exterior walls, with a catwalk across it to reach the electronic panels at the machine's apex.

Clive climbed the stairs, his footfalls on the metal grids echoing all the way to the top, the fillings in his teeth humming along with the intense vibration of the massive machine. God, he hated this place. If he could avoid it he would, but he had to check the building from top to bottom, and he just knew the one time he didn't was when someone from Hedgewood would be watching him on the feed, and he'd get written up or fired.

As he crossed the catwalk, craving one last cigarette before the end of his rounds, Clive spotted what at first looked like a stack of parcels on top of the machine. They had wires connecting them, and all the wires ended at the base of a cheap flip phone. The packages all had the same stamp: *C4 Explosives Block Demolition, M4.*

"Oh, you gotta be kidding m—"

The phone buzzed: 1 TEXT MESSAGE.

He had just enough time to think *Fucking Dougan* before the explosion practically vaporized him, leaving nothing but smoke and ash.

The massive boom made Jerry Dougan's ears pop. He swiveled in his chair as the ground beneath him shook, and every single thing that wasn't nailed down tipped over or fell to the floor. Even Clive's chair toppled, the base of it wide enough that it really shouldn't have. But it did, and that was enough to stir an emotion other than aggravation in Jerry for the first time in a long time.

That emotion was fear.

The monitors for quadrant three—the outbuildings and security station—had gone blue, the words NO INPUT along the top. Three cameras had been obliterated by whatever the hell had made that godawful boom. Now that his hearing had returned, he heard a new sound. It was something like a jet engine or a table saw winding down, but loud enough to make his eyeballs vibrate.

Frantic, he scanned the other monitors. Nothing on the rest of them, except for the parking lot camera in Q1, where that asshole deputy stood with some short pudgy guy, the stranger closer to the gates, the deputy leaning against his prowler. Jerry scanned the other monitors. Didn't look like much of anything was going on inside the park, except for maybe a high wind blowing a lot of trash and whatnot around. Looked like dust devils, in some places.

He saw the fireball rising over the north wall in one of

the Q2 feeds. Holy mackerel, she was a beaut: a big old ball of flame, like a mushroom cloud in miniature.

Jerry lowered his gaze to the big red panic button and the telephone receiver beside it.

The red button was a measure of last resort. Someone inside the park who shouldn't be there? Press the button, pick up the phone. Anything extremely out of the ordinary? Button, phone.

If anything was a red-button moment, this was it.

Still, Jerry hesitated. He hated talking to the boss on any job, and this phone went straight to the *boss's* boss. He'd have to try to explain what the hell was going on to Hedgewood, and he didn't even have the first inkling of a clue. Q3 could have dropped into a sinkhole for all he knew, like what happened to that house inside the park.

"No state to call the Big Boss, I'm still half-pissed," he muttered to himself. "I *knew* I shouldn'ta come in today, I *knew* I shouldn'ta *goddamn* come in today." He pounded his thigh with a fist, pacing the small room. "Wasn't for that prick Merritt, I'd be home right now."

Jerry still couldn't figure out how Bram had gotten the upper hand on him. One second, he'd been standing in the doorway and the next he'd found himself sprawled on the sofa, the ashtray and beer cans spilled all over the carpet. The guy had moved so fast Jerry hadn't even seen it coming. Then he'd picked Jerry up by his neck and whipped him around, hauling him right off the couch, even though Jerry had not once seen the man lift a finger. It was like he'd done it all with his mind, like something out of a Stephen King movie. Then he'd frog-marched Jerry straight into the shower, clothes and all, blasting him with ice-cold water.

Jerry shuddered at the memory. That Bram gave him

the creeps more than anyone he'd ever met. Even before this morning, something about him had seemed… *off*. Jerry couldn't quite put his finger on it, but he'd never really thought about it soberly.

He grabbed his walkie and depressed the TALK button. "Clive, it's Jerry. Where the hell are ya? C'mon back."

A squall of static met his request.

"Clive, it's Jerry," he shouted, the pitch of his voice rising in agitation. "C'mon back!"

Static.

"*Son of a bitch*," he spat, slamming the walkie down on the desk. He crossed to the red button and stood over it, scratching his head.

"Aw, hell…."

He slammed two fingers on the button and reached for the phone.

Something struck him on the base of his skull before he could grab the receiver, hard enough to send stars across his vision. He whipped around, blinking through tear-blurred eyes to get a look at his attacker.

"Clive, you mother—"

But Clive wasn't there. The security station was empty. Nobody had come in or out, he would have heard the click of the maglock. He would have heard them open the door.

A chill ran up his spine. He rubbed the bruises on his neck. "*Bram?*"

The engine whine from outside stopped suddenly. In the silence a voice called, distant and tinny, from the telephone receiver hanging over the edge of the desk, swaying like a pendulum. He must have knocked it off the hook when he'd spun around.

"*Hello? Can you confirm the breach?*"

He heard the ceramic scrape of his coffee mug full of

vodka and water a split second before it flew off the desk and struck him on the forehead.

"What the motherfuck?" He blinked at the shattered mug at his feet, rubbing the wound.

The computer mouse came next. Then the keyboard. Then the Styrofoam coffee cup full of pens, striking him one after another. In the barrage, Jerry thought back to those long-ago fights with Noreen after he'd stumble home drunk from the Blind Duck, when he'd maybe get a little handsy and she wasn't having any of it, and she'd chuck just about anything and everything in her reach at him to get him to stop.

"*Help!*" he cried at the swinging receiver. The desk drawer flung open and out came the takeout menus and condiment packets, the plastic cutlery, pennies and paperclips. "*Help me!*"

The voice on the phone no longer seemed concerned with him or their "breach." He was alone now, alone with whatever was chucking every-damn-thing in the security station at him like Noreen on a tear.

He stood abruptly and bolted for the door, his back and neck and legs pelted by heavy objects. They fell to the floor, smashing and cracking as he reached for his keycard, hanging on the retractable lanyard.

He heard the chairs rolling across the polished cement floor an instant before they struck him, slamming him face-first against the security door. His vision waned but he was still conscious enough to hear the groan of bending metal and the metallic pings of screws hitting the floor. When he finally turned to look at what could be causing such a horrendous sound, the first of the security monitors smashed screen-first into his face, erupting in a storm of plastic and blood.

It was the last thing he saw.

End of the Road

S AM BEADLE STOOD at Ghostland's front gate, thinking about her father.

From where she stood, she could see nothing of the inside of the park. The metal security door barred the entrance. It looked heavy and thick. She guessed it must have slammed down the moment things started getting hairy, trapping everyone inside the park. It didn't seem like a wise decision from a safety standpoint, but she supposed that since the gate remained closed and the Recurrence Field still on, protecting the outside world had been more of an imperative to the owners.

Stan would obviously have returned here first. Upon realizing he couldn't get through the gate he'd likely gone in search of the tunnels and the maintenance hatch. Sam tried to imagine him driving all the way across the country to be here on opening day. He'd been convinced Rex Garrote was alive, and a part of him had likely believed he'd encounter more than just the Doll's Head Killer here. She pictured him leading those kids through the tunnels toward safety, humming or singing to himself, and taking off his fedora every so often to scratch the few hairs left on his head.

He'd made it almost all the way to their destination

before meeting his end at the hands of the same man he'd come to apprehend. It was a sad, cosmic joke of a death. She'd always assumed her father would die on the job—she supposed it was a *gut feeling*, if she was being honest. His ailing health hadn't allowed him to work as a private investigator but he'd still continued picking at cold cases like the fabric pulls on his threadbare recliner: murders he hadn't been able to solve, killers he hadn't been able to put away. When the department had forced him into retirement, she'd known he wouldn't drop his unsolved cases. He was Ahab, like he'd said. They were his white whales. His albatrosses.

"You wanna know something weird?"

Sam started at the deputy's voice. He'd been so quiet for so long, leaning against his SUV with his arms crossed over his chest while she reminisced, that she'd nearly forgotten he was here.

"Sure," she said.

"When we found your dad, there was a whole bunch of weird stuff in those tunnels under that house. We came across this body, a male in his late-seventies. Looked like he'd been burned alive. Weird thing is, he had all these wires coming out of him, like electrodes, sorta snaking out of this glass pod. You ever see that movie *The Lawnmower Man*?"

Sam shook her head.

"No one ever says yes to that," he mused. "Anyway, I thought maybe with all those cables and wires, the Crispy Guy was connected to all the computers and whatnot around him. Like maybe he could control everything in the park with his mind." He shrugged, seemingly embarrassed by the admission. "I guess it sounds kinda stupid."

"You found all that under Garrote House?"

"Yeah-huh. They had to identify all the victims, some of them were so badly messed up they had to match em with dental records. Well, as it turns out, the Crispy Guy had false teeth. They found a match for em, made for a guy named Joseph M. Carruthers in Seattle about twenty years ago. Around the same time a horror writer named Rex Garrote burned alive in the same house that fell on top of Mr. Crisp twenty years later. Isn't that funny?"

Sam had only meant to chuckle but the chuckle turned into convulsive, guttural laughter. She looked up at the Ghostland sign, spanning the archway above the big metal gate, and laughed until tears spilled down her cheeks and the base of her skull started to ache.

"Guess I should try doin standup," Logan said once she'd settled down.

"All this time," Sam said, catching her breath, "all this time Stan was *convinced* Rex Garrote faked his own death, but nobody believed him. Not even me. Now it turns out he was right all along."

"Think so?"

"That's one monster of a coincidence if he didn't. Your Mr. Crisp was Rex Garrote, Deputy."

The deputy considered it a moment, then shrugged. "I guess you're probably right. It tracks, doesn't it? But why? And how does someone stay hidden in plain sight for twenty years? And why would Hedgewood keep that a secret?"

"Hell if I know, Logan," Sam said. "But that's the first thing we need to ask Hedgewood when we get him in a room—"

A massive boom cut her off midsentence, so forceful the ground beneath their feet shook, and the vehicles rocked on their wheels.

"What the hell was that?" Logan shouted over the rumble, gripping the front of his SUV to stay upright.

Sam careened back to her rental car, struggling to remain on her feet. *"I don't know! It sounded like an explosion!"*

When the earth stopped trembling, a loud whine arose in its wake. She turned toward the sound. A black cloud had filled the sky above the north wall, rising from a massive orange fireball. Fiery projectiles shot out in all directions like miniature comets.

"I'm heading over," Logan said, rounding the front of his SUV. "I'll call it in on the drive."

Sam nodded, preparing to follow. She had her hand on the door handle when she caught sight of someone standing in front of the gate in her peripheral vision.

As she turned, her heart leaped into her throat. She recognized the shape of him, the slump of his shoulders, even before she saw his face.

It was Stan. She didn't know how she was seeing him, how it was *possible*, but she couldn't deny what she was seeing. He stood beneath the archway in his wrinkled sport coat, the crumpled fedora held against his heart.

It was *him*.

"Dad?" she said, her voice soft and childlike with wonder and even fear.

Her dead father gave her an awkward smile. "Been a long time since you called me that, Samantha."

"You coming?" Deputy Lovett called, peering at her from his open passenger window.

Sam regarded him a moment then turned back to the gates, expecting Stan to be gone. But he was still there, with that sad, old hound dog expression.

Logan followed her gaze. He seemed to see nothing, or

at least he didn't react to the fact that an old man who wasn't there just a moment ago was suddenly standing by the ticket booths, seconds after a major explosion.

"I'll meet you over there," she said.

A scowl crossed the deputy's face. Then he nodded, flicked on the siren and strobes and backed out. She watched him drive across the lot, brightening the asphalt with blue and red as he headed toward the incident.

Once he was gone, she returned to her father. "How are you here?"

He gestured behind himself with his hat in his hand. "That racket a minute ago, loud enough to wake the dead?" He grinned. "I guess it musta worked."

"You're dead," she said.

"Bingo." His grin became a smile. "I tell ya, I sure didn't expect to see you again after the last time." The smile faltered. "Hang on a sec… you're not dead too, are you?"

She patted her arms and legs. "I don't think so."

"Huh. So you came all the way out to Maryland just to see your old man?"

"Not entirely."

His lips curled down at the edges.

"But I did come *here* for you. I guess I just needed some closure."

"Closure, huh?"

He took a step toward her. She took one step back, finally letting go of the door handle, afraid of what might happen if he tried to touch her.

"No need to be scared, sweetheart. If it's closure you want, I'm all ears."

He wiggled his ears to prove it, like he used to when she was little to make her laugh. She'd forgotten all about that. It had always made her think of Fozzie Bear, especially when he'd worn his hat. Tears stung her eyes.

"I missed you, Dad."

"I missed you, kid. I wish I'd been there for you when you needed me."

"You tried," she said.

He shrugged. "I coulda tried harder."

She smiled, fully crying now. "We both could have."

"You know how proud I am of you," he said. "Of who you became. Who woulda guessed you'd follow in my footsteps, huh? But maybe you'll do better than I did. Be a better cop and a better parent, if you ever roll the dice."

"I don't know how likely that is, Dad. But I appreciate you saying that."

Stan's smile suddenly faded. He jerked his head toward the park, gripping his hat in both hands. When he turned back, he looked frightened. "You oughta go, sweetheart. Don't follow your friend. Get as far away from this place as possible."

"Why? What's happening?"

"*The monsters are coming*," he said, the terror in his voice so profound she couldn't help but shiver.

"What about you?"

"Don't worry about me. I'll manage. I always do." He sat his fedora on his head and crushed it down. "Go. Before it's too late."

She wiped her eyes. "Okay." She opened the car door finally and sat behind the wheel. She took her eyes off her father just long enough to start the engine. When she looked up through the windshield he was gone.

Sam floored the accelerator all the way to the county road, with absolutely no idea which way she would go when she got there. Left would take her back to Duck

Falls. Right, toward escape.

Left or right, Sam. Fight or fright.

There was really no choice. If these people were in danger, as her dad seemed to believe, if *her friends* were in danger, she owed it to herself to help them.

She flicked the left-turn indicator and headed back the way she'd come. As she reached the town sign, an old civil defense siren began blaring from somewhere, probably the fire station or city hall. Sam knew a lot of small towns still used air-raid sirens for tornado warnings and to alert fire department volunteers. Usually it was nothing the average townsperson would pay much attention to, particularly outside of typical tornado zones.

But once she'd reached the outskirts of town, people were on the alert. They hurried everywhere: into cars, through traffic, into their homes and businesses, across the park to a fenced exit. Tourists took their cue from citizens to get their asses in gear, everyone looking fretfully toward the northwest, where the sky had turned black.

Sam supposed they must have all heard the explosion and felt the earth shake. They knew it meant something bad had happened at Ghostland.

The monsters are coming.

She'd felt a spike of fear when her father had spoken those words but it had lessened the further she'd gotten from Ghostland. The sheer state of panic in the streets put her on edge again. Clenching her jaw, Sam gripped the wheel tighter.

She wondered what would happen to Stan now. He hadn't been such a bad father, in retrospect. He'd been a bit neglectful and sometimes aloof, but he'd never abused her, never yelled at her. He'd instilled in her the same values she lived by today and she had followed in his footsteps, not just in her choice of career but by letting her gut lead her first to Vegas and finally here, where it had all begun. He was proud of her and she was proud of herself, for finally letting go of her anger and resentment. She felt happy for the first time in as long as she could remember, and all it had taken to get her there was the end of the damn world.

Two fire trucks blew past her, heading in the opposite direction. The sound of their sirens competed with the louder one from town hall until they were a good distance behind her.

Her cell phone rang in the dashboard cradle. She glanced at it. The caller ID said MOM.

Not the best timing but it could be worse, she thought. She answered it. "Hi, Mom."

"Oh!" Lucille Beadle said, startled. "I thought I'd get your voicemail again, Samantha."

Sam smiled. "Not today. I took some time off."

"You're on *vacation*?"

Another sheriff's department vehicle blew past with its siren blaring.

"Not really. I was in Vegas for a couple of days. I'm in Maryland now."

"Oh."

She heard the suspicion in her mother's tone. "Just trying to make peace, Mom. With Dad."

"Well, that's nice, I suppose." Her mother left a hefty pause. "And did you? Make peace?"

"I think so. Listen, Mom, I have to go but can we get a cup of coffee sometime when I get back?"

"I'd like that," her mother said.

Sam smiled. From the top of the hill—what locals called the "Duck Bill," according to Deputy Lovett—the buildings of downtown Duck Falls shimmered below her in the early-November sunset, framed by autumn leaves. It looked like something out of a postcard or painting. Genuine Norman Rockwell Americana. She began to understand why Deputy Lovett liked it here.

"Great," she said, smiling still. It had been too long since she'd spoken to her mom. Longer still since they'd had coffee together. "I'll let you know when I'm back in town, 'kay? I gotta get going now, I'm on the road. Love you, Mom."

"I love you, too."

As she returned her gaze to the road, the car struck something head-on, and the front end crumpled around it. Sam didn't even have an instant to wonder what it was, nor to realize she'd forgotten to buckle up in her rush to get clear of the explosion, before she catapulted out of the driver's seat. She reached out instinctively to protect her face, but her forehead struck the windshield first regardless. Her nose and both wrists shattered as she hurtled through the glass.

In a small mercy, Sam lost consciousness moments before her body collided roughly with the road. She didn't feel the final excruciating pain of her death, and didn't discover for herself whether Ron Thibodeau, the Seattle P.D. medical examiner, had been right about the eyes seeing for thirty seconds afterward.

She was gone. The vehicles surrounding the accident braked. Several occupants stepped out and marveled at her car, the windshield shattered, its front-end crumpled around an empty space.

On the phone, still secured in its cradle on the dash, Sam's mother called out her name several times before breaking down in tears and hanging up to call 9-1-1.

COUNTDOWN TO EXTINCTION

LOGAN'S PROWLER SCREECHED to a halt alongside the security station, where Jerry and Clive were on duty. This close to the burning building, the air surrounding the station was like standing hunched over a lit grill in contrast to the crisp November day. It felt like swimming into a warm undercurrent in the Atlantic Ocean. *Or piss in the pool*, Logan thought miserably.

He hammered a fist on the door, hoping neither of them had been in any of the outbuildings when whatever it was exploded. There was a lot of machinery in these buildings Logan had no knowledge of—for all he knew, the one that exploded could have been what was keeping all the ghosts from getting out.

For all he knew, they already had.

Three days, he thought. *It was supposed to be* three *days, not today.*

He'd forgotten all about what the desk nurse had told him earlier, until the explosion had rocked the ground beneath his feet: Elena Feliz's deathbed vision of the world coming to an end. He still couldn't exactly scoff, even if she may have gotten the date wrong. What he was looking at right now might not be the end of the world, but it was as close as he ever wanted to come to it. He felt like he was standing next to the fiery pits of Hell.

The noise from the burning machinery, a loud whine like a jet engine, had finally dissipated but the sound of the flames was immense. Huge chunks of twisted metal and debris littered the ground around the destroyed building. It reminded him of when he'd visited New York City a few months after 9/11 and had peered down into the pit at Ground Zero. Nearly the entire structure of the outbuilding was demolished, leaving only jigsaw patches of charred cinderblock and blackened steel support beams, bent outward like the petals of some ugly flower. He was close enough to see that whatever machinery had been inside the building had virtually disintegrated.

Logan pounded again on the door. "*Clive, open up, goddammit!*"

No answer.

Either the two of them had gotten themselves blown up or they'd both cut and run. Logan hoped for the latter. He couldn't blame them if they had.

Already sweating, he leaned closer to press his ear against the metal door and nearly burned it right off. He hissed in a pained breath.

Now what?

Get out of the area, that's what, he told himself. *Something else is liable to explode and then sayonara, Duck Falls' finest.*

He heeded his own advice, stepping out of the pocket of hot air and returning to the Suburban's cool interior. He drove far enough back to feel somewhat safe, then backed up even further until the only sign of trouble was the black smoke rising from behind the park wall.

It was clear now that Sam wasn't coming to meet him. She must have high-tailed it out of here the second he rounded the corner. He couldn't blame her, either. This wasn't her town. These weren't her people. They were his responsibility, and he couldn't just sit here waiting for someone of higher authority to take charge.

Go back to town. Someone'll be here soon. Let them deal with this mess. Duck Falls is Priority Numero Uno. This is federal business. Hedgewood's business.

He called it in as he peeled out of the lot, speeding toward town with the siren and strobe blasting.

On the way, a fire truck flew by, followed by the fire chief's van, headed toward the explosion. A sleek, black limousine was hot on their heels. Logan wasn't sure if Hedgewood himself was in town, but he suspected the limo belonged either to him or to Thea Petralia.

As he approached downtown, the traffic heading both ways thickened until he was driving at a crawl. Strobes flashed up ahead. He guessed they must have left a truck behind to deal with a traffic accident. The way people were driving, it was no wonder.

He rolled down his window and leaned out. About ten cars up, the fire truck was parked at the side of the road. He couldn't see the fender-bender. Gawkers stood around as the firefighters trudged back and forth in the road, dealing with the accident.

The car ahead of him moved up. Logan pulled into the ditch as far as he could and put on his blinkers. The minivan behind him honked as he got out.

He approached the accident, walking in the culvert along the right side of the road. The firefighters let traffic on his side pass through. The whole front end of the eastbound vehicle was crumpled. Glass everywhere in the road. A mangled bumper. A worn scrap of tire.

Logan recognized the car as he approached it. Silver

Ford Focus with Nevada plates. It was Sam Beadle's rental car.

"Oh, Jesus…." He sprinted toward it.

Sam lay in the middle of the spray of shattered glass, her body mangled, her jacket shredded. Her head had caved in from the impact with the road. A white van idled in the entrance to the parkette high up on the Duck Bill. He recognized the hard-faced man standing by it, talking to one of the firefighters, as a high-ranking member of GRP2. The van was undamaged. Logan couldn't figure what had caused the crash.

He approached Sam's broken body. She appeared to be staring back at the rental car, as if in disbelief. He followed her gaze. It looked like she'd hit a telephone pole, but there weren't any skid marks in the road, and the closest pole was ten, fifteen feet away.

What the hell did she hit then?

He crouched beside her, feeling her neck for a pulse. Her skin was already several degrees cooler than normal, and he knew he would feel nothing. Still, he held his hand there long enough to be sure. Once he was satisfied, he withdrew his fingers, wet with blood. With his clean hand he closed her eyes. He wiped his fingers on his uniform trousers.

How many times had she survived a high-speed chase after some badass only to end like this? Like him, he imagined she'd spent much of her day behind the wheel. To die like this felt unfair.

"Jesus, Sam. I'm so sorry."

"Deputy," a young firefighter said, returning from where he'd been speaking to the driver of the white van. "This is a real shitshow, ain't it?"

"It is," Logan agreed. "Ambulance on its way?"

"Just called em in from Hagerstown."

"Better call up Tom Browne, too."

Tom Browne ran the closest funeral home. He was also the county coroner. The young firefighter, a local named Bill James, nodded solemnly.

"And get a blanket, would you? She's one of us, goddamn it. No need for every damn rubberneck to see her like this. I'll deal with traffic."

While the firefighter ran off to grab one of the coarse gray blankets they kept in the storage compartments along the side of the truck, Logan returned to his prowler to grab some road flares from the back.

As he closed the hatch, he noticed the hard-faced Gurpy leaning against his van, staring grimly at Sam's lifeless body as the firefighter covered it with a blanket. He made a note to speak to the man as soon as the coroner arrived.

He lit one of the flares. He held it up a moment, burning brightly against the black smoke hovering over Ghostland.

Lord help us, he thought, holding the flame. *Lord help us all.*

Lamb may not have been able to see Andy's ghosts but she could feel their anxiety. They'd herded the two of them down the hill at a good pace, weaving through the streets and avenues. Why she and Andy couldn't have just stayed with the kids at the bomb shelter was beyond her, but she supposed Fate didn't work that way.

Fate had brought Andy to her door not so long ago, and taken her mother that same day. It had led them to save who knew how many lives at the psychic expo on Saturday, and joined them with the detective, a kindred spirit. Eventually, it had brought them here to Duck Falls.

The fact that Fate had arrived in the form of a Korean couple over thirty-years dead didn't matter. She and Andy had been brought here for a reason. Lamb hoped that reason would present itself at the Temple, though she supposed they may have already served their purpose, saving the lives of Lilian and Blake by directing them toward the bomb shelter.

The sun was already beginning to set by the time they reached the church. A sleek black SUV limousine idled directly out front, and a tractor-trailer had backed into the driveway at a steep angle. Two men lifted seemingly heavy boxes out of the rig and stacked them on a dolly. A third man rolled the dolly into the church while the other two stayed behind, awaiting the next load.

"Sweet whip!" Andy said, admiring the limo.

The driver's side window was down, and a Latino chauffer with a neatly trimmed goatee sat behind the wheel, reading the Duck Falls *Squawker*. He sucked on a vape and exhaled a plume of cotton-candy scented vapor. The smell reminded Lamb of the time her mom and one of her mother's old boyfriends had taken her to the Clark County Fair in Logandale when she was nine and the guy had tried to feel her up on the Ferris wheel.

Andy tried peering through the tinted back windows, the setting sun glinting off the dark glass. "I bet there's a celebrity in there."

"Hey!" The driver snapped his fingers, causing Andy to flinch and step back from the vehicle. "Look with your eyes, pal."

"Sorry." Andy hurried back to Lamb. "What a dick."

She ruffled his hair. "Aw. Did the big man scare you?"

He laughed and she joined him. One of the big church

doors opened as they climbed the steps. A white guy with blond dreads stood in the doorway. "Good, you're here," he said. "Thea wants to talk to you."

Andy shrugged at her. They followed the guy inside.

In the gloom directly beyond the door, a pale-faced woman wearing a turban made a rubber ball hover in the air nearly a foot above her hand. It took a moment for Lamb to realize there was another presence with the woman, keeping the ball from falling to the floor.

"People call me Coop," the man with the dreads said, as if the woman's trick was nothing new.

"I'm Lamb. This is Andy," she said, since he was too distracted by the floating ball.

"I know who you are."

"Did you see that?" Andy whispered.

"It's just an ethereal holding the ball," she told him.

His excitement deflated. "Spoilers," he groaned.

Inside the church, even stranger things transpired. A man in parachute pants floated inches above the pews, his arms held wide. Lamb sensed at least one presence with him, probably holding him up by the arms.

"Dude!" Andy marveled. "This is *awesome*." He turned to her. "Please don't ruin this for me…"

Lamb snorted laughter.

Elsewhere, other strange and amazing feats occurred. A woman placed the final champagne flute onto a pyramid and took two deliberate steps back. She signaled to someone Lamb couldn't see and the glasses began to tremble to the sound of a high-pitched whine. The whine grew louder, and the glasses shattered one after another like a bundle of fireworks. To their left, a shaggy-haired man wearing safety glasses held a lightbulb in one hand. The bulb grew impossibly bright, then suddenly burst in his hand. He gasped and shook out his fingers before bending to pick up another bulb from the box.

Among the pews, the pages of bibles and songbooks flipped from back to front, front to back, moving in precise coordination like a scene from *The Sorcerer's Apprentice*. On the other side of the pews, standing below the stained-glass windows, a man formed some kind of blue energy ball between his hands. When it seemed too erratic to contain, he launched it at a young girl with pigtails.

Lamb let out a little yelp of fright, but the girl caught the energy as easily as a lobbed ball. She held it a moment, laughing giddily, then fired it back at the man. The energy struck him in the chest and he fell to the floor as it dissipated.

"*Hadouken*," Andy said.

Coop chuckled as if he understood what Andy said. Lamb guessed it was Korean.

"Great shot," the energy-ball man said, apparently unharmed as he rose from the floor.

"Finish him!" Andy called over. The man scowled in Andy's direction and began forming another electric-blue ball.

"What's going on here?" Lamb asked finally.

Coop peered back with narrowed eyelids. "That's classified, dude." He stopped in front of a closed door to the right of the altar. "Thea's in a meeting right now. Soon as she's done, you two can go on in."

"So we just… wait here?" Andy asked.

"Until she's done, yeah."

"Cool."

"Cool," Coop agreed, then gave Andy a serious look. "*Don't go anywhere*."

"Got it," Lamb said.

Coop nodded and headed off. He gave the pigtailed girl a brief word of encouragement as he passed, then moved on to look over the shoulder of a man in a white suit scribbling on a large pad of paper at a school desk. Lamb figured he was a psychographer, performing automatic writing. She'd met several mediums at conventions over the years who'd claimed to have the ability.

"I don't care if it's ghosts doing all this," Andy said. "It's pretty friggin incredible anyway."

Lamb had to agree. She'd been exposed to psychics and spiritualists all her life and had never seen anything close to this. The raw power in this room was astounding.

As she turned to repeat the thought to Andy, a massive thunderclap startled everyone in the church. The bibles and song books fell to the floor with a sound like applause. The man hovering above the altar dropped to his knees, and the little girl let the energy ball she held loose. It blasted toward the vaulted ceiling and tore a hole through the roof.

The church floor shook a moment later, rattling the light fixtures and knocking the crucifix off the wall. Voices rose in screams and gasps of terror, followed by a confusion of anxious conversation:

"What's happening?"

"Did you feel that?"

"Was that an earthquake?"

"It sounded like an explosion!"

"Are we safe?"

"Omigod what was that?"

Lamb and Andy held each other as the Gurpies called out to friends and loved ones. The lights flickered and then brightened, as if from a power surge.

"Bright light, loud sound," Andy said.

"You caught that too, huh?"

The door to Thea's office burst open, nearly striking them. A tall, bald man in a three-piece suit emerged, holding a cell phone to his ear. He pushed past them, bumping Andy. He didn't even pause to excuse himself.

"Hello?" he shouted into the phone. "Can you confirm the breach?"

"*Breach?*" Andy repeated, his eyes wide.

Thea Petralia hurried out a moment later, calling for Coop. Coop hollered back, standing above a group of people huddled behind the pews.

"Get out to the park, now!" Thea said. "Bram will meet you there!"

"You think it was—?"

"I don't *know* what it was but we need to find out! Now *go*!" She scanned the frightened faces of her people, huddled in the pews and on the altar, reassuring each other, hugging each other. Finally, her gaze fell on Lamb and Andy. "I'm sorry we won't get a chance to speak," she said. "I need to deal with this."

"Of course," Andy said.

"You're welcome to stay while we figure out what happened. We'd certainly appreciate your help. We can speak later."

With that, she left, hurrying over to help the others.

Lamb squeezed Andy's arms. "What should we do?"

"Stay here, I guess. Wait it out. We came all this way...."

"But what if that was the Recurrence Field? I have a really bad feeling about this, Andy."

"If it was the Recurrence Field, this might the best place to be. You know, a church full of ghosts and people who know magic."

"The safest place was the bomb shelter," she said.

"You gettin any Nudges?"

He shook his head. "Nada."

"Then I guess we better stay here." She put an arm around his waist. "Whatever happens, we stay together."

He seemed surprised by the statement. "Are you kidding? I wouldn't leave you for anything."

"You promise?"

He held her gaze. "I promise. Okay?"

She smiled. "Okay. Then let's see if we can help."

Andy nodded, and the two of them headed out into the pews to see what they could do.

Thea Petralia sat behind her desk, waiting on her meeting with Hedgewood. She plucked Taffy out of the top desk drawer and set him on the blotter facing her.

"Tell me I'm doing the right thing," she said.

The pink unicorn stared at her with blank, brown-marble eyes, neither affirming nor denying it.

The detonator phone lay on the blotter beside Taffy. When Hedgewood arrived, she would text Bram. He'd wait exactly five minutes, then text her back. While pretending to respond to the text, she would message the phone attached to the explosives. The plan would have been simpler without her role, but she needed to be the one to push the button. It was important to her that the Recurrence Field would fall by her hand, while she looked Hedgewood straight in the eye.

A sharp knock on the door startled her. She dropped Taffy swiftly back into the drawer and closed it. "Who is it?"

"It's Coop. Mr. Hedgewood's here to see you."

She pressed Send on the burner phone. The message simply said READY. "Let him in, please." She stood quickly and strode around the desk as the door opened.

Hedgewood, a giant of a man in a gray three-piece suit, ducked to enter the room. "Ms. Petralia." He stuck out his left hand as he approached, wearing what looked as much like a grimace as a smile. "It's a pleasure to finally meet you."

Thea shot a scowl toward Coop, who still stood in the doorway, as she shook her enemy's hand. Coop caught the vibe and slinked back into the church, closing the door quietly behind himself.

"I can't say the feeling is entirely mutual, Mr. Hedgewood—"

"Ollie, please."

She sat behind the desk. "Ollie, then. Let's get down to business, shall we? I've got people out back waiting on your delivery."

The sickly smile widened. "The offloading is already in progress." Responding to her look of annoyance, he added, "I assumed you would be as eager as myself to make this meeting as brief as possible."

"You got my part of the bargain, I assume," she said.

"I did. It's currently contained in a pocket Recurrence Field two-hundred feet below the earth."

The statement confused her. "A pocket field?"

"Precisely. The future of tech is miniaturization, Ms. Petralia. Though in this case, the smaller field came first. They were used to contain and study the first entities."

Thea bit her lip. "The first guinea pigs, you mean."

The man shrugged his sharp shoulders. "If you wish. The Recurrence Field you know is an enlargement of the originals. Though, from what I understand, creating a larger version was far from an easy task. It certainly cost me quite a lot of money."

"That's what I don't understand about all of this," Thea said. "You seem to have no interest in ethereals at all. Why would you fund Ghostland in the first place?"

"I'm pleased you asked," Hedgewood said. His chair groaned as he leaned forward, over his knees. "Consider the lion. For quite some time it was arguably the most dangerous species in the animal kingdom, at least on land. Then man invented the rifle, and took his rightful place at the top of the food chain. He captured the lion and put them on display in zoos and the circus. He *tamed* the most ferocious beast in the wild, to an extent."

"Humans dominate what they fear," Thea said. "Are you afraid of ethereals, Hedgewood?"

The man sat back with his grimacing smile, tenting his index fingers below his purplish lips as if in thought. "I've brought the items you've requested," he said after a moment. "Two-hundred pairs of resonance-oscillation headsets—or ReOss glasses, as our development team calls them—two-hundred keeper suits, and a midsized Recurrence Field."

"Wait… we never requested a Recurrence Field."

"I'm aware. It's my insurance policy. I'm banking on you having a change of heart."

"What do you mean?"

"I mean, if you ever discover yourself in a situation in which your friends out there become your enemies," he said, nodding toward the door, "you may simply turn on the Recurrence Field, and every entity within a one-thousand square-foot bubble surrounding the device will be contained." The sickly smile returned. "Sooner or later, I suspect you'll use it."

The old flip phone buzzed on the desk, preventing her from snapping back at him with an angry retort. She glanced at it. Hedgewood followed her gaze.

"Just a second," she said. She picked up the phone and flipped to the pre-written message addressed to the detonation phone, ignoring whatever Bram had texted her. She paused only a moment, glancing at the phrase she'd typed, making sure it was exactly what she meant to send—even though it technically didn't matter. No one would read it in the split seconds before the blast.

She looked Hedgewood in the eyes as she pressed Send. "I'll never use it," she replied finally.

Hedgewood stood up and smiled or grimaced down at her. "In that case, I'll be proven wrong. Good day, Ms. Petral—"

The explosion shook the room, rocking the desk on its feet. Photos dropped off their hooks and smashed on the floor. Hedgewood staggered forward, grasping the edge of her desk to prevent himself from falling. Thea's chair rumbled beneath her like a seat in a 4D theater. She hadn't expected to feel anything from so far away. The result had startled her as much as it had her guest.

Commotion arose just beyond the door. Screams and gasps, followed by a loud clatter. Hedgewood locked eyes with her, his dour face working through several conflicting emotions.

What is he thinking? she wondered. *Does he know what I just did?*

"What the hell *was* that?" she said, finding it far easier to sound frightened than she'd imagined. Though she'd known the blast was coming, the aftermath made her anxious. The screams outside made it worse.

Hedgewood looked at the phone in her hand. She was gripping it tightly, without knowing it. She set it down quickly on the blotter.

His own phone rang as he turned and stormed toward the door, nearly tearing it off its hinges. She heard him answer it as he left the room: "Hello? Can you confirm the breach?"

Breach, she thought. *They're free. They're really free! I did it!*

She stood and hurried to the door. No time to chat with Sonya Curtis's daughter and her friend. Her people would expect her to lead them, to comfort them and assure them everything would be okay.

Will it?

Now was not the time to worry about what might happen in the future. The Recurrence Field was gone. Soon, every ethereal who'd been trapped inside that terrible place for so long would be looking for refuge, for salvation, for peace and freedom.

What better place to find it, Thea thought, *than here at my Temple?*

Bram Merritt stood on the hill overlooking town, in a parkette the residents of Duck Falls called Duck Bill Park. It wasn't much: aside from the view, there were two picnic tables, some pines and spruce with overhanging branches, a garbage can chained to a recycle bin, and a dinged-up guardrail along the ridge.

The view was all that mattered. From here he could see most of the town in the valley below, including the church and its steeple. To the northwest, he had an unencumbered view of the sprawling buildings and exhibits of Ghostland.

It was the perfect spot to watch the show.

He tracked Hedgewood's limousine and the semi-truck following it in his military binoculars as they rumbled through town toward the church. Hedgewood himself directed the men to unload the truck, then headed up the church steps. Coop opened the door for the man, and the door closed again behind them.

It wouldn't be long before he received the text from Thea. He would wait the agreed-upon five minutes and text her back. The sun was already setting to the west, though from here he could see much more of it than anyone in town. Already it was growing dark down in the valley, the shadows from buildings and trees stretching long, smothering the streets with a pre-winter chill.

It's gonna get a whole lot darker before nightfall.

Two kids came crashing out of the woods on bicycles as he thought this. Bram ducked behind the van, not sure why he was being so cautious. A passerby might wonder why he was up here alone, but nobody would make the leap of logic to link him to the explosion. Not that there would be much time to investigate in the aftermath. A couple of days at most, he figured, before it was all over.

The kids paused a moment. Bram could only see their backs, a boy and a girl, the boy on a bike much too small for him. The girl pointed toward Ghostland. When they started pedaling away, heading down the one-lane road he'd driven up to get here, he stepped out from behind the van and resumed his position by the edge of the hill.

In a way he felt sorry for these people, living their lives oblivious to the poison seeping into their town from above. This had always been much bigger than any of them. It was only due to bad luck and perhaps greed that it had happened here. Bram supposed Duck Falls was no better or worse a place for the end of life as it was currently known to transpire. Still, he didn't delight in the thought of kids being put through so much pain before this was all over.

His own childhood had been filled with trauma, and to know a similar fate would befall other children did trouble him. The fact that the pain wouldn't last for very long, and that the end justified the means, made it slightly more tolerable.

The view ahead of him was as perfect as a painting. Sundown cast its pinkish-orange hue over the arguably picturesque small town below, nestled among the vibrant colors of a changing season. Soon the leaves would fall and snow would linger, but before then a darkness would spread out across the state, the country, the world. And despite the many people whose obsessions or stupidity or naivety or greed had contributed toward the end, there was really only one person to blame for it all. As much as he would have liked to take credit, that person was not Bram Merritt.

The text came. He set a countdown on his watch: five minutes left.

As far back as he could remember, Bram had always sought a sense of purpose. A higher calling. He'd known the minute he'd first met his new friend that he had found his savior. The state hospital where he'd spent ten of the worst years of his life had been reluctant to let him go— they still believed he was insane—but his friend's money had changed their minds. Throughout all of their tests to disprove what they'd believed to be delusions he'd never been able to prove them wrong. The drugs they'd doped him up with had been so strong that he'd never been able to shift for them. To leave his body. The longer he'd lived that way, the more he'd wondered if they weren't right. If he was indeed *not sane*. He'd been given a gift, and that gift had been stolen from him. Unless he'd never had the gift to begin with.

When his new friend had freed him and the hospital drugs had finally worn off, he'd been elated to find himself able to transverse into the astral plane again.

He glanced at his watch.

One minute to go.

Bram was ready to achieve his higher purpose, his true calling. Knowing he would finally be free of his body, able to exist in the astral world without ever having to endure the mental exhaustion shifting caused him, he'd gladly offered his life in service to the man.

Thirty seconds left.

There would still be time to celebrate in this new world governed by the dead, but not long. When the boundary between the dead and the living came down, when the veil was finally lifted, there would be hours, maybe as long as a day, for the people below to make peace with their impending deaths.

Then, further work would need to be done.

"And three… two… one," Bram counted aloud.

He thumbed the Send button.

It was nearly a full minute between his text and the explosion. The fireball erupted over Ghostland moments before the sound reached his ears. He smiled as the shockwaves rolled across the valley, the flames reflected in his eyes. A blast of warm wind ruffled his hair and clothes, shaking the branches above him, rustling the dry leaves at his feet.

Satisfied it was done, he projected himself into the astral plane, where he could interact with ethereals as if he was one of them. In the material world he was as oblivious to their presence as most of the living were. It was yet another reason to detest his existence within this prison called the Self.

"Are you here?"

"I am," his friend said.

Bram rotated his astral body, hovering inches above the ground. In the physical world, he'd slumped over the picnic table, without regard to the clumps of bird shit and stains from picnics past on the wooden slats, covered in slashed curse words and scrawled initials.

His friend emerged from the gloom beneath the trees to the south. "It's good to see you, Bram," the man said.

"It's good to see you again, Rex."

Garrote's smile widened as he crossed the decaying grass between them. He shook Bram's hand, and in his friend's firm ethereal grip Bram felt all the power he would wield standing at the man's side. Fire reflected in Garrote's eyes as he held the man's gaze, though Bram knew it would not reflect in his own. It was almost as if the fire burned from *within* him. As if it had *started* there—which, Bram supposed, it had.

"It's glorious, isn't it?" Garrote said. "All of our brothers and sisters, free at last. All of us *together* at last."

Bram agreed that it was glorious.

"It won't be long now, Bram. But your work isn't finished just yet. You need to return to the Temple. We'll meet again when the moon is full. You know where."

He did. And before he could say as much, Garrote vanished from sight.

Bram returned to his body, blinking for a moment down at a black lump of guano in its glob of dried, white paste directly in front of his eyes. He jerked his head away and stood slowly, disgusted by the feel of his corporeal self, as he always was upon returning to it. The bone, the muscle, the tendons and skin were all too constraining. The feel of them constantly pulling and pushing against each other while they worked in tandem to create movement. The agonizing pressure in his temples from having spent mere minutes in the astral plane. The painful grumble of his stomach, begging for sustenance despite his distaste for food, for the process of mastication. Even the cool air fluttering the hairs on his arms, a feeling which might be subtle in a person who'd never experienced the lightness of their astral self, was too much for him to bear. His soul was not meant for the physical world.

When the moon is full, he thought. *Six days.*

From somewhere in town, an air-raid siren began to blare. Bram climbed in behind the wheel of his white Econoline van, and made a three-point turn to drive down the one-lane park road. More sirens joined the first. They rocketed past the intersection, red lights flashing, as he descended the hill.

He stopped at the county road, waiting for traffic to let him in. After the silver compact car, he'd be good. He watched it approach, and was about to press his foot on the accelerator when the silver car slammed to a halt with a crash of metal. Before he could blink, the driver shot through the windshield and landed heavily on the road, bones cracking, flesh grinding on asphalt.

"Jesus!" he gasped, looking at the broken woman, then at her car. The whole front-end had crumpled in the middle, as if something extremely large had punched right through it. Something that neither of them had apparently seen.

A middle-aged couple emerged from a station wagon in the opposite lane, wearing identical shell-shocked expressions. They looked at the woman in the street, then at Bram's van. The husband caught his eye in the side mirror.

He couldn't leave now. They would remember his van, maybe even notice the plates were out of state. He'd have to wait it out, tell his side of the story to the police. Besides, the crashed car had stopped right in front of him, blocking the lane. Even if he wanted to risk leaving the scene of an accident, he'd have to find some other way down the hill.

Bram gripped the wheel, his fingerbones aching, sweat burning his palms. Something very large and very dangerous had caused this wreck. If it was still here, he'd need to be cautious, even if they were playing for the same team.

He let his mind relax and shifted out of his body once more, waiting for the dead woman's ethereal to emerge.

While his driver chased the emergency vehicles to Ghostland, Oliver Hedgewood placed a call to General Zaydan at United States Central Command. Among all of his military contacts across the globe, making friends with Franklin "the Falcon" Zaydan had proved to be his most fruitful connection. Not only had CENTCOM commissioned several billion dollars' worth of state-of-the-art weaponry for its various forces over the three years of the general's term in office, but Ollie had known having Zaydan as a close personal friend would come in handy should something like what appeared to be occurring now ever come to pass.

In retrospect, he supposed a Recurrence Field breach had been inevitable. Like the bombings of Nagasaki and Hiroshima, a man could only hold a toy in his hand for so long without playing with it.

Following the Incident in April, and in light of the most recent deaths at Ghostland, Zaydan had assured Ollie he'd have the President's full support to contain the problem before it spiraled out of control—with brute force, if necessary. With the TANDY array ready to be deployed, brute force was exactly what Ollie had in mind.

He was on the phone with Danica Jackson as the limo weaved through traffic, following the firetrucks. "How close are you?" He waited for her reply. "Good. I need roadblocks at every exit and a perimeter set up with the array. This is it, Danica. This is the moment we've been preparing for."

He hung up and tossed his phone on the leather seat.

The vulgar display of raw power Thea had put on for him at the church still weighed heavily on his thoughts. Her sycophant with the awful blond dreadlocks had presented their circus sideshow to him as if Ollie was some rube off the street. As if he would be impressed by the tricks her people performed. As if his ancestors hadn't been contemporaries of P.T. Barnum and the Ringling Brothers.

"Looks like they're going into Ghostland," Manny said from the driver's seat, nodding at the emergency vehicles ahead of them. "Want me to stay on them?"

"Yes," Ollie said. He'd need to assess the damage himself before the cavalry arrived. With some good, old-fashioned hard work and an ounce of good luck, he could have the entire Duck Falls area quarantined before nightfall.

AND HELL FOLLOWED

LILIAN SAT WITH Blake on the Laramies' sofa, trying not to look as deeply on edge as she felt. Mr. Laramie—Michael, he'd said to call him, which felt odd to Lilian, as he'd been Mr. Laramie since she and Ben first met when they were little, still living on the same street—sat in his recliner, deep in thought. The three of them had been waiting for Mrs. Laramie to come home, and when the atmosphere had grown awkward, Lilian had hesitantly broached the subject of Ben and the afterlife. Michael Laramie had been sitting in silent contemplation of her words for nearly a minute.

Blake turned slightly toward her with his eyebrows raised. She patted his knee. The man needed time to process. She'd given him a lot to think about.

"I always knew it," Michael said finally. "Do you… still see him?"

"Well, he's not with us right now. But yeah, I still see him. We talk at least twice a week."

Or we did, she thought. *But now he's gone. This time, he's the one who ghosted me.*

Blake entwined his fingers with hers. She turned to him, unsure what had made him take her hand, if he was upset or jealous. But he was smiling. She smiled back.

"I felt him here, you know," Michael said, his eyes—which she'd only just now realized looked very much like Ben's—twinkling with joy and relief. "That morning in his bedroom, when the shelf broke and all of his horror figurines fell on the bed, I..." He swallowed hard, his sharp, stubbled Adam's apple rising and falling. "...I told myself I was imagining it." His eyes glistened, as if he might cry. "But it was Ben. He was showing me—showing *us* that he was still here."

"He loves both of you very much. I'm sure that if he was able to reach out to you, he probably has."

Michael smiled. A tear spilled from his right eye. He didn't interfere with its progress down his stubbled cheek. "Where is he now? Do you think we could talk to him if...? I mean, could you do that?"

"I don't know where he is," she said. Spoken out loud, the admission hurt her heart. "But we were told when he comes back, we'll all be in your tornado shelter."

"Told? Told by who?"

Lilian and Blake shared a look. How could they explain it without sounding absolutely crazy? "We met this guy today who's... well, I guess he's sort of like a ghost magnet. The ethereals he travels with—*ghosts*," she clarified, when Michael frowned, "I guess they're sort of psychic."

She turned to Blake, who nodded and shrugged as if it sounded accurate enough.

"I think maybe everything we look at as a paranormal ability—psychics, telepathy, telekinesis, all of that junk—I think some people are able to tap into those powers with the help of ethereals. In the astral world, those things are sort of innate, or at least teachable. That's from what I've seen, anyway."

Michael looked at Blake.

"It's true," Blake said. "The ethereals—the ghosts—they said we'd see a bright light and hear a loud sound, and I guess that must be what makes us go down into the shelter."

Ben's dad had sat bolt upright while Blake spoke, gripping the arms of his chair. "An explosion?" he asked, his voice calm but his gaze intensely focused.

"I guess it could be a tornado or something," Lilian said, concerned by the look in his eyes. "They never said, specifically. Is there something wrong, Mr. Laramie?"

Without answering, Michael snatched his cell phone from the end table. He swiped its cracked screen and speed-dialed a number. It rang. "Come on, pick up."

"*Hello?*"

Lilian recognized Ben's mother's voice.

Michael put the phone to his ear and stood, pacing the living room as he spoke. "Where are you right now?" He paused briefly. "I know you're showing a house, but where?" Another pause. He squinted toward the front windows. "How quickly can you pick up Mom and get back to the house?"

Her voice was sharp in the small speaker, though Lilian couldn't hear what she said. Michael held the phone away from his ear with a scowl.

"Because it's important, Wendy! Lilian is here. Yes, Lilian Roth, what other Lilian would I be—"

He waited as she spoke again. The call was beginning to make Lilian vaguely uncomfortable. She hoped it would end soon.

"Because she has news, and I'd like my mother to be here to hear it. It's news about Ben. *Yes*, our Ben. Jesus, Wen! Okay. *Thank* you."

He hung up and returned the phone to the end table. "Sorry about that," he said with a look of embarrassment. "Wendy will be back soon. We should get to the bunker."

"What d'you think is gonna happen, Mr. Laramie?"

With a faraway look in his eyes, Michael said: "The same thing that happened the day my son didn't come home. Only this time it's gonna be much, much worse."

Blake put up a hand timidly. "Excuse me, but how do you know that, sir?"

"I don't know," Michael said. He frowned. "But I believe it. Haven't you ever had a feeling you can't explain, but you know it's right?"

Lilian shot up from the sofa, pulling free of Blake's hand. She knew exactly what Michael meant about feelings that couldn't be explained. She'd lived with the unverifiable yet irrefutable belief that Rex Garrote would return, leading an army of ethereals through the streets of Duck Falls, ever since the night she'd inadvertently let them loose.

"How many people can fit in the shelter?" she asked.

"It's built for six but there's really only enough food and supplies for Wendy and I for a month or so. Why?"

"If we're supposed to be in that shelter when Ben comes back, I need to get my mom and dad."

Michael considered it, then nodded. "I guess there's room for two more. But the food won't last more than a week or two if we ration."

Blake's concern deepened. "The ghosts said it would happen *soon*."

Lilian ignored him, tugging out her phone from the back pocket of her jeans. She dialed her parents. The phone rang once, twice. By the third ring she started to worry. "Come on, Dad, pick up, *pick up*."

"Are they home?"

"Mom's at work, Dad should be home," Lilian said distantly. "Come *on*."

The old-school answering machine picked up. "Hi, you've reached the Roths," the three of them said cheerily, a happy family long before tragedy had struck. Lilian ended the call.

"They're not there," she said, staring at the blinded window. "Can you drive us to my house, Mr. Laramie?"

"Wendy has the car."

Her hopes sank. She couldn't just leave her parents out there to fend for themselves. There had to be a way to reach them—and *fast*.

"Ben's old bikes are in the garage, though," Michael said, sounding like someone who knew he was offering only a sliver of hope. "You need to get across town quick, short of a car that's the fastest way to do it."

"Will you wait for us?"

He nodded. "As long as we can."

"Then we'll be back soon," she said.

She and Blake headed out the back door and down the porch steps to the garage. The old BMX Ben used to ride around town, with her hanging off the back, would be too small for either of them to ride without banging their knees. The mountain bike his parents had bought him, before they thought he was too frail to ride it, would fit both of them fine.

"I'll ride the little one," Blake said. He was taller than her by a foot.

"That's not fair."

He shrugged. "I've always wanted a lowrider." He rolled it out of the garage and swung a leg over the seat, then sat with his knees bent sharply. "Actually, it's not that bad. Ready?"

Lilian had pulled out the mountain bike and straddled it. The seat was uncomfortable, but otherwise it was fine. "Ready," she said, gripping the handlebars.

They shot off down the driveway, Blake's little BMX wobbling, his knees coming up almost to his shoulders with every pump of his legs. She caught up to him quickly and they sped down the middle of the road side by side.

"I know a shortcut," she said, pedaling past him.

They blew past a car parked in front of her old house. Blake swerved to miss the door as the driver climbed out without looking. "Hey, watch it, Stranger Things!" Mr. Edison shouted after them.

Lilian ignored him, turning from Koestler to Becker Road. The road ended at the foot of Duck Bill Park, but a bike path had been worn through the bush up the hill. It was a steep but short climb, and cut out several small blocks, shaving at least two or three minutes off the route depending on the biker.

She led Blake up the hill through the trees, swatches of pine and spruce slapping their arms, low maples swishing over their heads. She supposed kids didn't use the trail much anymore. It had mostly overgrown with brush that tore off in the spokes, and the climb was tough but mercifully brief.

They emerged in the park, the breeze cooler up here with not a lot of tree covering. A white van was parked over by the picnic tables. She saw movement behind it in her peripherals, but when she turned it looked like there was no one there.

"Look," she said to Blake, pointing down at the spread of exhibits and rides to the northwest. Ghostland looked almost like the map view from up here.

Blake raised his eyebrows, clearly amazed. "That's awesome."

She had to admit the park was a pretty amazing feat of engineering and reconstruction, especially from up here. She saw the towers of Bright Falls Sanitarium, where Allison and Niko and Leonard had lost their lives, and the shattered glass dome of the prison, where Demont had met his untimely death, long before they'd reached him. She could even see the pit where Garrote House once stood, and the darkness below it, where Stan Beadle and the Doll's Head Killer and finally Ben had reached their own ends—though Ben's death had merely been a twist in the road, leading him down a different path.

Lilian hoped he was okay, wherever he was.

She turned away from the place, from the awful memories of that day, and pedaled toward the access road. Blake followed. The steep drop got them moving at a good, scary clip, the wind whipping strands of hair loose from her ponytail and into her face. Near the bottom she slowed, aware of the hidden entrance, where many a reckless kid had experienced their first brushes with death. She braked at the intersection, looked left for oncoming traffic, then pulled onto the main road.

They were downtown in less than two minutes, pulling the bikes up at the 86 Diner and dropping them below the plate-glass windows. She tore open the door, startling a group of older patrons near the front who'd been enjoying an early dinner until just then. She felt their stares as Blake followed her to the counter, the two of them sweaty and out of breath, looking like they could have just stumbled out of a heavy makeout session in the backseat of her car. Mr. Young, her mom's perpetually chipper boss, stood at the register in his apron and hair net, handing over change to a woman holding a boxed pie. The tables were already full with an early rush. It wasn't even five o'clock.

"Lilian!" Mr. Young said with a smile, while the woman with the pie sidled past them. "Good to see you!"

"Hi, Mr. Young. Is my mom here?"

"She's in back picking up an order. What can I do for you?"

"I need to see her. It's urgent."

"Well, she should be out any second."

Her mother came out as he spoke, dressed in her '50s diner uniform and holding a tray full of meals, pushing the door open with a hip.

"Speak of the devil and she shall appear," Mr. Young said gregariously.

"What did I do this time?" Maddy asked, before spotting Lilian at the counter. "Honey? What's wrong?"

"Mom, I need you."

"I'll be right there. Just let me serve these plates." She weaved through the tables, placed the meals in front of each diner. While she returned with the tray held vertical, her customers swapped their plates. She was normally a flawless server, but the anxiety Lilian could see on her own sweaty face in the mirrored bar behind the counter must have fazed her.

Her mother put a hand on her shoulder. "Are you okay?"

"Can you leave?"

"What do you mean, leave? What's happened? Are you hurt?"

"I'm fine. Can we talk outside?"

Maddy wiped her hands on her apron. "Sure, honey. Carl, I'm gonna take my break."

"Sure thing, Maddy."

Blake held the door and the three of them stepped outside.

"Mom, we need to find Dad."

"He wasn't home?"

Lilian shook her head.

"Then he's probably getting groceries. Why do you need him?"

"We have to go to the Laramies' house."

Maddy sneered. She'd never gotten along with Ben's mother, mentioning on more than one occasion that she thought the woman was a snob. "Mike and Wendy's? Why would we go there?"

"Something bad is going to happen, Mom. We have to go as soon as possible."

"Bad?" Maddy glanced back through the window. Inside, Mr. Young was serving one of her tables. "I can't leave work right now, honey. We're in the middle of rush."

"Mom, if you don't leave with us *right now*, we might never see each other again."

That got her attention. "What? Why would we never see each other?"

"I don't have time to explain. It's about Ghostland. Mr. Laramie thinks what happened that day is gonna happen again, only worse. He's built a bomb shelter—"

"So that's what he's been up to…."

"Mom, we need to get Dad *right now*."

Her mother seemed to see something in her eyes that changed her mind. She took off her apron. "I'll tell Carl you're sick or something," she said, opening the door. "Back in a sec."

Plenty of cars and pedestrians passed as Lilian shifted anxiously from one foot to another, waiting for her mom. She fought the urge to scream for everyone to get out of the street, to hurry home and lock all the doors, shutter the windows and hunker down to the basement. Nobody would believe her even if she did.

Blake squeezed her shoulder. "It's gonna be okay."

"Is it?"

He couldn't answer that.

The bell rang above the door and Maddy came out wearing her bulky fall jacket draped over the canary-yellow uniform. "Okay, let's go find your father."

Maddy called home while they rolled the bikes back to the apartment. "He's not answering. Must be still at the store."

They dropped the bikes in the vestibule and headed for the Food Market. The sun was setting by the time they reached the store, casting a pinkish-orange glow on the windows and puddles throughout town. They found Hiram Roth in the frozen foods section. His cart was half-full of groceries, enough to feed the four of them for a week.

"My darlings! And Blake," he said with a mimed hat tip. "What brings you here?"

Lilian told him what she'd told her mother. He eyed Maddy with curiosity, as if to gauge whether or not she believed what she was hearing.

"All right," he said once Lilian had finished. "Let's pay for these and get it in the car."

Lilian shook her head. "We have to go now."

He turned to her mother. Maddy shrugged.

"Then we leave it." The four of them returned to the checkout. "Turns out my lovely wife already bought groceries," Hiram said to the cashier, leaving the cart full of items. "Sorry about that."

The cashier, a girl Lilian knew from school, looked annoyed as she rang a customer's item over the scanner.

"Hey, Lilian," she muttered.

"Hey, Steph."

"Tell your mother I said 'hello,'" Maddy said as they slipped through the aisle behind the girl. Stephanie's mother, Jane Hawkins, had taught Lilian piano when she was little.

Stephanie Hawkins's dull-eyed reply was cut short by an earth-shattering boom that shook the entire store, rattling the plate-glass windows and shelves, and loosing insulation dust from the exposed pipes and ducts above their heads. Customers screamed as canned and bagged items rained down from the shelves. Split pop bottles sprayed foamy fountains in the snack aisle. Shopping carts overturned. A stack of water cooler jugs beside the automatic doors toppled and rolled, barring their escape. Out in the parking lot, vehicles began to honk and chirp, their alarms going off in a symphony of noise.

"Loud sound," Blake said, peering up at the swinging track lighting.

Lilian's mom and dad turned to her, shaken by the realization that what she'd told them had just come to pass. Mr. Laramie was right. It *had* sounded like an explosion.

Patrons were already running for the exit, knocking each other over, squeezing through the checkout aisles. Booting aside several heavy jugs, Blake hurried to the automatic doors. They didn't move when he approached. He pulled on them.

"They won't open!"

"Must be something wrong with the mechanism," Hiram said. He stepped over the errant jugs and pulled on the opposing door, but it still wouldn't budge. He stepped aside, looking for something along the jamb. Then he flicked a switch above a small black console. He switched it again and the doors opened, though only halfway.

The four of them dashed out sideways as a glut of customers rushed the doors. The crowd struck it in a huddled mass. One woman squeezed through, followed by a young boy, who fell on his knees and started crying. Frantic customers piled out, and would have trampled the child if Hiram hadn't bent quickly to scoop him up.

He handed the boy back to his mother. "There's the car," he said, pointing to the new black truck at the far end of the lot, close to the street.

Half of the vehicles in the lot were honking and chirping, the sound much louder out here than inside, their lights flashing. Customers scrambled toward them, while Blake hurried on ahead. He'd run track in high school and was faster than anyone in the lot. He leaped over a man who'd fallen and sprawled on the asphalt. He turned back, helped the man up, then held out his hands to her parents. "Throw me the keys, Mr. Roth!"

Jogging toward him, Lilian at his side, Hiram reached into a front pocket and tossed the keys. Blake caught them while running backwards and dashed on ahead.

The truck's engine was rumbling with the driver door open when Lilian and her parents arrived. "Is this a Hemi?" Blake asked, sitting behind the wheel.

"You bet your ass it is," Hiram said, puffing and doubled over from the jog.

"Killer," Blake said.

Maddy rolled her eyes at Lilian, opening the back door on the passenger side. "Boys," she said, and climbed in. Lilian sat in the front passenger seat, her feet on either side of her dad's toolbox. Hiram climbed in behind the driver's seat with a grunt.

Blake adjusted the rearview mirror and backed out of

the spot. The line was already ten-cars deep. The rear ends of two minivans ahead of them collided with a loud thud.

"How attached are you to this truck, Mr. Roth?"

"Why do you ask?" Hiram sounded cautious.

"Well, I think I can drive over those bumper blocks, but it might mess up the—"

"Do it," Hiram said, clapping Blake on the shoulder. He smiled at Lilian. "Your fella's a quick thinker."

Blake dropped the transmission into drive. He eased his foot down on the gas and the truck roared up and over the curb stopper. A man on the sidewalk leaped back out of their way.

"Sorry!" Blake called, waving at him.

The truck thumped down heavily onto the road, cutting in front of a cube van, whose driver honked.

Lilian gripped the armrest nervously, thinking back to another perilous journey in a truck not that long ago. At least then, she'd been behind the wheel and could only blame herself for any problems.

"Little rusty," Blake said with an anxious chuckle.

"Just keep your eyes on the road, Mario," Hiram said behind him.

The air-raid siren began to blare as soon as they turned onto Main Street. They passed by the Temple, where people she'd seen earlier hurried in an out, already boarding up the windows as if they'd been preparing for this. Traffic thickened the closer they got to Ben's house. The sidewalks were cluttered with people hurrying home, or shading their eyes to gawk at the black smoke choking the sky to the northwest, like charcoal smudged over a landscape portrait of the sunset over Duck Falls.

Eventually both lanes had filled with vehicles headed out of town, bumper to bumper, inching excruciatingly ahead. Blake slammed an open palm on the steering wheel. "We're not moving."

"What's going on up there?" Maddy asked, leaning forward so her head was between them.

Lilian opened her window and pulled herself up and out to get a better look, with her butt on the sill. Red lights flashed over the pickup truck and minivan ahead of them. "Looks like an accident," she said.

"Oy," Hiram muttered. "We could get there in five minutes if we walked at a brisk pace."

"Then why don't we?" Blake asked.

"Leave the truck?"

Blake shrugged.

Lilian looked back at her father. "He's right. We don't have much time left."

Hiram didn't give it a second's pause before patting Blake's shoulder. "Do it."

Blake pulled up onto the sidewalk. All four doors opened at once, and he and the Roths exited the brand-new Ram 1500, bought for her dad's business with their hefty settlement from Hedgewood. He kissed his fingers and touched them against the hood. Drivers honked madly as the four of them left the truck behind.

The accident was visible up ahead as they ascended the steep hill, a fire truck pulled to one side and a sheriff's department SUV on the other. From what Lilian could see, it looked bad. The silver hatchback was totaled. The windshield had a huge hole punched through it on the driver's side. In the road, a gray blanket had been draped over the shape of a person.

"Oh, my Lord," her father said. Her mother took his hand.

Lilian didn't see the first ethereal until the driver of a

convertible to their right screamed. The woman's curly brown hair was twisted up like the Bride of Frankenstein, in the grip of a skeleton dressed in shredded pirate garments. It lifted the woman several feet in the air, her fingers scrabbling at what to everyone but Lilian would seem to be an invisible presence holding her by the hair.

Lilian's skin crawled as she hurried away from the sight and bumped straight into her mother, who'd stopped to look back in terror. "What's happening?"

"*It's the Rapture!*" somebody cried from one of the vehicles in the road, having just seen the woman rise into the air.

"Run, Mom!"

Her mother and father ran hand-in-hand as fast as they could, Maddy taking the lead. Blake and Lilian did the same, turning on to Nagel Road. Dogs barked madly up and down the street. The windows of vehicles parked at the curb smashed one after another as orbs of multicolored light struck them from the sky. The doors tore open and they rocked on their suspensions, horns and alarms blaring, lights flashing. A fire hydrant popped out of the concrete like a champagne cork and a fountain spewed forth, the breeze creating a cold mist the four of them weren't quick enough to avoid.

At the corner house, Old Man Babbage scowled down from his upstairs window and quickly shut the blinds. Mrs. D'Addario ran into the street, avoiding the barrage of shattered glass. She scooped up her little girl under the armpits and ran back to her bungalow, leaving the tricycle in the street.

At the next house, a middle-aged man Lilian didn't recognize, his beer gut exposed below an ugly sweater, pulled down his rolling garage door. With his legs still visible from the knees down, a second pirate apparition plummeted from the sky and slammed into the door, leaving a good-sized dent. The man yelped and fell backwards onto his ass.

Maddy shrieked, shying away from the crash, barely pausing in her mad dash to the end of the street. Beneath the door, Lilian saw Beer Gut Man's look of horror and confusion in the seconds before the pirate swooped through the opening and dragged him into the dark.

At the next house, the newlywed McGowan couple hoisted a sofa up in front of their picture windows, blocking out the light. As Lilian watched, a bedraggled clown with a comically-large mallet materialized on their stoop and rang the doorbell. It turned and honked its nose at Lilian, its whole body shaking as it silently laughed. She didn't look back as they rounded the corner onto Ryle Avenue. She could only hope the McGowans were wise enough not to answer the door.

Blake was ahead of them, passing the thick hedge surrounding the house on the next corner. Lilian saw a long, thin branch dart out from the greenery toward him and shouted: "Look out!"

He jumped. The branch swung beneath his feet like a thrashing tentacle, grabbing at his heels as he darted past. Lilian and her parents dashed into the road. The hedge was alive, reaching out at them with a hundred vines, curling and twisting, grabbing and slashing at their arms and legs as they ran past.

"*What is happening?*" Maddy cried again, leaping into the road and dancing on her tiptoes to avoid the branches.

"Just keep running!" Lilian told her, remembering the ghost of Mrs. Crane, who'd spun victims into cocoons made from the vines of her hedge maze.

A cat yowled in the yard beyond the living bush and spray of red mist exploded from it. If they hadn't run into the road, they might have been splattered with gore.

"Come on!" Blake was waving them over, waiting at the corner of Ryle and Koestler.

They ran for him. Her dad was short of breath and her mom had a hard time pulling him along. Lilian turned back and took her father's other arm. "You're a dear," he said, his smile something like a grimace, and the three of them finally caught up with Blake.

The Laramies' house wasn't far now. Only six houses on either side to the end of the street. Her mother and father gave their old house a melancholic look as they passed. "Aw, the Edisons painted again," Maddy said, leaving Lilian and her dad to get a better look at the house.

Mr. Edison's car was still parked in the street, both the driver door and trunk wide open. No dogs barked here. There were no panicked cries or raised voices. The whole area was so quiet, with the air-raid siren still blaring and the sounds of chaos from the town below, it set Lilian on edge. Maybe everyone was at work, though she was pretty sure a handful of retirees lived on this street.

"Is it over?" her father asked.

Lilian shook her head. As much as she wished it was the end, she knew this was only the beginning. Garrote was out there, somewhere. And though she and Ben had inadvertently let him free, she didn't suspect he planned to thank them.

Maddy leaped back with a squawk of terror as the trellis of roses she'd planted after she'd given birth to Lilian overturned, and the bush tore up from the earth, exposing its roots.

"Let's go, Mom!"

"Get your caboose in gear, honey," Hiram said, breathing heavily.

Maddy returned, and the three of them hurried up to Blake, who'd again run ahead. He was peering up and down the road, into yards, at the sky. Watching him made her remember the keeper suit she'd brought to keep him safe in case something like this should ever happen. Now it was him looking out for them.

"He's a good man, your new beau," Hiram said between gulped breaths as they jogged for the house. "You know, I always thought you'd end up with Ben."

"Hiram!"

He turned to her mother with an apologetic look. "I wasn't finished, my dear. You've been through a lot this year, Lilian. I'm glad you found someone who makes you happy."

"Thanks, Dad." She swallowed hard. They were almost at the Laramies' house. Blake stood waiting for them at the foot of their driveway.

"All good here," he said. "You all right, Mr. Roth?"

"Hiram, please. And yes, I'll live. Thank you for asking."

He didn't look fine to Lilian. His face was flushed and slick with sweat, and there was a wheeze in his heavy breathing. But she supposed, like he said, he would live.

They headed along the side of the house to the backyard. The red Volvo was parked outside the open garage door with the driver door wide open.

"Lilian! Over here!"

Michael Laramie stood in the sunken alcove leading into the bunker, waving them over.

As the four of them crossed the driveway to the freshly sodded lawn, the asphalt began trembling beneath their feet. For a moment Lilian thought the ground might collapse beneath them, that all of Michael's digging had unearthed a fissure in the bedrock and the whole house was about to fall into a giant sinkhole, like when Garrote House collapsed into the tunnels.

"What was that?" Mrs. Laramie cried from inside the shelter.

"Come on!" Michael called to them. "Quickly!"

The silence that followed was shattered by a deep, resonant sound Lilian had hoped she would never hear again in her lifetime: something like a cross between an animal howl and an alpine horn. It chilled her as swiftly as if she'd just jumped into a cold lake. She knew the sound by heart, and understood now what the rumbling must have been.

"We have to get inside! Now!"

They ran. The springy sod made for wobbly terrain, particularly when the ground started trembling again. Lilian didn't dare look back. Of all the ethereals she never wanted to see again, the Behemoth was high on the list.

She reached the heavy door alongside Blake, and Mr. Laramie stepped aside, ushering them in. Outside the bunker had smelled like damp earth but inside it smelled of newness: new leather, clean chrome, fresh linens. This would be their home for who knew how long. Wendy Laramie sat on a sofa, dressed in a nice suit jacket, skirt and heels, looking shellshocked at what appeared to be a small toy in her hands. Ben's grandmother, frail and trembling in a wool sweater and shawl, sat beside her.

Lilian grasped the door frame, willing her parents to move faster. Her dad fell in the grass, dragging her mom down with him. Maddy got to her feet but Hiram remained on his knees. "My ankle!" he cried, holding it with a look of anguish.

"Dad!"

Her voice was lost in another blast of the Behemoth's horn. She covered her ears against the sound none of the others could hear. It was much closer this time but she still couldn't see the beast.

"I'll get him, Mrs. Roth!" Blake called over.

"Mom!" Lilian waved her over.

Reluctantly, Maddy left her husband behind. Blake squeezed Lilian's shoulder with a brief, anxious smile and ran up the alcove steps, hurrying over to her dad.

He was halfway there when the Volvo rocked aggressively on its wheels with a crash, as if something extremely large had smashed into it, lifting the passenger side so it stood at an angle on the driver's side wheels. Blake skidded on the grass and fell back on his butt, his heels digging up squares of fresh sod.

Maddy reached the door and slipped inside, terror in her eyes. "What is that?"

The Volvo flipped onto its roof with a jangle of metal and glass. Her mother shrieked at her side. Blake looked up from the grass. Her father whipped his head around to look.

None of the others saw the Behemoth, hunched and panting behind the flipped car, watching them through its masks of blood and metal.

"Blake!"

Lilian tried to go after him but her mom grabbed her arm, holding her put. "No," Maddy said firmly. "You *stay*."

Blake got to his feet and ran, closing the distance, while the Behemoth lumbered up onto the underside of the Volvo. It was even more terrifying than Lilian remembered it: a jumble of human parts, two torsos and eight hands, the inverse scold's bridle with mouthpiece shaped like a megaphone. In one hand it held the heavy, sculpted piece of iron. It blew its horn again, tilting back its female head like a wolf's. Then it leaped down off the car and ran, dragging the weapon in the grass.

Lilian screamed Blake's name.

He'd reached her father and had grabbed him by the arm. Hiram looked back from the still-wobbling Volvo and up at Blake. He smiled lightly, and wrapped an arm around Blake's shoulders as Blake helped him to his feet.

They hobbled toward the bunker but it was already far too late. The Behemoth hauled back with the sculpted iron and swung. The side of the blade struck her father in the hip with a heavy thud and a crunch of breaking bones, launching both men into the air. Blake struck the porch railing and her father sprawled over the stairs.

"*DADDY!*" Lilian wailed.

The Behemoth was upon him before he could roll over. It lifted him off the steps. His feet kicked madly, fighting off the incredibly strong presence he couldn't even see.

"*Hiram!*" Maddy cried.

Lilian screamed, tears blurring her vision. She was the only one to see the Behemoth grab her father by the feet with its two right hands and his shoulders with both of the left, and tear his body apart at the waist. She collapsed on the floor, still screaming as her weeping mother dropped beside her, grabbing her in a protective hug.

"*Daddy*," she moaned. She wanted to turn away, to not have to see the anguish in her father's face as his organs spilled out of him and the severed pieces of him fell on the lawn—but Blake was still in danger, sprawled on the lawn below the deck.

She called his name again, her throat raw. He roused. The Behemoth hulked over him, raising its gigantic, jagged weapon.

"*Move!*" she cried.

Blake rolled. The slab of iron slammed down and buried itself into the ground where he'd fallen. Blake got to his feet dazedly, wincing. He glanced at the trench in the grass, not seeing the blade nor the creature who wielded it, and bolted for the bunker.

The Behemoth jerked the iron out of the ground and lumbered after him. Within seconds it had closed the distance. Blake skidded down into the alcove, his butt thumping down the last few steps, and Mr. Laramie grabbed him by the hand, yanking him inside as Blake got to his feet again.

"Lilian!" He hugged her and her mom together.

She kissed his cheek. Behind him, Michael hauled on the door. She could see the Behemoth standing above the alcove as the hatch slammed shut and Michael spun the wheel—how closely the scene mirrored what she and Ben had gone through in Garrote House was not lost on her. This time, the stakes were much higher. She'd lost the one person she loved most of all. She wouldn't lose the others.

The Behemoth struck the door, causing the entire structure to shake. Michael staggered back. Sweating and visibly exhausted, he looked up nervously at the metal ceiling.

The horn sounded once more. Lilian thought she sensed defeat in it, as if the ethereal knew it had lost them. Then silence fell over the bunker.

"I'm so sorry, Lilian," Blake said.

He was crying. They all were.

"It's not your fault."

"We were almost *here*."

"Hush, both of you," Maddy said, smoothing down Lilian's hair. "You did the best you could. Your father just wanted you safe."

"We'll be safe in here," Michael said, crossing the small room to sit beside Wendy. She looked up from the toy in her hands and gave him a hopeful smile. "I packed the earth outside the shelter with salt. They won't be getting in here."

Wendy put an arm around her husband. He leaned into her shoulder. Lilian hugged her mother and Blake, the three of them dazed and grieving, while in the town below, the air-raid siren finally fell silent.

Something Ben said at Ghostland came back to her then: a line from a Rex Garrote book, she thought. "This town belongs to them now," she said, paraphrasing. "A town of the dead, a town full of ghosts."

The occupants of the shelter gave her quizzical looks but said nothing.

"Death isn't the end, Mom," she said, more certain of it than she'd ever been. "Dad will come back for us. You'll see."

DEARLY DEPARTED

Today.

BEN REAPPEARED ON Koestler Street, a few houses down from his own. The neighborhood was eerily silent. Cars doors stood open just like elsewhere in town. Household garbage had been strewn across the road, buzzing with flies. Only a blackened husk of the house Lilian grew up in remained. The rest had burned to ash and rubble. The front door of Lilian's old house had been smashed in. The windows were blocked by furniture, but that hadn't prevented whatever had wanted inside their house from entering.

He drifted up the street, mourning the signs of death and disaster of his neighbors and former friends. Wind blew through the shattered windows of the Ross's bungalow, curtains fluttering through broken panels. Their dog, often tied to the tree in the front yard in the summer, was missing. The leash and collar lay in the dead grass.

Ben sensed other ethereals nearby. It had been only moments since he'd left the Roths' apartment and he still hadn't seen a single entity besides the Swarm downtown. But there were signs of life here and there, hints of recent survival he promised himself he would investigate once he'd discovered whether or not Lilian and their parents had survived.

He reached his house and drifted through the front door, vaguely remembering the last time he'd been here, when his mom and dad found the Dracula collectible that he'd left for them as a sign he was okay. They'd argued over it, and he'd gotten upset and toppled the whole shelf of toys. He hadn't had the nerve to come home since.

The house was empty. Like the Roths's apartment, it seemed like nobody had been here in days, though it looked like his parents had been in a state of panic prior to the incident. He drifted from room to room, observing the opened drawers and cupboards and closets, clothing and dry goods spilled from them, sugar and socks on the floor.

He hoped they'd managed to get out of town. He hoped they were all together and safe with Grandma Laramie in some hotel in Hagerstown, or better yet, staying with Aunt Judy and Uncle Dave in West Virginia. Anywhere, so long as they were far away from Duck Falls.

He almost left the house behind, but as he drifted out of the kitchen, he noticed the backdoor was standing slightly ajar. He reached out to close it instinctively, as if it mattered anymore. As he did, he happened to glance through the window into the backyard.

The grass was back. The hole had been filled in, though the ground was uneven, with a large mound in the center. Clods of sod had been kicked up here and there.

He passed through the wall into the yard. The air was still and preternaturally quiet. His mom's Volvo was overturned in the driveway, a huge dent in the passenger side, all of the windows smashed. Something had split the patio stairs right down the middle.

He froze at the top, staring intently at what appeared to

be a pile of rotting innards on the lawn. Terror crawled over him like the flies and maggots picking away at the sunbaked organs. He brushed away the insects, hoping to discover who the entrails belonged to, hoping they belonged to a stranger and not to anyone he knew.

He pushed a hand into the fetid viscera up to the wrist, withdrawing it a moment later in shock.

"Oh no," he said.

What was Lilian's dad doing here? he thought. *And where's the rest of him?*

Crossing the lawn, searching for the rest of Hiram's remains, he spotted a trench dug into the mound, lined with cement. Within the trench was a hatch.

A shelter! That's what Dad was digging!

Brimming with excitement, he tried to descend into the shelter, but each attempt proved futile. He was able to reached a few inches into the grass and earth but something prevented him from going further. He tried going through the door and couldn't get in that way, either.

Dad must have salted the earth, like the salt-lined cinder blocks in the control room. He made a ghost-proof shelter!

Ben reached out to knock but realized his parents wouldn't hear him. After everything he'd been through, of course it couldn't be that easy. He'd need something heavy enough to make a loud noise, something that would sound like a friendly knock rather than a ravenous ethereal trying to gain entry.

He found his old baseball bat lying in the bushes by the back fence. It had probably lain there since before his cardiac arrest, when his dad used to pitch to him and he'd pop them back. "Dingers," his dad would call them. He brought the bat to the shelter and struck it against the door.

Clang! Clang! Clang!

Voices arose from within, too muffled to recognize.

He struck the bat against the door three more times.

The voices grew louder, arguing amongst each other. He recognized one of them as his dad, and felt a deep sense of relief knowing he was still alive. He thought he recognized Maddy's voice, as well. Lilian's mom.

"Hello?" he shouted in desperation. "Can anyone hear me?"

"Ben?"

"Lilian!"

She was here. She was safe and she was *here*. The relief he'd felt at hearing his father's voice doubled.

"Mr. Laramie, open the door! It's Ben!"

The door squeaked and squeaked until eventually a metallic mechanism inside made a hollow clunk, and the door came open a crack. His dad stood in the opening, peering out. Not seeing him.

"Ben!"

His dad moved out of the way and Lilian opened the door further. She hugged him. The other occupants of the shelter, both of his parents, Grandma Laramie, Lilian's mom and Blake, watched as she embraced what to them would have looked like thin air—except none of them seemed to doubt what she was seeing. Having spent however long trapped in a bunker by evil ghosts would have cured even the most ardent skeptic among them, Ben figured. And from the look of them, it had been several days. They seemed worn out, tired, scared.

"Ended up right where it all started, huh?" Ben said. "The two of us standing in front of a hatch."

Lilian ignored the joke. "Where *were* you? Le Mon was looking all over."

"It's a long story," he said. "I'm sorry about your dad. He was the best."

"He *is*," she said, looking down at her feet. It was difficult to tell if she was grieving or not. He supposed she'd already had several days to come to terms with her father's death. Then again, if Ben was able to come back, why couldn't her dad? It was entirely possible Hiram was somewhere in Duck Falls, hiding from ethereals and imagoes like everyone else in town.

"We buried his body beside the garage," Lilian said. "We had to do it in shifts. The Behemoth… the Swarm… they've been stalking us, Ben."

"The Behemoth…. Jeez. I saw part of the Swarm downtown a few minutes ago."

"They're everywhere. We were right, Ben. This is exactly what Garrote wanted."

He shook his head. "*Thea* did this. Thea and Bram. They played right into his hands."

"Why would *they* do this?"

"I don't know," Ben said. "Maybe they thought it was the only way to free the ethereals still in there. All I know is they were keeping a whole bunch of explosives out in a storage shed. I was heading back to warn everyone when Hedgewood captured me."

Lilian's jaw dropped. "He *kidnapped* you?"

"Kidnapped?" his dad cried. "Who kidnapped my boy?"

"Like I said, it's a long story," Ben repeated, ignoring his father, who wouldn't hear him anyhow. "Do you think you'll be okay here a while longer? I'm gonna see what's going on at the Temple. Check in on Le Mon and the others."

"We'll be okay. We've got food and water for a week,

at least. But Ben, they've quarantined the town. We saw it on the internet before they cut the phone and cable. They've got soldiers posted at roadblocks. They won't let people in or out. They're pretending it's an *infection*."

Ben looked at the others. They seemed resigned to the idea of being stuck in here for a long time. But there was a television and a DVD player. There was a laptop and enough food and water for at least a week.

"Hedgewood's supplied them with all kinds of tech stuff," Lilian said. "They said on the news. They've got these poles set up all around the town and nobody knows what they're for."

"Like the ESPs?"

"I don't think so. These look different. Like speakers or something."

"Speakers," Ben repeated. He thought he had a pretty good idea of what they might be. "Okay, I'll be back soon. I'm gonna try to find your dad. If he's out there and I can bring him back—"

The ground shook, cutting him off. Dirt sifted into the entrance between them.

"What was that?" his mother asked, her voice dulled. She'd been gripping something in her hands the whole time, and Ben finally realized what it was: his Dracula collectible. The one he'd left out the last time he saw them, to show them he was safe.

The rumbling intensified. The shelter's occupants hunkered down. His father wrapped an arm around his mother. Maddy and Blake hugged each other. Lilian crouched, cowering in the doorway.

"The Behemoth?" she said.

Ben shook his head. He knew exactly what it was: the speakers set up all over town. Everything he and

Cruikshank had endured at the Hedgewood Facility had merely been a test.

"Close the door," he said. The dull ache was already beginning to bloom in the center of his brain, creeping outward into his body, his limbs. It seemed as though the metal of the shelter itself was humming along with the imperceptible sound.

The ground trembled again. More dirt rained into the doorway.

"Ben?"

His mother's voice rose above the sound. She was looking *right at him*, the hope and love in her eyes unmistakable.

She can see me.

"Mom!" he cried.

His dad looked up at the sound of his voice and Michael's eyes grew very wide. "Ben! You're really here!"

"I'm here, Dad! I missed you both so much!"

The human eye has a resonant frequency of eighteen hertz, Hedgewood had said.

Ben's vision began to blur. There were two of each of them now. The stench of raw sewage, burnt hair and scorched rubber permeated the air, but he had to remain a moment longer. He had to hold this moment in his mind before it all disappeared.

His parents rushed to the door. Maddy, too. Elation and excitement exceeding their fear. Blake and Grandma Laramie remained at the kitchen table, but both of them stared at him in awe.

It's our contention that infrasound doesn't cause people to hallucinate ghosts, but rather causes ghosts to materialize within that range of sound, to some extent, thus rendering them visible to the human eye.

He saw his mom smile through the blur, tears spilling down her cheeks. "I thought I'd never see you again," she said.

He took her hand. She looked down at their hands entwined. "*I can feel you*," she said, in awe. His dad took his other hand and Michael's eyes widened even further.

I suppose we'll have to see how much infrasound you can handle before you just... wink out.

"I love you all so much," Ben said hurriedly, before it was too late.

In the next moment, he was gone.

EPILOGUE: GHOSTCEPTION

HARRISON HAD FELT unwell long before Oliver Hedgewood had showed him what Mr. Garrote had done with his head. For all he'd been a part of, for the hundreds of people he'd watched die that day in April, and the psychics Mr. Garrote and Oliver Hedgewood had convinced him to kill for in exchange for his freedom, all in the service of a Great Work he no longer fully understood—if he ever had at all—Harrison felt like maybe he deserved whatever eternal punishment he'd receive.

He hadn't believed it at first, that he was dead. But when Oliver had showed him what was happening in the outside world—the explosion and the mass ethereal exodus in its aftermath—he hadn't been able to deny it much longer. He *was* dead. And yet his consciousness endured within the construct despite his body already beginning to decay in the outside world, along with his former coworkers.

Do you ever wonder about the nature of the soul? Ms. Amblin had asked him. *Is it the dead energy? Or is consciousness itself the soul, and the dead energy just another shell? A different housing?*

Harrison knew the answer to her question now. He'd survived death. He'd *endured*. His consciousness—his *soul*—had merely been transferred to another shell. A different housing.

This house. Garrote House.

He stood in Oliver Hedgewood's sitting room, not a ghost within a ghost but a *completely digital being*. Like the others living here, inside Garrote's virtual mind.

"You understand now," Oliver said, seated in his red velvet armchair by the fire with a first edition of H.G. Wells's *The Time Machine* in his lap. "Mr. Garrote hasn't murdered you. He's *freed* you. And he'll return to free us all, very soon now. Just you wait and see."

The dark grin that spread across the ghost's face as he closed the book looked very much like Mr. Garrote's.

"But our work here isn't finished just yet, Harry, my boy," he said, affecting Garrote's pet name for him. "You and I have much to do and very little time in which to do it, I'm afraid."

The old ghost stood with a groan and gestured toward the door. "Shall we begin?"

TO BE CONTINUED...

A NotE FRom tHE AUtHoR

Here we are again, at the end of another book. This is my fifth novel and my eleventh book overall. I'd like to be able to tell you they get easier, but each one is its own challenge. I suppose it's much like any endeavor. If you start feeling like you're an expert, you're probably fooling yourself.

Like the last installment of what will forevermore be called the *Ghostland Trilogy*, this book ended up much different than it began. For one thing, I had no idea it would involve something called the Dark Rift (a creation that has had more names than Beelzebub—at one point it was called, unimaginatively, the Great Darkness). It also began with an extended sequence in a haunted mall in which Lilian and Ben and some folks from GRP2 tried to free ghosts who'd been trapped there by a magic-wielding security guard for some reason. There were several other sequences of them freeing ghosts but they'd never quite felt right for the tone of the novel, and I had no choice but to leave them on the "cutting-room floor" and plot over from scratch.

I guess here I should let you in on a little secret: I'd had a few ideas for a sequel I might write *eventually*, but I'd never intended *Ghostland* to be a trilogy. The ending, with its assertion that Garrote escaped, that he was out there preparing for war—I just thought it would be a fun, dark way to end the book, like Carrie's hand reaching out of the grave at the end of the movie. Just to leave you with a sense that the world had changed and would never be the same for these characters.

I'd never intended to fill in the details between the climax of the book and the epilogue—actually, that's not *quite* true. An earlier draft had that scene left in, but I just couldn't "show" Ben dying at the end of the book. Not that I didn't have the stomach for it—the scene is in this book almost verbatim—but like the ghost mall scene, it just didn't fit the tone of what I'd written, so I cut it. And I hoped no one would care that it was missing.

I think I mentioned in the notes of the last book that GRP2 were originally going to be the catalysts for the Ghostland Disaster, blowing up the Recurrence Field on opening day. It never felt right—the characters were also a little too *Thirteen Ghosts*—so I'd changed it to be a computer virus, which lead me to create the main antagonist, Rex Garrote. I still liked the idea enough that it felt right to have in the sequel. I hope you agree.

One last thing: it did feel kind of odd to write a pre-apocalypse novel set just after a "virus" during an actual pandemic, though there were details in this book and will be more in the next which have been informed by the bizarre and frightening events we've experienced this year. Hopefully by the time Book 3 arrives we'll live in a world where the virus is a distant memory, while the people we've lost to it remain in our hearts.

I need to thank some people, as always. In the first round are the folks who read an earlier draft and helped me beat it into shape. Without the invaluable input of my good friends and excellent writers Chad A. Clark and Erin Sweet-Al Mehairi, the book you've just read would have been an absolute mess. I can't thank them enough.

And as usual, I need to thank the first readers. Mom, Sherri, Marie Kirkland, Frank Spinney and John Rinaldi, especially. There are far more who I should thank for their kindness and support—the folks in the Horror Aficionados Goodreads group, the folks in the Books of Horror group on Facebook, friends and fellow writers on social media, Jeffrey Smith aka Ascending Storm, whose illustrations blew my mind—but it would be impossible to name all of you. Just know that if we interact regularly on social media or in real life, I appreciate you.

Until next time…

DR
November, 2020